THE BROTHERS KARAMAZOV

Abridged

Fyodor Dostoyevsky

Translated by Constance Garnett

pac ps
Pacific Publishing Studio

Published in the United States by Madison Park, an imprint of Pacific Publishing Studio.

www.PacPS.com

ISBN-13: 978-1463682156

ISBN-10: 1463682158

Contents

Chapter One
The History Of A Family

Alexey Fyodorovitch Karamazov was the third son of Fyodor Pavlovitch Karamazov, a land owner well known in our district in his own day, and still remembered among us owing to his gloomy and tragic death, which happened thirteen years ago, and which I shall describe in its proper place. For the present I will only say that this "landowner"—for so we used to call him, although he hardly spent a day of his life on his own estate—was a strange type, yet one pretty frequently to be met with, a type abject and vicious and at the same time senseless. But he was one of those senseless persons who are very well capable of looking after their worldly affairs, and, apparently, after nothing else. Fyodor Pavlovitch, for instance, began with next to nothing; his estate was of the smallest; he ran to dine at other men's tables, and fastened on them as a toady, yet at his death it appeared that he had a hundred thousand roubles in hard cash. At the same time, he was all his life one of the most senseless, fantastical fellows in the whole district. I repeat, it was not stupidity—the majority of these fantastical fellows are shrewd and intelligent enough—but just senselessness, and a peculiar national form of it.

He was married twice, and had three sons, the eldest, Dmitri, by his first wife, and two, Ivan and Alexey, by his second. Fyodor Pavlovitch's first wife, Adelaïda Ivanovna, belonged to a fairly rich and distinguished noble family, also landowners in our district, the Miüsovs. How it came to pass that an heiress, who was also a beauty, and moreover one of those vigorous, intelligent girls, so common in this generation, but sometimes also to be found in the last, could have married such a worthless, puny weakling, as we all called him, I won't attempt to explain. I knew a young lady of the last "romantic" generation who after some years of an enigmatic passion for a gentleman, whom she might quite easily have married at any moment, invented insuperable obstacles to their union, and ended by throwing herself one stormy night into a rather deep and rapid river from a high bank, almost a precipice, and so perished, entirely to satisfy her own caprice, and to be like Shakespeare's Ophelia. Indeed, if this precipice, a chosen and favorite spot of hers, had been less picturesque, if there had been a prosaic flat bank in its place, most likely the suicide would never have taken place. This is a fact, and probably there have been not a few similar instances in the last two or three generations. Adelaïda Ivanovna Miüsov's action was similarly, no doubt, an echo of other people's ideas, and was due to the irritation caused by lack of mental freedom. She wanted, perhaps, to show her feminine independence, to override class distinctions and the despotism of her family. And a pliable imagination persuaded her, we must suppose, for a brief moment, that Fyodor Pavlovitch, in spite of his parasitic position, was one of the bold and ironical spirits of that progressive epoch, though he was, in fact, an ill-natured buffoon and nothing more. What gave the marriage piquancy was that it was preceded by an elopement, and this greatly captivated Adelaïda Ivanovna's fancy. Fyodor Pavlovitch's position at the time made him specially eager for any such enterprise, for he was passionately anxious to make a career in one way or another. To attach himself to a good family and obtain a dowry was an alluring prospect. As for mutual love it did not exist apparently, either in the bride or in him, in spite of Adelaïda Ivanovna's beauty. This was, perhaps, a unique case of the kind in the life of Fyodor Pavlovitch, who was always of a voluptuous temper, and ready to run after any petticoat on the slightest encouragement. She seems to have been the only woman who made no particular appeal to his senses.

Immediately after the elopement Adelaïda Ivanovna discerned in a flash that she had no feeling for her husband but contempt. The marriage accordingly showed itself in its true colors with extraordinary rapidity. Although the family accepted the event pretty quickly and apportioned the runaway bride her dowry, the husband and wife began to lead a most disorderly life, and there were everlasting scenes between them. It was said that the young wife showed incomparably more generosity and dignity than Fyodor Pavlovitch, who, as is now known, got hold of all her money up to twenty-five thousand roubles as soon as she received it, so that those thousands were lost to her for ever. The little village and the rather fine town house which formed part of her dowry he did his utmost for a long time to transfer to his name, by means of some deed of conveyance. He would probably have succeeded, merely from her moral fatigue and desire to get rid of him, and from the contempt and loathing he aroused by his persistent and shameless importunity. But, fortunately, Adelaïda Ivanovna's family intervened and circumvented his greediness. It is known for a fact that frequent fights took place between the husband and wife, but rumor had it that Fyodor Pavlovitch did not beat his wife but was beaten by her, for she was a hot-tempered, bold, dark-browed, impatient woman, possessed of remarkable physical strength. Finally, she left the house and ran away from Fyodor Pavlovitch with a destitute divinity student, leaving Mitya, a child of three years old, in her husband's hands. Immediately Fyodor Pavlovitch introduced a regular harem into the house, and abandoned himself to orgies of drunkenness. In the intervals he used to drive all over the province, complaining tearfully to each and all of Adelaïda Ivanovna's having left him, going into details too disgraceful for a husband to mention in regard to his own married life. What seemed to gratify him and flatter his self-love most was to play the ridiculous part of the injured husband, and to parade his woes with embellishments.

"One would think that you'd got a promotion, Fyodor Pavlovitch, you seem so pleased in spite of your sorrow," scoffers said to him. Many even added that he was glad of a new comic part in which to play the buffoon, and that it was simply to make it funnier that he pretended to be unaware of his ludicrous position. But, who knows, it may have been simplicity. At last he succeeded in getting on the track of his runaway wife. The poor woman turned out to be in Petersburg, where she had gone with her divinity student, and where she had thrown herself into a life of complete emancipation. Fyodor Pavlovitch at once began bustling about, making preparations to go to Petersburg, with what object he could not himself have said. He would perhaps have really gone; but having determined to do so he felt at once entitled to fortify himself for the journey by another bout of reckless drinking. And just at that time his wife's family received the news of her death in Petersburg. She had died quite suddenly in a garret, according to one story, of typhus, or as another version had it, of starvation. Fyodor Pavlovitch was drunk when he heard of his wife's death, and the story is that he ran out into the street and began shouting with joy, raising his hands to Heaven: "Lord, now lettest Thou Thy servant depart in peace," but others say he wept without restraint like a little child, so much so that people were sorry for him, in spite of the repulsion he inspired. It is quite possible that both versions were true, that he rejoiced at his release, and at the same time wept for her who released him. As a general rule, people, even the wicked, are much more naïve and simple-hearted than we suppose. And we ourselves are, too.

You can easily imagine what a father such a man could be and how he would bring up his children. His behavior as a father was exactly what might be expected. He completely abandoned the child of his marriage with Adelaïda Ivanovna, not from malice, nor because of his matrimonial grievances, but simply because he forgot him. While he was wearying every one with his tears and complaints, and turning his house into a sink of debauchery, a faithful servant of the family, Grigory, took the three-year-old Mitya into his care. If he hadn't looked after him there would have been no one even to change the baby's little shirt.

It happened moreover that the child's relations on his mother's side forgot him too at first. His grandfather was no longer living, his widow, Mitya's grandmother, had moved to Moscow, and was seriously ill, while his daughters were married, so that Mitya remained for almost a whole year in old Grigory's charge and lived with him in the servant's cottage. But if his father had remembered him (he could not, indeed, have been altogether unaware of his existence) he would have sent him back to the cottage, as the child would only have been in the way of his debaucheries. But a cousin of Mitya's mother, Pyotr Alexandrovitch Miüsov, happened to return from Paris. He lived for many years afterwards abroad, but was at that time quite a young man, and distinguished among the Miüsovs as a man of enlightened ideas and of European culture, who had been in the capitals and abroad.

Towards the end of his life he became a Liberal of the type common in the forties and fifties. In the course of his career he had come into contact with many of the most Liberal men of his epoch, both in Russia and abroad. He had known Proudhon and Bakunin personally, and in his declining years was very fond of describing the three days of the Paris Revolution of February 1848, hinting that he himself had almost taken part in the fighting on the barricades. This was one of the most grateful recollections of his youth. He had an independent property of about a thousand souls, to reckon in the old style. His splendid estate lay on the outskirts of our little town and bordered on the lands of our famous monastery, with which Pyotr Alexandrovitch began an endless lawsuit, almost as soon as he came into the estate, concerning the rights of fishing in the river or wood-cutting in the forest, I don't know exactly which. He regarded it as his duty as a citizen and a man of culture to open an attack upon the "clericals." Hearing all about Adelaïda Ivanovna, whom he, of course, remembered, and in whom he had at one time been interested, and learning of the existence of Mitya, he intervened, in spite of all his youthful indignation and contempt for Fyodor Pavlovitch. He made the latter's acquaintance for the first time, and told him directly that he wished to undertake the child's education. He used long afterwards to tell as a characteristic touch, that when he began to speak of Mitya, Fyodor Pavlovitch looked for some time as though he did not understand what child he was talking about, and even as though he was surprised to hear that he had a little son in the house. The story may have been exaggerated, yet it must have been something like the truth.

Fyodor Pavlovitch was all his life fond of acting, of suddenly playing an unexpected part, sometimes without any motive for doing so, and even to his own direct disadvantage, as, for instance, in the present case. This habit, however, is characteristic of a very great number of people, some of them very clever ones, not like Fyodor Pavlovitch. Pyotr Alexandrovitch carried the business through vigorously, and was appointed, with Fyodor Pavlovitch, joint guardian of the child, who had a small property, a house and land, left him by his mother. Mitya did, in fact, pass into this cousin's keeping, but as the latter had no family of his own, and after securing the revenues of his estates was in haste to return at once to Paris, he left the boy in charge of one of his cousins, a lady living in Moscow. It came to pass that, settling permanently in Paris he, too, forgot the child, especially when the Revolution of February broke out, making an impression on his mind that he remembered all the rest of his life. The Moscow lady died, and Mitya passed into the care of one of her married daughters. I believe he changed his home a fourth time later on. I won't enlarge upon that now, as I shall have much to tell later of Fyodor Pavlovitch's firstborn, and must confine myself now to the most essential facts about him, without which I could not begin my story.

In the first place, this Mitya, or rather Dmitri Fyodorovitch, was the only one of Fyodor Pavlovitch's three sons who grew up in the belief that he had property, and that he would be independent on coming of age. He spent an irregular boyhood and youth. He did not finish his studies at the gymnasium, he got into a military school, then went to the Caucasus, was promoted, fought a duel, and was degraded to the ranks, earned promotion again, led a wild life, and spent a good deal of money. He did not begin to receive any income from Fyodor Pavlovitch until he came of age, and until then got into debt. He saw and knew his father, Fyodor Pavlovitch, for the first time on coming of age, when he visited our neighborhood on purpose to settle with him about his property. He seems not to have liked his father. He did not stay long with him, and made haste to get away, having only succeeded in obtaining a sum of money, and entering into an agreement for future payments from the estate, of the revenues and value of which he was unable (a fact worthy of note), upon this occasion, to get a statement from his father. Fyodor Pavlovitch remarked for the first time then (this, too, should be noted) that Mitya had a vague and exaggerated idea of his property. Fyodor Pavlovitch was very well satisfied with this, as it fell in with his own designs. He gathered only that the young man was frivolous, unruly, of violent passions, impatient, and dissipated, and that if he could only obtain ready money he would be satisfied, although only, of course, for a short time. So Fyodor Pavlovitch began to take advantage of this fact, sending him from time to time small doles, installments. In the end, when four years later, Mitya, losing patience, came a second time to our little town to settle up once for all with his father, it turned out to his amazement that he had nothing, that it was difficult to get an account even, that he had received the whole value of his property in sums of money from Fyodor Pavlovitch, and was perhaps even in debt to him, that by various agreements into which he had, of his own desire, entered at various previous dates, he had no right to expect anything more, and so on, and so on. The young man was overwhelmed, suspected deceit and cheating, and was almost beside himself. And, indeed, this circumstance led to the catastrophe, the account of which forms the subject of my first introductory story, or rather the external side of it. But before I pass to that story I must say a little of Fyodor Pavlovitch's other two sons, and of their origin.

Very shortly after getting his four-year-old Mitya off his hands Fyodor Pavlovitch married a second time. His second marriage lasted eight years. He took this second wife, Sofya Ivanovna, also a very young girl, from another province, where he had gone upon some small piece of business in company with a Jew. Though Fyodor Pavlovitch was a drunkard and a vicious debauchee he never neglected investing his capital, and managed his business affairs very successfully, though, no doubt, not over-scrupulously. Sofya Ivanovna was the daughter of an obscure deacon, and was left from childhood an orphan without relations. She grew up in the house of a general's widow, a wealthy old lady of good position, who was at once her benefactress and tormentor. I do not know the details, but I have only heard that the orphan girl, a meek and gentle creature, was once cut down from a halter in which she was hanging from a nail in the loft, so terrible were her sufferings from the caprice and everlasting nagging of this old woman, who was apparently not bad-hearted but had become an insufferable tyrant through idleness.

Fyodor Pavlovitch made her an offer; inquiries were made about him and he was refused. But again, as in his first marriage, he proposed an elopement to the orphan girl. There is very little doubt that she would not on any account have married him if she had known a little more about him in time. But she lived in another province; besides, what could a little girl of sixteen know about it, except that she would be better at the bottom of the river than remaining with her benefactress. So the poor child exchanged a benefactress for a benefactor. Fyodor Pavlovitch did not get a penny this time, for the general's widow was furious. She gave them nothing and cursed them both. But he had not reckoned on a dowry; what allured him was the remarkable beauty of the innocent girl, above all her innocent appearance, which had a peculiar attraction for a vicious profligate, who had hitherto admired only the coarser types of feminine beauty.

"Those innocent eyes slit my soul up like a razor," he used to say afterwards, with his loathsome snigger. In a man so depraved this might, of course, mean no more than sensual attraction. As he had received no dowry with his wife, and had, so to speak, taken her "from the halter," he did not stand on ceremony with her. Making her feel that she had "wronged" him, he took advantage of her phenomenal meekness and submissiveness to trample on the elementary decencies of marriage. He gathered loose women into his house, and carried on orgies of debauchery in his wife's presence. To show what a pass things had come to, I may mention that Grigory, the gloomy, stupid, obstinate, argumentative servant, who had always hated his first mistress, Adelaïda Ivanovna, took the side of his new mistress. He championed her cause, abusing Fyodor Pavlovitch in a manner little befitting a servant, and on one occasion broke up the revels and drove all the disorderly women out of the house. In the end this unhappy young woman, kept in terror from her childhood, fell into that kind of nervous disease which is most frequently found in peasant women who are said to be "possessed by devils." At times after terrible fits of hysterics she even lost her reason. Yet she bore Fyodor Pavlovitch two sons, Ivan and Alexey, the eldest in the first year of marriage and the second three years later. When she died, little Alexey was in his fourth year, and, strange as it seems, I know that he remembered his mother all his life, like a dream, of course. At her death almost exactly the same thing happened to the two little boys as to their elder brother, Mitya. They were completely forgotten and abandoned by their father. They were looked after by the same Grigory and lived in his cottage, where they were found by the tyrannical old lady who had brought up their mother. She was still alive, and had not, all those eight years, forgotten the insult done her. All that time she was obtaining exact information as to her Sofya's manner of life, and hearing of her illness and hideous surroundings she declared aloud two or three times to her retainers:

"It serves her right. God has punished her for her ingratitude."

Exactly three months after Sofya Ivanovna's death the general's widow suddenly appeared in our town, and went straight to Fyodor Pavlovitch's house. She spent only half an hour in the town but she did a great deal. It was evening. Fyodor Pavlovitch, whom she had not seen for those eight years, came in to her drunk. The story is that instantly upon seeing him, without any sort of explanation, she gave him two good, resounding slaps on the face, seized him by a tuft of hair, and shook him three times up and down. Then, without a word, she went straight to the cottage to the two boys. Seeing, at the first glance, that they were unwashed and in dirty linen, she promptly gave Grigory, too, a box on the ear, and announcing that she would carry off both the children she wrapped them just as they were in a rug, put them in the carriage, and drove off to her own town. Grigory accepted the blow like a devoted slave, without a word, and when he escorted the old lady to her carriage he made her a low bow and pronounced impressively that, "God would repay her for the orphans." "You are a blockhead all the same," the old lady shouted to him as she drove away.

Fyodor Pavlovitch, thinking it over, decided that it was a good thing, and did not refuse the general's widow his formal consent to any proposition in regard to his children's education. As for the slaps she had given him, he drove all over the town telling the story.

It happened that the old lady died soon after this, but she left the boys in her will a thousand roubles each "for their instruction, and so that all be spent on them exclusively, with the condition that it be so portioned out as to last till they are twenty-one, for it is more than adequate provision for such children. If other people think fit to throw away their money, let them." I have not read the will myself, but I heard there was something queer of the sort, very whimsically expressed. The principal heir, Yefim Petrovitch Polenov, the Marshal of Nobility of the province, turned out, however, to be an honest man. Writing to Fyodor Pavlovitch, and discerning at once that he could extract nothing from him for his children's education (though the latter never directly refused but only procrastinated as he always did in such cases, and was, indeed, at times effusively sentimental), Yefim Petrovitch took a personal interest in the orphans. He became especially fond of the younger, Alexey, who lived for a long while as one of his family. I beg the reader to note this from the beginning. And to Yefim Petrovitch, a man of a generosity and humanity rarely to be met with, the young people were more indebted for their education and bringing up than to any one. He kept the two thousand roubles left to them by the general's widow intact, so that by the time they came of age their portions had been doubled by the accumulation of interest. He educated them both at his own expense, and certainly spent far more than a thousand roubles upon each of them. I won't enter into a detailed account of their boyhood and youth, but will only mention a few of the most important events. Of the elder, Ivan, I will only say that he grew into a somewhat morose and reserved, though far from timid boy. At ten years old he had realized that they were living not in their own home but on other people's charity, and that their father was a man of whom it was disgraceful to speak. This boy began very early, almost in his infancy (so they say at least), to show a brilliant and unusual aptitude for learning. I don't know precisely why, but he left the family of Yefim Petrovitch when he was hardly thirteen, entering a Moscow gymnasium, and boarding with an experienced and celebrated teacher, an old friend of Yefim Petrovitch. Ivan used to declare afterwards that this was all due to the "ardor for good works" of Yefim Petrovitch, who was captivated by the idea that the boy's genius should be trained by a teacher of genius. But neither Yefim Petrovitch nor this teacher was living when the young man finished at the gymnasium and entered the university. As Yefim Petrovitch had made no provision for the payment of the tyrannical old lady's legacy, which had grown from one thousand to two, it was delayed, owing to formalities inevitable in Russia, and the young man was in great straits for the first two years at the university, as he was forced to keep himself all the time he was studying. It must be noted that he did not even attempt to communicate with his father, perhaps from pride, from contempt for him, or perhaps from his cool common sense, which told him that from such a father he would get no real assistance. However that may have been, the young man was by no means despondent and succeeded in getting work, at first giving sixpenny lessons and afterwards getting paragraphs on street incidents into the newspapers under the signature of "Eye-Witness." These paragraphs, it was said, were so interesting and piquant that they were soon taken. This alone showed the young man's practical and intellectual superiority over the masses of needy and unfortunate students of both sexes who hang about the offices of the newspapers and journals, unable to think of anything better than everlasting entreaties for copying and translations from the French. Having once got into touch with the editors Ivan Fyodorovitch always kept up his connection with them, and in his latter years at the university he published brilliant reviews of books upon various special subjects, so that he became well known in literary circles. But only in his last year he suddenly succeeded in attracting the attention of a far wider circle of readers, so that a great many people noticed and remembered him. It was rather a curious incident. When he had just left the university and was preparing to go abroad upon his two thousand roubles, Ivan Fyodorovitch published in one of the more important journals a strange article, which attracted general notice, on a subject of which he might have been supposed to know nothing, as he was a student of natural science. The article dealt with a subject which was being debated everywhere at the time—the position of the ecclesiastical courts. After discussing several opinions on the subject he went on to explain his own view. What was most striking about the article was its tone, and its unexpected conclusion. Many of the Church party regarded him unquestioningly as on their side. And yet not only the secularists but even atheists joined them in their applause. Finally some sagacious persons opined that the article was nothing but an impudent satirical burlesque. I mention this incident particularly because this article penetrated into the famous monastery in our neighborhood, where the inmates, being particularly interested in the question of the ecclesiastical courts, were completely bewildered by it. Learning the author's name, they were interested in his being a native of the town and the son of "that Fyodor Pavlovitch." And just then it was that the author himself made his appearance among us.

Why Ivan Fyodorovitch had come amongst us I remember asking myself at the time with a certain uneasiness. This fateful visit, which was the first step leading to so many consequences, I never fully explained to myself. It seemed strange on the face of it that a young man so learned, so proud, and apparently so cautious, should suddenly visit such an infamous house and a father who had ignored him all his life, hardly knew him, never thought of him, and would not under any circumstances have given him money, though he was always afraid that his sons Ivan and Alexey would also come to ask him for it. And here the young man was staying in the house of such a father, had been living with him for two months, and they were on the best possible terms. This last fact was a special cause of wonder to many others as well as to me. Pyotr Alexandrovitch Miüsov, of whom we have spoken already, the cousin of Fyodor Pavlovitch's first wife, happened to be in the neighborhood again on a visit to his estate. He had come from Paris, which was his permanent home. I remember that he was more surprised than any one when he made the acquaintance of the young man, who interested him extremely, and with whom he sometimes argued and not without an inner pang compared himself in acquirements.

"He is proud," he used to say, "he will never be in want of pence; he has got money enough to go abroad now. What does he want here? Every one can see that he hasn't come for money, for his father would never give him any. He has no taste for drink and dissipation, and yet his father can't do without him. They get on so well together!"

That was the truth; the young man had an unmistakable influence over his father, who positively appeared to be behaving more decently and even seemed at times ready to obey his son, though often extremely and even spitefully perverse.

It was only later that we learned that Ivan had come partly at the request of, and in the interests of, his elder brother, Dmitri, whom he saw for the first time on this very visit, though he had before leaving Moscow been in correspondence with him about an important matter of more concern to Dmitri than himself. What that business was the reader will learn fully in due time. Yet even when I did know of this special circumstance I still felt Ivan Fyodorovitch to be an enigmatic figure, and thought his visit rather mysterious.

I may add that Ivan appeared at the time in the light of a mediator between his father and his elder brother Dmitri, who was in open quarrel with his father and even planning to bring an action against him.

The family, I repeat, was now united for the first time, and some of its members met for the first time in their lives. The younger brother, Alexey, had been a year already among us, having been the first of the three to arrive. It is of that brother Alexey I find it most difficult to speak in this introduction. Yet I must give some preliminary account of him, if only to explain one queer fact, which is that I have to introduce my hero to the reader wearing the cassock of a novice. Yes, he had been for the last year in our monastery, and seemed willing to be cloistered there for the rest of his life.

He was only twenty, his brother Ivan was in his twenty-fourth year at the time, while their elder brother Dmitri was twenty-seven. First of all, I must explain that this young man, Alyosha, was not a fanatic, and, in my opinion at least, was not even a mystic. I may as well give my full opinion from the beginning. He was simply an early lover of humanity, and that he adopted the monastic life was simply because at that time it struck him, so to say, as the ideal escape for his soul struggling from the darkness of worldly wickedness to the light of love. And the reason this life struck him in this way was that he found in it at that time, as he thought, an extraordinary being, our celebrated elder, Zossima, to whom he became attached with all the warm first love of his ardent heart. But I do not dispute that he was very strange even at that time, and had been so indeed from his cradle. I have mentioned already, by the way, that though he lost his mother in his fourth year he remembered her all his life—her face, her caresses, "as though she stood living before me." Such memories may persist, as every one knows, from an even earlier age, even from two years old, but scarcely standing out through a whole lifetime like spots of light out of darkness, like a corner torn out of a huge picture, which has all faded and disappeared except that fragment. That is how it was with him. He remembered one still summer evening, an open window, the slanting rays of the setting sun (that he recalled most vividly of all); in a corner of the room the holy image, before it a lighted lamp, and on her knees before the image his mother, sobbing hysterically with cries and moans, snatching him up in both arms, squeezing him close till it hurt, and praying for him to the Mother of God, holding him out in both arms to the image as though to put him under the Mother's protection ... and suddenly a nurse runs in and snatches him from her in terror. That was the picture! And Alyosha remembered his mother's face at that minute. He used to say that it was frenzied but beautiful as he remembered. But he rarely cared to speak of this memory to any one. In his childhood and youth he was by no means expansive, and talked little indeed, but not from shyness or a sullen unsociability; quite the contrary, from something different, from a sort of inner preoccupation entirely personal and unconcerned with other people, but so important to him that he seemed, as it were, to forget others on account of it. But he was fond of people: he seemed throughout his life to put implicit trust in people: yet no one ever looked on him as a simpleton or naïve person. There was something about him which made one feel at once (and it was so all his life afterwards) that he did not care to be a judge of others—that he would never take it upon himself to criticize and would never condemn any one for anything. He seemed, indeed, to accept everything without the least condemnation though often grieving bitterly: and this was so much so that no one could surprise or frighten him even in his earliest youth. Coming at twenty to his father's house, which was a very sink of filthy debauchery, he, chaste and pure as he was, simply withdrew in silence when to look on was unbearable, but without the slightest sign of contempt or condemnation. His father, who had once been in a dependent position, and so was sensitive and ready to take offense, met him at first with distrust and sullenness. "He does not say much," he used to say, "and thinks the more." But soon, within a fortnight indeed, he took to embracing him and kissing him terribly often, with drunken tears, with sottish sentimentality, yet he evidently felt a real and deep affection for him, such as he had never been capable of feeling for any one before.

Every one, indeed, loved this young man wherever he went, and it was so from his earliest childhood. When he entered the household of his patron and benefactor, Yefim Petrovitch Polenov, he gained the hearts of all the family, so that they looked on him quite as their own child. Yet he entered the house at such a tender age that he could not have acted from design nor artfulness in winning affection. So that the gift of making himself loved directly and unconsciously was inherent in him, in his very nature, so to speak. It was the same at school, though he seemed to be just one of those children who are distrusted, sometimes ridiculed, and even disliked by their schoolfellows. He was dreamy, for instance, and rather solitary. From his earliest childhood he was fond of creeping into a corner to read, and yet he was a general favorite all the while he was at school. He was rarely playful or merry, but any one could see at the first glance that this was not from any sullenness. On the contrary he was bright and good-tempered. He never tried to show off among his schoolfellows. Perhaps because of this, he was never afraid of any one, yet the boys immediately understood that he was not proud of his fearlessness and seemed to be unaware that he was bold and courageous. He never resented an insult. It would happen that an hour after the offense he would address the offender or answer some question with as trustful and candid an expression as though nothing had happened between them. And it was not that he seemed to have forgotten or intentionally forgiven the affront, but simply that he did not regard it as an affront, and this completely conquered and captivated the boys. He had one characteristic which made all his schoolfellows from the bottom class to the top want to mock at him, not from malice but because it amused them. This characteristic was a wild fanatical modesty and chastity. He could not bear to hear certain words and certain conversations about women. There are "certain" words and conversations unhappily impossible to eradicate in schools. Boys pure in mind and heart, almost children, are fond of talking in school among themselves, and even aloud, of things, pictures, and images of which even soldiers would sometimes hesitate to speak. More than that, much that soldiers have no knowledge or conception of is familiar to quite young children of our intellectual and higher classes. There is no moral depravity, no real corrupt inner cynicism in it, but there is the appearance of it, and it is often looked upon among them as something refined, subtle, daring, and worthy of imitation. Seeing that Alyosha Karamazov put his fingers in his ears when they talked of "that," they used sometimes to crowd round him, pull his hands away, and shout nastiness into both ears, while he struggled, slipped to the floor, tried to hide himself without uttering one word of abuse, enduring their insults in silence. But at last they left him alone and gave up taunting him with being a "regular girl," and what's more they looked upon it with compassion as a weakness. He was always one of the best in the class but was never first.

At the time of Yefim Petrovitch's death Alyosha had two more years to complete at the provincial gymnasium. The inconsolable widow went almost immediately after his death for a long visit to Italy with her whole family, which consisted only of women and girls. Alyosha went to live in the house of two distant relations of Yefim Petrovitch, ladies whom he had never seen before. On what terms he lived with them he did not know himself. It was very characteristic of him, indeed, that he never cared at whose expense he was living. In that respect he was a striking contrast to his elder brother Ivan, who struggled with poverty for his first two years in the university, maintained himself by his own efforts, and had from childhood been bitterly conscious of living at the expense of his benefactor. But this strange trait in Alyosha's character must not, I think, be criticized too severely, for at the slightest acquaintance with him any one would have perceived that Alyosha was one of those youths, almost of the type of religious enthusiast, who, if they were suddenly to come into possession of a large fortune, would not hesitate to give it away for the asking, either for good works or perhaps to a clever rogue. In general he seemed scarcely to know the value of money, not, of course, in a literal sense. When he was given pocket-money, which he never asked for, he was either terribly careless of it so that it was gone in a moment, or he kept it for weeks together, not knowing what to do with it.

In later years Pyotr Alexandrovitch Miüsov, a man very sensitive on the score of money and bourgeois honesty, pronounced the following judgment, after getting to know Alyosha:

"Here is perhaps the one man in the world whom you might leave alone without a penny, in the center of an unknown town of a million inhabitants, and he would not come to harm, he would not die of cold and hunger, for he would be fed and sheltered at once; and if he were not, he would find a shelter for himself, and it would cost him no effort or humiliation. And to shelter him would be no burden, but, on the contrary, would probably be looked on as a pleasure."

He did not finish his studies at the gymnasium. A year before the end of the course he suddenly announced to the ladies that he was going to see his father about a plan which had occurred to him. They were sorry and unwilling to let him go. The journey was not an expensive one, and the ladies would not let him pawn his watch, a parting present from his benefactor's family. They provided him liberally with money and even fitted him out with new clothes and linen. But he returned half the money they gave him, saying that he intended to go third class. On his arrival in the town he made no answer to his father's first inquiry why he had come before completing his studies, and seemed, so they say, unusually thoughtful. It soon became apparent that he was looking for his mother's tomb. He practically acknowledged at the time that that was the only object of his visit. But it can hardly have been the whole reason of it. It is more probable that he himself did not understand and could not explain what had suddenly arisen in his soul, and drawn him irresistibly into a new, unknown, but inevitable path. Fyodor Pavlovitch could not show him where his second wife was buried, for he had never visited her grave since he had thrown earth upon her coffin, and in the course of years had entirely forgotten where she was buried.

Fyodor Pavlovitch, by the way, had for some time previously not been living in our town. Three or four years after his wife's death he had gone to the south of Russia and finally turned up in Odessa, where he spent several years. He made the acquaintance at first, in his own words, "of a lot of low Jews, Jewesses, and Jewkins," and ended by being received by "Jews high and low alike." It may be presumed that at this period he developed a peculiar faculty for making and hoarding money. He finally returned to our town only three years before Alyosha's arrival. His former acquaintances found him looking terribly aged, although he was by no means an old man. He behaved not exactly with more dignity but with more effrontery. The former buffoon showed an insolent propensity for making buffoons of others. His depravity with women was not simply what it used to be, but even more revolting. In a short time he opened a great number of new taverns in the district. It was evident that he had perhaps a hundred thousand roubles or not much less. Many of the inhabitants of the town and district were soon in his debt, and, of course, had given good security. Of late, too, he looked somehow bloated and seemed more irresponsible, more uneven, had sunk into a sort of incoherence, used to begin one thing and go on with another, as though he were letting himself go altogether. He was more and more frequently drunk. And, if it had not been for the same servant Grigory, who by that time had aged considerably too, and used to look after him sometimes almost like a tutor, Fyodor Pavlovitch might have got into terrible scrapes. Alyosha's arrival seemed to affect even his moral side, as though something had awakened in this prematurely old man which had long been dead in his soul.

"Do you know," he used often to say, looking at Alyosha, "that you are like her, 'the crazy woman'"—that was what he used to call his dead wife, Alyosha's mother. Grigory it was who pointed out the "crazy woman's" grave to Alyosha. He took him to our town cemetery and showed him in a remote corner a cast-iron tombstone, cheap but decently kept, on which were inscribed the name and age of the deceased and the date of her death, and below a four-lined verse, such as are commonly used on old-fashioned middle-class tombs. To Alyosha's amazement this tomb turned out to be Grigory's doing. He had put it up on the poor "crazy woman's" grave at his own expense, after Fyodor Pavlovitch, whom he had often pestered about the grave, had gone to Odessa, abandoning the grave and all his memories. Alyosha showed no particular emotion at the sight of his mother's grave. He only listened to Grigory's minute and solemn account of the erection of the tomb; he stood with bowed head and walked away without uttering a word. It was perhaps a year before he visited the cemetery again. But this little episode was not without an influence upon Fyodor Pavlovitch—and a very original one. He suddenly took a thousand roubles to our monastery to pay for requiems for the soul of his wife; but not for the second, Alyosha's mother, the "crazy woman," but for the first, Adelaïda Ivanovna, who used to thrash him. In the evening of the same day he got drunk and abused the monks to Alyosha. He himself was far from being religious; he had probably never put a penny candle before the image of a saint. Strange impulses of sudden feeling and sudden thought are common in such types.

I have mentioned already that he looked bloated. His countenance at this time bore traces of something that testified unmistakably to the life he had led. Besides the long fleshy bags under his little, always insolent, suspicious, and ironical eyes; besides the multitude of deep wrinkles in his little fat face, the Adam's apple hung below his sharp chin like a great, fleshy goiter, which gave him a peculiar, repulsive, sensual appearance; add to that a long rapacious mouth with full lips, between which could be seen little stumps of black decayed teeth. He slobbered every time he began to speak. He was fond indeed of making fun of his own face, though, I believe, he was well satisfied with it. He used particularly to point to his nose, which was not very large, but very delicate and conspicuously aquiline. "A regular Roman nose," he used to say, "with my goiter I've quite the countenance of an ancient Roman patrician of the decadent period." He seemed proud of it.

Not long after visiting his mother's grave Alyosha suddenly announced that he wanted to enter the monastery, and that the monks were willing to receive him as a novice. He explained that this was his strong desire, and that he was solemnly asking his consent as his father. The old man knew that the elder Zossima, who was living in the monastery hermitage, had made a special impression upon his "gentle boy."

"That is the most honest monk among them, of course," he observed, after listening in thoughtful silence to Alyosha, and seeming scarcely surprised at his request. "H'm!... So that's where you want to be, my gentle boy?"

He was half drunk, and suddenly he grinned his slow half-drunken grin, which was not without a certain cunning and tipsy slyness. "H'm!... I had a presentiment that you would end in something like this. Would you believe it? You were making straight for it. Well, to be sure you have your own two thousand. That's a dowry for you. And I'll never desert you, my angel. And I'll pay what's wanted for you there, if they ask for it. But, of course, if they don't ask, why should we worry them? What do you say? You know, you spend money like a canary, two grains a week. H'm!... Do you know that near one monastery there's a place outside the town where every baby knows there are none but 'the monks' wives' living, as they are called. Thirty women, I believe. I have been there myself. You know, it's interesting in its own way, of course, as a variety. The worst of it is it's awfully Russian. There are no French women there. Of course they could get them fast enough, they have plenty of money. If they get to hear of it they'll come along. Well, there's nothing of that sort here, no 'monks' wives,' and two hundred monks. They're honest. They keep the fasts. I admit it.... H'm.... So you want to be a monk? And do you know I'm sorry to lose you, Alyosha; would you believe it, I've really grown fond of you? Well, it's a good opportunity. You'll pray for us sinners; we have sinned too much here. I've always been thinking who would pray for me, and whether there's any one in the world to do it. My dear boy, I'm awfully stupid about that. You wouldn't believe it. Awfully. You see, however stupid I am about it, I keep thinking, I keep thinking—from time to time, of course, not all the while. It's impossible, I think, for the devils to forget to drag me down to hell with their hooks when I die. Then I wonder—hooks? Where would they get them? What of? Iron hooks? Where do they forge them? Have they a foundry there of some sort? The monks in the monastery probably believe that there's a ceiling in hell, for instance. Now I'm ready to believe in hell, but without a ceiling. It makes it more refined, more enlightened, more Lutheran that is. And, after all, what does it matter whether it has a ceiling or hasn't? But, do you know, there's a damnable question involved in it? If there's no ceiling there can be no hooks, and if there are no hooks it all breaks down, which is unlikely again, for then there would be none to drag me down to hell, and if they don't drag me down what justice is there in the world? *Il faudrait les inventer*, those hooks, on purpose for me alone, for, if you only knew, Alyosha, what a blackguard I am."

"But there are no hooks there," said Alyosha, looking gently and seriously at his father.

"Yes, yes, only the shadows of hooks, I know, I know. That's how a Frenchman described hell: '*J'ai bu l'ombre d'un cocher qui avec l'ombre d'une brosse frottait l'ombre d'une carrosse.*' How do you know there are no hooks, darling? When you've lived with the monks you'll sing a different tune. But go and get at the truth there, and then come and tell me. Anyway it's easier going to the other world if one knows what there is there. Besides, it will be more seemly for you with the monks than here with me, with a drunken old man and young harlots ... though you're like an angel, nothing touches you. And I dare say nothing will touch you there. That's why I let you go, because I hope for that. You've got all your wits about you. You will burn and you will burn out; you will be healed and come back again. And I will wait for you. I feel that you're the only creature in the world who has not condemned me. My dear boy, I feel it, you know. I can't help feeling it."

And he even began blubbering. He was sentimental. He was wicked and sentimental.

Chapter Two
An Unfortunate Gathering

It was a warm, bright day at the end of August. The interview with the elder had been fixed for half-past eleven, immediately after late mass. Our visitors did not take part in the service, but arrived just as it was over. First an elegant open carriage, drawn by two valuable horses, drove up with Miüsov and a distant relative of his, a young man of twenty, called Pyotr Fomitch Kalganov. This young man was preparing to enter the university. Miüsov, with whom he was staying for the time, was trying to persuade him to go abroad to the university of Zurich or Jena. The young man was still undecided. He was thoughtful and absent-minded. He was nice-looking, strongly built, and rather tall. There was a strange fixity in his gaze at times. Like all very absent-minded people he would sometimes stare at a person without seeing him. He was silent and rather awkward, but sometimes, when he was alone with any one, he became talkative and effusive, and would laugh at anything or nothing. But his animation vanished as quickly as it appeared. He was always well and even elaborately dressed; he had already some independent fortune and expectations of much more. He was a friend of Alyosha's.

In an ancient, jolting, but roomy, hired carriage, with a pair of old pinkish-gray horses, a long way behind Miüsov's carriage, came Fyodor Pavlovitch, with his son Ivan. Dmitri was late, though he had been informed of the time the evening before. The visitors left their carriage at the hotel, outside the precincts, and went to the gates of the monastery on foot. Except Fyodor Pavlovitch, none of the party had ever seen the monastery, and Miüsov had probably not even been to church for thirty years. He looked about him with curiosity, together with assumed ease. But, except the church and the domestic buildings, though these too were ordinary enough, he found nothing of interest in the interior of the monastery. The last of the worshippers were coming out of the church, bareheaded and crossing themselves. Among the humbler people were a few of higher rank—two or three ladies and a very old general. They were all staying at the hotel. Our visitors were at once surrounded by beggars, but none of them gave them anything, except young Kalganov, who took a ten-copeck piece out of his purse, and, nervous and embarrassed—God knows why!—hurriedly gave it to an old woman, saying: "Divide it equally." None of his companions made any remark upon it, so that he had no reason to be embarrassed; but, perceiving this, he was even more overcome.

It was strange that their arrival did not seem expected, and that they were not received with special honor, though one of them had recently made a donation of a thousand roubles, while another was a very wealthy and highly cultured landowner, upon whom all in the monastery were in a sense dependent, as a decision of the lawsuit might at any moment put their fishing rights in his hands. Yet no official personage met them.

Miüsov looked absent-mindedly at the tombstones round the church, and was on the point of saying that the dead buried here must have paid a pretty penny for the right of lying in this "holy place," but refrained. His liberal irony was rapidly changing almost into anger.

"Who the devil is there to ask in this imbecile place? We must find out, for time is passing," he observed suddenly, as though speaking to himself.

All at once there came up a bald-headed, elderly man with ingratiating little eyes, wearing a full, summer overcoat. Lifting his hat, he introduced himself with a honeyed lisp as Maximov, a landowner of Tula. He at once entered into our visitors' difficulty.

"Father Zossima lives in the hermitage, apart, four hundred paces from the monastery, the other side of the copse."

"I know it's the other side of the copse," observed Fyodor Pavlovitch, "but we don't remember the way. It is a long time since we've been here."

"This way, by this gate, and straight across the copse ... the copse. Come with me, won't you? I'll show you. I have to go.... I am going myself. This way, this way."

They came out of the gate and turned towards the copse. Maximov, a man of sixty, ran rather than walked, turning sideways to stare at them all, with an incredible degree of nervous curiosity. His eyes looked starting out of his head.

"You see, we have come to the elder upon business of our own," observed Miüsov severely. "That personage has granted us an audience, so to speak, and so, though we thank you for showing us the way, we cannot ask you to accompany us."

"I've been there. I've been already; *un chevalier parfait*," and Maximov snapped his fingers in the air.

"Who is a *chevalier*?" asked Miüsov.

"The elder, the splendid elder, the elder! The honor and glory of the monastery, Zossima. Such an elder!"

But his incoherent talk was cut short by a very pale, wan-looking monk of medium height, wearing a monk's cap, who overtook them. Fyodor Pavlovitch and Miüsov stopped.

The monk, with an extremely courteous, profound bow, announced:

"The Father Superior invites all of you gentlemen to dine with him after your visit to the hermitage. At one o'clock, not later. And you also," he added, addressing Maximov.

"That I certainly will, without fail," cried Fyodor Pavlovitch, hugely delighted at the invitation. "And, believe me, we've all given our word to behave properly here.... And you, Pyotr Alexandrovitch, will you go, too?"

"Yes, of course. What have I come for but to study all the customs here? The only obstacle to me is your company...."

"Yes, Dmitri Fyodorovitch is non-existent as yet."

"It would be a capital thing if he didn't turn up. Do you suppose I like all this business, and in your company, too? So we will come to dinner. Thank the Father Superior," he said to the monk.

"No, it is my duty now to conduct you to the elder," answered the monk.

"If so I'll go straight to the Father Superior—to the Father Superior," babbled Maximov.

"The Father Superior is engaged just now. But as you please—" the monk hesitated.

"Impertinent old man!" Miüsov observed aloud, while Maximov ran back to the monastery.

"He's like von Sohn," Fyodor Pavlovitch said suddenly.

"Is that all you can think of?... In what way is he like von Sohn? Have you ever seen von Sohn?"

"I've seen his portrait. It's not the features, but something indefinable. He's a second von Sohn. I can always tell from the physiognomy."

"Ah, I dare say you are a connoisseur in that. But, look here, Fyodor Pavlovitch, you said just now that we had given our word to behave properly. Remember it. I advise you to control yourself. But, if you begin to play the fool I don't intend to be associated with you here.... You see what a man he is"—he turned to the monk—"I'm afraid to go among decent people with him." A fine smile, not without a certain slyness, came on to the pale, bloodless lips of the monk, but he made no reply, and was evidently silent from a sense of his own dignity. Miüsov frowned more than ever.

"Oh, devil take them all! An outer show elaborated through centuries, and nothing but charlatanism and nonsense underneath," flashed through Miüsov's mind.

"Here's the hermitage. We've arrived," cried Fyodor Pavlovitch. "The gates are shut."

And he repeatedly made the sign of the cross to the saints painted above and on the sides of the gates.

"When you go to Rome you must do as the Romans do. Here in this hermitage there are twenty-five saints being saved. They look at one another, and eat cabbages. And not one woman goes in at this gate. That's what is remarkable. And that really is so. But I did hear that the elder receives ladies," he remarked suddenly to the monk.

"Women of the people are here too now, lying in the portico there waiting. But for ladies of higher rank two rooms have been built adjoining the portico, but outside the precincts—you can see the windows—and the elder goes out to them by an inner passage when he is well enough. They are always outside the precincts. There is a Harkov lady, Madame Hohlakov, waiting there now with her sick daughter. Probably he has promised to come out to her, though of late he has been so weak that he has hardly shown himself even to the people."

"So then there are loopholes, after all, to creep out of the hermitage to the ladies. Don't suppose, holy father, that I mean any harm. But do you know that at Athos not only the visits of women are not allowed, but no creature of the female sex—no hens, nor turkey-hens, nor cows."

"Fyodor Pavlovitch, I warn you I shall go back and leave you here. They'll turn you out when I'm gone."

"But I'm not interfering with you, Pyotr Alexandrovitch. Look," he cried suddenly, stepping within the precincts, "what a vale of roses they live in!"

Though there were no roses now, there were numbers of rare and beautiful autumn flowers growing wherever there was space for them, and evidently tended by a skillful hand; there were flower-beds round the church, and between the tombs; and the one-storied wooden house where the elder lived was also surrounded with flowers.

"And was it like this in the time of the last elder, Varsonofy? He didn't care for such elegance. They say he used to jump up and thrash even ladies with a stick," observed Fyodor Pavlovitch, as he went up the steps.

"The elder Varsonofy did sometimes seem rather strange, but a great deal that's told is foolishness. He never thrashed any one," answered the monk. "Now, gentlemen, if you will wait a minute I will announce you."

"Fyodor Pavlovitch, for the last time, your compact, do you hear? Behave properly or I will pay you out!" Miüsov had time to mutter again.

"I can't think why you are so agitated," Fyodor Pavlovitch observed sarcastically. "Are you uneasy about your sins? They say he can tell by one's eyes what one has come about. And what a lot you think of their opinion! you, a Parisian, and so advanced. I'm surprised at you."

But Miüsov had no time to reply to this sarcasm. They were asked to come in. He walked in, somewhat irritated.

"Now, I know myself, I am annoyed, I shall lose my temper and begin to quarrel—and lower myself and my ideas," he reflected.

They entered the room almost at the same moment that the elder came in from his bedroom. There were already in the cell, awaiting the elder, two monks of the hermitage, one the Father Librarian, and the other Father Païssy, a very learned man, so they said, in delicate health, though not old. There was also a tall young man, who looked about two and twenty, standing in the corner throughout the interview. He had a broad, fresh face, and clever, observant, narrow brown eyes, and was wearing ordinary dress. He was a divinity student, living under the protection of the monastery. His expression was one of unquestioning, but self-respecting, reverence. Being in a subordinate and dependent position, and so not on an equality with the guests, he did not greet them with a bow.

Father Zossima was accompanied by a novice, and by Alyosha. The two monks rose and greeted him with a very deep bow, touching the ground with their fingers; then kissed his hand. Blessing them, the elder replied with as deep a reverence to them, and asked their blessing. The whole ceremony was performed very seriously and with an appearance of feeling, not like an everyday rite. But Miüsov fancied that it was all done with intentional impressiveness. He stood in front of the other visitors. He ought—he had reflected upon it the evening before—from simple politeness, since it was the custom here, to have gone up to receive the elder's blessing, even if he did not kiss his hand. But when he saw all this bowing and kissing on the part of the monks he instantly changed his mind. With dignified gravity he made a rather deep, conventional bow, and moved away to a chair. Fyodor Pavlovitch did the same, mimicking Miüsov like an ape. Ivan bowed with great dignity and courtesy, but he too kept his hands at his sides, while Kalganov was so confused that he did not bow at all. The elder let fall the hand raised to bless them, and bowing to them again, asked them all to sit down. The blood rushed to Alyosha's cheeks. He was ashamed. His forebodings were coming true.

Father Zossima sat down on a very old-fashioned mahogany sofa, covered with leather, and made his visitors sit down in a row along the opposite wall on four mahogany chairs, covered with shabby black leather. The monks sat, one at the door and the other at the window. The divinity student, the novice, and Alyosha remained standing. The cell was not very large and had a faded look. It contained nothing but the most necessary furniture, of coarse and poor quality. There were two pots of flowers in the window, and a number of holy pictures in the corner. Before one huge ancient ikon of the Virgin a lamp was burning. Near it were two other holy pictures in shining settings, and, next them, carved cherubims, china eggs, a Catholic cross of ivory, with a Mater Dolorosa embracing it, and several foreign engravings from the great Italian artists of past centuries. Next to these costly and artistic engravings were several of the roughest Russian prints of saints and martyrs, such as are sold for a few farthings at all the fairs. On the other walls were portraits of Russian bishops, past and present.

Miüsov took a cursory glance at all these "conventional" surroundings and bent an intent look upon the elder. He had a high opinion of his own insight, a weakness excusable in him as he was fifty, an age at which a clever man of the world of established position can hardly help taking himself rather seriously. At the first moment he did not like Zossima. There was, indeed, something in the elder's face which many people besides Miüsov might not have liked. He was a short, bent, little man, with very weak legs, and though he was only sixty-five, he looked at least ten years older. His face was very thin and covered with a network of fine wrinkles, particularly numerous about his eyes, which were small, light-colored, quick, and shining like two bright points. He had a sprinkling of gray hair about his temples. His pointed beard was small and scanty, and his lips, which smiled frequently, were as thin as two threads. His nose was not long, but sharp, like a bird's beak.

"To all appearances a malicious soul, full of petty pride," thought Miüsov. He felt altogether dissatisfied with his position.

A cheap little clock on the wall struck twelve hurriedly, and served to begin the conversation.

"Precisely to our time," cried Fyodor Pavlovitch, "but no sign of my son, Dmitri. I apologize for him, sacred elder!" (Alyosha shuddered all over at "sacred elder.") "I am always punctual myself, minute for minute, remembering that punctuality is the courtesy of kings...."

"But you are not a king, anyway," Miüsov muttered, losing his self-restraint at once.

"Yes; that's true. I'm not a king, and, would you believe it, Pyotr Alexandrovitch, I was aware of that myself. But, there! I always say the wrong thing. Your reverence," he cried, with sudden pathos, "you behold before you a buffoon in earnest! I introduce myself as such. It's an old habit, alas! And if I sometimes talk nonsense out of place it's with an object, with the object of amusing people and making myself agreeable. One must be agreeable, mustn't one? I was seven years ago in a little town where I had business, and I made friends with some merchants there. We went to the captain of police because we had to see him about something, and to ask him to dine with us. He was a tall, fat, fair, sulky man, the most dangerous type in such cases. It's their liver. I went straight up to him, and with the ease of a man of the world, you know, 'Mr. Ispravnik,' said I, 'be our Napravnik.' 'What do you mean by Napravnik?' said he. I saw, at the first half-second, that it had missed fire. He stood there so glum. 'I wanted to make a joke,' said I, 'for the general diversion, as Mr. Napravnik is our well-known Russian orchestra conductor and what we need for the harmony of our undertaking is some one of that sort.' And I explained my comparison very reasonably, didn't I? 'Excuse me,' said he, 'I am an Ispravnik, and I do not allow puns to be made on my calling.' He turned and walked away. I followed him, shouting, 'Yes, yes, you are an Ispravnik, not a Napravnik.' 'No,' he said, 'since you called me a Napravnik I am one.' And would you believe it, it ruined our business! And I'm always like that, always like that. Always injuring myself with my politeness. Once, many years ago, I said to an influential person: 'Your wife is a ticklish lady,' in an honorable sense, of the moral qualities, so to speak. But he asked me, 'Why, have you tickled her?' I thought I'd be polite, so I couldn't help saying, 'Yes,' and he gave me a fine tickling on the spot. Only that happened long ago, so I'm not ashamed to tell the story. I'm always injuring myself like that."

"You're doing it now," muttered Miüsov, with disgust.

Father Zossima scrutinized them both in silence.

"Am I? Would you believe it, I was aware of that, too, Pyotr Alexandrovitch, and let me tell you, indeed, I foresaw I should as soon as I began to speak. And do you know I foresaw, too, that you'd be the first to remark on it. The minute I see my joke isn't coming off, your reverence, both my cheeks feel as though they were drawn down to the lower jaw and there is almost a spasm in them. That's been so since I was young, when I had to make jokes for my living in noblemen's families. I am an inveterate buffoon, and have been from birth up, your reverence, it's as though it were a craze in me. I dare say it's a devil within me. But only a little one. A more serious one would have chosen another lodging. But not your soul, Pyotr Alexandrovitch; you're not a lodging worth having either. But I do believe—I believe in God, though I have had doubts of late. But now I sit and await words of wisdom. I'm like the philosopher, Diderot, your reverence. Did you ever hear, most Holy Father, how Diderot went to see the Metropolitan Platon, in the time of the Empress Catherine? He went in and said straight out, 'There is no God.' To which the great bishop lifted up his finger and answered, 'The fool hath said in his heart there is no God.' And he fell down at his feet on the spot. 'I believe,' he cried, 'and will be christened.' And so he was. Princess Dashkov was his godmother, and Potyomkin his godfather."

"Fyodor Pavlovitch, this is unbearable! You know you're telling lies and that that stupid anecdote isn't true. Why are you playing the fool?" cried Miüsov in a shaking voice.

"I suspected all my life that it wasn't true," Fyodor Pavlovitch cried with conviction. "But I'll tell you the whole truth, gentlemen. Great elder! Forgive me, the last thing about Diderot's christening I made up just now. I never thought of it before. I made it up to add piquancy. I play the fool, Pyotr Alexandrovitch, to make myself agreeable. Though I really don't know myself, sometimes, what I do it for. And as for Diderot, I heard as far as 'the fool hath said in his heart' twenty times from the gentry about here when I was young. I heard your aunt, Pyotr Alexandrovitch, tell the story. They all believe to this day that the infidel Diderot came to dispute about God with the Metropolitan Platon...."

Miüsov got up, forgetting himself in his impatience. He was furious, and conscious of being ridiculous.

What was taking place in the cell was really incredible. For forty or fifty years past, from the times of former elders, no visitors had entered that cell without feelings of the profoundest veneration. Almost every one admitted to the cell felt that a great favor was being shown him. Many remained kneeling during the whole visit. Of those visitors, many had been men of high rank and learning, some even freethinkers, attracted by curiosity, but all without exception had shown the profoundest reverence and delicacy, for here there was no question of money, but only, on the one side love and kindness, and on the other penitence and eager desire to decide some spiritual problem or crisis. So that such buffoonery amazed and bewildered the spectators, or at least some of them. The monks, with unchanged countenances, waited, with earnest attention, to hear what the elder would say, but seemed on the point of standing up, like Miüsov. Alyosha stood, with hanging head, on the verge of tears. What seemed to him strangest of all was that his brother Ivan, on whom alone he had rested his hopes, and who alone had such influence on his father that he could have stopped him, sat now quite unmoved, with downcast eyes, apparently waiting with interest to see how it would end, as though he had nothing to do with it. Alyosha did not dare to look at Rakitin, the divinity student, whom he knew almost intimately. He alone in the monastery knew Rakitin's thoughts.

"Forgive me," began Miüsov, addressing Father Zossima, "for perhaps I seem to be taking part in this shameful foolery. I made a mistake in believing that even a man like Fyodor Pavlovitch would understand what was due on a visit to so honored a personage. I did not suppose I should have to apologize simply for having come with him...."

Pyotr Alexandrovitch could say no more, and was about to leave the room, overwhelmed with confusion.

"Don't distress yourself, I beg." The elder got on to his feeble legs, and taking Pyotr Alexandrovitch by both hands, made him sit down again. "I beg you not to disturb yourself. I particularly beg you to be my guest." And with a bow he went back and sat down again on his little sofa.

"Great elder, speak! Do I annoy you by my vivacity?" Fyodor Pavlovitch cried suddenly, clutching the arms of his chair in both hands, as though ready to leap up from it if the answer were unfavorable.

"I earnestly beg you, too, not to disturb yourself, and not to be uneasy," the elder said impressively. "Do not trouble. Make yourself quite at home. And, above all, do not be so ashamed of yourself, for that is at the root of it all."

"Quite at home? To be my natural self? Oh, that is much too much, but I accept it with grateful joy. Do you know, blessed Father, you'd better not invite me to be my natural self. Don't risk it.... I will not go so far as that myself. I warn you for your own sake. Well, the rest is still plunged in the mists of uncertainty, though there are people who'd be pleased to describe me for you. I mean that for you, Pyotr Alexandrovitch. But as for you, holy being, let me tell you, I am brimming over with ecstasy."

He got up, and throwing up his hands, declaimed, "Blessed be the womb that bare thee, and the paps that gave thee suck—the paps especially. When you said just now, 'Don't be so ashamed of yourself, for that is at the root of it all,' you pierced right through me by that remark, and read me to the core. Indeed, I always feel when I meet people that I am lower than all, and that they all take me for a buffoon. So I say, 'Let me really play the buffoon. I am not afraid of your opinion, for you are every one of you worse than I am.' That is why I am a buffoon. It is from shame, great elder, from shame; it's simply over-sensitiveness that makes me rowdy. If I had only been sure that every one would accept me as the kindest and wisest of men, oh, Lord, what a good man I should have been then! Teacher!" he fell suddenly on his knees, "what must I do to gain eternal life?"

It was difficult even now to decide whether he was joking or really moved.

Father Zossima, lifting his eyes, looked at him, and said with a smile:

"You have known for a long time what you must do. You have sense enough: don't give way to drunkenness and incontinence of speech; don't give way to sensual lust; and, above all, to the love of money. And close your taverns. If you can't close all, at least two or three. And, above all—don't lie."

"You mean about Diderot?"

"No, not about Diderot. Above all, don't lie to yourself. The man who lies to himself and listens to his own lie comes to such a pass that he cannot distinguish the truth within him, or around him, and so loses all respect for himself and for others. And having no respect he ceases to love, and in order to occupy and distract himself without love he gives way to passions and coarse pleasures, and sinks to bestiality in his vices, all from continual lying to other men and to himself. The man who lies to himself can be more easily offended than any one. You know it is sometimes very pleasant to take offense, isn't it? A man may know that nobody has insulted him, but that he has invented the insult for himself, has lied and exaggerated to make it picturesque, has caught at a word and made a mountain out of a molehill—he knows that himself, yet he will be the first to take offense, and will revel in his resentment till he feels great pleasure in it, and so pass to genuine vindictiveness. But get up, sit down, I beg you. All this, too, is deceitful posturing...."

"Blessed man! Give me your hand to kiss."

Fyodor Pavlovitch skipped up, and imprinted a rapid kiss on the elder's thin hand. "It is, it is pleasant to take offense. You said that so well, as I never heard it before. Yes, I have been all my life taking offense, to please myself, taking offense on esthetic grounds, for it is not so much pleasant as distinguished sometimes to be insulted—that you had forgotten, great elder, it is distinguished! I shall make a note of that. But I have been lying, lying positively my whole life long, every day and hour of it. Of a truth, I am a lie, and the father of lies. Though I believe I am not the father of lies. I am getting mixed in my texts. Say, the son of lies, and that will be enough. Only ... my angel ... I may sometimes talk about Diderot! Diderot will do no harm, though sometimes a word will do harm. Great elder, by the way, I was forgetting, though I had been meaning for the last two years to come here on purpose to ask and to find out something. Only do tell Pyotr Alexandrovitch not to interrupt me. Here is my question: Is it true, great Father, that the story is told somewhere in the *Lives of the Saints* of a holy saint martyred for his faith who, when his head was cut off at last, stood up, picked up his head, and, 'courteously kissing it,' walked a long way, carrying it in his hands. Is that true or not, honored Father?"

"No, it is untrue," said the elder.

"There is nothing of the kind in all the lives of the saints. What saint do you say the story is told of?" asked the Father Librarian.

"I do not know what saint. I do not know, and can't tell. I was deceived. I was told the story. I had heard it, and do you know who told it? Pyotr Alexandrovitch Miüsov here, who was so angry just now about Diderot. He it was who told the story."

"I have never told it you, I never speak to you at all."

"It is true you did not tell me, but you told it when I was present. It was three years ago. I mentioned it because by that ridiculous story you shook my faith, Pyotr Alexandrovitch. You knew nothing of it, but I went home with my faith shaken, and I have been getting more and more shaken ever since. Yes, Pyotr Alexandrovitch, you were the cause of a great fall. That was not a Diderot!"

Fyodor Pavlovitch got excited and pathetic, though it was perfectly clear to every one by now that he was playing a part again. Yet Miüsov was stung by his words.

"What nonsense, and it is all nonsense," he muttered. "I may really have told it, some time or other ... but not to you. I was told it myself. I heard it in Paris from a Frenchman. He told me it was read at our mass from the *Lives of the Saints* ... he was a very learned man who had made a special study of Russian statistics and had lived a long time in Russia.... I have not read the *Lives of the Saints* myself, and I am not going to read them ... all sorts of things are said at dinner—we were dining then."

"Yes, you were dining then, and so I lost my faith!" said Fyodor Pavlovitch, mimicking him.

"What do I care for your faith?" Miüsov was on the point of shouting, but he suddenly checked himself, and said with contempt, "You defile everything you touch."

The elder suddenly rose from his seat. "Excuse me, gentlemen, for leaving you a few minutes," he said, addressing all his guests. "I have visitors awaiting me who arrived before you. But don't you tell lies all the same," he added, turning to Fyodor Pavlovitch with a good-humored face. He went out of the cell. Alyosha and the novice flew to escort him down the steps. Alyosha was breathless: he was glad to get away, but he was glad, too, that the elder was good-humored and not offended. Father Zossima was going towards the portico to bless the people waiting for him there. But Fyodor Pavlovitch persisted in stopping him at the door of the cell.

"Blessed man!" he cried, with feeling. "Allow me to kiss your hand once more. Yes, with you I could still talk, I could still get on. Do you think I always lie and play the fool like this? Believe me, I have been acting like this all the time on purpose to try you. I have been testing you all the time to see whether I could get on with you. Is there room for my humility beside your pride? I am ready to give you a testimonial that one can get on with you! But now, I'll be quiet; I will keep quiet all the time. I'll sit in a chair and hold my tongue. Now it is for you to speak, Pyotr Alexandrovitch. You are the principal person left now—for ten minutes."

Near the wooden portico below, built on to the outer wall of the precinct, there was a crowd of about twenty peasant women. They had been told that the elder was at last coming out, and they had gathered together in anticipation. Two ladies, Madame Hohlakov and her daughter, had also come out into the portico to wait for the elder, but in a separate part of it set aside for women of rank.

Madame Hohlakov was a wealthy lady, still young and attractive, and always dressed with taste. She was rather pale, and had lively black eyes. She was not more than thirty-three, and had been five years a widow. Her daughter, a girl of fourteen, was partially paralyzed. The poor child had not been able to walk for the last six months, and was wheeled about in a long reclining chair. She had a charming little face, rather thin from illness, but full of gayety. There was a gleam of mischief in her big dark eyes with their long lashes. Her mother had been intending to take her abroad ever since the spring, but they had been detained all the summer by business connected with their estate. They had been staying a week in our town, where they had come more for purposes of business than devotion, but had visited Father Zossima once already, three days before. Though they knew that the elder scarcely saw any one, they had now suddenly turned up again, and urgently entreated "the happiness of looking once again on the great healer."

The mother was sitting on a chair by the side of her daughter's invalid carriage, and two paces from her stood an old monk, not one of our monastery, but a visitor from an obscure religious house in the far north. He too sought the elder's blessing.

But Father Zossima, on entering the portico, went first straight to the peasants who were crowded at the foot of the three steps that led up into the portico. Father Zossima stood on the top step, put on his stole, and began blessing the women who thronged about him. One crazy woman was led up to him. As soon as she caught sight of the elder she began shrieking and writhing as though in the pains of childbirth. Laying the stole on her forehead, he read a short prayer over her, and she was at once soothed and quieted.

I do not know how it may be now, but in my childhood I often happened to see and hear these "possessed" women in the villages and monasteries. They used to be brought to mass; they would squeal and bark like a dog so that they were heard all over the church. But when the sacrament was carried in and they were led up to it, at once the "possession" ceased, and the sick women were always soothed for a time. I was greatly impressed and amazed at this as a child; but then I heard from country neighbors and from my town teachers that the whole illness was simulated to avoid work, and that it could always be cured by suitable severity; various anecdotes were told to confirm this. But later on I learnt with astonishment from medical specialists that there is no pretense about it, that it is a terrible illness to which women are subject, specially prevalent among us in Russia, and that it is due to the hard lot of the peasant women. It is a disease, I was told, arising from exhausting toil too soon after hard, abnormal and unassisted labor in childbirth, and from the hopeless misery, from beatings, and so on, which some women were not able to endure like others. The strange and instant healing of the frantic and struggling woman as soon as she was led up to the holy sacrament, which had been explained to me as due to malingering and the trickery of the "clericals," arose probably in the most natural manner. Both the women who supported her and the invalid herself fully believed as a truth beyond question that the evil spirit in possession of her could not hold out if the sick woman were brought to the sacrament and made to bow down before it. And so, with a nervous and psychically deranged woman, a sort of convulsion of the whole organism always took place, and was bound to take place, at the moment of bowing down to the sacrament, aroused by the expectation of the miracle of healing and the implicit belief that it would come to pass; and it did come to pass, though only for a moment. It was exactly the same now as soon as the elder touched the sick woman with the stole.

Many of the women in the crowd were moved to tears of ecstasy by the effect of the moment: some strove to kiss the hem of his garment, others cried out in sing-song voices.

He blessed them all and talked with some of them. The "possessed" woman he knew already. She came from a village only six versts from the monastery, and had been brought to him before.

"But here is one from afar." He pointed to a woman by no means old but very thin and wasted, with a face not merely sunburnt but almost blackened by exposure. She was kneeling and gazing with a fixed stare at the elder; there was something almost frenzied in her eyes.

"From afar off, Father, from afar off! From two hundred miles from here. From afar off, Father, from afar off!" the woman began in a sing-song voice as though she were chanting a dirge, swaying her head from side to side with her cheek resting in her hand.

There is silent and long-suffering sorrow to be met with among the peasantry. It withdraws into itself and is still. But there is a grief that breaks out, and from that minute it bursts into tears and finds vent in wailing. This is particularly common with women. But it is no lighter a grief than the silent. Lamentations comfort only by lacerating the heart still more. Such grief does not desire consolation. It feeds on the sense of its hopelessness. Lamentations spring only from the constant craving to reopen the wound.

"You are of the tradesman class?" said Father Zossima, looking curiously at her.

"Townfolk we are, Father, townfolk. Yet we are peasants though we live in the town. I have come to see you, O Father! We heard of you, Father, we heard of you. I have buried my little son, and I have come on a pilgrimage. I have been in three monasteries, but they told me, 'Go, Nastasya, go to them'—that is to you. I have come; I was yesterday at the service, and to-day I have come to you."

"What are you weeping for?"

"It's my little son I'm grieving for, Father. He was three years old—three years all but three months. For my little boy, Father, I'm in anguish, for my little boy. He was the last one left. We had four, my Nikita and I, and now we've no children, our dear ones have all gone. I buried the first three without grieving overmuch, and now I have buried the last I can't forget him. He seems always standing before me. He never leaves me. He has withered my heart. I look at his little clothes, his little shirt, his little boots, and I wail. I lay out all that is left of him, all his little things. I look at them and wail. I say to Nikita, my husband, 'Let me go on a pilgrimage, master.' He is a driver. We're not poor people, Father, not poor; he drives our own horse. It's all our own, the horse and the carriage. And what good is it all to us now? My Nikita has begun drinking while I am away. He's sure to. It used to be so before. As soon as I turn my back he gives way to it. But now I don't think about him. It's three months since I left home. I've forgotten him. I've forgotten everything. I don't want to remember. And what would our life be now together? I've done with him, I've done. I've done with them all. I don't care to look upon my house and my goods. I don't care to see anything at all!"

"Listen, mother," said the elder. "Once in olden times a holy saint saw in the Temple a mother like you weeping for her little one, her only one, whom God had taken. 'Knowest thou not,' said the saint to her, 'how bold these little ones are before the throne of God? Verily there are none bolder than they in the Kingdom of Heaven. "Thou didst give us life, O Lord," they say, "and scarcely had we looked upon it when Thou didst take it back again." And so boldly they ask and ask again that God gives them at once the rank of angels. Therefore,' said the saint, 'thou, too, O mother, rejoice and weep not, for thy little son is with the Lord in the fellowship of the angels.' That's what the saint said to the weeping mother of old. He was a great saint and he could not have spoken falsely. Therefore you too, mother, know that your little one is surely before the throne of God, is rejoicing and happy, and praying to God for you, and therefore weep not, but rejoice."

The woman listened to him, looking down with her cheek in her hand. She sighed deeply.

"My Nikita tried to comfort me with the same words as you. 'Foolish one,' he said, 'why weep? Our son is no doubt singing with the angels before God.' He says that to me, but he weeps himself. I see that he cries like me. 'I know, Nikita,' said I. 'Where could he be if not with the Lord God? Only, here with us now he is not as he used to sit beside us before.' And if only I could look upon him one little time, if only I could peep at him one little time, without going up to him, without speaking, if I could be hidden in a corner and only see him for one little minute, hear him playing in the yard, calling in his little voice, 'Mammy, where are you?' If only I could hear him pattering with his little feet about the room just once, only once; for so often, so often I remember how he used to run to me and shout and laugh, if only I could hear his little feet I should know him! But he's gone, Father, he's gone, and I shall never hear him again. Here's his little sash, but him I shall never see or hear now."

She drew out of her bosom her boy's little embroidered sash, and as soon as she looked at it she began shaking with sobs, hiding her eyes with her fingers through which the tears flowed in a sudden stream.

"It is Rachel of old," said the elder, "weeping for her children, and will not be comforted because they are not. Such is the lot set on earth for you mothers. Be not comforted. Consolation is not what you need. Weep and be not consoled, but weep. Only every time that you weep be sure to remember that your little son is one of the angels of God, that he looks down from there at you and sees you, and rejoices at your tears, and points at them to the Lord God; and a long while yet will you keep that great mother's grief. But it will turn in the end into quiet joy, and your bitter tears will be only tears of tender sorrow that purifies the heart and delivers it from sin. And I shall pray for the peace of your child's soul. What was his name?"

"Alexey, Father."

"A sweet name. After Alexey, the man of God?"

"Yes, Father."

"What a saint he was! I will remember him, mother, and your grief in my prayers, and I will pray for your husband's health. It is a sin for you to leave him. Your little one will see from heaven that you have forsaken his father, and will weep over you. Why do you trouble his happiness? He is living, for the soul lives for ever, and though he is not in the house he is near you, unseen. How can he go into the house when you say that the house is hateful to you? To whom is he to go if he find you not together, his father and mother? He comes to you in dreams now, and you grieve. But then he will send you gentle dreams. Go to your husband, mother; go this very day."

"I will go, Father, at your word. I will go. You've gone straight to my heart. My Nikita, my Nikita, you are waiting for me," the woman began in a sing-song voice; but the elder had already turned away to a very old woman, dressed like a dweller in the town, not like a pilgrim. Her eyes showed that she had come with an object, and in order to say something. She said she was the widow of a non-commissioned officer, and lived close by in the town. Her son Vasenka was in the commissariat service, and had gone to Irkutsk in Siberia. He had written twice from there, but now a year had passed since he had written. She did inquire about him, but she did not know the proper place to inquire.

"Only the other day Stepanida Ilyinishna—she's a rich merchant's wife—said to me, 'You go, Prohorovna, and put your son's name down for prayer in the church, and pray for the peace of his soul as though he were dead. His soul will be troubled,' she said, 'and he will write you a letter.' And Stepanida Ilyinishna told me it was a certain thing which had been many times tried. Only I am in doubt.... Oh, you light of ours! is it true or false, and would it be right?"

"Don't think of it. It's shameful to ask the question. How is it possible to pray for the peace of a living soul? And his own mother too! It's a great sin, akin to sorcery. Only for your ignorance it is forgiven you. Better pray to the Queen of Heaven, our swift defense and help, for his good health, and that she may forgive you for your error. And another thing I will tell you, Prohorovna. Either he will soon come back to you, your son, or he will be sure to send a letter. Go, and henceforward be in peace. Your son is alive, I tell you."

"Dear Father, God reward you, our benefactor, who prays for all of us and for our sins!"

But the elder had already noticed in the crowd two glowing eyes fixed upon him. An exhausted, consumptive-looking, though young peasant woman was gazing at him in silence. Her eyes besought him, but she seemed afraid to approach.

"What is it, my child?"

"Absolve my soul, Father," she articulated softly, and slowly sank on her knees and bowed down at his feet. "I have sinned, Father. I am afraid of my sin."

The elder sat down on the lower step. The woman crept closer to him, still on her knees.

"I am a widow these three years," she began in a half-whisper, with a sort of shudder. "I had a hard life with my husband. He was an old man. He used to beat me cruelly. He lay ill; I thought looking at him, if he were to get well, if he were to get up again, what then? And then the thought came to me—"

"Stay!" said the elder, and he put his ear close to her lips.

The woman went on in a low whisper, so that it was almost impossible to catch anything. She had soon done.

"Three years ago?" asked the elder.

"Three years. At first I didn't think about it, but now I've begun to be ill, and the thought never leaves me."

"Have you come from far?"

"Over three hundred miles away."

"Have you told it in confession?"

"I have confessed it. Twice I have confessed it."

"Have you been admitted to Communion?"

"Yes. I am afraid. I am afraid to die."

"Fear nothing and never be afraid; and don't fret. If only your penitence fail not, God will forgive all. There is no sin, and there can be no sin on all the earth, which the Lord will not forgive to the truly repentant! Man cannot commit a sin so great as to exhaust the infinite love of God. Can there be a sin which could exceed the love of God? Think only of repentance, continual repentance, but dismiss fear altogether. Believe that God loves you as you cannot conceive; that He loves you with your sin, in your sin. It has been said of old that over one repentant sinner there is more joy in heaven than over ten righteous men. Go, and fear not. Be not bitter against men. Be not angry if you are wronged. Forgive the dead man in your heart what wrong he did you. Be reconciled with him in truth. If you are penitent, you love. And if you love you are of God. All things are atoned for, all things are saved by love. If I, a sinner, even as you are, am tender with you and have pity on you, how much more will God. Love is such a priceless treasure that you can redeem the whole world by it, and expiate not only your own sins but the sins of others."

He signed her three times with the cross, took from his own neck a little ikon and put it upon her. She bowed down to the earth without speaking.

He got up and looked cheerfully at a healthy peasant woman with a tiny baby in her arms.

"From Vyshegorye, dear Father."

"Five miles you have dragged yourself with the baby. What do you want?"

"I've come to look at you. I have been to you before—or have you forgotten? You've no great memory if you've forgotten me. They told us you were ill. Thinks I, I'll go and see him for myself. Now I see you, and you're not ill! You'll live another twenty years. God bless you! There are plenty to pray for you; how should you be ill?"

"I thank you for all, daughter."

"By the way, I have a thing to ask, not a great one. Here are sixty copecks. Give them, dear Father, to some one poorer than me. I thought as I came along, better give through him. He'll know whom to give to."

"Thanks, my dear, thanks! You are a good woman. I love you. I will do so certainly. Is that your little girl?"

"My little girl, Father, Lizaveta."

"May the Lord bless you both, you and your babe Lizaveta! You have gladdened my heart, mother. Farewell, dear children, farewell, dear ones."

He blessed them all and bowed low to them.

A visitor looking on the scene of his conversation with the peasants and his blessing them shed silent tears and wiped them away with her handkerchief. She was a sentimental society lady of genuinely good disposition in many respects. When the elder went up to her at last she met him enthusiastically.

"Ah, what I have been feeling, looking on at this touching scene!..." She could not go on for emotion. "Oh, I understand the people's love for you. I love the people myself. I want to love them. And who could help loving them, our splendid Russian people, so simple in their greatness!"

"How is your daughter's health? You wanted to talk to me again?"

"Oh, I have been urgently begging for it, I have prayed for it! I was ready to fall on my knees and kneel for three days at your windows until you let me in. We have come, great healer, to express our ardent gratitude. You have healed my Lise, healed her completely, merely by praying over her last Thursday and laying your hands upon her. We have hastened here to kiss those hands, to pour out our feelings and our homage."

"What do you mean by healed? But she is still lying down in her chair."

"But her night fevers have entirely ceased ever since Thursday," said the lady with nervous haste. "And that's not all. Her legs are stronger. This morning she got up well; she had slept all night. Look at her rosy cheeks, her bright eyes! She used to be always crying, but now she laughs and is gay and happy. This morning she insisted on my letting her stand up, and she stood up for a whole minute without any support. She wagers that in a fortnight she'll be dancing a quadrille. I've called in Doctor Herzenstube. He shrugged his shoulders and said, 'I am amazed; I can make nothing of it.' And would you have us not come here to disturb you, not fly here to thank you? Lise, thank him—thank him!"

Lise's pretty little laughing face became suddenly serious. She rose in her chair as far as she could and, looking at the elder, clasped her hands before him, but could not restrain herself and broke into laughter.

"It's at him," she said, pointing to Alyosha, with childish vexation at herself for not being able to repress her mirth.

If any one had looked at Alyosha standing a step behind the elder, he would have caught a quick flush crimsoning his cheeks in an instant. His eyes shone and he looked down.

"She has a message for you, Alexey Fyodorovitch. How are you?" the mother went on, holding out her exquisitely gloved hand to Alyosha.

The elder turned round and all at once looked attentively at Alyosha. The latter went nearer to Lise and, smiling in a strangely awkward way, held out his hand to her too. Lise assumed an important air.

"Katerina Ivanovna has sent you this through me." She handed him a little note. "She particularly begs you to go and see her as soon as possible; that you will not fail her, but will be sure to come."

"She asks me to go and see her? Me? What for?" Alyosha muttered in great astonishment. His face at once looked anxious. "Oh, it's all to do with Dmitri Fyodorovitch and—what has happened lately," the mother explained hurriedly. "Katerina Ivanovna has made up her mind, but she must see you about it.... Why, of course, I can't say. But she wants to see you at once. And you will go to her, of course. It is a Christian duty."

"I have only seen her once," Alyosha protested with the same perplexity.

"Oh, she is such a lofty, incomparable creature! If only for her suffering.... Think what she has gone through, what she is enduring now! Think what awaits her! It's all terrible, terrible!"

"Very well, I will come," Alyosha decided, after rapidly scanning the brief, enigmatic note, which consisted of an urgent entreaty that he would come, without any sort of explanation.

"Oh, how sweet and generous that would be of you!" cried Lise with sudden animation. "I told mamma you'd be sure not to go. I said you were saving your soul. How splendid you are! I've always thought you were splendid. How glad I am to tell you so!"

"Lise!" said her mother impressively, though she smiled after she had said it.

"You have quite forgotten us, Alexey Fyodorovitch," she said; "you never come to see us. Yet Lise has told me twice that she is never happy except with you."

Alyosha raised his downcast eyes and again flushed, and again smiled without knowing why. But the elder was no longer watching him. He had begun talking to a monk who, as mentioned before, had been awaiting his entrance by Lise's chair. He was evidently a monk of the humblest, that is of the peasant, class, of a narrow outlook, but a true believer, and, in his own way, a stubborn one. He announced that he had come from the far north, from Obdorsk, from Saint Sylvester, and was a member of a poor monastery, consisting of only ten monks. The elder gave him his blessing and invited him to come to his cell whenever he liked.

"How can you presume to do such deeds?" the monk asked suddenly, pointing solemnly and significantly at Lise. He was referring to her "healing."

"It's too early, of course, to speak of that. Relief is not complete cure, and may proceed from different causes. But if there has been any healing, it is by no power but God's will. It's all from God. Visit me, Father," he added to the monk. "It's not often I can see visitors. I am ill, and I know that my days are numbered."

"Oh, no, no! God will not take you from us. You will live a long, long time yet," cried the lady. "And in what way are you ill? You look so well, so gay and happy."

"I am extraordinarily better to-day. But I know that it's only for a moment. I understand my disease now thoroughly. If I seem so happy to you, you could never say anything that would please me so much. For men are made for happiness, and any one who is completely happy has a right to say to himself, 'I am doing God's will on earth.' All the righteous, all the saints, all the holy martyrs were happy."

"Oh, how you speak! What bold and lofty words!" cried the lady. "You seem to pierce with your words. And yet—happiness, happiness—where is it? Who can say of himself that he is happy? Oh, since you have been so good as to let us see you once more to-day, let me tell you what I could not utter last time, what I dared not say, all I am suffering and have been for so long! I am suffering! Forgive me! I am suffering!"

And in a rush of fervent feeling she clasped her hands before him.

"From what specially?"

"I suffer ... from lack of faith."

"Lack of faith in God?"

"Oh, no, no! I dare not even think of that. But the future life—it is such an enigma! And no one, no one can solve it. Listen! You are a healer, you are deeply versed in the human soul, and of course I dare not expect you to believe me entirely, but I assure you on my word of honor that I am not speaking lightly now. The thought of the life beyond the grave distracts me to anguish, to terror. And I don't know to whom to appeal, and have not dared to all my life. And now I am so bold as to ask you. Oh, God! What will you think of me now?"

She clasped her hands.

"Don't distress yourself about my opinion of you," said the elder. "I quite believe in the sincerity of your suffering."

"Oh, how thankful I am to you! You see, I shut my eyes and ask myself if every one has faith, where did it come from? And then they do say that it all comes from terror at the menacing phenomena of nature, and that none of it's real. And I say to myself, 'What if I've been believing all my life, and when I come to die there's nothing but the burdocks growing on my grave?' as I read in some author. It's awful! How—how can I get back my faith? But I only believed when I was a little child, mechanically, without thinking of anything. How, how is one to prove it? I have come now to lay my soul before you and to ask you about it. If I let this chance slip, no one all my life will answer me. How can I prove it? How can I convince myself? Oh, how unhappy I am! I stand and look about me and see that scarcely any one else cares; no one troubles his head about it, and I'm the only one who can't stand it. It's deadly—deadly!"

"No doubt. But there's no proving it, though you can be convinced of it."

"How?"

"By the experience of active love. Strive to love your neighbor actively and indefatigably. In as far as you advance in love you will grow surer of the reality of God and of the immortality of your soul. If you attain to perfect self-forgetfulness in the love of your neighbor, then you will believe without doubt, and no doubt can possibly enter your soul. This has been tried. This is certain."

"In active love? There's another question—and such a question! You see, I so love humanity that—would you believe it?—I often dream of forsaking all that I have, leaving Lise, and becoming a sister of mercy. I close my eyes and think and dream, and at that moment I feel full of strength to overcome all obstacles. No wounds, no festering sores could at that moment frighten me. I would bind them up and wash them with my own hands. I would nurse the afflicted. I would be ready to kiss such wounds."

"It is much, and well that your mind is full of such dreams and not others. Sometime, unawares, you may do a good deed in reality."

"Yes. But could I endure such a life for long?" the lady went on fervently, almost frantically. "That's the chief question—that's my most agonizing question. I shut my eyes and ask myself, 'Would you persevere long on that path? And if the patient whose wounds you are washing did not meet you with gratitude, but worried you with his whims, without valuing or remarking your charitable services, began abusing you and rudely commanding you, and complaining to the superior authorities of you (which often happens when people are in great suffering)—what then? Would you persevere in your love, or not?' And do you know, I came with horror to the conclusion that, if anything could dissipate my love to humanity, it would be ingratitude. In short, I am a hired servant, I expect my payment at once—that is, praise, and the repayment of love with love. Otherwise I am incapable of loving any one."

She was in a very paroxysm of self-castigation, and, concluding, she looked with defiant resolution at the elder.

"It's just the same story as a doctor once told me," observed the elder. "He was a man getting on in years, and undoubtedly clever. He spoke as frankly as you, though in jest, in bitter jest. 'I love humanity,' he said, 'but I wonder at myself. The more I love humanity in general, the less I love man in particular. In my dreams,' he said, 'I have often come to making enthusiastic schemes for the service of humanity, and perhaps I might actually have faced crucifixion if it had been suddenly necessary; and yet I am incapable of living in the same room with any one for two days together, as I know by experience. As soon as any one is near me, his personality disturbs my self-complacency and restricts my freedom. In twenty-four hours I begin to hate the best of men: one because he's too long over his dinner; another because he has a cold and keeps on blowing his nose. I become hostile to people the moment they come close to me. But it has always happened that the more I detest men individually the more ardent becomes my love for humanity.'"

"But what's to be done? What can one do in such a case? Must one despair?"

"No. It is enough that you are distressed at it. Do what you can, and it will be reckoned unto you. Much is done already in you since you can so deeply and sincerely know yourself. If you have been talking to me so sincerely, simply to gain approbation for your frankness, as you did from me just now, then of course you will not attain to anything in the achievement of real love; it will all get no further than dreams, and your whole life will

Fyodor Dostoyevsky   23

slip away like a phantom. In that case you will naturally cease to think of the future life too, and will of yourself grow calmer after a fashion in the end."

"You have crushed me! Only now, as you speak, I understand that I was really only seeking your approbation for my sincerity when I told you I could not endure ingratitude. You have revealed me to myself. You have seen through me and explained me to myself!"

"Are you speaking the truth? Well, now, after such a confession, I believe that you are sincere and good at heart. If you do not attain happiness, always remember that you are on the right road, and try not to leave it. Above all, avoid falsehood, every kind of falsehood, especially falseness to yourself. Watch over your own deceitfulness and look into it every hour, every minute. Avoid being scornful, both to others and to yourself. What seems to you bad within you will grow purer from the very fact of your observing it in yourself. Avoid fear, too, though fear is only the consequence of every sort of falsehood. Never be frightened at your own faint-heartedness in attaining love. Don't be frightened overmuch even at your evil actions. I am sorry I can say nothing more consoling to you, for love in action is a harsh and dreadful thing compared with love in dreams. Love in dreams is greedy for immediate action, rapidly performed and in the sight of all. Men will even give their lives if only the ordeal does not last long but is soon over, with all looking on and applauding as though on the stage. But active love is labor and fortitude, and for some people too, perhaps, a complete science. But I predict that just when you see with horror that in spite of all your efforts you are getting farther from your goal instead of nearer to it—at that very moment I predict that you will reach it and behold clearly the miraculous power of the Lord who has been all the time loving and mysteriously guiding you. Forgive me for not being able to stay longer with you. They are waiting for me. Good-by."

The lady was weeping.

"Lise, Lise! Bless her—bless her!" she cried, starting up suddenly.

"She does not deserve to be loved. I have seen her naughtiness all along," the elder said jestingly. "Why have you been laughing at Alexey?"

Lise had in fact been occupied in mocking at him all the time. She had noticed before that Alyosha was shy and tried not to look at her, and she found this extremely amusing. She waited intently to catch his eye. Alyosha, unable to endure her persistent stare, was irresistibly and suddenly drawn to glance at her, and at once she smiled triumphantly in his face. Alyosha was even more disconcerted and vexed. At last he turned away from her altogether and hid behind the elder's back. After a few minutes, drawn by the same irresistible force, he turned again to see whether he was being looked at or not, and found Lise almost hanging out of her chair to peep sideways at him, eagerly waiting for him to look. Catching his eye, she laughed so that the elder could not help saying, "Why do you make fun of him like that, naughty girl?"

Lise suddenly and quite unexpectedly blushed. Her eyes flashed and her face became quite serious. She began speaking quickly and nervously in a warm and resentful voice:

"Why has he forgotten everything, then? He used to carry me about when I was little. We used to play together. He used to come to teach me to read, do you know. Two years ago, when he went away, he said that he would never forget me, that we were friends for ever, for ever, for ever! And now he's afraid of me all at once. Am I going to eat him? Why doesn't he want to come near me? Why doesn't he talk? Why won't he come and see us? It's not that you won't let him. We know that he goes everywhere. It's not good manners for me to invite him. He ought to have thought of it first, if he hasn't forgotten me. No, now he's saving his soul! Why have you put that long gown on him? If he runs he'll fall."

And suddenly she hid her face in her hand and went off into irresistible, prolonged, nervous, inaudible laughter. The elder listened to her with a smile, and blessed her tenderly. As she kissed his hand she suddenly pressed it to her eyes and began crying.

"Don't be angry with me. I'm silly and good for nothing ... and perhaps Alyosha's right, quite right, in not wanting to come and see such a ridiculous girl."

"I will certainly send him," said the elder.

Chapter Three
Alyosha

The body of Father Zossima was prepared for burial according to the established ritual. As is well known, the bodies of dead monks and hermits are not washed. In the words of the Church Ritual: "If any one of the monks depart in the Lord, the monk designated (that is, whose office it is) shall wipe the body with warm water, making first the sign of the cross with a sponge on the forehead of the deceased, on the breast, on the hands and feet and on the knees, and that is enough." All this was done by Father Païssy, who then clothed the deceased in his monastic garb and wrapped him in his cloak, which was, according to custom, somewhat slit to allow of its being folded about him in the form of a cross. On his head he put a hood with an eight-cornered cross. The hood was left open and the dead man's face was covered with black gauze. In his hands was put an ikon of the Saviour. Towards morning he was put in the coffin which had been made ready long before. It was decided to leave the coffin all day in the cell, in the larger room in which the elder used to receive his visitors and fellow monks. As the deceased was a priest and monk of the strictest rule, the Gospel, not the Psalter, had to be read over his body by monks in holy orders. The reading was begun by Father Iosif immediately after the requiem service. Father Païssy desired later on to read the Gospel all day and night over his dead friend, but for the present he, as well as the Father Superintendent of the Hermitage, was very busy and occupied, for something extraordinary, an unheard-of, even "unseemly" excitement and impatient expectation began to be apparent in the monks, and the visitors from the monastery hostels, and the crowds of people flocking from the town. And as time went on, this grew more and more marked. Both the Superintendent and Father Païssy did their utmost to calm the general bustle and agitation.

When it was fully daylight, some people began bringing their sick, in most cases children, with them from the town—as though they had been waiting expressly for this moment to do so, evidently persuaded that the dead elder's remains had a power of healing, which would be immediately made manifest in accordance with their faith. It was only then apparent how unquestionably every one in our town had accepted Father Zossima during his lifetime as a great saint. And those who came were far from being all of the humbler classes.

This intense expectation on the part of believers displayed with such haste, such openness, even with impatience and almost insistence, impressed Father Païssy as unseemly. Though he had long foreseen something of the sort, the actual manifestation of the feeling was beyond anything he had looked for. When he came across any of the monks who displayed this excitement, Father Païssy began to reprove them. "Such immediate expectation of something extraordinary," he said, "shows a levity, possible to worldly people but unseemly in us."

But little attention was paid him and Father Païssy noticed it uneasily. Yet he himself (if the whole truth must be told), secretly at the bottom of his heart, cherished almost the same hopes and could not but be aware of it, though he was indignant at the too impatient expectation around him, and saw in it light-mindedness and vanity. Nevertheless, it was particularly unpleasant to him to meet certain persons, whose presence aroused in him great misgivings. In the crowd in the dead man's cell he noticed with inward aversion (for which he immediately reproached himself) the presence of Rakitin and of the monk from Obdorsk, who was still staying in the monastery. Of both of them Father Païssy felt for some reason suddenly suspicious—though, indeed, he might well have felt the same about others.

The monk from Obdorsk was conspicuous as the most fussy in the excited crowd. He was to be seen everywhere; everywhere he was asking questions, everywhere he was listening, on all sides he was whispering with a peculiar, mysterious air. His expression showed the greatest impatience and even a sort of irritation.

As for Rakitin, he, as appeared later, had come so early to the hermitage at the special request of Madame Hohlakov. As soon as that good-hearted but weak-minded woman, who could not herself have been admitted to the hermitage, waked and heard of the death of Father Zossima, she was overtaken with such intense curiosity that she promptly dispatched Rakitin to the hermitage, to keep a careful look out and report to her by letter every half-hour or so *everything that takes place.* She regarded Rakitin as a most religious and devout young man. He was particularly clever in getting round people and assuming whatever part he thought most to their taste, if he detected the slightest advantage to himself from doing so.

It was a bright, clear day, and many of the visitors were thronging about the tombs, which were particularly numerous round the church and scattered here and there about the hermitage. As he walked round the hermitage, Father Païssy remembered Alyosha and that he had not seen him for some time, not since the night. And he had no sooner thought of him than he at once noticed him in the farthest corner of the hermitage garden, sitting on the tombstone of a monk who had been famous long ago for his saintliness. He sat with his back to the hermitage and his face to the wall, and seemed to be hiding behind the tombstone. Going up to him, Father Païssy saw that he was weeping quietly but bitterly, with his face hidden in his hands, and that his whole frame was shaking with sobs. Father Païssy stood over him for a little.

"Enough, dear son, enough, dear," he pronounced with feeling at last. "Why do you weep? Rejoice and weep not. Don't you know that this is the greatest of his days? Think only where he is now, at this moment!"

Alyosha glanced at him, uncovering his face, which was swollen with crying like a child's, but turned away at once without uttering a word and hid his face in his hands again.

"Maybe it is well," said Father Païssy thoughtfully; "weep if you must, Christ has sent you those tears."

"Your touching tears are but a relief to your spirit and will serve to gladden your dear heart," he added to himself, walking away from Alyosha, and thinking lovingly of him. He moved away quickly, however, for he felt that he too might weep looking at him.

Meanwhile the time was passing; the monastery services and the requiems for the dead followed in their due course. Father Païssy again took Father Iosif's place by the coffin and began reading the Gospel. But before three o'clock in the afternoon that something took place to which I alluded at the end of the last book, something so unexpected by all of us and so contrary to the general hope, that, I repeat, this trivial incident has been minutely remembered to this day in our town and all the surrounding neighborhood. I may add here, for myself personally, that I feel it almost repulsive to recall that event which caused such frivolous agitation and was such a stumbling-block to many, though in reality it was the most natural and trivial matter. I should, of course, have omitted all mention of it in my story, if it had not exerted a very strong influence on the heart and soul of the chief, though future, hero of my story, Alyosha, forming a crisis and turning-point in his spiritual development, giving a shock to his intellect, which finally strengthened it for the rest of his life and gave it a definite aim.

And so, to return to our story. When before dawn they laid Father Zossima's body in the coffin and brought it into the front room, the question of opening the windows was raised among those who were around the coffin. But this suggestion made casually by some one was unanswered and almost unnoticed. Some of those present may perhaps have inwardly noticed it, only to reflect that the anticipation of decay and corruption from the body of such a saint was an actual absurdity, calling for compassion (if not a smile) for the lack of faith and the frivolity it implied. For they expected something quite different.

And, behold, soon after midday there were signs of something, at first only observed in silence by those who came in and out and were evidently each afraid to communicate the thought in his mind. But by three o'clock those signs had become so clear and unmistakable, that the news swiftly reached all the monks and visitors in the hermitage, promptly penetrated to the monastery, throwing all the monks into amazement, and finally, in the shortest possible time, spread to the town, exciting every one in it, believers and unbelievers alike. The unbelievers rejoiced, and as for the believers some of them rejoiced even more than the unbelievers, for "men love the downfall and disgrace of the righteous," as the deceased elder had said in one of his exhortations.

The fact is that a smell of decomposition began to come from the coffin, growing gradually more marked, and by three o'clock it was quite unmistakable. In all the past history of our monastery, no such scandal could be recalled, and in no other circumstances could such a scandal have been possible, as showed itself in unseemly disorder immediately after this discovery among the very monks themselves. Afterwards, even many years afterwards, some sensible monks were amazed and horrified, when they recalled that day, that the scandal could have reached such proportions. For in the past, monks of very holy life had died, God-fearing old men, whose saintliness was acknowledged by all, yet from their humble coffins, too, the breath of corruption had come, naturally, as from all dead bodies, but that had caused no scandal nor even the slightest excitement. Of course there had been, in former times, saints in the monastery whose memory was carefully preserved and whose relics, according to tradition, showed no signs of corruption. This fact was regarded by the monks as touching and mysterious, and the tradition of it was cherished as something blessed and miraculous, and as a promise, by God's grace, of still greater glory from their tombs in the future.

One such, whose memory was particularly cherished, was an old monk, Job, who had died seventy years before at the age of a hundred and five. He had been a celebrated ascetic, rigid in fasting and silence, and his tomb was pointed out to all visitors on their arrival with peculiar respect and mysterious hints of great hopes connected with it. (That was the very tomb on which Father Païssy had found Alyosha sitting in the morning.) Another memory cherished in the monastery was that of the famous Father Varsonofy, who was only recently dead and had preceded Father Zossima in the eldership. He was reverenced during his lifetime as a crazy saint by all the pilgrims to the monastery. There was a tradition that both of these had lain in their coffins as though alive, that they had shown no signs of decomposition when they were buried and that there had been a holy light in their faces. And some people even insisted that a sweet fragrance came from their bodies.

Yet, in spite of these edifying memories, it would be difficult to explain the frivolity, absurdity and malice that were manifested beside the coffin of Father Zossima. It is my private opinion that several different causes were simultaneously at work, one of which was the deeply-rooted hostility to the institution of elders as a pernicious innovation, an antipathy hidden deep in the hearts of many of the monks. Even more powerful was jealousy of the dead man's saintliness, so firmly established during his lifetime that it was almost a forbidden thing to question it. For though the late elder had won over many hearts, more by love than by miracles, and had gathered round him a mass of loving adherents, none the less, in fact, rather the more on that account he had awakened jealousy and so had come to have bitter enemies, secret and open, not only in the monastery but in the world outside it. He did no one any harm, but "Why do they think him so saintly?" And that question alone, gradually repeated, gave rise at last to an intense, insatiable hatred of him. That, I believe, was why many people were extremely delighted at the smell of decomposition which came so quickly, for not a day had passed since his death. At the same time there were some among those who had been hitherto reverently devoted to the elder, who were almost mortified and personally affronted by this incident. This was how the thing happened.

As soon as signs of decomposition had begun to appear, the whole aspect of the monks betrayed their secret motives in entering the cell. They went in, stayed a little while and hastened out to confirm the news to the crowd of other monks waiting outside. Some of the latter shook their heads mournfully, but others did not even care to conceal the delight which gleamed unmistakably in their malignant eyes. And now no one reproached them for it, no one raised his voice in protest, which was strange, for the majority of the monks had been devoted to the dead elder. But it seemed as though God had in this case let the minority get the upper hand for a time.

Visitors from outside, particularly of the educated class, soon went into the cell, too, with the same spying intent. Of the peasantry few went into the cell, though there were crowds of them at the gates of the hermitage. After three o'clock the rush of worldly visitors was greatly increased and this was no doubt owing to the shocking news. People were attracted who would not otherwise have come on that day and had not intended to come, and among them were some personages of high standing. But external decorum was still preserved and Father Païssy, with a stern face, continued firmly and distinctly reading aloud the Gospel, apparently not noticing what was taking place around him, though he had, in fact, observed something unusual long before. But at last the murmurs, first subdued but gradually louder and more confident, reached even him. "It shows God's judgment is not as man's," Father Païssy heard suddenly. The first to give utterance to this sentiment was a layman, an elderly official from the town, known to be a man of great piety. But he only repeated aloud what the monks had long been whispering. They had long before formulated this damning conclusion, and the worst of it was that a sort of triumphant satisfaction at that conclusion became more and more apparent every moment. Soon they began to lay aside even external decorum and almost seemed to feel they had a sort of right to discard it.

"And for what reason can *this* have happened," some of the monks said, at first with a show of regret; "he had a small frame and his flesh was dried up on his bones, what was there to decay?"

"It must be a sign from heaven," others hastened to add, and their opinion was adopted at once without protest. For it was pointed out, too, that if the decomposition had been natural, as in the case of every dead sinner, it would have been apparent later, after a lapse of at least twenty-four hours, but this premature corruption "was in excess of nature," and so the finger of God was evident. It was meant for a sign. This conclusion seemed irresistible.

Gentle Father Iosif, the librarian, a great favorite of the dead man's, tried to reply to some of the evil speakers that "this is not held everywhere alike," and that the incorruptibility of the bodies of the just was not a dogma of the Orthodox Church, but only an opinion, and that even in the most Orthodox regions, at Athos for instance, they were not greatly confounded by the smell of corruption, and there the chief sign of the glorification of the saved was not bodily incorruptibility, but the color of the bones when the bodies have lain many years in the earth and have decayed in it. "And if the bones are yellow as wax, that is the great sign that the Lord has glorified the dead saint, if they are not yellow but black, it shows that God has not deemed him worthy of such glory—that is the belief in Athos, a great place, where the Orthodox doctrine has been preserved from of old, unbroken and in its greatest purity," said Father Iosif in conclusion.

But the meek Father's words had little effect and even provoked a mocking retort. "That's all pedantry and innovation, no use listening to it," the monks decided. "We stick to the old doctrine, there are all sorts of innovations nowadays, are we to follow them all?" added others.

"We have had as many holy fathers as they had. There they are among the Turks, they have forgotten everything. Their doctrine has long been impure and they have no bells even," the most sneering added.

Father Iosif walked away, grieving the more since he had put forward his own opinion with little confidence as though scarcely believing in it himself. He foresaw with distress that something very unseemly was beginning and that there were positive signs of disobedience. Little by little, all the sensible monks were reduced to silence like Father Iosif. And so it came to pass that all who loved the elder and had accepted with devout obedience the institution of the eldership were all at once terribly cast down and glanced timidly in one another's faces, when they met. Those who were hostile to the institution of elders, as a novelty, held up their heads proudly. "There was no smell of corruption from the late elder Varsonofy, but a sweet fragrance," they recalled malignantly. "But he gained that glory not because he was an elder, but because he was a holy man."

And this was followed by a shower of criticism and even blame of Father Zossima. "His teaching was false; he taught that life is a great joy and not a vale of tears," said some of the more unreasonable. "He followed the fashionable belief, he did not recognize material fire in hell," others, still more unreasonable, added. "He was not strict in fasting, allowed himself sweet things, ate cherry jam with his tea, ladies used to send it to him. Is it for a monk of strict rule to drink tea?" could be heard among some of the envious. "He sat in pride," the most malignant declared vindictively; "he considered himself a saint and he took it as his due when people knelt before him." "He abused the sacrament of confession," the fiercest opponents of the institution of elders added in a malicious whisper. And among these were some of the oldest monks, strictest in their devotion, genuine ascetics, who had kept silent during the life of the deceased elder, but now suddenly unsealed their lips. And this was terrible, for their words had great influence on young monks who were not yet firm in their convictions. The monk from Obdorsk heard all this attentively, heaving deep sighs and nodding his head. "Yes, clearly Father Ferapont was right in his judgment yesterday," and at that moment Father Ferapont himself made his appearance, as though on purpose to increase the confusion.

I have mentioned already that he rarely left his wooden cell by the apiary. He was seldom even seen at church and they overlooked this neglect on the ground of his craziness, and did not keep him to the rules binding on all the rest. But if the whole truth is to be told, they hardly had a choice about it. For it would have been discreditable to insist on burdening with the common regulations so great an ascetic, who prayed day and night (he even dropped asleep on his knees). If they had insisted, the monks would have said, "He is holier than all of us and he follows a rule harder than ours. And if he does not go to church, it's because he knows when he ought to; he has his own rule." It was to avoid the chance of these sinful murmurs that Father Ferapont was left in peace.

As every one was aware, Father Ferapont particularly disliked Father Zossima. And now the news had reached him in his hut that "God's judgment is not the same as man's," and that something had happened which was "in excess of nature." It may well be supposed that among the first to run to him with the news was the monk from Obdorsk, who had visited him the evening before and left his cell terror-stricken.

I have mentioned above, that though Father Païssy, standing firm and immovable reading the Gospel over the coffin, could not hear nor see what was passing outside the cell, he gauged most of it correctly in his heart, for he knew the men surrounding him, well. He was not shaken by it, but awaited what would come next without fear, watching with penetration and insight for the outcome of the general excitement.

Suddenly an extraordinary uproar in the passage in open defiance of decorum burst on his ears. The door was flung open and Father Ferapont appeared in the doorway. Behind him there could be seen accompanying him a crowd of monks, together with many people from the town. They did not, however, enter the cell, but stood at the bottom of the steps, waiting to see what Father Ferapont would say or do. For they felt with a certain awe, in spite of their audacity, that he had not come for nothing. Standing in the doorway, Father Ferapont raised his arms, and under his right arm the keen inquisitive little eyes of the monk from Obdorsk peeped in. He alone, in his intense curiosity, could not resist running up the steps after Father Ferapont. The others, on the contrary, pressed farther back in sudden alarm when the door was noisily flung open. Holding his hands aloft, Father Ferapont suddenly roared:

"Casting out I cast out!" and, turning in all directions, he began at once making the sign of the cross at each of the four walls and four corners of the cell in succession. All who accompanied Father Ferapont immediately understood his action. For they knew he always did this wherever he went, and that he would not sit down or say a word, till he had driven out the evil spirits.

"Satan, go hence! Satan, go hence!" he repeated at each sign of the cross. "Casting out I cast out," he roared again.

He was wearing his coarse gown girt with a rope. His bare chest, covered with gray hair, could be seen under his hempen shirt. His feet were bare. As soon as he began waving his arms, the cruel irons he wore under his gown could be heard clanking.

Father Païssy paused in his reading, stepped forward and stood before him waiting.

"What have you come for, worthy Father? Why do you offend against good order? Why do you disturb the peace of the flock?" he said at last, looking sternly at him.

"What have I come for? You ask why? What is your faith?" shouted Father Ferapont crazily. "I've come here to drive out your visitors, the unclean devils. I've come to see how many have gathered here while I have been away. I want to sweep them out with a birch broom."

"You cast out the evil spirit, but perhaps you are serving him yourself," Father Païssy went on fearlessly. "And who can say of himself 'I am holy'? Can you, Father?"

"I am unclean, not holy. I would not sit in an arm-chair and would not have them bow down to me as an idol," thundered Father Ferapont. "Nowadays folk destroy the true faith. The dead man, your saint," he turned to the crowd, pointing with his finger to the coffin, "did not believe in devils. He gave medicine to keep off the devils. And so they have become as common as spiders in the corners. And now he has begun to stink himself. In that we see a great sign from God."

The incident he referred to was this. One of the monks was haunted in his dreams and, later on, in waking moments, by visions of evil spirits. When in the utmost terror he confided this to Father Zossima, the elder had advised continual prayer and rigid fasting. But when that was of no use, he advised him, while persisting in prayer and fasting, to take a special medicine. Many persons were shocked at the time and wagged their heads as they talked over it—and most of all Father Ferapont, to whom some of the censorious had hastened to report this "extraordinary" counsel on the part of the elder.

"Go away, Father!" said Father Païssy, in a commanding voice, "it's not for man to judge but for God. Perhaps we see here a 'sign' which neither you, nor I, nor any one of us is able to comprehend. Go, Father, and do not trouble the flock!" he repeated impressively.

"He did not keep the fasts according to the rule and therefore the sign has come. That is clear and it's a sin to hide it," the fanatic, carried away by a zeal that outstripped his reason, would not be quieted. "He was seduced by sweetmeats, ladies brought them to him in their pockets, he sipped tea, he worshiped his belly, filling it with sweet things and his mind with haughty thoughts.... And for this he is put to shame...."

"You speak lightly, Father." Father Païssy, too, raised his voice. "I admire your fasting and severities, but you speak lightly like some frivolous youth, fickle and childish. Go away, Father, I command you!" Father Païssy thundered in conclusion.

"I will go," said Ferapont, seeming somewhat taken aback, but still as bitter. "You learned men! You are so clever you look down upon my humbleness. I came hither with little learning and here I have forgotten what I did know, God Himself has preserved me in my weakness from your subtlety."

Father Païssy stood over him, waiting resolutely. Father Ferapont paused and, suddenly leaning his cheek on his hand despondently, pronounced in a sing-song voice, looking at the coffin of the dead elder:

"To-morrow they will sing over him 'Our Helper and Defender'—a splendid anthem—and over me when I die all they'll sing will be 'What earthly joy'—a little canticle,"[6] he added with tearful regret. "You are proud and puffed up, this is a vain place!" he shouted suddenly like a madman, and with a wave of his hand he turned quickly and quickly descended the steps. The crowd awaiting him below wavered; some followed him at once and some lingered, for the cell was still open, and Father Païssy, following Father Ferapont on to the steps, stood watching him. But the excited old fanatic was not completely silenced. Walking twenty steps away, he suddenly turned towards the setting sun, raised both his arms and, as though some one had cut him down, fell to the ground with a loud scream.

"My God has conquered! Christ has conquered the setting sun!" he shouted frantically, stretching up his hands to the sun, and falling face downwards on the ground, he sobbed like a little child, shaken by his tears and spreading out his arms on the ground. Then all rushed up to him; there were exclamations and sympathetic sobs ... a kind of frenzy seemed to take possession of them all.

"This is the one who is a saint! This is the one who is a holy man!" some cried aloud, losing their fear. "This is he who should be an elder," others added malignantly.

"He wouldn't be an elder ... he would refuse ... he wouldn't serve a cursed innovation ... he wouldn't imitate their foolery," other voices chimed in at once. And it is hard to say how far they might have gone, but at that moment the bell rang summoning them to service. All began crossing themselves at once. Father Ferapont, too, got up and crossing himself went back to his cell without looking round, still uttering exclamations which were utterly incoherent. A few followed him, but the greater number dispersed, hastening to service. Father Païssy let Father Iosif read in his place and went down. The frantic outcries of bigots could not shake him, but his heart was suddenly filled with melancholy for some special reason and he felt that. He stood still and suddenly wondered, "Why am I sad even to dejection?" and immediately grasped with surprise that his sudden sadness was due to a very small and special cause. In the crowd thronging at the entrance to the cell, he had noticed Alyosha and he remembered that he had felt at once a pang at heart on seeing him. "Can that boy mean so much to my heart now?" he asked himself, wondering.

At that moment Alyosha passed him, hurrying away, but not in the direction of the church. Their eyes met. Alyosha quickly turned away his eyes and dropped them to the ground, and from the boy's look alone, Father Païssy guessed what a great change was taking place in him at that moment.

"Have you, too, fallen into temptation?" cried Father Païssy. "Can you be with those of little faith?" he added mournfully.

Alyosha stood still and gazed vaguely at Father Païssy, but quickly turned his eyes away again and again looked on the ground. He stood sideways and did not turn his face to Father Païssy, who watched him attentively.

"Where are you hastening? The bell calls to service," he asked again, but again Alyosha gave no answer.

"Are you leaving the hermitage? What, without asking leave, without asking a blessing?"

Alyosha suddenly gave a wry smile, cast a strange, very strange, look at the Father to whom his former guide, the former sovereign of his heart and mind, his beloved elder, had confided him as he lay dying. And suddenly, still without speaking, waved his hand, as though not caring even to be respectful, and with rapid steps walked towards the gates away from the hermitage.

"You will come back again!" murmured Father Païssy, looking after him with sorrowful surprise.

Father Païssy, of course, was not wrong when he decided that his "dear boy" would come back again. Perhaps indeed, to some extent, he penetrated with insight into the true meaning of Alyosha's spiritual condition. Yet I must frankly own that it would be very difficult for me to give a clear account of that strange, vague moment in the life of the young hero I love so much. To Father Païssy's sorrowful question, "Are you too with those of little faith?" I could of course confidently answer for Alyosha, "No, he is not with those of little faith. Quite the contrary." Indeed, all his trouble came from the fact that he was of great faith. But still the trouble was there and was so agonizing that even long afterwards Alyosha thought of that sorrowful day as one of the bitterest and most fatal days of his life. If the question is asked: "Could all his grief and disturbance have been only due to the fact that his elder's body had shown signs of premature decomposition instead of at once performing miracles?" I must answer without beating about the bush, "Yes, it certainly was." I would only beg the reader not to be in too great a hurry to laugh at my young hero's pure heart. I am far from intending to apologize for him or to justify his innocent faith on the ground of his youth, or the little progress he had made in his studies, or any such reason. I must declare, on the contrary, that I have genuine respect for the qualities of his heart. No doubt a youth who received impressions cautiously, whose love was lukewarm, and whose mind was too prudent for his age and so of little value, such a young man might, I admit, have avoided what happened to my hero. But in some cases it is really more creditable to be carried away by an emotion, however unreasonable, which springs from a great love, than to be unmoved. And this is even truer in youth, for a young man who is always sensible is to be suspected and is of little worth—that's my opinion!

"But," reasonable people will exclaim perhaps, "every young man cannot believe in such a superstition and your hero is no model for others."

To this I reply again, "Yes! my hero had faith, a faith holy and steadfast, but still I am not going to apologize for him."

Though I declared above, and perhaps too hastily, that I should not explain or justify my hero, I see that some explanation is necessary for the understanding of the rest of my story. Let me say then, it was not a question of miracles. There was no frivolous and impatient expectation of miracles in his mind. And Alyosha needed no miracles at the time, for the triumph of some preconceived idea—oh, no, not at all—what he saw before all was one figure—the figure of his beloved elder, the figure of that holy man whom he revered with such adoration. The fact is that all the love that lay concealed in his pure young heart for every one and everything had, for the past year, been concentrated—and perhaps wrongly so—on one being, his beloved elder. It is true that being had for so long been accepted by him as his ideal, that all his young strength and energy could not but turn towards that ideal, even to the forgetting at the moment "of every one and everything." He remembered afterwards how, on that terrible day, he had entirely forgotten his brother Dmitri, about whom he had been so anxious and troubled the day before; he had forgotten, too, to take the two hundred roubles to Ilusha's father, though he had so warmly intended to do so the preceding evening. But again it was not miracles he needed but only "the higher justice" which had been in his belief outraged by the blow that had so suddenly and cruelly wounded his heart. And what does it signify that this "justice" looked for by Alyosha inevitably took the shape of miracles to be wrought immediately by the ashes of his adored teacher? Why, every one in the monastery cherished the same thought and the same hope, even those whose intellects Alyosha revered, Father Païssy himself, for instance. And so Alyosha, untroubled by doubts, clothed his dreams too in the same form as all the rest. And a whole year of life in the monastery had formed the habit of this expectation in his heart. But it was justice, justice, he thirsted for, not simply miracles.

And now the man who should, he believed, have been exalted above every one in the whole world, that man, instead of receiving the glory that was his due, was suddenly degraded and dishonored! What for? Who had judged him? Who could have decreed this? Those were the questions that wrung his inexperienced and virginal heart. He could not endure without mortification, without resentment even, that the holiest of holy men should have been exposed to the jeering and spiteful mockery of the frivolous crowd so inferior to him. Even had there been no miracles, had there been nothing marvelous to justify his hopes, why this indignity, why this humiliation, why this premature decay, "in excess of nature," as the spiteful monks said? Why this "sign from heaven," which they so triumphantly acclaimed in company with Father Ferapont, and why did they believe they had gained the right to acclaim it? Where is the finger of Providence? Why did Providence hide its face "at the most critical moment" (so Alyosha thought it), as though voluntarily submitting to the blind, dumb, pitiless laws of nature?

That was why Alyosha's heart was bleeding, and, of course, as I have said already, the sting of it all was that the man he loved above everything on earth should be put to shame and humiliated! This murmuring may have been shallow and unreasonable in my hero, but I repeat again for the third time—and am prepared to admit that it might be difficult to defend my feeling—I am glad that my hero showed himself not too reasonable at that moment, for any man of sense will always come back to reason in time, but, if love does not gain the upper hand in a boy's heart at such an exceptional moment, when will it? I will not, however, omit to mention something strange, which came for a time to the surface of Alyosha's mind at this fatal and obscure moment. This new something was the harassing impression left by the conversation with Ivan, which now persistently haunted Alyosha's mind. At this moment it haunted him. Oh, it was not that something of the fundamental, elemental, so to speak, faith of his soul had been shaken. He loved his God and believed in Him steadfastly, though he was suddenly murmuring against Him. Yet a vague but tormenting and evil impression left by his conversation with Ivan the day before, suddenly revived again now in his soul and seemed forcing its way to the surface of his consciousness.

It had begun to get dusk when Rakitin, crossing the pine copse from the hermitage to the monastery, suddenly noticed Alyosha, lying face downwards on the ground under a tree, not moving and apparently asleep. He went up and called him by his name.

"You here, Alexey? Can you have—" he began wondering but broke off. He had meant to say, "Can you have come to this?"

Alyosha did not look at him, but from a slight movement Rakitin at once saw that he heard and understood him.

"What's the matter?" he went on; but the surprise in his face gradually passed into a smile that became more and more ironical.

"I say, I've been looking for you for the last two hours. You suddenly disappeared. What are you about? What foolery is this? You might just look at me..."

Alyosha raised his head, sat up and leaned his back against the tree. He was not crying, but there was a look of suffering and irritability in his face. He did not look at Rakitin, however, but looked away to one side of him.

"Do you know your face is quite changed? There's none of your famous mildness to be seen in it. Are you angry with some one? Have they been ill-treating you?"

"Let me alone," said Alyosha suddenly, with a weary gesture of his hand, still looking away from him.

"Oho! So that's how we are feeling! So you can shout at people like other mortals. That is a come-down from the angels. I say, Alyosha, you have surprised me, do you hear? I mean it. It's long since I've been surprised at anything here. I always took you for an educated man...."

Alyosha at last looked at him, but vaguely, as though scarcely understanding what he said.

"Can you really be so upset simply because your old man has begun to stink? You don't mean to say you seriously believed that he was going to work miracles?" exclaimed Rakitin, genuinely surprised again.

"I believed, I believe, I want to believe, and I will believe, what more do you want?" cried Alyosha irritably.

"Nothing at all, my boy. Damn it all! why, no schoolboy of thirteen believes in that now. But there.... So now you are in a temper with your God, you are rebelling against Him; He hasn't given promotion, He hasn't bestowed the order of merit! Eh, you are a set!"

Alyosha gazed a long while with his eyes half closed at Rakitin, and there was a sudden gleam in his eyes ... but not of anger with Rakitin.

"I am not rebelling against my God; I simply 'don't accept His world.'" Alyosha suddenly smiled a forced smile.

"How do you mean, you don't accept the world?" Rakitin thought a moment over his answer. "What idiocy is this?"

Alyosha did not answer.

"Come, enough nonsense, now to business. Have you had anything to eat to-day?"

"I don't remember.... I think I have."

"You need keeping up, to judge by your face. It makes one sorry to look at you. You didn't sleep all night either, I hear, you had a meeting in there. And then all this bobbery afterwards. Most likely you've had nothing to eat but a mouthful of holy bread. I've got some sausage in my pocket; I've brought it from the town in case of need, only you won't eat sausage...."

"Give me some."

"I say! You are going it! Why, it's a regular mutiny, with barricades! Well, my boy, we must make the most of it. Come to my place.... I shouldn't mind a drop of vodka myself, I am tired to death. Vodka is going too far for you, I suppose ... or would you like some?"

"Give me some vodka too."

"Hullo! You surprise me, brother!" Rakitin looked at him in amazement. "Well, one way or another, vodka or sausage, this is a jolly fine chance and mustn't be missed. Come along."

Alyosha got up in silence and followed Rakitin.

"If your little brother Ivan could see this—wouldn't he be surprised! By the way, your brother Ivan set off to Moscow this morning, did you know?"

"Yes," answered Alyosha listlessly, and suddenly the image of his brother Dmitri rose before his mind. But only for a minute, and though it reminded him of something that must not be put off for a moment, some duty, some terrible obligation, even that reminder made no impression on him, did not reach his heart and instantly faded out of his mind and was forgotten. But, a long while afterwards, Alyosha remembered this.

"Your brother Ivan declared once that I was a 'liberal booby with no talents whatsoever.' Once you, too, could not resist letting me know I was 'dishonorable.' Well! I should like to see what your talents and sense of honor will do for you now." This phrase Rakitin finished to himself in a whisper.

"Listen!" he said aloud, "let's go by the path beyond the monastery straight to the town. Hm! I ought to go to Madame Hohlakov's by the way. Only fancy, I've written to tell her everything that happened, and would you believe it, she answered me instantly in pencil (the lady has a passion for writing notes) that 'she would never have expected *such conduct* from a man of such a reverend character as Father Zossima.' That was her very word: 'conduct.' She is angry too. Eh, you are a set! Stay!" he cried suddenly again. He suddenly stopped and taking Alyosha by the shoulder made him stop too.

"Do you know, Alyosha," he peeped inquisitively into his eyes, absorbed in a sudden new thought which had dawned on him, and though he was laughing outwardly he was evidently afraid to utter that new idea aloud, so difficult he still found it to believe in the strange and unexpected mood in which he now saw Alyosha. "Alyosha, do you know where we had better go?" he brought out at last timidly, and insinuatingly.

"I don't care ... where you like."

"Let's go to Grushenka, eh? Will you come?" pronounced Rakitin at last, trembling with timid suspense.

"Let's go to Grushenka," Alyosha answered calmly, at once, and this prompt and calm agreement was such a surprise to Rakitin that he almost started back.

"Well! I say!" he cried in amazement, but seizing Alyosha firmly by the arm he led him along the path, still dreading that he would change his mind.

They walked along in silence, Rakitin was positively afraid to talk.

"And how glad she will be, how delighted!" he muttered, but lapsed into silence again. And indeed it was not to please Grushenka he was taking Alyosha to her. He was a practical person and never undertook anything without a prospect of gain for himself. His object in this case was twofold, first a revengeful desire to see "the downfall of the righteous," and Alyosha's fall "from the saints to the sinners," over which he was already gloating in his imagination, and in the second place he had in view a certain material gain for himself, of which more will be said later.

"So the critical moment has come," he thought to himself with spiteful glee, "and we shall catch it on the hop, for it's just what we want."

Grushenka lived in the busiest part of the town, near the cathedral square, in a small wooden lodge in the courtyard belonging to the house of the widow Morozov. The house was a large stone building of two stories, old and very ugly. The widow led a secluded life with her two unmarried nieces, who were also elderly women. She had no need to let her lodge, but every one knew that she had taken in Grushenka as a lodger, four years before, solely to please her kinsman, the merchant Samsonov, who was known to be the girl's protector. It was said that the jealous old man's object in placing his "favorite" with the widow Morozov was that the old woman should keep a sharp eye on her new lodger's conduct. But this sharp eye soon proved to be unnecessary, and in the end the widow Morozov seldom met Grushenka and did not worry her by looking after her in any way. It is true that four years had passed since the old man had brought the slim, delicate, shy, timid, dreamy, and sad girl of eighteen from the chief town of the province, and much had happened since then. Little was known of the girl's history in the town and that little was vague. Nothing more had been learnt during the last four years, even after many persons had become interested in the beautiful young woman into whom Agrafena Alexandrovna had meanwhile developed. There were rumors that she had been at seventeen betrayed by some one, some sort of officer, and immediately afterwards abandoned by him. The officer had gone away and afterwards married, while Grushenka had been left in poverty and disgrace. It was said, however, that though Grushenka had been raised from destitution by the old man, Samsonov, she came of a respectable family belonging to the clerical class, that she was the daughter of a deacon or something of the sort.

And now after four years the sensitive, injured and pathetic little orphan had become a plump, rosy beauty of the Russian type, a woman of bold and determined character, proud and insolent. She had a good head for business, was acquisitive, saving and careful, and by fair means or foul had succeeded, it was said, in amassing a little fortune. There was only one point on which all were agreed. Grushenka was not easily to be approached and except her aged protector there had not been one man who could boast of her favors during those four years. It was a positive fact, for there had been a good many, especially during the last two years, who had attempted to obtain those favors. But all their efforts had been in vain and some of these suitors had been forced to beat an undignified and even comic retreat, owing to the firm and ironical resistance they met from the strong-willed young person. It was known, too, that the young person had, especially of late, been given to what is called "speculation," and that she had shown marked abilities in that direction, so that many people began to say that she was no better than a Jew. It was not that she lent money on interest, but it was known, for instance, that she had for some time past, in partnership with old Karamazov, actually invested in the purchase of bad debts for a trifle, a tenth of their nominal value, and afterwards had made out of them ten times their value.

The old widower Samsonov, a man of large fortune, was stingy and merciless. He tyrannized over his grown-up sons, but, for the last year during which he had been ill and lost the use of his swollen legs, he had fallen greatly under the influence of his protégée, whom he had at first kept strictly and in humble surroundings, "on Lenten fare," as the wits said at the time. But Grushenka had succeeded in emancipating herself, while she established in him a boundless belief in her fidelity. The old man, now long since dead, had had a large business in his day and was also a noteworthy character, miserly and hard as flint. Though Grushenka's hold upon him was so strong that he could not live without her (it had been so especially for the last two years), he did not settle any considerable fortune on her and would not have been moved to do so, if she had threatened to leave him. But he had presented her with a small sum, and even that was a surprise to every one when it became known.

"You are a wench with brains," he said to her, when he gave her eight thousand roubles, "and you must look after yourself, but let me tell you that except your yearly allowance as before, you'll get nothing more from me to the day of my death, and I'll leave you nothing in my will either."

And he kept his word; he died and left everything to his sons, whom, with their wives and children, he had treated all his life as servants. Grushenka was not even mentioned in his will. All this became known afterwards. He helped Grushenka with his advice to increase her capital and put business in her way.

When Fyodor Pavlovitch, who first came into contact with Grushenka over a piece of speculation, ended to his own surprise by falling madly in love with her, old Samsonov, gravely ill as he was, was immensely amused. It is remarkable that throughout their whole acquaintance Grushenka was absolutely and spontaneously open with the old man, and he seems to have been the only person in the world with whom she was so. Of late, when Dmitri too had come on the scene with his love, the old man left off laughing. On the contrary, he once gave Grushenka a stern and earnest piece of advice.

"If you have to choose between the two, father or son, you'd better choose the old man, if only you make sure the old scoundrel will marry you and settle some fortune on you beforehand. But don't keep on with the captain, you'll get no good out of that."

These were the very words of the old profligate, who felt already that his death was not far off and who actually died five months later.

I will note, too, in passing, that although many in our town knew of the grotesque and monstrous rivalry of the Karamazovs, father and son, the object of which was Grushenka, scarcely any one understood what really underlay her attitude to both of them. Even Grushenka's two servants (after the catastrophe of which we will speak later) testified in court that she received Dmitri Fyodorovitch simply from fear because "he threatened to murder her." These servants were an old cook, invalidish and almost deaf, who came from Grushenka's old home, and her granddaughter, a smart young girl of twenty, who performed the duties of a maid. Grushenka lived very economically and her surroundings were anything but luxurious. Her lodge consisted of three rooms furnished with mahogany furniture in the fashion of 1820, belonging to her landlady.

It was quite dark when Rakitin and Alyosha entered her rooms, yet they were not lighted up. Grushenka was lying down in her drawing-room on the big, hard, clumsy sofa, with a mahogany back. The sofa was covered with shabby and ragged leather. Under her head she had two white down pillows taken from her bed. She was lying stretched out motionless on her back with her hands behind her head. She was dressed as though expecting some one, in a black silk dress, with a dainty lace fichu on her head, which was very becoming. Over her shoulders was thrown a lace shawl pinned with a massive gold brooch. She certainly was expecting some one. She lay as though impatient and weary, her face rather pale and her lips and eyes hot, restlessly tapping the arm of the sofa with the tip of her right foot. The appearance of Rakitin and Alyosha caused a slight excitement. From the hall they could hear Grushenka leap up from the sofa and cry out in a frightened voice, "Who's there?" But the maid met the visitors and at once called back to her mistress.

"It's not he, it's nothing, only other visitors."

"What can be the matter?" muttered Rakitin, leading Alyosha into the drawing-room.

Grushenka was standing by the sofa as though still alarmed. A thick coil of her dark brown hair escaped from its lace covering and fell on her right shoulder, but she did not notice it and did not put it back till she had gazed at her visitors and recognized them.

"Ah, it's you, Rakitin? You quite frightened me. Whom have you brought? Who is this with you? Good heavens, you have brought him!" she exclaimed, recognizing Alyosha.

"Do send for candles!" said Rakitin, with the free-and-easy air of a most intimate friend, who is privileged to give orders in the house.

"Candles ... of course, candles.... Fenya, fetch him a candle.... Well, you have chosen a moment to bring him!" she exclaimed again, nodding towards Alyosha, and turning to the looking-glass she began quickly fastening up her hair with both hands. She seemed displeased.

"Haven't I managed to please you?" asked Rakitin, instantly almost offended.

"You frightened me, Rakitin, that's what it is." Grushenka turned with a smile to Alyosha. "Don't be afraid of me, my dear Alyosha, you cannot think how glad I am to see you, my unexpected visitor. But you frightened me, Rakitin, I thought it was Mitya breaking in. You see, I deceived him just now, I made him promise to believe me and I told him a lie. I told him that I was going to spend the evening with my old man, Kuzma Kuzmitch, and should be there till late counting up his money. I always spend one whole evening a week with him making up his accounts. We lock ourselves in and he counts on the reckoning beads while I sit and put things down in the book. I am the only person he trusts. Mitya believes that I am there, but I came back and have been sitting locked in here, expecting some news. How was it Fenya let you in? Fenya, Fenya, run out to the gate, open it and look about whether the captain is to be seen! Perhaps he is hiding and spying, I am dreadfully frightened."

"There's no one there, Agrafena Alexandrovna, I've just looked out, I keep running to peep through the crack, I am in fear and trembling myself."

"Are the shutters fastened, Fenya? And we must draw the curtains—that's better!" She drew the heavy curtains herself. "He'd rush in at once if he saw a light. I am afraid of your brother Mitya to-day, Alyosha."

Grushenka spoke aloud, and, though she was alarmed, she seemed very happy about something.

"Why are you so afraid of Mitya to-day?" inquired Rakitin. "I should have thought you were not timid with him, you'd twist him round your little finger."

"I tell you, I am expecting news, priceless news, so I don't want Mitya at all. And he didn't believe, I feel he didn't, that I should stay at Kuzma Kuzmitch's. He must be in his ambush now, behind Fyodor Pavlovitch's, in the garden, watching for me. And if he's there, he won't come here, so much the better! But I really have been to Kuzma Kuzmitch's, Mitya escorted me there. I told him I should stay there till midnight, and I asked him to be sure to come at midnight to fetch me home. He went away and I sat ten minutes with Kuzma Kuzmitch and came back here again. Ugh, I was afraid, I ran for fear of meeting him."

"And why are you so dressed up? What a curious cap you've got on!"

"How curious you are yourself, Rakitin! I tell you, I am expecting a message. If the message comes, I shall fly, I shall gallop away and you will see no more of me. That's why I am dressed up, so as to be ready."

"And where are you flying to?"

"If you know too much, you'll get old too soon."

"Upon my word! You are highly delighted ... I've never seen you like this before. You are dressed up as if you were going to a ball." Rakitin looked her up and down.

"Much you know about balls."

"And do you know much about them?"

"I have seen a ball. The year before last, Kuzma Kuzmitch's son was married and I looked on from the gallery. Do you suppose I want to be talking to you, Rakitin, while a prince like this is standing here. Such a visitor! Alyosha, my dear boy, I gaze at you and can't believe my eyes. Good heavens, can you have come here to see me! To tell you the truth, I never had a thought of seeing you and I didn't think that you would ever come and see me. Though this is not the moment now, I am awfully glad to see you. Sit down on the sofa, here, that's right, my bright young moon. I really can't take it in even now.... Eh, Rakitin, if only you had brought him yesterday or the day before! But I am glad as it is! Perhaps it's better he has come now, at such a moment, and not the day before yesterday."

She gayly sat down beside Alyosha on the sofa, looking at him with positive delight. And she really was glad, she was not lying when she said so. Her eyes glowed, her lips laughed, but it was a good-hearted merry laugh. Alyosha had not expected to see such a kind expression in her face.... He had hardly met her till the day before, he had formed an alarming idea of her, and had been horribly distressed the day before by the spiteful and treacherous trick she had played on Katerina Ivanovna. He was greatly surprised to find her now altogether different from what he had expected. And, crushed as he was by his own sorrow, his eyes involuntarily rested on her with attention. Her whole manner seemed changed for the better since yesterday, there was scarcely any trace of that mawkish sweetness in her speech, of that voluptuous softness in her movements. Everything was simple and good-natured, her gestures were rapid, direct, confiding, but she was greatly excited.

"Dear me, how everything comes together to-day!" she chattered on again. "And why I am so glad to see you, Alyosha, I couldn't say myself! If you ask me, I couldn't tell you."

"Come, don't you know why you're glad?" said Rakitin, grinning. "You used to be always pestering me to bring him, you'd some object, I suppose."

"I had a different object once, but now that's over, this is not the moment. I say, I want you to have something nice. I am so good-natured now. You sit down, too, Rakitin; why are you standing? You've sat down already? There's no fear of Rakitin's forgetting to look after himself. Look, Alyosha, he's sitting there opposite us, so offended that I didn't ask him to sit down before you. Ugh, Rakitin is such a one to take offense!" laughed Grushenka. "Don't be angry, Rakitin, I'm kind to-day. Why are you so depressed, Alyosha? Are you afraid of me?" She peeped into his eyes with merry mockery"

"He's sad. The promotion has not been given," boomed Rakitin.

"What promotion?"

"His elder stinks."

"What? You are talking some nonsense, you want to say something nasty. Be quiet, you stupid! Let me sit on your knee, Alyosha, like this." She suddenly skipped forward and jumped, laughing, on his knee, like a nestling kitten, with her right arm about his neck. "I'll cheer you up, my pious boy. Yes, really, will you let me sit on your knee? You won't be angry? If you tell me, I'll get off?"

Alyosha did not speak. He sat afraid to move, he heard her words, "If you tell me, I'll get off," but he did not answer. But there was nothing in his heart such as Rakitin, for instance, watching him malignantly from his corner, might have expected or fancied. The great grief in his heart swallowed up every sensation that might have been aroused, and, if only he could have thought clearly at that moment, he would have realized that he had now the strongest armor to protect him from every lust and temptation. Yet in spite of the vague irresponsiveness of his spiritual condition and the sorrow that overwhelmed him, he could not help wondering at a new and strange sensation in his heart. This woman, this "dreadful" woman, had no terror for him now, none of that terror that had stirred in his soul at any passing thought of woman. On the contrary, this woman, dreaded above all women, sitting now on his knee, holding him in her arms, aroused in him now a quite different, unexpected, peculiar feeling, a feeling of the intensest and purest interest without a trace of fear, of his former terror. That was what instinctively surprised him.

"You've talked nonsense enough," cried Rakitin, "you'd much better give us some champagne. You owe it me, you know you do!"

"Yes, I really do. Do you know, Alyosha, I promised him champagne on the top of everything, if he'd bring you? I'll have some too! Fenya, Fenya, bring us the bottle Mitya left! Look sharp! Though I am so stingy, I'll stand a bottle, not for you, Rakitin, you're a toadstool, but he is a falcon! And though my heart is full of something very different, so be it, I'll drink with you. I long for some dissipation."

"But what is the matter with you? And what is this message, may I ask, or is it a secret?" Rakitin put in inquisitively, doing his best to pretend not to notice the snubs that were being continually aimed at him.

"Ech, it's not a secret, and you know it, too," Grushenka said, in a voice suddenly anxious, turning her head towards Rakitin, and drawing a little away from Alyosha, though she still sat on his knee with her arm round his neck. "My officer is coming, Rakitin, my officer is coming."

"I heard he was coming, but is he so near?"

"He is at Mokroe now; he'll send a messenger from there, so he wrote; I got a letter from him to-day. I am expecting the messenger every minute."

"You don't say so! Why at Mokroe?"

"That's a long story, I've told you enough."

"Mitya'll be up to something now—I say! Does he know or doesn't he?"

"He know! Of course he doesn't. If he know, there would be murder. But I am not afraid of that now, I am not afraid of his knife. Be quiet, Rakitin, don't remind me of Dmitri Fyodorovitch, he has bruised my heart. And I don't want to think of that at this moment. I can think of Alyosha here, I can look at Alyosha ... smile at me, dear, cheer up, smile at my foolishness, at my pleasure.... Ah, he's smiling, he's smiling! How kindly he looks at me! And you know, Alyosha, I've been thinking all this time you were angry with me, because of the day before yesterday, because of that young lady. I was a cur, that's the truth.... But it's a good thing it happened so. It was a horrid thing, but a good thing too." Grushenka smiled dreamily and a little cruel line showed in her smile. "Mitya told me that she screamed out that I 'ought to be flogged.' I did insult her dreadfully. She sent for me, she wanted to make a conquest of me, to win me over with her chocolate.... No, it's a good thing it did end like that." She smiled again. "But I am still afraid of your being angry."

"Yes, that's really true," Rakitin put in suddenly with genuine surprise. "Alyosha, she is really afraid of a chicken like you."

"He is a chicken to you, Rakitin ... because you've no conscience, that's what it is! You see, I love him with all my soul, that's how it is! Alyosha, do you believe I love you with all my soul?"

"Ah, you shameless woman! She is making you a declaration, Alexey!"

"Well, what of it, I love him!"

"And what about your officer? And the priceless message from Mokroe?"

"That is quite different."

"That's a woman's way of looking at it!"

"Don't you make me angry, Rakitin." Grushenka caught him up hotly. "This is quite different. I love Alyosha in a different way. It's true, Alyosha, I had sly designs on you before. For I am a horrid, violent creature. But at other times I've looked upon you, Alyosha, as my conscience. I've kept thinking 'how any one like that must despise a nasty thing like me.' I thought that the day before yesterday, as I ran home from the young lady's. I have thought of you a long time in that way, Alyosha, and Mitya knows, I've talked to him about it. Mitya understands. Would you believe it, I sometimes look at you and feel ashamed, utterly ashamed of myself.... And how, and since when, I began to think about you like that, I can't say, I don't remember...."

Fenya came in and put a tray with an uncorked bottle and three glasses of champagne on the table.

"Here's the champagne!" cried Rakitin. "You're excited, Agrafena Alexandrovna, and not yourself. When you've had a glass of champagne, you'll be ready to dance. Eh, they can't even do that properly," he added, looking at the bottle. "The old woman's poured it out in the kitchen and the bottle's been brought in warm and without a cork. Well, let me have some, anyway."

He went up to the table, took a glass, emptied it at one gulp and poured himself out another.

"One doesn't often stumble upon champagne," he said, licking his lips. "Now, Alyosha, take a glass, show what you can do! What shall we drink to? The gates of paradise? Take a glass, Grushenka, you drink to the gates of paradise, too."

"What gates of paradise?"

She took a glass, Alyosha took his, tasted it and put it back.

"No, I'd better not," he smiled gently.

"And you bragged!" cried Rakitin.

"Well, if so, I won't either," chimed in Grushenka, "I really don't want any. You can drink the whole bottle alone, Rakitin. If Alyosha has some, I will."

"What touching sentimentality!" said Rakitin tauntingly; "and she's sitting on his knee, too! He's got something to grieve over, but what's the matter with you? He is rebelling against his God and ready to eat sausage...."

"How so?"

"His elder died to-day, Father Zossima, the saint."

"So Father Zossima is dead," cried Grushenka. "Good God, I did not know!" She crossed herself devoutly. "Goodness, what have I been doing, sitting on his knee like this at such a moment!" She started up as though in dismay, instantly slipped off his knee and sat down on the sofa.

Alyosha bent a long wondering look upon her and a light seemed to dawn in his face.

"Rakitin," he said suddenly, in a firm and loud voice; "don't taunt me with having rebelled against God. I don't want to feel angry with you, so you must be kinder, too, I've lost a treasure such as you have never had, and you cannot judge me now. You had much better look at her—do you see how she has pity on me? I came here to find a wicked soul—I felt drawn to evil because I was base and evil myself, and I've found a true sister, I have found a treasure—a loving heart. She had pity on me just now.... Agrafena Alexandrovna, I am speaking of you. You've raised my soul from the depths."

Alyosha's lips were quivering and he caught his breath.

"She has saved you, it seems," laughed Rakitin spitefully. "And she meant to get you in her clutches, do you realize that?"

"Stay, Rakitin." Grushenka jumped up. "Hush, both of you. Now I'll tell you all about it. Hush, Alyosha, your words make me ashamed, for I am bad and not good—that's what I am. And you hush, Rakitin, because you are telling lies. I had the low idea of trying to get him in my clutches, but now you are lying, now it's all different. And don't let me hear anything more from you, Rakitin."

All this Grushenka said with extreme emotion.

"They are both crazy," said Rakitin, looking at them with amazement. "I feel as though I were in a madhouse. They're both getting so feeble they'll begin crying in a minute."

"I shall begin to cry, I shall," repeated Grushenka. "He called me his sister and I shall never forget that. Only let me tell you, Rakitin, though I am bad, I did give away an onion."

"An onion? Hang it all, you really are crazy."

Rakitin wondered at their enthusiasm. He was aggrieved and annoyed, though he might have reflected that each of them was just passing through a spiritual crisis such as does not come often in a lifetime. But though Rakitin was very sensitive about everything that concerned himself, he was very obtuse as regards the feelings and sensations of others—partly from his youth and inexperience, partly from his intense egoism.

"You see, Alyosha," Grushenka turned to him with a nervous laugh. "I was boasting when I told Rakitin I had given away an onion, but it's not to boast I tell you about it. It's only a story, but it's a nice story. I used to hear it when I was a child from Matryona, my cook, who is still with me. It's like this. Once upon a time there was a peasant woman and a very wicked woman she was. And she died and did not leave a single good deed behind. The devils caught her and plunged her into the lake of fire. So her guardian angel stood and wondered what good deed of hers he could remember to tell to God; 'She once pulled up an onion in her garden,' said he, 'and gave it to a beggar woman.' And God answered: 'You take that onion then, hold it out to her in the lake, and let her take hold and be pulled out. And if you can pull her out of the lake, let her come to Paradise, but if the onion breaks, then the woman must stay where she is.' The angel ran to the woman and held out the onion to her. 'Come,' said he, 'catch hold and I'll pull you out.' And he began cautiously pulling her out. He had just pulled her right out, when the other sinners in the lake, seeing how she was being drawn out, began catching hold of her so as to be pulled out with her. But she was a very wicked woman and she began kicking them. 'I'm to be pulled out, not you. It's my onion, not yours.' As soon as she said that, the onion broke. And the woman fell into the lake and she is burning there to this day. So the angel wept and went away. So that's the story, Alyosha; I know it by heart, for I am that wicked woman myself. I boasted to Rakitin that I had given away an onion, but to you I'll say: 'I've done nothing but give away one onion all my life, that's the only good deed I've done.' So don't praise me,

Alyosha, don't think me good, I am bad, I am a wicked woman and you make me ashamed if you praise me. Eh, I must confess everything. Listen, Alyosha. I was so anxious to get hold of you that I promised Rakitin twenty-five roubles if he would bring you to me. Stay, Rakitin, wait!"

She went with rapid steps to the table, opened a drawer, pulled out a purse and took from it a twenty-five rouble note.

"What nonsense! What nonsense!" cried Rakitin, disconcerted.

"Take it. Rakitin, I owe it you, there's no fear of your refusing it, you asked for it yourself." And she threw the note to him.

"Likely I should refuse it," boomed Rakitin, obviously abashed, but carrying off his confusion with a swagger. "That will come in very handy; fools are made for wise men's profit."

"And now hold your tongue, Rakitin, what I am going to say now is not for your ears. Sit down in that corner and keep quiet. You don't like us, so hold your tongue."

"What should I like you for?" Rakitin snarled, not concealing his ill-humor. He put the twenty-five rouble note in his pocket and he felt ashamed at Alyosha's seeing it. He had reckoned on receiving his payment later, without Alyosha's knowing of it, and now, feeling ashamed, he lost his temper. Till that moment he had thought it discreet not to contradict Grushenka too flatly in spite of her snubbing, since he had something to get out of her. But now he, too, was angry:

"One loves people for some reason, but what have either of you done for me?"

"You should love people without a reason, as Alyosha does."

"How does he love you? How has he shown it, that you make such a fuss about it?"

Grushenka was standing in the middle of the room; she spoke with heat and there were hysterical notes in her voice.

"Hush, Rakitin, you know nothing about us! And don't dare to speak to me like that again. How dare you be so familiar! Sit in that corner and be quiet, as though you were my footman! And now, Alyosha, I'll tell you the whole truth, that you may see what a wretch I am! I am not talking to Rakitin, but to you. I wanted to ruin you, Alyosha, that's the holy truth; I quite meant to. I wanted to so much, that I bribed Rakitin to bring you. And why did I want to do such a thing? You knew nothing about it, Alyosha, you turned away from me; if you passed me, you dropped your eyes. And I've looked at you a hundred times before to-day; I began asking every one about you. Your face haunted my heart. 'He despises me,' I thought; 'he won't even look at me.' And I felt it so much at last that I wondered at myself for being so frightened of a boy. I'll get him in my clutches and laugh at him. I was full of spite and anger. Would you believe it, nobody here dares talk or think of coming to Agrafena Alexandrovna with any evil purpose. Old Kuzma is the only man I have anything to do with here; I was bound and sold to him; Satan brought us together, but there has been no one else. But looking at you, I thought, I'll get him in my clutches and laugh at him. You see what a spiteful cur I am, and you called me your sister! And now that man who wronged me has come; I sit here waiting for a message from him. And do you know what that man has been to me? Five years ago, when Kuzma brought me here, I used to shut myself up, that no one might have sight or sound of me. I was a silly slip of a girl; I used to sit here sobbing; I used to lie awake all night, thinking: 'Where is he now, the man who wronged me? He is laughing at me with another woman, most likely. If only I could see him, if I could meet him again, I'd pay him out, I'd pay him out!' At night I used to lie sobbing into my pillow in the dark, and I used to brood over it; I used to tear my heart on purpose and gloat over my anger. 'I'll pay him out, I'll pay him out!' That's what I used to cry out in the dark. And when I suddenly thought that I should really do nothing to him, and that he was laughing at me then, or perhaps had utterly forgotten me, I would fling myself on the floor, melt into helpless tears, and lie there shaking till dawn. In the morning I would get up more spiteful than a dog, ready to tear the whole world to pieces. And then what do you think? I began saving money, I became hard-hearted, grew stout— grew wiser, would you say? No, no one in the whole world sees it, no one knows it, but when night comes on, I sometimes lie as I did five years ago, when I was a silly girl, clenching my teeth and crying all night, thinking, 'I'll pay him out, I'll pay him out!' Do you hear? Well then, now you understand me. A month ago a letter came to me—he was coming, he was a widower, he wanted to see me. It took my breath away; then I suddenly thought: 'If he comes and whistles to call me, I shall creep back to him like a beaten dog.' I couldn't believe myself. Am I so abject? Shall I run to him or not? And I've been in such a rage with myself all this month that I am worse than I was five years ago. Do you see now, Alyosha, what a violent, vindictive creature I am? I have shown you the whole truth! I played with Mitya to keep me from running to that other. Hush, Rakitin, it's not for you to judge me, I am not speaking to you. Before you came in, I was lying here waiting, brooding, deciding my whole future life, and you can never know what was in my heart. Yes, Alyosha, tell your young lady not to be angry with me for what happened the day before yesterday.... Nobody in the whole world knows what I am going through now, and no one ever can know.... For perhaps I shall take a knife with me to-day, I can't make up my mind ..."

And at this "tragic" phrase Grushenka broke down, hid her face in her hands, flung herself on the sofa pillows, and sobbed like a little child.

Alyosha got up and went to Rakitin.

"Misha," he said, "don't be angry. She wounded you, but don't be angry. You heard what she said just now? You mustn't ask too much of human endurance, one must be merciful."

Alyosha said this at the instinctive prompting of his heart. He felt obliged to speak and he turned to Rakitin. If Rakitin had not been there, he would have spoken to the air. But Rakitin looked at him ironically and Alyosha stopped short.

"You were so primed up with your elder's teaching last night that now you have to let it off on me, Alexey, man of God!" said Rakitin, with a smile of hatred.

"Don't laugh, Rakitin, don't smile, don't talk of the dead—he was better than any one in the world!" cried Alyosha, with tears in his voice. "I didn't speak to you as a judge but as the lowest of the judged. What am I beside her? I came here seeking my ruin, and said to myself, 'What does it matter?' in my cowardliness, but she, after five years in torment, as soon as any one says a word from the heart to her—it makes her forget everything, forgive everything, in her tears! The man who has wronged her has come back, he sends for her and she forgives him everything, and hastens joyfully to meet him and she won't take a knife with her. She won't! No, I am not like that. I don't know whether you are, Misha, but I am not like that. It's a lesson to me.... She is more loving than we.... Have you heard her speak before of what she has just told us? No, you haven't; if you had, you'd have understood her long ago ... and the person insulted the day before yesterday must forgive her, too! She will, when she knows ... and she shall know.... This soul is not yet at peace with itself, one must be tender with it ... there may be a treasure in that soul...."

Alyosha stopped, because he caught his breath. In spite of his ill-humor Rakitin looked at him with astonishment. He had never expected such a tirade from the gentle Alyosha.

"She's found some one to plead her cause! Why, are you in love with her? Agrafena Alexandrovna, our monk's really in love with you, you've made a conquest!" he cried, with a coarse laugh.

Grushenka lifted her head from the pillow and looked at Alyosha with a tender smile shining on her tear-stained face.

"Let him alone, Alyosha, my cherub; you see what he is, he is not a person for you to speak to. Mihail Osipovitch," she turned to Rakitin, "I meant to beg your pardon for being rude to you, but now I don't want to. Alyosha, come to me, sit down here." She beckoned to him with a happy smile. "That's right, sit here. Tell me," she shook him by the hand and peeped into his face, smiling, "tell me, do I love that man or not? the man who wronged me, do I love him or not? Before you came, I lay here in the dark, asking my heart whether I loved him. Decide for me, Alyosha, the time has come, it shall be as you say. Am I to forgive him or not?"

"But you have forgiven him already," said Alyosha, smiling.

"Yes, I really have forgiven him," Grushenka murmured thoughtfully. "What an abject heart! To my abject heart!" She snatched up a glass from the table, emptied it at a gulp, lifted it in the air and flung it on the floor. The glass broke with a crash. A little cruel line came into her smile.

"Perhaps I haven't forgiven him, though," she said, with a sort of menace in her voice, and she dropped her eyes to the ground as though she were talking to herself. "Perhaps my heart is only getting ready to forgive. I shall struggle with my heart. You see, Alyosha, I've grown to love my tears in these five years.... Perhaps I only love my resentment, not him ..."

"Well, I shouldn't care to be in his shoes," hissed Rakitin.

"Well, you won't be, Rakitin, you'll never be in his shoes. You shall black my shoes, Rakitin, that's the place you are fit for. You'll never get a woman like me ... and he won't either, perhaps ..."

"Won't he? Then why are you dressed up like that?" said Rakitin, with a venomous sneer.

"Don't taunt me with dressing up, Rakitin, you don't know all that is in my heart! If I choose to tear off my finery, I'll tear it off at once, this minute," she cried in a resonant voice. "You don't know what that finery is for, Rakitin! Perhaps I shall see him and say: 'Have you ever seen me look like this before?' He left me a thin, consumptive cry-baby of seventeen. I'll sit by him, fascinate him and work him up. 'Do you see what I am like now?' I'll say to him; 'well, and that's enough for you, my dear sir, there's many a slip twixt the cup and the lip!' That may be what the finery is for, Rakitin." Grushenka finished with a malicious laugh. "I'm violent and resentful, Alyosha, I'll tear off my finery, I'll destroy my beauty, I'll scorch my face, slash it with a knife, and turn beggar. If I choose, I won't go anywhere now to see any one. If I choose, I'll send Kuzma back all he has ever given me, to-morrow, and all his money and I'll go out charing for the rest of my life. You think I wouldn't do it, Rakitin, that I would not dare to do it? I would, I would, I could do it directly, only don't exasperate me ... and I'll send him about his business, I'll snap my fingers in his face, he shall never see me again!"

She uttered the last words in an hysterical scream, but broke down again, hid her face in her hands, buried it in the pillow and shook with sobs.

Rakitin got up.

"It's time we were off," he said, "it's late, we shall be shut out of the monastery."

Grushenka leapt up from her place.

"Surely you don't want to go, Alyosha!" she cried, in mournful surprise. "What are you doing to me? You've stirred up my feeling, tortured me, and now you'll leave me to face this night alone!"

"He can hardly spend the night with you! Though if he wants to, let him! I'll go alone," Rakitin scoffed jeeringly.

"Hush, evil tongue!" Grushenka cried angrily at him; "you never said such words to me as he has come to say."

"What has he said to you so special?" asked Rakitin irritably.

"I can't say, I don't know. I don't know what he said to me, it went straight to my heart; he has wrung my heart.... He is the first, the only one who has pitied me, that's what it is. Why did you not come before, you angel?" She fell on her knees before him as though in a sudden frenzy. "I've been waiting all my life for some one like you, I knew that some one like you would come and forgive me. I believed that, nasty as I am, some one would really love me, not only with a shameful love!"

"What have I done to you?" answered Alyosha, bending over her with a tender smile, and gently taking her by the hands; "I only gave you an onion, nothing but a tiny little onion, that was all!"

He was moved to tears himself as he said it. At that moment there was a sudden noise in the passage, some one came into the hall. Grushenka jumped up, seeming greatly alarmed. Fenya ran noisily into the room, crying out:

"Mistress, mistress darling, a messenger has galloped up," she cried, breathless and joyful. "A carriage from Mokroe for you, Timofey the driver, with three horses, they are just putting in fresh horses.... A letter, here's the letter, mistress."

A letter was in her hand and she waved it in the air all the while she talked. Grushenka snatched the letter from her and carried it to the candle. It was only a note, a few lines. She read it in one instant.

"He has sent for me," she cried, her face white and distorted, with a wan smile; "he whistles! Crawl back, little dog!"

But only for one instant she stood as though hesitating; suddenly the blood rushed to her head and sent a glow to her cheeks.

"I will go," she cried; "five years of my life! Good-by! Good-by, Alyosha, my fate is sealed. Go, go, leave me all of you, don't let me see you again! Grushenka is flying to a new life.... Don't you remember evil against me either, Rakitin. I may be going to my death! Ugh! I feel as though I were drunk!"

She suddenly left them and ran into her bedroom.

"Well, she has no thoughts for us now!" grumbled Rakitin. "Let's go, or we may hear that feminine shriek again. I am sick of all these tears and cries."

Alyosha mechanically let himself be led out. In the yard stood a covered cart. Horses were being taken out of the shafts, men were running to and fro with a lantern. Three fresh horses were being led in at the open gate. But when Alyosha and Rakitin reached the bottom of the steps, Grushenka's bedroom window was suddenly opened and she called in a ringing voice after Alyosha:

"Alyosha, give my greetings to your brother Mitya and tell him not to remember evil against me, though I have brought him misery. And tell him, too, in my words: 'Grushenka has fallen to a scoundrel, and not to you, noble heart.' And add, too, that Grushenka loved him only one hour, only one short hour she loved him—so let him remember that hour all his life—say, 'Grushenka tells you to!' "

She ended in a voice full of sobs. The window was shut with a slam.

"H'm, h'm!" growled Rakitin, laughing, "she murders your brother Mitya and then tells him to remember it all his life! What ferocity!"

Alyosha made no reply, he seemed not to have heard. He walked fast beside Rakitin as though in a terrible hurry. He was lost in thought and moved mechanically. Rakitin felt a sudden twinge as though he had been touched on an open wound. He had expected something quite different by bringing Grushenka and Alyosha together. Something very different from what he had hoped for had happened.

"He is a Pole, that officer of hers," he began again, restraining himself; "and indeed he is not an officer at all now. He served in the customs in Siberia, somewhere on the Chinese frontier, some puny little beggar of a Pole, I expect. Lost his job, they say. He's heard now that Grushenka's saved a little money, so he's turned up again—that's the explanation of the mystery."

Again Alyosha seemed not to hear. Rakitin could not control himself.

"Well, so you've saved the sinner?" he laughed spitefully. "Have you turned the Magdalene into the true path? Driven out the seven devils, eh? So you see the miracles you were looking out for just now have come to pass!"

"Hush, Rakitin," Alyosha answered with an aching heart.

"So you despise me now for those twenty-five roubles? I've sold my friend, you think. But you are not Christ, you know, and I am not Judas."

"Oh, Rakitin, I assure you I'd forgotten about it," cried Alyosha, "you remind me of it yourself...."

But this was the last straw for Rakitin.

"Damnation take you all and each of you!" he cried suddenly, "why the devil did I take you up? I don't want to know you from this time forward. Go alone, there's your road!"

And he turned abruptly into another street, leaving Alyosha alone in the dark. Alyosha came out of the town and walked across the fields to the monastery.

It was very late, according to the monastery ideas, when Alyosha returned to the hermitage; the door-keeper let him in by a special entrance. It had struck nine o'clock—the hour of rest and repose after a day of such agitation for all. Alyosha timidly opened the door and went into the elder's cell where his coffin was now standing. There was no one in the cell but Father Païssy, reading the Gospel in solitude over the coffin, and the young novice Porfiry, who, exhausted by the previous night's conversation and the disturbing incidents of the day, was sleeping the deep sound sleep of youth on the floor of the other room. Though Father Païssy heard Alyosha come in, he did not even look in his direction. Alyosha turned to the right from the door to the corner, fell on his knees and began to pray.

His soul was overflowing but with mingled feelings; no single sensation stood out distinctly; on the contrary, one drove out another in a slow, continual rotation. But there was a sweetness in his heart and, strange to say, Alyosha was not surprised at it. Again he saw that coffin before him, the hidden dead figure so precious to him, but the weeping and poignant grief of the morning was no longer aching in his soul. As soon as he came in, he fell down before the coffin as before a holy shrine, but joy, joy was glowing in his mind and in his heart. The one window of the cell was open, the air was fresh and cool. "So the smell must have become stronger, if they opened the window," thought Alyosha. But even this thought of the smell of corruption, which had seemed to him so awful and humiliating a few hours before, no longer made him feel miserable or indignant. He began quietly praying, but he soon felt that he was praying almost mechanically. Fragments of thought floated through his soul, flashed like stars and went out again at once, to be succeeded by others. But yet there was reigning in his soul a sense of the wholeness of things— something steadfast and comforting—and he was aware of it himself. Sometimes he began praying ardently, he longed to pour out his thankfulness and love....

But when he had begun to pray, he passed suddenly to something else, and sank into thought, forgetting both the prayer and what had interrupted it. He began listening to what Father Païssy was reading, but worn out with exhaustion he gradually began to doze.

"And the third day there was a marriage in Cana of Galilee;" read Father Païssy. "And the mother of Jesus was there; And both Jesus was called, and his disciples, to the marriage."

"Marriage? What's that?... A marriage!" floated whirling through Alyosha's mind. "There is happiness for her, too.... She has gone to the feast.... No, she has not taken the knife.... That was only a tragic phrase.... Well ... tragic phrases should be forgiven, they must be. Tragic phrases comfort the heart.... Without them, sorrow would be too heavy for men to bear. Rakitin has gone off to the back alley. As long as Rakitin broods over his wrongs, he will always go off to the back alley.... But the high road ... The road is wide and straight and bright as crystal, and the sun is at the end of it.... Ah!... What's being read?"...

"And when they wanted wine, the mother of Jesus saith unto him, They have no wine" ... Alyosha heard.

"Ah, yes, I was missing that, and I didn't want to miss it, I love that passage: it's Cana of Galilee, the first miracle.... Ah, that miracle! Ah, that sweet miracle! It was not men's grief, but their joy Christ visited, He worked His first miracle to help men's gladness.... 'He who loves men loves their gladness, too' ... He was always repeating that, it was one of his leading ideas.... 'There's no living without joy,' Mitya says.... Yes, Mitya.... 'Everything that is true and good is always full of forgiveness,' he used to say that, too" ...

"Jesus saith unto her, Woman, what has it to do with thee or me? Mine hour is not yet come.

"His mother saith unto the servants, Whatsoever he saith unto you, do it" ...

"Do it.... Gladness, the gladness of some poor, very poor, people.... Of course they were poor, since they hadn't wine enough even at a wedding.... The historians write that, in those days, the people living about the Lake of Gennesaret were the poorest that can possibly be imagined ... and another great heart, that other great being, His Mother, knew that He had come not only to make His great terrible sacrifice. She knew that His heart was open even to the simple, artless merrymaking of some obscure and unlearned people, who had warmly bidden Him to their poor wedding. 'Mine hour is not yet come,' He said, with a soft smile (He must have smiled gently to her). And, indeed, was it to make wine abundant at poor weddings He had come down to earth? And yet He went and did as she asked Him.... Ah, he is reading again"....

"Jesus saith unto them, Fill the waterpots with water. And they filled them up to the brim.

"And he saith unto them, Draw out now and bear unto the governor of the feast. And they bare it.

"When the ruler of the feast had tasted the water that was made wine, and knew not whence it was; (but the servants which drew the water knew;) the governor of the feast called the bridegroom,

"And saith unto him, Every man at the beginning doth set forth good wine; and when men have well drunk, that which is worse; but thou hast kept the good wine until now."

"But what's this, what's this? Why is the room growing wider?... Ah, yes ... It's the marriage, the wedding ... yes, of course. Here are the guests, here are the young couple sitting, and the merry crowd and ... Where is the wise governor of the feast? But who is this? Who? Again the walls are receding.... Who is getting up there from the great table?

What!... He here, too? But he's in the coffin ... but he's here, too. He has stood up, he sees me, he is coming here.... God!"...

Yes, he came up to him, to him, he, the little, thin old man, with tiny wrinkles on his face, joyful and laughing softly. There was no coffin now, and he was in the same dress as he had worn yesterday sitting with them, when the visitors had gathered about him. His face was uncovered, his eyes were shining. How was this, then? He, too, had been called to the feast. He, too, at the marriage of Cana in Galilee....

"Yes, my dear, I am called, too, called and bidden," he heard a soft voice saying over him. "Why have you hidden yourself here, out of sight? You come and join us too."

It was his voice, the voice of Father Zossima. And it must be he, since he called him!

The elder raised Alyosha by the hand and he rose from his knees.

"We are rejoicing," the little, thin old man went on. "We are drinking the new wine, the wine of new, great gladness; do you see how many guests? Here are the bride and bridegroom, here is the wise governor of the feast, he is tasting the new wine. Why do you wonder at me? I gave an onion to a beggar, so I, too, am here. And many here have given only an onion each—only one little onion.... What are all our deeds? And you, my gentle one, you, my kind boy, you too have known how to give a famished woman an onion to-day. Begin your work, dear one, begin it, gentle one!... Do you see our Sun, do you see Him?"

"I am afraid ... I dare not look," whispered Alyosha.

"Do not fear Him. He is terrible in His greatness, awful in His sublimity, but infinitely merciful. He has made Himself like unto us from love and rejoices with us. He is changing the water into wine that the gladness of the guests may not be cut short. He is expecting new guests, He is calling new ones unceasingly for ever and ever.... There they are bringing new wine. Do you see they are bringing the vessels...."

Something glowed in Alyosha's heart, something filled it till it ached, tears of rapture rose from his soul.... He stretched out his hands, uttered a cry and waked up.

Again the coffin, the open window, and the soft, solemn, distinct reading of the Gospel. But Alyosha did not listen to the reading. It was strange, he had fallen asleep on his knees, but now he was on his feet, and suddenly, as though thrown forward, with three firm rapid steps he went right up to the coffin. His shoulder brushed against Father Païssy without his noticing it. Father Païssy raised his eyes for an instant from his book, but looked away again at once, seeing that something strange was happening to the boy. Alyosha gazed for half a minute at the coffin, at the covered, motionless dead man that lay in the coffin, with the ikon on his breast and the peaked cap with the octangular cross, on his head. He had only just been hearing his voice, and that voice was still ringing in his ears. He was listening, still expecting other words, but suddenly he turned sharply and went out of the cell.

He did not stop on the steps either, but went quickly down; his soul, overflowing with rapture, yearned for freedom, space, openness. The vault of heaven, full of soft, shining stars, stretched vast and fathomless above him. The Milky Way ran in two pale streams from the zenith to the horizon. The fresh, motionless, still night enfolded the earth. The white towers and golden domes of the cathedral gleamed out against the sapphire sky. The gorgeous autumn flowers, in the beds round the house, were slumbering till morning. The silence of earth seemed to melt into the silence of the heavens. The mystery of earth was one with the mystery of the stars....

Alyosha stood, gazed, and suddenly threw himself down on the earth. He did not know why he embraced it. He could not have told why he longed so irresistibly to kiss it, to kiss it all. But he kissed it weeping, sobbing and watering it with his tears, and vowed passionately to love it, to love it for ever and ever. "Water the earth with the tears of your joy and love those tears," echoed in his soul.

What was he weeping over?

Oh! in his rapture he was weeping even over those stars, which were shining to him from the abyss of space, and "he was not ashamed of that ecstasy." There seemed to be threads from all those innumerable worlds of God, linking his soul to them, and it was trembling all over "in contact with other worlds." He longed to forgive every one and for everything, and to beg forgiveness. Oh, not for himself, but for all men, for all and for everything. "And others are praying for me too," echoed again in his soul. But with every instant he felt clearly and, as it were, tangibly, that something firm and unshakable as that vault of heaven had entered into his soul. It was as though some idea had seized the sovereignty of his mind—and it was for all his life and for ever and ever. He had fallen on the earth a weak boy, but he rose up a resolute champion, and he knew and felt it suddenly at the very moment of his ecstasy. And never, never, all his life long, could Alyosha forget that minute.

"Some one visited my soul in that hour," he used to say afterwards, with implicit faith in his words.

Within three days he left the monastery in accordance with the words of his elder, who had bidden him "sojourn in the world."

Chapter Four
Mitya

But Dmitri, to whom Grushenka, flying away to a new life, had left her last greetings, bidding him remember the hour of her love for ever, knew nothing of what had happened to her, and was at that moment in a condition of feverish agitation and activity. For the last two days he had been in such an inconceivable state of mind that he might easily have fallen ill with brain fever, as he said himself afterwards. Alyosha had not been able to find him the morning before, and Ivan had not succeeded in meeting him at the tavern on the same day. The people at his lodgings, by his orders, concealed his movements.

He had spent those two days literally rushing in all directions, "struggling with his destiny and trying to save himself," as he expressed it himself afterwards, and for some hours he even made a dash out of the town on urgent business, terrible as it was to him to lose sight of Grushenka for a moment. All this was explained afterwards in detail, and confirmed by documentary evidence; but for the present we will only note the most essential incidents of those two terrible days immediately preceding the awful catastrophe, that broke so suddenly upon him.

Though Grushenka had, it is true, loved him for an hour, genuinely and sincerely, yet she tortured him sometimes cruelly and mercilessly. The worst of it was that he could never tell what she meant to do. To prevail upon her by force or kindness was also impossible: she would yield to nothing. She would only have become angry and turned away from him altogether, he knew that well already. He suspected, quite correctly, that she, too, was passing through an inward struggle, and was in a state of extraordinary indecision, that she was making up her mind to something, and unable to determine upon it. And so, not without good reason, he divined, with a sinking heart, that at moments she must simply hate him and his passion. And so, perhaps, it was, but what was distressing Grushenka he did not understand. For him the whole tormenting question lay between him and Fyodor Pavlovitch.

Here, we must note, by the way, one certain fact: he was firmly persuaded that Fyodor Pavlovitch would offer, or perhaps had offered, Grushenka lawful wedlock, and did not for a moment believe that the old voluptuary hoped to gain his object for three thousand roubles. Mitya had reached this conclusion from his knowledge of Grushenka and her character. That was how it was that he could believe at times that all Grushenka's uneasiness rose from not knowing which of them to choose, which was most to her advantage.

Strange to say, during those days it never occurred to him to think of the approaching return of the "officer," that is, of the man who had been such a fatal influence in Grushenka's life, and whose arrival she was expecting with such emotion and dread. It is true that of late Grushenka had been very silent about it. Yet he was perfectly aware of a letter she had received a month ago from her seducer, and had heard of it from her own lips. He partly knew, too, what the letter contained. In a moment of spite Grushenka had shown him that letter, but to her astonishment he attached hardly any consequence to it. It would be hard to say why this was. Perhaps, weighed down by all the hideous horror of his struggle with his own father for this woman, he was incapable of imagining any danger more terrible, at any rate for the time. He simply did not believe in a suitor who suddenly turned up again after five years' disappearance, still less in his speedy arrival. Moreover, in the "officer's" first letter which had been shown to Mitya, the possibility of his new rival's visit was very vaguely suggested. The letter was very indefinite, high-flown, and full of sentimentality. It must be noted that Grushenka had concealed from him the last lines of the letter, in which his return was alluded to more definitely. He had, besides, noticed at that moment, he remembered afterwards, a certain involuntary proud contempt for this missive from Siberia on Grushenka's face. Grushenka told him nothing of what had passed later between her and this rival; so that by degrees he had completely forgotten the officer's existence.

He felt that whatever might come later, whatever turn things might take, his final conflict with Fyodor Pavlovitch was close upon him, and must be decided before anything else. With a sinking heart he was expecting every moment Grushenka's decision, always believing that it would come suddenly, on the impulse of the moment. All of a sudden she would say to him: "Take me, I'm yours for ever," and it would all be over. He would seize her and bear her away at once to the ends of the earth. Oh, then he would bear her away at once, as far, far away as possible; to the farthest end of Russia, if not of the earth, then he would marry her, and settle down with her incognito, so that no one would know anything about them, there, here, or anywhere. Then, oh, then, a new life would begin at once!

Of this different, reformed and "virtuous" life ("it must, it must be virtuous") he dreamed feverishly at every moment. He thirsted for that reformation and renewal. The filthy morass, in which he had sunk of his own free will, was too revolting to him, and, like very many men in such cases, he put faith above all in change of place. If only it were not for these people, if only it were not for these circumstances, if only he could fly away from this accursed place—he would be altogether regenerated, would enter on a new path. That was what he believed in, and what he was yearning for.

But all this could only be on condition of the first, the *happy* solution of the question. There was another possibility, a different and awful ending. Suddenly she might say to him: "Go away. I have just come to terms with Fyodor Pavlovitch. I am going to marry him and don't want you"—and then ... but then.... But Mitya did not know what would happen then. Up to the last hour he didn't know. That must be said to his credit. He had no definite intentions, had planned no crime. He was simply watching and spying in agony, while he prepared himself for the first, happy solution of his destiny. He drove away any other idea, in fact. But for that ending a quite different anxiety arose, a new, incidental, but yet fatal and insoluble difficulty presented itself.

If she were to say to him: "I'm yours; take me away," how could he take her away? Where had he the means, the money to do it? It was just at this time that all sources of revenue from Fyodor Pavlovitch, doles which had gone on without interruption for so many years, ceased. Grushenka had money, of course, but with regard to this Mitya suddenly evinced extraordinary pride; he wanted to carry her away and begin the new life with her himself, at his own expense, not at hers. He could not conceive of taking her money, and the very idea caused him a pang of intense repulsion. I won't enlarge on this fact or analyze it here, but confine myself to remarking that this was his attitude at the moment. All this may have arisen indirectly and unconsciously from the secret stings of his conscience for the money of Katerina Ivanovna that he had dishonestly appropriated. "I've been a scoundrel to one of them, and I shall be a scoundrel again to the other directly," was his feeling then, as he explained after: "and when Grushenka knows, she won't care for such a scoundrel."

Where then was he to get the means, where was he to get the fateful money? Without it, all would be lost and nothing could be done, "and only because I hadn't the money. Oh, the shame of it!"

To anticipate things: he did, perhaps, know where to get the money, knew, perhaps, where it lay at that moment. I will say no more of this here, as it will all be clear later. But his chief trouble, I must explain however obscurely, lay in the fact that to have that sum he knew of, to *have the right* to take it, he must first restore Katerina Ivanovna's three thousand—if not, "I'm a common pickpocket, I'm a scoundrel, and I don't want to begin a new life as a scoundrel," Mitya decided. And so he made up his mind to move heaven and earth to return Katerina Ivanovna that three thousand, and that *first of all*. The final stage of this decision, so to say, had been reached only during the last hours, that is, after his last interview with Alyosha, two days before, on the high-road, on the evening when Grushenka had insulted Katerina Ivanovna, and Mitya, after hearing Alyosha's account of it, had admitted that he was a scoundrel, and told him to tell Katerina Ivanovna so, if it could be any comfort to her. After parting from his brother on that night, he had felt in his frenzy that it would be better "to murder and rob some one than fail to pay my debt to Katya. I'd rather every one thought me a robber and a murderer, I'd rather go to Siberia than that Katya should have the right to say that I deceived her and stole her money, and used her money to run away with Grushenka and begin a new life! That I can't do!" So Mitya decided, grinding his teeth, and he might well fancy at times that his brain would give way. But meanwhile he went on struggling....

Strange to say, though one would have supposed there was nothing left for him but despair—for what chance had he, with nothing in the world, to raise such a sum?—yet to the very end he persisted in hoping that he would get that three thousand, that the money would somehow come to him of itself, as though it might drop from heaven. That is just how it is with people who, like Dmitri, have never had anything to do with money, except to squander what has come to them by inheritance without any effort of their own, and have no notion how money is obtained. A whirl of the most fantastic notions took possession of his brain immediately after he had parted with Alyosha two days before, and threw his thoughts into a tangle of confusion. This is how it was he pitched first on a perfectly wild enterprise. And perhaps to men of that kind in such circumstances the most impossible, fantastic schemes occur first, and seem most practical.

He suddenly determined to go to Samsonov, the merchant who was Grushenka's protector, and to propose a "scheme" to him, and by means of it to obtain from him at once the whole of the sum required. Of the commercial value of his scheme he had no doubt, not the slightest, and was only uncertain how Samsonov would look upon his freak, supposing he were to consider it from any but the commercial point of view. Though Mitya knew the merchant by sight, he was not acquainted with him and had never spoken a word to him. But for some unknown reason he had long entertained the conviction that the old reprobate, who was lying at death's door, would perhaps not at all object now to Grushenka's securing a respectable position, and marrying a man "to be depended upon." And he believed not only that he would not object, but that this was what he desired, and, if opportunity arose, that he would be ready to help. From some rumor, or perhaps from some stray word of Grushenka's, he had gathered further that the old man would perhaps prefer him to Fyodor Pavlovitch for Grushenka.

Possibly many of the readers of my novel will feel that in reckoning on such assistance, and being ready to take his bride, so to speak, from the hands of her protector, Dmitri showed great coarseness and want of delicacy. I will only observe that Mitya looked upon Grushenka's past as something completely over. He looked on that past with infinite pity and resolved with all the fervor of his passion that when once Grushenka told him she loved him and would marry him, it would mean the beginning of a new Grushenka and a new Dmitri, free from every vice. They would forgive one another and would begin their lives afresh. As for Kuzma Samsonov, Dmitri looked upon him as a man who had exercised a fateful influence in that remote past of Grushenka's, though she had never loved him, and who was now himself a thing of the past, completely done with, and, so to say, non-existent. Besides, Mitya hardly looked upon him as a man at all, for it was known to every one in the town that he was only a shattered wreck, whose relations with Grushenka had changed their character and were now simply paternal, and that this had been so for a long time.

In any case there was much simplicity on Mitya's part in all this, for in spite of all his vices, he was a very simple-hearted man. It was an instance of this simplicity that Mitya was seriously persuaded that, being on the eve of his departure for the next world, old Kuzma must sincerely repent of his past relations with Grushenka, and that she had no more devoted friend and protector in the world than this, now harmless old man.

After his conversation with Alyosha, at the cross-roads, he hardly slept all night, and at ten o'clock next morning, he was at the house of Samsonov and telling the servant to announce him. It was a very large and gloomy old house of two stories, with a lodge and outhouses. In the lower story lived Samsonov's two married sons with their families, his old sister, and his unmarried daughter. In the lodge lived two of his clerks, one of whom also had a large family. Both the lodge and the lower story were overcrowded, but the old man kept the upper floor to himself, and would not even let the daughter live there with him, though she waited upon him, and in spite of her asthma was obliged at certain fixed hours, and at any time he might call her, to run upstairs to him from below.

This upper floor contained a number of large rooms kept purely for show, furnished in the old-fashioned merchant style, with long monotonous rows of clumsy mahogany chairs along the walls, with glass chandeliers under shades, and gloomy mirrors on the walls. All these rooms were entirely empty and unused, for the old man kept to one room, a small, remote bedroom, where he was waited upon by an old servant with a kerchief on her head, and by a lad, who used to sit on the locker in the passage. Owing to his swollen legs, the old man could hardly walk at all, and was only rarely lifted from his leather arm-chair, when the old woman supporting him led him up and down the room once or twice. He was morose and taciturn even with this old woman.

When he was informed of the arrival of the "captain," he at once refused to see him. But Mitya persisted and sent his name up again. Samsonov questioned the lad minutely: What he looked like? Whether he was drunk? Was he going to make a row? The answer he received was: that he was sober, but wouldn't go away. The old man again refused to see him. Then Mitya, who had foreseen this, and purposely brought pencil and paper with him, wrote clearly on the piece of paper the words: "On most important business closely concerning Agrafena Alexandrovna," and sent it up to the old man.

After thinking a little Samsonov told the lad to take the visitor to the drawing-room, and sent the old woman downstairs with a summons to his younger son to come upstairs to him at once. This younger son, a man over six foot and of exceptional physical strength, who was closely-shaven and dressed in the European style, though his father still wore a kaftan and a beard, came at once without a comment. All the family trembled before the father. The old man had sent for this giant, not because he was afraid of the "captain" (he was by no means of a timorous temper), but in order to have a witness in case of any emergency. Supported by his son and the servant-lad, he waddled at last into the drawing-room. It may be assumed that he felt considerable curiosity. The drawing-room in which Mitya was awaiting him was a vast, dreary room that laid a weight of depression on the heart. It had a double row of windows, a gallery, marbled walls, and three immense chandeliers with glass lusters covered with shades.

Mitya was sitting on a little chair at the entrance, awaiting his fate with nervous impatience. When the old man appeared at the opposite door, seventy feet away, Mitya jumped up at once, and with his long, military stride walked to meet him. Mitya was well dressed, in a frock-coat, buttoned up, with a round hat and black gloves in his hands, just as he had been three days before at the elder's, at the family meeting with his father and brothers. The old man waited for him, standing dignified and unbending, and Mitya felt at once that he had looked him through and through as he advanced. Mitya was greatly impressed, too, with Samsonov's immensely swollen face. His lower lip, which had always been thick, hung down now, looking like a bun. He bowed to his guest in dignified silence, motioned him to a low chair by the sofa, and, leaning on his son's arm he began lowering himself on to the sofa opposite, groaning painfully, so that Mitya, seeing his painful exertions, immediately felt remorseful and sensitively conscious of his insignificance in the presence of the dignified person he had ventured to disturb.

"What is it you want of me, sir?" said the old man, deliberately, distinctly, severely, but courteously, when he was at last seated.

Mitya started, leapt up, but sat down again. Then he began at once speaking with loud, nervous haste, gesticulating, and in a positive frenzy. He was unmistakably a man driven into a corner, on the brink of ruin, catching at the last straw, ready to sink if he failed. Old Samsonov probably grasped all this in an instant, though his face remained cold and immovable as a statue's.

"Most honored sir, Kuzma Kuzmitch, you have no doubt heard more than once of my disputes with my father, Fyodor Pavlovitch Karamazov, who robbed me of my inheritance from my mother ... seeing the whole town is gossiping about it ... for here every one's gossiping of what they shouldn't ... and besides, it might have reached you through Grushenka ... I beg your pardon, through Agrafena Alexandrovna ... Agrafena Alexandrovna, the lady for whom I have the highest respect and esteem ..."

So Mitya began, and broke down at the first sentence. We will not reproduce his speech word for word, but will only summarize the gist of it. Three months ago, he said, he had of express intention (Mitya purposely used these words instead of "intentionally") consulted a lawyer in the chief town of the province, "a distinguished lawyer, Kuzma Kuzmitch, Pavel Pavlovitch Korneplodov. You have perhaps heard of him? A man of vast intellect, the mind of a statesman ... he knows you, too ... spoke of you in the highest terms ..." Mitya broke

down again. But these breaks did not deter him. He leapt instantly over the gaps, and struggled on and on.

This Korneplodov, after questioning him minutely, and inspecting the documents he was able to bring him (Mitya alluded somewhat vaguely to these documents, and slurred over the subject with special haste), reported that they certainly might take proceedings concerning the village of Tchermashnya, which ought, he said, to have come to him, Mitya, from his mother, and so checkmate the old villain, his father ... "because every door was not closed and justice might still find a loophole." In fact, he might reckon on an additional sum of six or even seven thousand roubles from Fyodor Pavlovitch, as Tchermashnya was worth, at least, twenty-five thousand, he might say twenty-eight thousand, in fact, "thirty, thirty, Kuzma Kuzmitch, and would you believe it, I didn't get seventeen from that heartless man!" So he, Mitya, had thrown the business up, for the time, knowing nothing about the law, but on coming here was struck dumb by a cross-claim made upon him (here Mitya went adrift again and again took a flying leap forward), "so will not you, excellent and honored Kuzma Kuzmitch, be willing to take up all my claims against that unnatural monster, and pay me a sum down of only three thousand?... You see, you cannot, in any case, lose over it. On my honor, my honor, I swear that. Quite the contrary, you may make six or seven thousand instead of three." Above all, he wanted this concluded that very day.

"I'll do the business with you at a notary's, or whatever it is ... in fact, I'm ready to do anything.... I'll hand over all the deeds ... whatever you want, sign anything ... and we could draw up the agreement at once ... and if it were possible, if it were only possible, that very morning.... You could pay me that three thousand, for there isn't a capitalist in this town to compare with you, and so would save me from ... would save me, in fact ... for a good, I might say an honorable action.... For I cherish the most honorable feelings for a certain person, whom you know well, and care for as a father. I would not have come, indeed, if it had not been as a father. And, indeed, it's a struggle of three in this business, for it's fate—that's a fearful thing, Kuzma Kuzmitch! A tragedy, Kuzma Kuzmitch, a tragedy! And as you've dropped out long ago, it's a tug-of-war between two. I'm expressing it awkwardly, perhaps, but I'm not a literary man. You see, I'm on the one side, and that monster on the other. So you must choose. It's either I or the monster. It all lies in your hands—the fate of three lives, and the happiness of two.... Excuse me, I'm making a mess of it, but you understand ... I see from your venerable eyes that you understand ... and if you don't understand, I'm done for ... so you see!"

Mitya broke off his clumsy speech with that, "so you see!" and jumping up from his seat, awaited the answer to his foolish proposal. At the last phrase he had suddenly become hopelessly aware that it had all fallen flat, above all, that he had been talking utter nonsense.

"How strange it is! On the way here it seemed all right, and now it's nothing but nonsense." The idea suddenly dawned on his despairing mind. All the while he had been talking, the old man sat motionless, watching him with an icy expression in his eyes. After keeping him for a moment in suspense, Kuzma Kuzmitch pronounced at last in the most positive and chilling tone:

"Excuse me, we don't undertake such business."

Mitya suddenly felt his legs growing weak under him.

"What am I to do now, Kuzma Kuzmitch?" he muttered, with a pale smile. "I suppose it's all up with me—what do you think?"

"Excuse me...."

Mitya remained standing, staring motionless. He suddenly noticed a movement in the old man's face. He started.

"You see, sir, business of that sort's not in our line," said the old man slowly. "There's the court, and the lawyers—it's a perfect misery. But if you like, there is a man here you might apply to."

"Good heavens! Who is it? You're my salvation, Kuzma Kuzmitch," faltered Mitya.

"He doesn't live here, and he's not here just now. He is a peasant, he does business in timber. His name is Lyagavy. He's been haggling with Fyodor Pavlovitch for the last year, over your copse at Tchermashnya. They can't agree on the price, maybe you've heard? Now he's come back again and is staying with the priest at Ilyinskoe, about twelve versts from the Volovya station. He wrote to me, too, about the business of the copse, asking my advice. Fyodor Pavlovitch means to go and see him himself. So if you were to be beforehand with Fyodor Pavlovitch and to make Lyagavy the offer you've made me, he might possibly—"

"A brilliant idea!" Mitya interrupted ecstatically. "He's the very man, it would just suit him. He's haggling with him for it, being asked too much, and here he would have all the documents entitling him to the property itself. Ha ha ha!"

And Mitya suddenly went off into his short, wooden laugh, startling Samsonov.

"How can I thank you, Kuzma Kuzmitch?" cried Mitya effusively.

"Don't mention it," said Samsonov, inclining his head.

"But you don't know, you've saved me. Oh, it was a true presentiment brought me to you.... So now to this priest!"

"No need of thanks."

"I'll make haste and fly there. I'm afraid I've overtaxed your strength. I shall never forget it. It's a Russian says that, Kuzma Kuzmitch, a R-r-russian!"

"To be sure!"

Mitya seized his hand to press it, but there was a malignant gleam in the old man's eye. Mitya drew back his hand, but at once blamed himself for his mistrustfulness.

"It's because he's tired," he thought.

"For her sake! For her sake, Kuzma Kuzmitch! You understand that it's for her," he cried, his voice ringing through the room. He bowed, turned sharply round, and with the same long stride walked to the door without looking back. He was trembling with delight.

"Everything was on the verge of ruin and my guardian angel saved me," was the thought in his mind. And if such a business man as Samsonov (a most worthy old man, and what dignity!) had suggested this course, then ... then success was assured. He would fly off immediately. "I will be back before night, I shall be back at night and the thing is done. Could the old man have been laughing at me?" exclaimed Mitya, as he strode towards his lodging. He could, of course, imagine nothing, but that the advice was practical "from such a business man" with an understanding of the business, with an understanding of this Lyagavy (curious surname!). Or—the old man was laughing at him.

Alas! The second alternative was the correct one. Long afterwards, when the catastrophe had happened, old Samsonov himself confessed, laughing, that he had made a fool of the "captain." He was a cold, spiteful and sarcastic man, liable to violent antipathies. Whether it was the "captain's" excited face, or the foolish conviction of the "rake and spendthrift," that he, Samsonov, could be taken in by such a cock-and-bull story as his scheme, or his jealousy of Grushenka, in whose name this "scapegrace" had rushed in on him with such a tale to get money which worked on the old man, I can't tell. But at the instant when Mitya stood before him, feeling his legs grow weak under him, and frantically exclaiming that he was ruined, at that moment the old man looked at him with intense spite, and resolved to make a laughing-stock of him. When Mitya had gone, Kuzma Kuzmitch, white with rage, turned to his son and bade him see to it that that beggar be never seen again, and never admitted even into the yard, or else he'd—

He did not utter his threat. But even his son, who often saw him enraged, trembled with fear. For a whole hour afterwards, the old man was shaking with anger, and by evening he was worse, and sent for the doctor.

Where was he running? "Where could she be except at Fyodor Pavlovitch's? She must have run straight to him from Samsonov's, that was clear now. The whole intrigue, the whole deceit was evident." ... It all rushed whirling through his mind. He did not run to Marya Kondratyevna's. "There was no need to go there ... not the slightest need ... he must raise no alarm ... they would run and tell directly.... Marya Kondratyevna was clearly in the plot, Smerdyakov too, he too, all had been bought over!"

He formed another plan of action: he ran a long way round Fyodor Pavlovitch's house, crossing the lane, running down Dmitrovsky Street, then over the little bridge, and so came straight to the deserted alley at the back, which was empty and uninhabited, with, on one side the hurdle fence of a neighbor's kitchen-garden, on the other the strong high fence, that ran all round Fyodor Pavlovitch's garden. Here he chose a spot, apparently the very place, where according to the tradition, he knew Lizaveta had once climbed over it: "If she could climb over it," the thought, God knows why, occurred to him, "surely I can." He did in fact jump up, and instantly contrived to catch hold of the top of the fence. Then he vigorously pulled himself up and sat astride on it. Close by, in the garden stood the bath-house, but from the fence he could see the lighted windows of the house too.

"Yes, the old man's bedroom is lighted up. She's there!" and he leapt from the fence into the garden. Though he knew Grigory was ill and very likely Smerdyakov, too, and that there was no one to hear him, he instinctively hid himself, stood still, and began to listen. But there was dead silence on all sides and, as though of design, complete stillness, not the slightest breath of wind.

"And naught but the whispering silence," the line for some reason rose to his mind. "If only no one heard me jump over the fence! I think not." Standing still for a minute, he walked softly over the grass in the garden, avoiding the trees and shrubs. He walked slowly, creeping stealthily at every step, listening to his own footsteps. It took him five minutes to reach the lighted window. He remembered that just under the window there were several thick and high bushes of elder and whitebeam. The door from the house into the garden on the left-hand side, was shut; he had carefully looked on purpose to see, in passing. At last he reached the bushes and hid behind them. He held his breath. "I must wait now," he thought, "to reassure them, in case they heard my footsteps and are listening ... if only I don't cough or sneeze."

He waited two minutes. His heart was beating violently, and, at moments, he could scarcely breathe. "No, this throbbing at my heart won't stop," he thought. "I can't wait any longer." He was standing behind a bush in the shadow. The light of the window fell on the front part of the bush.

"How red the whitebeam berries are!" he murmured, not knowing why. Softly and noiselessly, step by step, he approached the window, and raised himself on tiptoe. All Fyodor Pavlovitch's bedroom lay open before him. It was not a large room, and was divided in two parts by a red screen, "Chinese," as Fyodor Pavlovitch used to call it. The word "Chinese" flashed into Mitya's mind, "and behind the screen, is Grushenka," thought Mitya. He began watching Fyodor Pavlovitch, who was wearing his new striped-silk dressing-gown, which Mitya had never seen, and a silk cord with tassels round the waist. A clean, dandified shirt of fine linen with gold studs peeped out under the collar of the dressing-gown. On his head Fyodor Pavlovitch had the same red bandage which Alyosha had seen.

"He has got himself up," thought Mitya.

His father was standing near the window, apparently lost in thought. Suddenly he jerked up his head, listened a moment, and hearing nothing went up to the table, poured out half a glass of brandy from a decanter and drank it off. Then he uttered a deep sigh, again stood still a moment, walked carelessly up to the looking-glass on the wall, with his right hand raised the red bandage on his forehead a little, and began examining his bruises and scars, which had not yet disappeared.

"He's alone," thought Mitya, "in all probability he's alone."

Fyodor Pavlovitch moved away from the looking-glass, turned suddenly to the window and looked out. Mitya instantly slipped away into the shadow.

"She may be there behind the screen. Perhaps she's asleep by now," he thought, with a pang at his heart. Fyodor Pavlovitch moved away from the window. "He's looking for her out of the window, so she's not there. Why should he stare out into the dark? He's wild with impatience." ... Mitya slipped back at once, and fell to gazing in at the window again. The old man was sitting down at the table, apparently disappointed. At last he put his elbow on the table, and laid his right cheek against his hand. Mitya watched him eagerly.

"He's alone, he's alone!" he repeated again. "If she were here, his face would be different."

Strange to say, a queer, irrational vexation rose up in his heart that she was not here. "It's not that she's not here," he explained to himself, immediately, "but that I can't tell for certain whether she is or not." Mitya remembered afterwards that his mind was at that moment exceptionally clear, that he took in everything to the slightest detail, and missed no point. But a feeling of misery, the misery of uncertainty and indecision, was growing in his heart with every instant. "Is she here or not?" The angry doubt filled his heart, and suddenly, making up his mind, he put out his hand and softly knocked on the window frame. He knocked the signal the old man had agreed upon with Smerdyakov, twice slowly and then three times more quickly, the signal that meant "Grushenka is here!"

The old man started, jerked up his head, and, jumping up quickly, ran to the window. Mitya slipped away into the shadow. Fyodor Pavlovitch opened the window and thrust his whole head out.

"Grushenka, is it you? Is it you?" he said, in a sort of trembling half-whisper. "Where are you, my angel, where are you?" He was fearfully agitated and breathless.

"He's alone." Mitya decided.

"Where are you?" cried the old man again; and he thrust his head out farther, thrust it out to the shoulders, gazing in all directions, right and left. "Come here, I've a little present for you. Come, I'll show you...."

"He means the three thousand," thought Mitya.

"But where are you? Are you at the door? I'll open it directly."

And the old man almost climbed out of the window, peering out to the right, where there was a door into the garden, trying to see into the darkness. In another second he would certainly have run out to open the door without waiting for Grushenka's answer.

Mitya looked at him from the side without stirring. The old man's profile that he loathed so, his pendent Adam's apple, his hooked nose, his lips that smiled in greedy expectation, were all brightly lighted up by the slanting lamplight falling on the left from the room. A horrible fury of hatred suddenly surged up in Mitya's heart: "There he was, his rival, the man who had tormented him, had ruined his life!" It was a rush of that sudden, furious, revengeful anger of which he had spoken, as though foreseeing it, to Alyosha, four days ago in the arbor, when, in answer to Alyosha's question, "How can you say you'll kill our father?" "I don't know, I don't know," he had said then. "Perhaps I shall not kill him, perhaps I shall. I'm afraid he'll suddenly be so loathsome to me at that moment. I hate his double chin, his nose, his eyes, his shameless grin. I feel a personal repulsion. That's what I'm afraid of, that's what may be too much for me." ... This personal repulsion was growing unendurable. Mitya was beside himself, he suddenly pulled the brass pestle out of his pocket.

"God was watching over me then," Mitya himself said afterwards. At that very moment Grigory waked up on his bed of sickness. Earlier in the evening he had undergone the treatment which Smerdyakov had described to Ivan. He had rubbed himself all over with vodka mixed with a secret, very strong decoction, had drunk what was left of the mixture while his wife repeated a "certain prayer" over him, after which he had gone to bed. Marfa Ignatyevna had tasted the stuff, too, and, being unused to strong drink, slept like the dead beside her husband.

But Grigory waked up in the night, quite suddenly, and, after a moment's reflection, though he immediately felt a sharp pain in his back, he sat up in bed. Then he deliberated again, got up and dressed hurriedly. Perhaps his conscience was uneasy at the thought of sleeping while the house was unguarded "in such perilous times." Smerdyakov, exhausted by his fit, lay motionless in the next room. Marfa Ignatyevna did not stir. "The stuff's been too much for the woman," Grigory thought, glancing at her, and groaning, he went out on the steps. No doubt he only intended to look out from the steps, for he was hardly able to walk, the pain in his back and his right leg was intolerable. But he suddenly remembered that he had not locked the little gate into the garden that evening. He was the most punctual and precise of men, a man who adhered to an unchangeable routine, and habits that lasted for years. Limping and writhing with pain he went down the steps and towards the garden. Yes, the gate stood wide open. Mechanically he stepped into the garden. Perhaps he fancied something, perhaps caught some sound, and, glancing to the left he saw his master's window open. No one was looking out of it then.

"What's it open for? It's not summer now," thought Grigory, and suddenly, at that very instant he caught a glimpse of something extraordinary before him in the garden. Forty paces in front of him a man seemed to be running in the dark, a sort of shadow was moving very fast.

"Good Lord!" cried Grigory beside himself, and forgetting the pain in his back, he hurried to intercept the running figure. He took a short cut, evidently he knew the garden better; the flying figure went towards the bath-house, ran behind it and rushed to the garden fence. Grigory followed, not losing sight of him, and ran, forgetting everything. He reached the fence at the very moment the man was climbing over it. Grigory cried out, beside himself, pounced on him, and clutched his leg in his two hands.

Yes, his foreboding had not deceived him. He recognized him, it was he, the "monster," the "parricide."

"Parricide!" the old man shouted so that the whole neighborhood could hear, but he had not time to shout more, he fell at once, as though struck by lightning.

Mitya jumped back into the garden and bent over the fallen man. In Mitya's hands was a brass pestle, and he flung it mechanically in the grass. The pestle fell two paces from Grigory, not in the grass but on the path, in a most conspicuous place. For some seconds he examined the prostrate figure before him. The old man's head was covered with blood. Mitya put out his hand and began feeling it. He remembered afterwards clearly, that he had been awfully anxious to make sure whether he had broken the old man's skull, or simply stunned him with the pestle. But the blood was flowing horribly; and in a moment Mitya's fingers were drenched with the hot stream. He remembered taking out of his pocket the clean white handkerchief with which he had provided himself for his visit to Madame Hohlakov, and putting it to the old man's head, senselessly trying to wipe the blood from his face and temples. But the handkerchief was instantly soaked with blood.

"Good heavens! what am I doing it for?" thought Mitya, suddenly pulling himself together. "If I have broken his skull, how can I find out now? And what difference does it make now?" he added, hopelessly. "If I've killed him, I've killed him.... You've come to grief, old man, so there you must lie!" he said aloud. And suddenly turning to the fence, he vaulted over it into the lane and fell to running—the handkerchief soaked with blood he held, crushed up in his right fist, and as he ran he thrust it into the back pocket of his coat. He ran headlong, and the few passers-by who met him in the dark, in the streets, remembered afterwards that they had met a man running that night. He flew back again to the widow Morozov's house.

Immediately after he had left it that evening, Fenya had rushed to the chief porter, Nazar Ivanovitch, and besought him, for Christ's sake, "not to let the captain in again to-day or to-morrow." Nazar Ivanovitch promised, but went upstairs to his mistress who had suddenly sent for him, and meeting his nephew, a boy of twenty, who had recently come from the country, on the way up told him to take his place, but forgot to mention "the captain." Mitya, running up to the gate, knocked. The lad instantly recognized him, for Mitya had more than once tipped him. Opening the gate at once, he let him in, and hastened to inform him with a good-humored smile that "Agrafena Alexandrovna is not at home now, you know."

"Where is she then, Prohor?" asked Mitya, stopping short.

"She set off this evening, some two hours ago, with Timofey, to Mokroe."

"What for?" cried Mitya.

"That I can't say. To see some officer. Some one invited her and horses were sent to fetch her."

Mitya left him, and ran like a madman to Fenya.

Dmitri Fyodorovitch was speeding along the road. It was a little more than twenty versts to Mokroe, but Andrey's three horses galloped at such a pace that the distance might be covered in an hour and a quarter. The swift motion revived Mitya. The air was fresh and cool, there were big stars shining in the sky. It was the very night, and perhaps the very hour, in which Alyosha fell on the earth, and rapturously swore to love it for ever and ever.

All was confusion, confusion, in Mitya's soul, but although many things were goading his heart, at that moment his whole being was yearning for her, his queen, to whom he was flying to look on her for the last time. One thing I can say for certain; his heart did not waver for one instant. I shall perhaps not be believed when I say that this jealous lover felt not the slightest jealousy of this new rival, who seemed to have sprung out of the earth. If any other had appeared on the scene, he would have been jealous at once, and would perhaps have stained his fierce hands with blood again. But as he flew through the night, he felt no envy, no hostility even, for the man who had been her first lover.... It is true he had not yet seen him.

"Here there was no room for dispute: it was her right and his; this was her first love which, after five years, she had not forgotten; so she had loved him only for those five years, and I, how do I come in? What right have I? Step aside, Mitya, and make way! What am I now? Now everything is over apart from the officer—even if he had not appeared, everything would be over ..."

These words would roughly have expressed his feelings, if he had been capable of reasoning. But he could not reason at that moment. His present plan of action had arisen without reasoning. At Fenya's first words, it had sprung from feeling, and been adopted in a flash, with all its consequences. And yet, in spite of his resolution, there was confusion in his soul, an agonizing confusion: his resolution did not give him peace. There was so much behind that tortured him. And it seemed strange to him, at moments, to think that he had written his own sentence of death with pen and paper: "I punish myself," and the paper was lying there in his pocket, ready; the pistol was loaded; he had already resolved how, next morning, he would meet the first warm ray of "golden-haired Phœbus."

And yet he could not be quit of the past, of all that he had left behind and that tortured him. He felt that miserably, and the thought of it sank into his heart with despair. There was one moment when he felt an impulse to stop Andrey, to jump out of the cart, to pull out his loaded pistol, and to make an end of everything without waiting for the dawn. But that moment flew by like a spark. The horses galloped on, "devouring space," and as he drew near his goal, again the thought of her, of her alone, took more and more complete possession of his soul, chasing away the fearful images that had been haunting it. Oh, how he longed to look upon her, if only for a moment, if only from a distance!

"She's now with *him*," he thought, "now I shall see what she looks like with him, her first love, and that's all I want." Never had this woman, who was such a fateful influence in his life, aroused such love in his breast, such new and unknown feeling, surprising even to himself, a feeling tender to devoutness, to self-effacement before her! "I will efface myself!" he said, in a rush of almost hysterical ecstasy.

They had been galloping nearly an hour. Mitya was silent, and though Andrey was, as a rule, a talkative peasant, he did not utter a word, either. He seemed afraid to talk, he only whipped up smartly his three lean, but mettlesome, bay horses. Suddenly Mitya cried out in horrible anxiety:

"Andrey! What if they're asleep?"

This thought fell upon him like a blow. It had not occurred to him before.

"It may well be that they're gone to bed, by now, Dmitri Fyodorovitch."

Mitya frowned as though in pain. Yes, indeed ... he was rushing there ... with such feelings ... while they were asleep ... she was asleep, perhaps, there too.... An angry feeling surged up in his heart.

"Drive on, Andrey! Whip them up! Look alive!" he cried, beside himself.

"But maybe they're not in bed!" Andrey went on after a pause. "Timofey said they were a lot of them there—"

"At the station?"

"Not at the posting-station, but at Plastunov's, at the inn, where they let out horses, too."

"I know. So you say there are a lot of them? How's that? Who are they?" cried Mitya, greatly dismayed at this unexpected news.

"Well, Timofey was saying they're all gentlefolk. Two from our town—who they are I can't say—and there are two others, strangers, maybe more besides. I didn't ask particularly. They've set to playing cards, so Timofey said."

"Cards?"

"So, maybe they're not in bed if they're at cards. It's most likely not more than eleven."

"Quicker, Andrey! Quicker!" Mitya cried again, nervously.

"May I ask you something, sir?" said Andrey, after a pause. "Only I'm afraid of angering you, sir."

"What is it?"

"Why, Fenya threw herself at your feet just now, and begged you not to harm her mistress, and some one else, too ... so you see, sir— It's I am taking you there ... forgive me, sir, it's my conscience ... maybe it's stupid of me to speak of it—"

Mitya suddenly seized him by the shoulders from behind.

"Are you a driver?" he asked frantically.

"Yes, sir."

"Then you know that one has to make way. What would you say to a driver who wouldn't make way for any one, but would just drive on and crush people? No, a driver mustn't run over people. One can't run over a man. One can't spoil people's lives. And if you have spoilt a life—punish yourself.... If only you've spoilt, if only you've ruined any one's life—punish yourself and go away."

These phrases burst from Mitya almost hysterically. Though Andrey was surprised at him, he kept up the conversation.

"That's right, Dmitri Fyodorovitch, you're quite right, one mustn't crush or torment a man, or any kind of creature, for every creature is created by God. Take a horse, for instance, for some folks, even among us drivers, drive anyhow. Nothing will restrain them, they just force it along."

"To hell?" Mitya interrupted, and went off into his abrupt, short laugh. "Andrey, simple soul," he seized him by the shoulders again, "tell me, will Dmitri Fyodorovitch Karamazov go to hell, or not, what do you think?"

"I don't know, darling, it depends on you, for you are ... you see, sir, when the Son of God was nailed on the Cross and died, He went straight down to hell from the Cross, and set free all sinners that were in agony. And the devil groaned, because he thought that he would get no more sinners in hell. And God said to him, then, 'Don't groan, for you shall have all the mighty of the earth, the rulers, the chief judges, and the rich men, and shall be filled up as you have been in all the ages till I come again.' Those were His very words ..."

"A peasant legend! Capital! Whip up the left, Andrey!"

"So you see, sir, who it is hell's for," said Andrey, whipping up the left horse, "but you're like a little child ... that's how we look on you ... and though you're hasty-tempered, sir, yet God will forgive you for your kind heart."

"And you, do you forgive me, Andrey?"

"What should I forgive you for, sir? You've never done me any harm."

"No, for every one, for every one, you here alone, on the road, will you forgive me for every one? Speak, simple peasant heart!"

"Oh, sir! I feel afraid of driving you, your talk is so strange."

But Mitya did not hear. He was frantically praying and muttering to himself.

"Lord, receive me, with all my lawlessness, and do not condemn me. Let me pass by Thy judgment ... do not condemn me, for I have condemned myself, do not condemn me, for I love Thee, O Lord. I am a wretch, but I love Thee. If Thou sendest me to hell, I shall love Thee there, and from there I shall cry out that I love Thee for ever and ever.... But let me love to the end.... Here and now for just five hours ... till the first light of Thy day ... for I love the queen of my soul ... I love her and I cannot help loving her. Thou seest my whole heart.... I shall gallop up, I shall fall before her and say, 'You are right to pass on and leave me. Farewell and forget your victim ... never fret yourself about me!' "

"Mokroe!" cried Andrey, pointing ahead with his whip.

Through the pale darkness of the night loomed a solid black mass of buildings, flung down, as it were, in the vast plain. The village of Mokroe numbered two thousand inhabitants, but at that hour all were asleep, and only here and there a few lights still twinkled.

"Drive on, Andrey, I come!" Mitya exclaimed, feverishly.

"They're not asleep," said Andrey again, pointing with his whip to the Plastunovs' inn, which was at the entrance to the village. The six windows, looking on the street, were all brightly lighted up.

"They're not asleep," Mitya repeated joyously. "Quicker, Andrey! Gallop! Drive up with a dash! Set the bells ringing! Let all know that I have come. I'm coming! I'm coming, too!"

Andrey lashed his exhausted team into a gallop, drove with a dash and pulled up his steaming, panting horses at the high flight of steps.

Mitya jumped out of the cart just as the innkeeper, on his way to bed, peeped out from the steps curious to see who had arrived.

"Trifon Borissovitch, is that you?"

The innkeeper bent down, looked intently, ran down the steps, and rushed up to the guest with obsequious delight.

"Dmitri Fyodorovitch, your honor! Do I see you again?"

Trifon Borissovitch was a thick-set, healthy peasant, of middle height, with a rather fat face. His expression was severe and uncompromising, especially with the peasants of Mokroe, but he had the power of assuming the most obsequious countenance, when he had an inkling that it was to his interest. He dressed in Russian style, with a shirt buttoning down on one side, and a full-skirted coat. He had saved a good sum of money, but was for ever dreaming of improving his position. More than half the peasants were in his clutches, every one in the neighborhood was in debt to him. From the neighboring landowners he bought and rented lands which were worked by the peasants, in payment of debts which they could never shake off. He was a widower, with four grown-up daughters. One of them was already a widow and lived in the inn with her two children, his grandchildren, and worked for him like a charwoman. Another of his daughters was married to a petty official, and in one of the rooms of the inn, on the wall could be seen, among the family photographs, a miniature photograph of this official in uniform and official epaulettes. The two younger daughters used to wear fashionable blue or green dresses, fitting tight at the back, and with trains a yard long, on Church holidays or when they went to pay visits. But next morning they would get up at dawn, as usual, sweep out the rooms with a birch-broom, empty the slops, and clean up after lodgers.

In spite of the thousands of roubles he had saved, Trifon Borissovitch was very fond of emptying the pockets of a drunken guest, and remembering that not a month ago he had, in twenty-four hours, made two if not three hundred roubles out of Dmitri, when he had come on his escapade with Grushenka, he met him now with eager welcome, scenting his prey the moment Mitya drove up to the steps.

"Dmitri Fyodorovitch, dear sir, we see you once more!"

"Stay, Trifon Borissovitch," began Mitya, "first and foremost, where is she?"

"Agrafena Alexandrovna?" The inn-keeper understood at once, looking sharply into Mitya's face. "She's here, too ..."

"With whom? With whom?"

"Some strangers. One is an official gentleman, a Pole, to judge from his speech. He sent the horses for her from here; and there's another with him, a friend of his, or a fellow traveler, there's no telling. They're dressed like civilians."

"Well, are they feasting? Have they money?"

"Poor sort of a feast! Nothing to boast of, Dmitri Fyodorovitch."

"Nothing to boast of? And who are the others?"

"They're two gentlemen from the town.... They've come back from Tcherny, and are putting up here. One's quite a young gentleman, a relative of Mr. Miüsov, he must be, but I've forgotten his name ... and I expect you know the other, too, a gentleman called Maximov. He's been on a pilgrimage, so he says, to the monastery in the town. He's traveling with this young relation of Mr. Miüsov."

"Is that all?"

"Yes."

"Stay, listen, Trifon Borissovitch. Tell me the chief thing: What of her? How is she?"

"Oh, she's only just come. She's sitting with them."

"Is she cheerful? Is she laughing?"

"No, I think she's not laughing much. She's sitting quite dull. She's combing the young gentleman's hair."

"The Pole—the officer?"

"He's not young, and he's not an officer, either. Not him, sir. It's the young gentleman that's Mr. Miüsov's relation ... I've forgotten his name."

"Kalganov."

"That's it, Kalganov!"

"All right. I'll see for myself. Are they playing cards?"

"They have been playing, but they've left off. They've been drinking tea, the official gentleman asked for liqueurs."

"Stay, Trifon Borissovitch, stay, my good soul, I'll see for myself. Now answer one more question: are the gypsies here?"

"You can't have the gypsies now, Dmitri Fyodorovitch. The authorities have sent them away. But we've Jews that play the cymbals and the fiddle in the village, so one might send for them. They'd come."

"Send for them. Certainly send for them!" cried Mitya. "And you can get the girls together as you did then, Marya especially, Stepanida, too, and Arina. Two hundred roubles for a chorus!"

"Oh, for a sum like that I can get all the village together, though by now they're asleep. Are the peasants here worth such kindness, Dmitri Fyodorovitch, or the girls either? To spend a sum like that on such coarseness and rudeness! What's the good of giving a peasant a cigar to smoke, the stinking ruffian! And the girls are all lousy. Besides, I'll get my daughters up for nothing, let alone a sum like that. They've only just gone to bed, I'll give them a kick and set them singing for you. You gave the peasants champagne to drink the other day, e—ech!"

For all his pretended compassion for Mitya, Trifon Borissovitch had hidden half a dozen bottles of champagne on that last occasion, and had picked up a hundred-rouble note under the table, and it had remained in his clutches.

"Trifon Borissovitch, I sent more than one thousand flying last time I was here. Do you remember?"

"You did send it flying. I may well remember. You must have left three thousand behind you."

"Well, I've come to do the same again, do you see?"

And he pulled out his roll of notes, and held them up before the innkeeper's nose.

"Now, listen and remember. In an hour's time the wine will arrive, savories, pies, and sweets—bring them all up at once. That box Andrey has got is to be brought up at once, too. Open it, and hand champagne immediately. And the girls, we must have the girls, Marya especially."

He turned to the cart and pulled out the box of pistols.

"Here, Andrey, let's settle. Here's fifteen roubles for the drive, and fifty for vodka ... for your readiness, for your love.... Remember Karamazov!"

"I'm afraid, sir," faltered Andrey. "Give me five roubles extra, but more I won't take. Trifon Borissovitch, bear witness. Forgive my foolish words ..."

"What are you afraid of?" asked Mitya, scanning him. "Well, go to the devil, if that's it!" he cried, flinging him five roubles. "Now, Trifon Borissovitch, take me up quietly and let me first get a look at them, so that they don't see me. Where are they? In the blue room?"

Trifon Borissovitch looked apprehensively at Mitya, but at once obediently did his bidding. Leading him into the passage, he went himself into the first large room, adjoining that in which the visitors were sitting, and took the light away. Then he stealthily led Mitya in, and put him in a corner in the dark, whence he could freely watch the company without being seen. But Mitya did not look long, and, indeed, he could not see them, he saw her, his heart throbbed violently, and all was dark before his eyes.

She was sitting sideways to the table in a low chair, and beside her, on the sofa, was the pretty youth, Kalganov. She was holding his hand and seemed to be laughing, while he, seeming vexed and not looking at her, was saying something in a loud voice to Maximov, who sat the other side of the table, facing Grushenka. Maximov was laughing violently at something. On the sofa sat *he*, and on a chair by the sofa there was another stranger. The one on the sofa was lolling backwards, smoking a pipe, and Mitya had an impression of a stoutish, broad-faced, short little man, who was apparently angry about something. His friend, the other stranger, struck Mitya as extraordinarily tall, but he could make out nothing more. He caught his breath. He could not bear it for a minute, he put the pistol-case on a chest, and with a throbbing heart he walked, feeling cold all over, straight into the blue room to face the company.

"Aie!" shrieked Grushenka, the first to notice him.

With his long, rapid strides, Mitya walked straight up to the table.

"Gentlemen," he said in a loud voice, almost shouting, yet stammering at every word, "I … I'm all right! Don't be afraid!" he exclaimed, "I—there's nothing the matter," he turned suddenly to Grushenka, who had shrunk back in her chair towards Kalganov, and clasped his hand tightly. "I … I'm coming, too. I'm here till morning. Gentlemen, may I stay with you till morning? Only till morning, for the last time, in this same room?"

So he finished, turning to the fat little man, with the pipe, sitting on the sofa. The latter removed his pipe from his lips with dignity and observed severely:

"*Panie*, we're here in private. There are other rooms."

"Why, it's you, Dmitri Fyodorovitch! What do you mean?" answered Kalganov suddenly. "Sit down with us. How are you?"

"Delighted to see you, dear … and precious fellow, I always thought a lot of you." Mitya responded, joyfully and eagerly, at once holding out his hand across the table.

"Aie! How tight you squeeze! You've quite broken my fingers," laughed Kalganov.

"He always squeezes like that, always," Grushenka put in gayly, with a timid smile, seeming suddenly convinced from Mitya's face that he was not going to make a scene. She was watching him with intense curiosity and still some uneasiness. She was impressed by something about him, and indeed the last thing she expected of him was that he would come in and speak like this at such a moment.

"Good evening," Maximov ventured blandly on the left. Mitya rushed up to him, too.

"Good evening. You're here, too! How glad I am to find you here, too! Gentlemen, gentlemen, I—" (He addressed the Polish gentleman with the pipe again, evidently taking him for the most important person present.) "I flew here.... I wanted to spend my last day, my last hour in this room, in this very room … where I, too, adored … my queen.... Forgive me, *panie*," he cried wildly, "I flew here and vowed— Oh, don't be afraid, it's my last night! Let's drink to our good understanding. They'll bring the wine at once.... I brought this with me." (Something made him pull out his bundle of notes.) "Allow me, *panie*! I want to have music, singing, a revel, as we had before. But the worm, the unnecessary worm, will crawl away, and there'll be no more of him. I will commemorate my day of joy on my last night."

He was almost choking. There was so much, so much he wanted to say, but strange exclamations were all that came from his lips. The Pole gazed fixedly at him, at the bundle of notes in his hand; looked at Grushenka, and was in evident perplexity.

"If my suverin lady is permitting—" he was beginning.

"What does 'suverin' mean? 'Sovereign,' I suppose?" interrupted Grushenka. "I can't help laughing at you, the way you talk. Sit down, Mitya, what are you talking about? Don't frighten us, please. You won't frighten us, will you? If you won't, I am glad to see you …"

"Me, me frighten you?" cried Mitya, flinging up his hands. "Oh, pass me by, go your way, I won't hinder you!..."

And suddenly he surprised them all, and no doubt himself as well, by flinging himself on a chair, and bursting into tears, turning his head away to the opposite wall, while his arms clasped the back of the chair tight, as though embracing it.

"Come, come, what a fellow you are!" cried Grushenka reproachfully. "That's just how he comes to see me—he begins talking, and I can't make out what he means. He cried like that once before, and now he's crying again! It's shameful! Why are you crying? *As though you had anything to cry for!*" she added enigmatically, emphasizing each word with some irritability.

"I … I'm not crying.... Well, good evening!" He instantly turned round in his chair, and suddenly laughed, not his abrupt wooden laugh, but a long, quivering, inaudible nervous laugh.

"Well, there you are again.... Come, cheer up, cheer up!" Grushenka said to him persuasively. "I'm very glad you've come, very glad, Mitya, do you hear, I'm very glad! I want him to stay here with us," she said peremptorily, addressing the whole company, though her words were obviously meant for the man sitting on the sofa. "I wish it, I wish it! And if he goes away I shall go, too!" she added with flashing eyes.

"What my queen commands is law!" pronounced the Pole, gallantly kissing Grushenka's hand. "I beg you, *panie*, to join our company," he added politely, addressing Mitya.

Mitya was jumping up with the obvious intention of delivering another tirade, but the words did not come.

"Let's drink, *panie*," he blurted out instead of making a speech. Every one laughed.

"Good heavens! I thought he was going to begin again!" Grushenka exclaimed nervously. "Do you hear, Mitya," she went on insistently, "don't prance about, but it's nice you've brought the champagne. I want some myself, and I can't bear liqueurs. And best of all, you've come yourself. We were fearfully dull here.... You've come for a spree again, I suppose? But put your money in your pocket. Where did you get such a lot?"

Mitya had been, all this time, holding in his hand the crumpled bundle of notes on which the eyes of all, especially of the Poles, were fixed. In confusion he thrust them hurriedly into his pocket. He flushed. At that moment the innkeeper brought in an uncorked bottle of champagne, and glasses on a tray. Mitya snatched up the bottle, but he was so bewildered that he did not know what to do with it. Kalganov took it from him and poured out the champagne.

"Another! Another bottle!" Mitya cried to the innkeeper, and, forgetting to clink glasses with the Pole whom he had so solemnly invited to drink to their good understanding, he drank off his glass without waiting for any one else. His whole countenance suddenly changed. The solemn and tragic expression with which he had entered vanished completely, and a look of something childlike came into his face. He seemed to have become suddenly gentle and subdued. He looked shyly and happily at every one, with a continual nervous little laugh, and the blissful expression of a dog who has done wrong, been punished, and forgiven. He seemed to have forgotten everything, and was looking round at every one with a childlike smile of delight. He looked at Grushenka, laughing continually, and bringing his chair close up to her. By degrees he had gained some idea of the two Poles, though he had formed no definite conception of them yet.

The Pole on the sofa struck him by his dignified demeanor and his Polish accent; and, above all, by his pipe. "Well, what of it? It's a good thing he's smoking a pipe," he reflected. The Pole's puffy, middle-aged face, with its tiny nose and two very thin, pointed, dyed and impudent-looking mustaches, had not so far roused the faintest doubts in Mitya. He was not even particularly struck by the Pole's absurd wig made in Siberia, with love-locks foolishly combed forward over the temples. "I suppose it's all right since he wears a wig," he went on, musing blissfully. The other, younger Pole, who was staring insolently and defiantly at the company and listening to the conversation with silent contempt, still only impressed Mitya by his great height, which was in striking contrast to the Pole on the sofa. "If he stood up he'd be six foot three." The thought flitted through Mitya's mind. It occurred to him, too, that this Pole must be the friend of the other, as it were, a "bodyguard," and no doubt the big Pole was at the disposal of the little Pole with the pipe. But this all seemed to Mitya perfectly right and not to be questioned. In his mood of doglike submissiveness all feeling of rivalry had died away.

Grushenka's mood and the enigmatic tone of some of her words he completely failed to grasp. All he understood, with thrilling heart, was that she was kind to him, that she had forgiven him, and made him sit by her. He was beside himself with delight, watching her sip her glass of champagne. The silence of the company seemed somehow to strike him, however, and he looked round at every one with expectant eyes.

"Why are we sitting here though, gentlemen? Why don't you begin doing something?" his smiling eyes seemed to ask.

"He keeps talking nonsense, and we were all laughing," Kalganov began suddenly, as though divining his thought, and pointing to Maximov.

Mitya immediately stared at Kalganov and then at Maximov.

"He's talking nonsense?" he laughed, his short, wooden laugh, seeming suddenly delighted at something—"ha ha!"

"Yes. Would you believe it, he will have it that all our cavalry officers in the twenties married Polish women. That's awful rot, isn't it?"

"Polish women?" repeated Mitya, perfectly ecstatic.

Kalganov was well aware of Mitya's attitude to Grushenka, and he guessed about the Pole, too, but that did not so much interest him, perhaps did not interest him at all; what he was interested in was Maximov. He had come here with Maximov by chance, and he met the Poles here at the inn for the first time in his life. Grushenka he knew before, and had once been with some one to see her; but she had not taken to him. But here she looked at him very affectionately: before Mitya's arrival, she had been making much of him, but he seemed somehow to be unmoved by it. He was a boy, not over twenty, dressed like a dandy, with a very charming fair-skinned face, and splendid thick, fair hair. From his fair face looked out beautiful pale blue eyes, with an intelligent and sometimes even deep expression, beyond his age indeed, although the young man sometimes looked and talked quite like a child, and was not at all ashamed of it, even when he was aware of it himself. As a rule he was very willful, even capricious, though always friendly. Sometimes there was something fixed and obstinate in his expression. He would look at you and listen, seeming all the while to be persistently dreaming over something else. Often he was listless and lazy, at other times he would grow excited, sometimes, apparently, over the most trivial matters.

"Only imagine, I've been taking him about with me for the last four days," he went on, indolently drawling his words, quite naturally though, without the slightest affectation. "Ever since your brother, do you remember, shoved him off the carriage and sent him flying. That made me take an interest in him at the time, and I took him into the country, but he keeps talking such rot I'm ashamed to be with him. I'm taking him back."

"The gentleman has not seen Polish ladies, and says what is impossible," the Pole with the pipe observed to Maximov.

He spoke Russian fairly well, much better, anyway, than he pretended. If he used Russian words, he always distorted them into a Polish form.

"But I was married to a Polish lady myself," tittered Maximov.

"But did you serve in the cavalry? You were talking about the cavalry. Were you a cavalry officer?" put in Kalganov at once.

"Was he a cavalry officer indeed? Ha ha!" cried Mitya, listening eagerly, and turning his inquiring eyes to each as he spoke, as though there were no knowing what he might hear from each.

"No, you see," Maximov turned to him. "What I mean is that those pretty Polish ladies ... when they danced the mazurka with our Uhlans ... when one of them dances a mazurka with a Uhlan she jumps on his knee like a kitten ... a little white one ... and the *pan*-father and *pan*-mother look on and allow it.... They allow it ... and next day the Uhlan comes and offers her his hand.... That's how it is ... offers her his hand, he he!" Maximov ended, tittering.

"The *pan* is a *lajdak*!" the tall Pole on the chair growled suddenly and crossed one leg over the other. Mitya's eye was caught by his huge greased boot, with its thick, dirty sole. The dress of both the Poles looked rather greasy.

"Well, now it's *lajdak*! What's he scolding about?" said Grushenka, suddenly vexed.

"*Pani* Agrippina, what the gentleman saw in Poland were servant girls, and not ladies of good birth," the Pole with the pipe observed to Grushenka.

"You can reckon on that," the tall Pole snapped contemptuously.

"What next! Let him talk! People talk, why hinder them? It makes it cheerful," Grushenka said crossly.

"I'm not hindering them, *pani*," said the Pole in the wig, with a long look at Grushenka, and relapsing into dignified silence he sucked his pipe again.

"No, no. The Polish gentleman spoke the truth." Kalganov got excited again, as though it were a question of vast import. "He's never been in Poland, so how can he talk about it? I suppose you weren't married in Poland, were you?"

"No, in the Province of Smolensk. Only, a Uhlan had brought her to Russia before that, my future wife, with her mamma and her aunt, and another female relation with a grown-up son. He brought her straight from Poland and gave her up to me. He was a lieutenant in our regiment, a very nice young man. At first he meant to marry her himself. But he didn't marry her, because she turned out to be lame."

"So you married a lame woman?" cried Kalganov.

"Yes. They both deceived me a little bit at the time, and concealed it. I thought she was hopping; she kept hopping.... I thought it was for fun."

"So pleased she was going to marry you!" yelled Kalganov, in a ringing, childish voice.

"Yes, so pleased. But it turned out to be quite a different cause. Afterwards, when we were married, after the wedding, that very evening, she confessed, and very touchingly asked forgiveness. 'I once jumped over a puddle when I was a child,' she said, 'and injured my leg.' He he!"

Kalganov went off into the most childish laughter, almost falling on the sofa. Grushenka, too, laughed. Mitya was at the pinnacle of happiness.

"Do you know, that's the truth, he's not lying now," exclaimed Kalganov, turning to Mitya; "and do you know, he's been married twice; it's his first wife he's talking about. But his second wife, do you know, ran away, and is alive now."

"Is it possible?" said Mitya, turning quickly to Maximov with an expression of the utmost astonishment.

"Yes. She did run away. I've had that unpleasant experience," Maximov modestly assented, "with a *monsieur*. And what was worse, she'd had all my little property transferred to her beforehand. 'You're an educated man,' she said to me. 'You can always get your living.' She settled my business with that. A venerable bishop once said to me: 'One of your wives was lame, but the other was too light-footed.' He he!"

"Listen, listen!" cried Kalganov, bubbling over, "if he's telling lies—and he often is—he's only doing it to amuse us all. There's no harm in that, is there? You know, I sometimes like him. He's awfully low, but it's natural to him, eh? Don't you think so? Some people are low from self-interest, but he's simply so, from nature. Only fancy, he claims (he was arguing about it all the way yesterday) that Gogol wrote *Dead Souls* about him. Do you remember, there's a landowner called Maximov in it, whom Nozdryov thrashed. He was charged, do you remember, 'for inflicting bodily injury with rods on the landowner Maximov in a drunken condition.' Would you believe it, he claims that he was that Maximov and that he was beaten! Now can it be so? Tchitchikov made his journey, at the very latest, at the beginning of the twenties, so that the dates don't fit. He couldn't have been thrashed then, he couldn't, could he?"

It was difficult to imagine what Kalganov was excited about, but his excitement was genuine. Mitya followed his lead without protest.

"Well, but if they did thrash him!" he cried, laughing.

"It's not that they thrashed me exactly, but what I mean is—" put in Maximov.

"What do you mean? Either they thrashed you or they didn't."

"What o'clock is it, *panie*?" the Pole, with the pipe, asked his tall friend, with a bored expression. The other shrugged his shoulders in reply. Neither of them had a watch.

"Why not talk? Let other people talk. Mustn't other people talk because you're bored?" Grushenka flew at him with evident intention of finding fault. Something seemed for the first time to flash upon Mitya's mind. This time the Pole answered with unmistakable irritability.

"*Pani*, I didn't oppose it. I didn't say anything."

"All right then. Come, tell us your story," Grushenka cried to Maximov. "Why are you all silent?"

"There's nothing to tell, it's all so foolish," answered Maximov at once, with evident satisfaction, mincing a little. "Besides, all that's by way of allegory in Gogol, for he's made all the names have a meaning. Nozdryov was really called Nosov, and Kuvshinikov had quite a different name, he was called Shkvornev. Fenardi really was called Fenardi, only he wasn't an Italian but a Russian, and Mamsel Fenardi was a pretty girl with her pretty little legs in tights, and she had a little short skirt with spangles, and she kept turning round and round, only not for four hours but for four minutes only, and she bewitched every one..."

"But what were you beaten for?" cried Kalganov.

"For Piron!" answered Maximov.

"What Piron?" cried Mitya.

"The famous French writer, Piron. We were all drinking then, a big party of us, in a tavern at that very fair. They'd invited me, and first of all I began quoting epigrams. 'Is that you, Boileau? What a funny get-up!' and Boileau answers that he's going to a masquerade, that is to the baths, he he! And they took it to themselves, so I made haste to repeat another, very sarcastic, well known to all educated people:

Yes, Sappho and Phaon are we!
But one grief is weighing on me.
You don't know your way to the sea!

They were still more offended and began abusing me in the most unseemly way for it. And as ill-luck would have it, to set things right, I began telling a very cultivated anecdote about Piron, how he was not accepted into the French Academy, and to revenge himself wrote his own epitaph:

Ci-gît Piron qui ne fut rien,
Pas même académicien.

They seized me and thrashed me."

"But what for? What for?"

"For my education. People can thrash a man for anything," Maximov concluded, briefly and sententiously.

"Eh, that's enough! That's all stupid, I don't want to listen. I thought it would be amusing," Grushenka cut them short, suddenly.

Mitya started, and at once left off laughing. The tall Pole rose upon his feet, and with the haughty air of a man, bored and out of his element, began pacing from corner to corner of the room, his hands behind his back.

"Ah, he can't sit still," said Grushenka, looking at him contemptuously. Mitya began to feel anxious. He noticed besides, that the Pole on the sofa was looking at him with an irritable expression.

"*Panie!*" cried Mitya, "let's drink! and the other *pan*, too! Let us drink."

In a flash he had pulled three glasses towards him, and filled them with champagne.

"To Poland, *panovie*, I drink to your Poland!" cried Mitya.

"I shall be delighted, *panie*," said the Pole on the sofa, with dignity and affable condescension, and he took his glass.

"And the other *pan*, what's his name? Drink, most illustrious, take your glass!" Mitya urged.

"Pan Vrublevsky," put in the Pole on the sofa.

Pan Vrublevsky came up to the table, swaying as he walked.

"To Poland, *panovie!*" cried Mitya, raising his glass. "Hurrah!"

All three drank. Mitya seized the bottle and again poured out three glasses.

"Now to Russia, *panovie*, and let us be brothers!"

"Pour out some for us," said Grushenka; "I'll drink to Russia, too!"

"So will I," said Kalganov.

"And I would, too ... to Russia, the old grandmother!" tittered Maximov.

"All! All!" cried Mitya. "Trifon Borissovitch, some more bottles!"

The other three bottles Mitya had brought with him were put on the table. Mitya filled the glasses.

"To Russia! Hurrah!" he shouted again. All drank the toast except the Poles, and Grushenka tossed off her whole glass at once. The Poles did not touch theirs.

"How's this, *panovie*?" cried Mitya, "won't you drink it?"

Pan Vrublevsky took the glass, raised it and said with a resonant voice:

"To Russia as she was before 1772."

"Come, that's better!" cried the other Pole, and they both emptied their glasses at once.

"You're fools, you *panovie*," broke suddenly from Mitya.

"*Panie!*" shouted both the Poles, menacingly, setting on Mitya like a couple of cocks. Pan Vrublevsky was specially furious.

"Can one help loving one's own country?" he shouted.

"Be silent! Don't quarrel! I won't have any quarreling!" cried Grushenka imperiously, and she stamped her foot on the floor. Her face glowed, her eyes were shining. The effects of the glass she had just drunk were apparent. Mitya was terribly alarmed.

"*Panovie*, forgive me! It was my fault, I'm sorry. Vrublevsky, *panie* Vrublevsky, I'm sorry."

"Hold your tongue, you, anyway! Sit down, you stupid!" Grushenka scolded with angry annoyance.

Every one sat down, all were silent, looking at one another.

"Gentlemen, I was the cause of it all," Mitya began again, unable to make anything of Grushenka's words. "Come, why are we sitting here? What shall we do ... to amuse ourselves again?"

"Ach, it's certainly anything but amusing!" Kalganov mumbled lazily.

"Let's play faro again, as we did just now," Maximov tittered suddenly.

"Faro? Splendid!" cried Mitya. "If only the *panovie*—"

"It's lite, *panovie*," the Pole on the sofa responded, as it were unwillingly.

"That's true," assented Pan Vrublevsky.

"Lite? What do you mean by 'lite'?" asked Grushenka.

"Late, *pani*! 'a late hour' I mean," the Pole on the sofa explained.

"It's always late with them. They can never do anything!" Grushenka almost shrieked in her anger. "They're dull themselves, so they want others to be dull. Before you came, Mitya, they were just as silent and kept turning up their noses at me."

"My goddess!" cried the Pole on the sofa, "I see you're not well-disposed to me, that's why I'm gloomy. I'm ready, *panie*," added he, addressing Mitya.

"Begin, *panie*," Mitya assented, pulling his notes out of his pocket, and laying two hundred-rouble notes on the table. "I want to lose a lot to you. Take your cards. Make the bank."

"We'll have cards from the landlord, *panie*," said the little Pole, gravely and emphatically.

"That's much the best way," chimed in Pan Vrublevsky.

"From the landlord? Very good, I understand, let's get them from him. Cards!" Mitya shouted to the landlord.

The landlord brought in a new, unopened pack, and informed Mitya that the girls were getting ready, and that the Jews with the cymbals would most likely be here soon; but the cart with the provisions had not yet arrived. Mitya jumped up from the table and ran into the next room to give orders, but only three girls had arrived, and Marya was not there yet. And he did not know himself what orders to give and why he had run out. He only told them to take out of the box the presents for the girls, the sweets, the toffee and the fondants. "And vodka for Andrey, vodka for Andrey!" he cried in haste. "I was rude to Andrey!"

Suddenly Maximov, who had followed him out, touched him on the shoulder.

"Give me five roubles," he whispered to Mitya. "I'll stake something at faro, too, he he!"

"Capital! Splendid! Take ten, here!"

Again he took all the notes out of his pocket and picked out one for ten roubles. "And if you lose that, come again, come again."

"Very good," Maximov whispered joyfully, and he ran back again. Mitya, too, returned, apologizing for having kept them waiting. The Poles had already sat down, and opened the pack. They looked much more amiable, almost cordial. The Pole on the sofa had lighted another pipe and was preparing to throw. He wore an air of solemnity.

"To your places, gentlemen," cried Pan Vrublevsky.

"No, I'm not going to play any more," observed Kalganov, "I've lost fifty roubles to them just now."

"The *pan* had no luck, perhaps he'll be lucky this time," the Pole on the sofa observed in his direction.

"How much in the bank? To correspond?" asked Mitya.

"That's according, *panie*, maybe a hundred, maybe two hundred, as much as you will stake."

"A million!" laughed Mitya.

"The Pan Captain has heard of Pan Podvysotsky, perhaps?"

"What Podvysotsky?"

"In Warsaw there was a bank and any one comes and stakes against it. Podvysotsky comes, sees a thousand gold pieces, stakes against the bank. The banker says, '*Panie* Podvysotsky, are you laying down the gold, or must we trust to your honor?' 'To my honor, *panie*,' says Podvysotsky. 'So much the better.' The banker throws the dice. Podvysotsky wins. 'Take it, *panie*,' says the banker, and pulling out the drawer he gives him a million. 'Take it, *panie*, this is your gain.' There was a million in the bank. 'I didn't know that,' says Podvysotsky. '*Panie* Podvysotsky,' said the banker, 'you pledged your honor and we pledged ours.' Podvysotsky took the million."

"That's not true," said Kalganov.

"*Panie* Kalganov, in gentlemanly society one doesn't say such things."

"As if a Polish gambler would give away a million!" cried Mitya, but checked himself at once. "Forgive me, *panie*, it's my fault again, he would, he would give away a million, for honor, for Polish honor. You see how I talk Polish, ha ha! Here, I stake ten roubles, the knave leads."

"And I put a rouble on the queen, the queen of hearts, the pretty little *panienotchka*, he he!" laughed Maximov, pulling out his queen, and, as though trying to conceal it from every one, he moved right up and crossed himself hurriedly under the table. Mitya won. The rouble won, too.

"A corner!" cried Mitya.

"I'll bet another rouble, a 'single' stake," Maximov muttered gleefully, hugely delighted at having won a rouble.

"Lost!" shouted Mitya. "A 'double' on the seven!"

The seven too was trumped.

"Stop!" cried Kalganov suddenly.

"Double! Double!" Mitya doubled his stakes, and each time he doubled the stake, the card he doubled was trumped by the Poles. The rouble stakes kept winning.

"On the double!" shouted Mitya furiously.

"You've lost two hundred, *panie*. Will you stake another hundred?" the Pole on the sofa inquired.

"What? Lost two hundred already? Then another two hundred! All doubles!"

And pulling his money out of his pocket, Mitya was about to fling two hundred roubles on the queen, but Kalganov covered it with his hand.

"That's enough!" he shouted in his ringing voice.

"What's the matter?" Mitya stared at him.

"That's enough! I don't want you to play any more. Don't!"

"Why?"

"Because I don't. Hang it, come away. That's why. I won't let you go on playing."

Mitya gazed at him in astonishment.

"Give it up, Mitya. He may be right. You've lost a lot as it is," said Grushenka, with a curious note in her voice. Both the Poles rose from their seats with a deeply offended air.

"Are you joking, *panie*?" said the short man, looking severely at Kalganov.

"How dare you!" Pan Vrublevsky, too, growled at Kalganov.

"Don't dare to shout like that," cried Grushenka. "Ah, you turkey-cocks!"

Mitya looked at each of them in turn. But something in Grushenka's face suddenly struck him, and at the same instant something new flashed into his mind—a strange new thought!

"*Pani* Agrippina," the little Pole was beginning, crimson with anger, when Mitya suddenly went up to him and slapped him on the shoulder.

"Most illustrious, two words with you."

"What do you want?"

"In the next room, I've two words to say to you, something pleasant, very pleasant. You'll be glad to hear it."

The little *pan* was taken aback and looked apprehensively at Mitya. He agreed at once, however, on condition that Pan Vrublevsky went with them.

"The bodyguard? Let him come, and I want him, too. I must have him!" cried Mitya. "March, *panovie*!"

"Where are you going?" asked Grushenka, anxiously.

"We'll be back in one moment," answered Mitya.

There was a sort of boldness, a sudden confidence shining in his eyes. His face had looked very different when he entered the room an hour before.

He led the Poles, not into the large room where the chorus of girls was assembling and the table was being laid, but into the bedroom on the right, where the trunks and packages were kept, and there were two large beds, with pyramids of cotton pillows on each. There was a lighted candle on a small deal table in the corner. The small man and Mitya sat down to this table, facing each other, while the huge Vrublevsky stood beside them, his hands behind his back. The Poles looked severe but were evidently inquisitive.

"What can I do for you, *panie*?" lisped the little Pole.

"Well, look here, *panie*, I won't keep you long. There's money for you," he pulled out his notes. "Would you like three thousand? Take it and go your way."

The Pole gazed open-eyed at Mitya, with a searching look.

"Three thousand, *panie*?" He exchanged glances with Vrublevsky.

"Three, *panovie*, three! Listen, *panie*, I see you're a sensible man. Take three thousand and go to the devil, and Vrublevsky with you—d'you hear? But, at once, this very minute, and for ever. You understand that, *panie*, for ever. Here's the door, you go out of it. What have you got there, a great-coat, a fur coat? I'll bring it out to you. They'll get the horses out directly, and then—good-by, *panie*!"

Mitya awaited an answer with assurance. He had no doubts. An expression of extraordinary resolution passed over the Pole's face.

"And the money, *panie*?"

"The money, *panie*? Five hundred roubles I'll give you this moment for the journey, and as a first installment, and two thousand five hundred to-morrow, in the town—I swear on my honor, I'll get it, I'll get it at any cost!" cried Mitya.

The Poles exchanged glances again. The short man's face looked more forbidding.

"Seven hundred, seven hundred, not five hundred, at once, this minute, cash down!" Mitya added, feeling something wrong. "What's the matter, *panie*? Don't you trust me? I can't give you the whole three thousand straight off. If I give it, you may come back to her to-morrow.... Besides, I haven't the three thousand with me. I've got it at home in the town," faltered Mitya, his spirit sinking at every word he uttered. "Upon my word, the money's there, hidden."

In an instant an extraordinary sense of personal dignity showed itself in the little man's face.

"What next?" he asked ironically. "For shame!" and he spat on the floor. Pan Vrublevsky spat too.

"You do that, *panie*," said Mitya, recognizing with despair that all was over, "because you hope to make more out of Grushenka? You're a couple of capons, that's what you are!"

"This is a mortal insult!" The little Pole turned as red as a crab, and he went out of the room, briskly, as though unwilling to hear another word. Vrublevsky swung out after him, and Mitya followed, confused and crestfallen. He was afraid of Grushenka, afraid that the *pan* would at once raise an outcry. And so indeed he did. The Pole walked into the room and threw himself in a theatrical attitude before Grushenka.

"*Pani* Agrippina, I have received a mortal insult!" he exclaimed. But Grushenka suddenly lost all patience, as though they had wounded her in the tenderest spot.

"Speak Russian! Speak Russian!" she cried, "not another word of Polish! You used to talk Russian. You can't have forgotten it in five years."

She was red with passion.

"*Pani* Agrippina—"

"My name's Agrafena, Grushenka, speak Russian or I won't listen!"

The Pole gasped with offended dignity, and quickly and pompously delivered himself in broken Russian:

"*Pani* Agrafena, I came here to forget the past and forgive it, to forget all that has happened till to-day—"

"Forgive? Came here to forgive me?" Grushenka cut him short, jumping up from her seat.

"Just so, *pani*, I'm not pusillanimous, I'm magnanimous. But I was astounded when I saw your lovers. Pan Mitya offered me three thousand, in the other room to depart. I spat in the *pan's* face."

"What? He offered you money for me?" cried Grushenka, hysterically. "Is it true, Mitya? How dare you? Am I for sale?"

"*Panie*, *panie*!" yelled Mitya, "she's pure and shining, and I have never been her lover! That's a lie...."

"How dare you defend me to him?" shrieked Grushenka. "It wasn't virtue kept me pure, and it wasn't that I was afraid of Kuzma, but that I might hold up my head when I met him, and tell him he's a scoundrel. And he did actually refuse the money?"

"He took it! He took it!" cried Mitya; "only he wanted to get the whole three thousand at once, and I could only give him seven hundred straight off."

"I see: he heard I had money, and came here to marry me!"

"*Pani* Agrippina!" cried the little Pole. "I'm—a knight, I'm—a nobleman, and not a *lajdak*. I came here to make you my wife and I find you a different woman, perverse and shameless."

"Oh, go back where you came from! I'll tell them to turn you out and you'll be turned out," cried Grushenka, furious. "I've been a fool, a fool, to have been miserable these five years! And it wasn't for his sake, it was my anger made me miserable. And this isn't he at all! Was he like this? It might be his father! Where did you get your wig from? He was a falcon, but this is a gander. He used to laugh and sing to me.... And I've been crying for five years, damned fool, abject, shameless I was!"

She sank back in her low chair and hid her face in her hands. At that instant the chorus of Mokroe began singing in the room on the left—a rollicking dance song.

"A regular Sodom!" Vrublevsky roared suddenly. "Landlord, send the shameless hussies away!"

The landlord, who had been for some time past inquisitively peeping in at the door, hearing shouts and guessing that his guests were quarreling, at once entered the room.

"What are you shouting for? D'you want to split your throat?" he said, addressing Vrublevsky, with surprising rudeness.

"Animal!" bellowed Pan Vrublevsky.

"Animal? And what sort of cards were you playing with just now? I gave you a pack and you hid it. You played with marked cards! I could send you to Siberia for playing with false cards, d'you know that, for it's just the same as false banknotes...."

And going up to the sofa he thrust his fingers between the sofa back and the cushion, and pulled out an unopened pack of cards.

"Here's my pack unopened!"

He held it up and showed it to all in the room. "From where I stood I saw him slip my pack away, and put his in place of it—you're a cheat and not a gentleman!"

"And I twice saw the *pan* change a card!" cried Kalganov.

"How shameful! How shameful!" exclaimed Grushenka, clasping her hands, and blushing for genuine shame. "Good Lord, he's come to that!"

"I thought so, too!" said Mitya. But before he had uttered the words, Vrublevsky, with a confused and infuriated face, shook his fist at Grushenka, shouting:

"You low harlot!"

Mitya flew at him at once, clutched him in both hands, lifted him in the air, and in one instant had carried him into the room on the right, from which they had just come.

"I've laid him on the floor, there," he announced, returning at once, gasping with excitement. "He's struggling, the scoundrel! But he won't come back, no fear of that!..."

He closed one half of the folding doors, and holding the other ajar called out to the little Pole:

"Most illustrious, will you be pleased to retire as well?"

"My dear Dmitri Fyodorovitch," said Trifon Borissovitch, "make them give you back the money you lost. It's as good as stolen from you."

"I don't want my fifty roubles back," Kalganov declared suddenly.

"I don't want my two hundred, either," cried Mitya, "I wouldn't take it for anything! Let him keep it as a consolation."

"Bravo, Mitya! You're a trump, Mitya!" cried Grushenka, and there was a note of fierce anger in the exclamation.

The little *pan*, crimson with fury but still mindful of his dignity, was making for the door, but he stopped short and said suddenly, addressing Grushenka:

"*Pani*, if you want to come with me, come. If not, good-by."

And swelling with indignation and importance he went to the door. This was a man of character: he had so good an opinion of himself that after all that had passed, he still expected that she would marry him. Mitya slammed the door after him.

"Lock it," said Kalganov. But the key clicked on the other side, they had locked it from within.

"That's capital!" exclaimed Grushenka relentlessly. "Serve them right!"

Chapter Five
The Preliminary Investigation

Something utterly unexpected and amazing to Mitya happened. He could never, even a minute before, have conceived that any one could behave like that to him, Mitya Karamazov. What was worst of all, there was something humiliating in it, and on their side something "supercilious and scornful." It was nothing to take off his coat, but he was asked to undress further, or rather not asked but "commanded," he quite understood that. From pride and contempt he submitted without a word. Several peasants accompanied the lawyers and remained on the same side of the curtain. "To be ready if force is required," thought Mitya, "and perhaps for some other reason, too."

"Well, must I take off my shirt, too?" he asked sharply, but Nikolay Parfenovitch did not answer. He was busily engaged with the prosecutor in examining the coat, the trousers, the waistcoat and the cap; and it was evident that they were both much interested in the scrutiny. "They make no bones about it," thought Mitya, "they don't keep up the most elementary politeness."

"I ask you for the second time—need I take off my shirt or not?" he said, still more sharply and irritably.

"Don't trouble yourself. We will tell you what to do," Nikolay Parfenovitch said, and his voice was positively peremptory, or so it seemed to Mitya.

Meantime a consultation was going on in undertones between the lawyers. There turned out to be on the coat, especially on the left side at the back, a huge patch of blood, dry, and still stiff. There were bloodstains on the trousers, too. Nikolay Parfenovitch, moreover, in the presence of the peasant witnesses, passed his fingers along the collar, the cuffs, and all the seams of the coat and trousers, obviously looking for something—money, of course. He didn't even hide from Mitya his suspicion that he was capable of sewing money up in his clothes.

"He treats me not as an officer but as a thief," Mitya muttered to himself. They communicated their ideas to one another with amazing frankness. The secretary, for instance, who was also behind the curtain, fussing about and listening, called Nikolay Parfenovitch's attention to the cap, which they were also fingering.

"You remember Gridyenko, the copying-clerk," observed the secretary. "Last summer he received the wages of the whole office, and pretended to have lost the money when he was drunk. And where was it found? Why, in just such pipings in his cap. The hundred-rouble notes were screwed up in little rolls and sewed in the piping."

Both the lawyers remembered Gridyenko's case perfectly, and so laid aside Mitya's cap, and decided that all his clothes must be more thoroughly examined later.

"Excuse me," cried Nikolay Parfenovitch, suddenly, noticing that the right cuff of Mitya's shirt was turned in, and covered with blood, "excuse me, what's that, blood?"

"Yes," Mitya jerked out.

"That is, what blood? ... and why is the cuff turned in?"

Mitya told him how he had got the sleeve stained with blood looking after Grigory, and had turned it inside when he was washing his hands at Perhotin's.

"You must take off your shirt, too. That's very important as material evidence."

Mitya flushed red and flew into a rage.

"What, am I to stay naked?" he shouted.

"Don't disturb yourself. We will arrange something. And meanwhile take off your socks."

"You're not joking? Is that really necessary?" Mitya's eyes flashed.

"We are in no mood for joking," answered Nikolay Parfenovitch sternly.

"Well, if I must—" muttered Mitya, and sitting down on the bed, he took off his socks. He felt unbearably awkward. All were clothed, while he was naked, and strange to say, when he was undressed he felt somehow guilty in their presence, and was almost ready to believe himself that he was inferior to them, and that now they had a perfect right to despise him.

"When all are undressed, one is somehow not ashamed, but when one's the only one undressed and everybody is looking, it's degrading," he kept repeating to himself, again and again. "It's like a dream, I've sometimes dreamed of being in such degrading positions." It was a misery to him to take off his socks. They were very dirty, and so were his underclothes, and now every one could see it. And what was worse, he disliked his feet. All his life he had thought both his big toes hideous. He particularly loathed the coarse, flat, crooked nail on the right one, and now they would all see it. Feeling intolerably ashamed made him, at once and intentionally, rougher. He pulled off his shirt, himself.

"Would you like to look anywhere else if you're not ashamed to?"

"No, there's no need to, at present."

"Well, am I to stay naked like this?" he added savagely.

"Yes, that can't be helped for the time.... Kindly sit down here for a while. You can wrap yourself in a quilt from the bed, and I ... I'll see to all this."

All the things were shown to the witnesses. The report of the search was drawn up, and at last Nikolay Parfenovitch went out, and the clothes were carried out after him. Ippolit Kirillovitch went out, too. Mitya was left alone with the peasants, who stood in silence, never taking their eyes off him. Mitya wrapped himself up in the quilt. He felt cold. His bare feet stuck out, and he couldn't pull the quilt over so as to cover them. Nikolay Parfenovitch seemed to be gone a long time, "an insufferable time." "He thinks of me as a puppy," thought Mitya, gnashing his teeth. "That rotten prosecutor has gone, too, contemptuous no doubt, it disgusts him to see me naked!"

Mitya imagined, however, that his clothes would be examined and returned to him. But what was his indignation when Nikolay Parfenovitch came back with quite different clothes, brought in behind him by a peasant.

"Here are clothes for you," he observed airily, seeming well satisfied with the success of his mission. "Mr. Kalganov has kindly provided these for this unusual emergency, as well as a clean shirt. Luckily he had them all in his trunk. You can keep your own socks and underclothes."

Mitya flew into a passion.

"I won't have other people's clothes!" he shouted menacingly, "give me my own!"

"It's impossible!"

"Give me my own. Damn Kalganov and his clothes, too!"

It was a long time before they could persuade him. But they succeeded somehow in quieting him down. They impressed upon him that his clothes, being stained with blood, must be "included with the other material evidence," and that they "had not even the right to let him have them now ... taking into consideration the possible outcome of the case." Mitya at last understood this. He subsided into gloomy silence and hurriedly dressed himself. He merely observed, as he put them on, that the clothes were much better than his old ones, and that he disliked "gaining by the change." The coat was, besides, "ridiculously tight. Am I to be dressed up like a fool ... for your amusement?"

They urged upon him again that he was exaggerating, that Kalganov was only a little taller, so that only the trousers might be a little too long. But the coat turned out to be really tight in the shoulders.

"Damn it all! I can hardly button it," Mitya grumbled. "Be so good as to tell Mr. Kalganov from me that I didn't ask for his clothes, and it's not my doing that they've dressed me up like a clown."

"He understands that, and is sorry ... I mean, not sorry to lend you his clothes, but sorry about all this business," mumbled Nikolay Parfenovitch.

"Confound his sorrow! Well, where now? Am I to go on sitting here?"

He was asked to go back to the "other room." Mitya went in, scowling with anger, and trying to avoid looking at any one. Dressed in another man's clothes he felt himself disgraced, even in the eyes of the peasants, and of Trifon Borissovitch, whose face appeared, for some reason, in the doorway, and vanished immediately. "He's come to look at me dressed up," thought Mitya. He sat down on the same chair as before. He had an absurd nightmarish feeling, as though he were out of his mind.

"Well, what now? Are you going to flog me? That's all that's left for you," he said, clenching his teeth and addressing the prosecutor. He would not turn to Nikolay Parfenovitch, as though he disdained to speak to him.

"He looked too closely at my socks, and turned them inside out on purpose to show every one how dirty they were—the scoundrel!"

"Well, now we must proceed to the examination of witnesses," observed Nikolay Parfenovitch, as though in reply to Mitya's question.

"Yes," said the prosecutor thoughtfully, as though reflecting on something.

"We've done what we could in your interest, Dmitri Fyodorovitch," Nikolay Parfenovitch went on, "but having received from you such an uncompromising refusal to explain to us the source from which you obtained the money found upon you, we are, at the present moment—"

"What is the stone in your ring?" Mitya interrupted suddenly, as though awakening from a reverie. He pointed to one of the three large rings adorning Nikolay Parfenovitch's right hand.

"Ring?" repeated Nikolay Parfenovitch with surprise.

"Yes, that one ... on your middle finger, with the little veins in it, what stone is that?" Mitya persisted, like a peevish child.

"That's a smoky topaz," said Nikolay Parfenovitch, smiling. "Would you like to look at it? I'll take it off ..."

"No, don't take it off," cried Mitya furiously, suddenly waking up, and angry with himself. "Don't take it off ... there's no need.... Damn it!... Gentlemen, you've sullied my heart! Can you suppose that I would conceal it from you, if I had really killed my father, that I would shuffle, lie, and hide myself? No, that's not like Dmitri Karamazov, that he couldn't do, and if I were guilty, I swear I shouldn't have waited for your coming, or for the sunrise as I meant at first, but should have killed myself before this, without waiting for the dawn! I know that about myself now. I couldn't have learnt so much in twenty years as I've found out in this accursed night!... And should I have been like this on this night, and at this moment, sitting with you, could I have talked like this, could I have moved like this, could I have looked at you and at the world like this, if I had really been the murderer of my father, when the very thought of having accidentally killed Grigory gave me no peace all night—not from fear—oh, not simply from fear of your punishment! The disgrace of it! And you expect me to be open with such scoffers as you, who see nothing and believe in nothing, blind moles and scoffers, and to tell you another nasty thing I've done, another disgrace, even if that would save me from your accusation! No, better Siberia! The man who opened the door to my father and went in at that door, he killed him, he robbed him. Who was he? I'm racking my brains and can't think who. But I can tell you it was not Dmitri Karamazov, and that's all I can tell you, and that's enough, enough, leave me alone.... Exile me, punish me, but don't bother me any more. I'll say no more. Call your witnesses!"

Mitya uttered his sudden monologue as though he were determined to be absolutely silent for the future. The prosecutor watched him the whole time and only when he had ceased speaking, observed, as though it were the most ordinary thing, with the most frigid and composed air:

"Oh, about the open door of which you spoke just now, we may as well inform you, by the way, now, of a very interesting piece of evidence of the greatest importance both to you and to us, that has been given us by Grigory, the old man you wounded. On his recovery, he clearly and emphatically stated, in reply to our questions, that when, on coming out to the steps, and hearing a noise in the garden, he made up his mind to go into it through the little gate which stood open, before he noticed you running, as you have told us already, in the dark from the open window where you saw your father, he, Grigory, glanced to the left, and, while noticing the open window, observed at the same time, much nearer to him, the door, standing wide open—that door which you have stated to have been shut the whole time you were in the garden. I will not conceal from you that Grigory himself confidently affirms and bears witness that you must have run from that door, though, of course, he did not see you do so with his own eyes, since he only noticed you first some distance away in the garden, running towards the fence."

Mitya had leapt up from his chair half-way through this speech.

"Nonsense!" he yelled, in a sudden frenzy, "it's a barefaced lie. He couldn't have seen the door open because it was shut. He's lying!"

"I consider it my duty to repeat that he is firm in his statement. He does not waver. He adheres to it. We've cross-examined him several times."

"Precisely. I have cross-examined him several times," Nikolay Parfenovitch confirmed warmly.

"It's false, false! It's either an attempt to slander me, or the hallucination of a madman," Mitya still shouted. "He's simply raving, from loss of blood, from the wound. He must have fancied it when he came to.... He's raving."

"Yes, but he noticed the open door, not when he came to after his injuries, but before that, as soon as he went into the garden from the lodge."

"But it's false, it's false! It can't be so! He's slandering me from spite.... He couldn't have seen it ... I didn't come from the door," gasped Mitya.

The prosecutor turned to Nikolay Parfenovitch and said to him impressively:

"Confront him with it."

"Do you recognize this object?"

Nikolay Parfenovitch laid upon the table a large and thick official envelope, on which three seals still remained intact. The envelope was empty, and slit open at one end. Mitya stared at it with open eyes.

"It ... it must be that envelope of my father's, the envelope that contained the three thousand roubles ... and if there's inscribed on it, allow me, 'For my little chicken' ... yes—three thousand!" he shouted, "do you see, three thousand, do you see?"

"Of course, we see. But we didn't find the money in it. It was empty, and lying on the floor by the bed, behind the screen."

For some seconds Mitya stood as though thunderstruck.

"Gentlemen, it's Smerdyakov!" he shouted suddenly, at the top of his voice. "It's he who's murdered him! He's robbed him! No one else knew where the old man hid the envelope. It's Smerdyakov, that's clear, now!"

"But you, too, knew of the envelope and that it was under the pillow."

"I never knew it. I've never seen it. This is the first time I've looked at it. I'd only heard of it from Smerdyakov.... He was the only one who knew where the old man kept it hidden, I didn't know ..." Mitya was completely breathless.

"But you told us yourself that the envelope was under your deceased father's pillow. You especially stated that it was under the pillow, so you must have known it."

"We've got it written down," confirmed Nikolay Parfenovitch.

"Nonsense! It's absurd! I'd no idea it was under the pillow. And perhaps it wasn't under the pillow at all.... It was just a chance guess that it was under the pillow. What does Smerdyakov say? Have you asked him where it was? What does Smerdyakov say? that's the chief point.... And I went out of my way to tell lies against myself.... I told you without thinking that it was under the pillow, and now you— Oh, you know how one says the wrong thing, without meaning it. No one knew but Smerdyakov, only Smerdyakov, and no one else.... He didn't even tell me where it was! But it's his doing, his doing; there's no doubt about it, he murdered him, that's as clear as daylight now," Mitya exclaimed more and more frantically, repeating himself incoherently, and growing more and more exasperated and excited. "You must understand that, and arrest him at once.... He must have killed him while I was running away and while Grigory was unconscious, that's clear now.... He gave the signal and father opened to him ... for no one but he knew the signal, and without the signal father would never have opened the door...."

"But you're again forgetting the circumstance," the prosecutor observed, still speaking with the same restraint, though with a note of triumph, "that there was no need to give the signal if the door already stood open when you were there, while you were in the garden...."

"The door, the door," muttered Mitya, and he stared speechless at the prosecutor. He sank back helpless in his chair. All were silent.

"Yes, the door!... It's a nightmare! God is against me!" he exclaimed, staring before him in complete stupefaction.

"Come, you see," the prosecutor went on with dignity, "and you can judge for yourself, Dmitri Fyodorovitch. On the one hand we have the evidence of the open door from which you ran out, a fact which overwhelms you and us. On the other side your incomprehensible, persistent, and, so to speak, obdurate silence with regard to the source from which you obtained the money which was so suddenly seen in your hands, when only three hours earlier, on your own showing, you pledged your pistols for the sake of ten roubles! In view of all these facts, judge for yourself. What are we to believe, and what can we depend upon? And don't accuse us of being 'frigid, cynical, scoffing people,' who are incapable of believing in the generous impulses of your heart.... Try to enter into our position ..."

Mitya was indescribably agitated. He turned pale.

"Very well!" he exclaimed suddenly. "I will tell you my secret. I'll tell you where I got the money!... I'll reveal my shame, that I may not have to blame myself or you hereafter."

"And believe me, Dmitri Fyodorovitch," put in Nikolay Parfenovitch, in a voice of almost pathetic delight, "that every sincere and complete confession on your part at this moment may, later on, have an immense influence in your favor, and may, indeed, moreover—"

But the prosecutor gave him a slight shove under the table, and he checked himself in time. Mitya, it is true, had not heard him.

"Gentlemen," he began, still in the same agitation, "I want to make a full confession: that money was *my own*." The lawyers' faces lengthened. That was not at all what they expected.

"How do you mean?" faltered Nikolay Parfenovitch, "when at five o'clock on the same day, from your own confession—"

"Damn five o'clock on the same day and my own confession! That's nothing to do with it now! That money was my own, my own, that is, stolen by me ... not mine, I mean, but stolen by me, and it was fifteen hundred roubles, and I had it on me all the time, all the time ..."

"But where did you get it?"

"I took it off my neck, gentlemen, off this very neck ... it was here, round my neck, sewn up in a rag, and I'd had it round my neck a long time, it's a month since I put it round my neck ... to my shame and disgrace!"

"And from whom did you ... appropriate it?"

"You mean, 'steal it'? Speak out plainly now. Yes, I consider that I practically stole it, but, if you prefer, I 'appropriated it.' I consider I stole it. And last night I stole it finally."

"Last night? But you said that it's a month since you ... obtained it?..."

"Yes. But not from my father. Not from my father, don't be uneasy. I didn't steal it from my father, but from her. Let me tell you without interrupting. It's hard to do, you know. You see, a month ago, I was sent for by Katerina Ivanovna, formerly my betrothed. Do you know her?"

"Yes, of course."

"I know you know her. She's a noble creature, noblest of the noble. But she has hated me ever so long, oh, ever so long ... and hated me with good reason, good reason!"

"Katerina Ivanovna!" Nikolay Parfenovitch exclaimed with wonder. The prosecutor, too, stared.

"Oh, don't take her name in vain! I'm a scoundrel to bring her into it. Yes, I've seen that she hated me ... a long while.... From the very first, even that evening at my lodging ... but enough, enough. You're unworthy even to know of that. No need of that at all.... I need only tell you that she sent for me a month ago, gave me three thousand roubles to send off to her sister and another relation in Moscow (as though she couldn't have sent it off herself!) and I ... it was just at that fatal moment in my life when I ... well, in fact, when I'd just come to love another, her, she's sitting down below now, Grushenka. I carried her off here to Mokroe then, and wasted here in two days half that damned three thousand, but the other half I kept on me. Well, I've kept that other half, that fifteen hundred, like a locket round my neck, but yesterday I undid it, and spent it. What's left of it, eight hundred roubles, is in your hands now, Nikolay Parfenovitch. That's the change out of the fifteen hundred I had yesterday."

"Excuse me. How's that? Why, when you were here a month ago you spent three thousand, not fifteen hundred, everybody knows that."

"Who knows it? Who counted the money? Did I let any one count it?"

"Why, you told every one yourself that you'd spent exactly three thousand."

"It's true, I did. I told the whole town so, and the whole town said so. And here, at Mokroe, too, every one reckoned it was three thousand. Yet I didn't spend three thousand, but fifteen hundred. And the other fifteen hundred I sewed into a little bag. That's how it was, gentlemen. That's where I got that money yesterday...."

"This is almost miraculous," murmured Nikolay Parfenovitch.

"Allow me to inquire," observed the prosecutor at last, "have you informed any one whatever of this circumstance before, I mean that you had fifteen hundred left about you a month ago?"

"I told no one."

"That's strange. Do you mean absolutely no one?"

"Absolutely no one. No one and nobody."

"What was your reason for this reticence? What was your motive for making such a secret of it? To be more precise: You have told us at last your secret, in your words, so 'disgraceful,' though in reality—that is, of course, comparatively speaking—this action, that is, the appropriation of three thousand roubles belonging to some one else, and, of course, only for a time is, in my view at least, only an act of the greatest recklessness and not so disgraceful, when one takes into consideration your character.... Even admitting that it was an action in the highest degree discreditable, still, discreditable is not 'disgraceful.'... Many people have already guessed, during this last month, about the three thousand of Katerina Ivanovna's, that you have spent, and I heard the legend myself, apart from your confession.... Mihail Makarovitch, for instance, had heard it, too, so that indeed, it was scarcely a legend, but the gossip of the whole town. There are indications, too, if I am not mistaken, that you confessed this yourself to some one, I mean that the money was Katerina Ivanovna's, and so, it's extremely surprising to me that hitherto, that is, up to the present moment, you have made such an extraordinary secret of the fifteen hundred you say you put by, apparently connecting a feeling of positive horror with that secret.... It's not easy to believe that it could cost you such distress to confess such a secret.... You cried out, just now, that Siberia would be better than confessing it ..."

The prosecutor ceased speaking. He was provoked. He did not conceal his vexation, which was almost anger, and gave vent to all his accumulated spleen, disconnectedly and incoherently, without choosing words.

"It's not the fifteen hundred that's the disgrace, but that I put it apart from the rest of the three thousand," said Mitya firmly.

"Why?" smiled the prosecutor irritably. "What is there disgraceful, to your thinking, in your having set aside half of the three thousand you had discreditably, if you prefer, 'disgracefully,' appropriated? Your taking the three thousand is more important than what you did with it. And by the way, why did you do that—why did you set apart that half, for what purpose, for what object did you do it? Can you explain that to us?"

"Oh, gentlemen, the purpose is the whole point!" cried Mitya. "I put it aside because I was vile, that is, because I was calculating, and to be calculating in such a case is vile ... and that vileness has been going on a whole month."

"It's incomprehensible."

"I wonder at you. But I'll make it clearer. Perhaps it really is incomprehensible. You see, attend to what I say. I appropriate three thousand entrusted to my honor, I spend it on a spree, say I spend it all, and next morning I go to her and say, 'Katya, I've done wrong, I've squandered your three thousand,' well, is that right? No, it's not right—it's dishonest and cowardly, I'm a beast, with no more self-control than a beast, that's so, isn't it? But still I'm not a thief? Not a downright thief, you'll admit! I squandered it, but I didn't steal it. Now a second, rather more favorable alternative: follow me carefully, or I may get confused again—my head's going round—and so, for the second alternative: I spend here only fifteen hundred out of the three thousand, that is, only half. Next day I go and take that half to her: 'Katya, take this fifteen hundred from me, I'm a low beast, and an untrustworthy scoundrel, for I've wasted half the money, and I shall waste this, too, so keep me from temptation!' Well, what of that alternative? I should be a beast and a scoundrel, and whatever you like; but not a thief, not altogether a thief, or I should not have brought back what was left, but have kept that, too. She would see at once that since I brought back half, I should pay back what I'd spent, that I should never give up trying to, that I should work to get it and pay it back. So in that case I should be a scoundrel, but not a thief, you may say what you like, not a thief!"

"I admit that there is a certain distinction," said the prosecutor, with a cold smile. "But it's strange that you see such a vital difference."

"Yes, I see a vital difference! Every man may be a scoundrel, and perhaps every man is a scoundrel, but not every one can be a thief, it takes an arch-scoundrel to be that. Oh, of course, I don't know how to make these fine distinctions ... but a thief is lower than a scoundrel, that's my conviction. Listen, I carry the money about me a whole month, I may make up my mind to give it back to-morrow, and I'm a scoundrel no longer, but I cannot make up my mind, you see, though I'm making up my mind every day, and every day spurring myself on to do it, and yet for a whole month I can't bring myself to it, you see. Is that right to your thinking, is that right?"

"Certainly, that's not right, that I can quite understand, and that I don't dispute," answered the prosecutor with reserve. "And let us give up all discussion of these subtleties and distinctions, and, if you will be so kind, get back to the point. And the point is, that you have still not told us, altogether we've asked you, why, in the first place, you halved the money, squandering one half and hiding the other? For what purpose exactly did you hide it, what did you mean to do with that fifteen hundred? I insist upon that question, Dmitri Fyodorovitch."

"Yes, of course!" cried Mitya, striking himself on the forehead; "forgive me, I'm worrying you, and am not explaining the chief point, or you'd understand in a minute, for it's just the motive of it that's the disgrace! You see, it was all to do with the old man, my dead father. He was always pestering Agrafena Alexandrovna, and I was jealous; I thought then that she was hesitating between me and him. So I kept thinking every day, suppose she were to make up her mind all of a sudden, suppose she were to leave off tormenting me, and were suddenly to say to me, 'I love you, not him; take me to the other end of the world.' And I'd only forty copecks; how could I take her away, what could I do? Why, I'd be lost. You see, I didn't know her then, I didn't understand her, I thought she wanted money, and that she wouldn't forgive my poverty. And so I fiendishly counted out the half of that three thousand, sewed it up, calculating on it, sewed it up before I was drunk, and after I had sewn it up, I went off to get drunk on the rest. Yes, that was base. Do you understand now?"

Both the lawyers laughed aloud.

"I should have called it sensible and moral on your part not to have squandered it all," chuckled Nikolay Parfenovitch, "for after all what does it amount to?"

"Why, that I stole it, that's what it amounts to! Oh, God, you horrify me by not understanding! Every day that I had that fifteen hundred sewn up round my neck, every day and every hour I said to myself, 'You're a thief! you're a thief!' Yes, that's why I've been so savage all this month, that's why I fought in the tavern, that's why I attacked my father, it was because I felt I was a thief. I couldn't make up my mind, I didn't dare even to tell Alyosha, my brother, about that fifteen hundred: I felt I was such a scoundrel and such a pickpocket. But, do you know, while I carried it I said to myself at the same time every hour: 'No, Dmitri Fyodorovitch, you may yet not be a thief.' Why? Because I might go next day and pay back that fifteen hundred to Katya. And only yesterday I made up my mind to tear my amulet off my neck, on my way from Fenya's to Perhotin. I hadn't been able till that moment to bring myself to it. And it was only when I tore it off that I became a downright thief, a thief and a dishonest man for the rest of my life. Why? Because, with that I destroyed, too, my dream of going to Katya and saying, 'I'm a scoundrel, but not a thief!' Do you understand now? Do you understand?"

"What was it made you decide to do it yesterday?" Nikolay Parfenovitch interrupted.

"Why? It's absurd to ask. Because I had condemned myself to die at five o'clock this morning, here, at dawn. I thought it made no difference whether I died a thief or a man of honor. But I see it's not so, it turns out that it does make a difference. Believe me, gentlemen, what has tortured me most during this night has not been the thought that I'd killed the old servant, and that I was in danger of Siberia just when my love was being rewarded, and Heaven was open to me again. Oh, that did torture me, but not in the same way: not so much as the damned consciousness that I had torn that damned money off my breast at last and spent it, and had become a downright thief! Oh, gentlemen, I tell you again, with a bleeding heart, I have learnt a great deal this night. I have learnt that it's not only impossible to live a scoundrel, but impossible to die a scoundrel.... No, gentlemen, one must die honest...."

Mitya was pale. His face had a haggard and exhausted look, in spite of his being intensely excited.

"I am beginning to understand you, Dmitri Fyodorovitch," the prosecutor said slowly, in a soft and almost compassionate tone. "But all this, if you'll excuse my saying so, is a matter of nerves, in my opinion ... your overwrought nerves, that's what it is. And why, for instance, should you not have saved yourself such misery for almost a month, by going and returning that fifteen hundred to the lady who had entrusted it to you? And why could you not have explained things to her, and in view of your position, which you describe as being so awful, why could you not have had recourse to the plan which would so naturally have occurred to one's mind, that is, after honorably confessing your errors to her, why could you not have asked her to lend you the sum needed for your expenses, which, with her generous heart, she would certainly not have refused you in your distress, especially if it had been with some guarantee, or even on the security you offered to the merchant Samsonov, and to Madame Hohlakov? I suppose you still regard that security as of value?"

Mitya suddenly crimsoned.

"Surely you don't think me such an out and out scoundrel as that? You can't be speaking in earnest?" he said, with indignation, looking the prosecutor straight in the face, and seeming unable to believe his ears.

"I assure you I'm in earnest.... Why do you imagine I'm not serious?" It was the prosecutor's turn to be surprised.

"Oh, how base that would have been! Gentlemen, do you know, you are torturing me! Let me tell you everything, so be it. I'll confess all my infernal wickedness, but to put you to shame, and you'll be surprised yourselves at the depth of ignominy to which a medley of human passions can sink. You must know that I already had that plan myself, that plan you spoke of, just now, prosecutor! Yes, gentlemen, I, too, have had that thought in my mind all this current month, so that I was on the point of deciding to go to Katya—I was mean enough for that. But to go to her, to tell her of my treachery, and for that very treachery, to carry it out, for the expenses of that treachery, to beg for money from her, Katya (to beg, do you hear, to beg), and go straight from her to run away with the other, the rival, who hated and insulted her—to think of it! You must be mad, prosecutor!"

"Mad I am not, but I did speak in haste, without thinking ... of that feminine jealousy ... if there could be jealousy in this case, as you assert ... yes, perhaps there is something of the kind," said the prosecutor, smiling.

"But that would have been so infamous!" Mitya brought his fist down on the table fiercely. "That would have been filthy beyond everything! Yes, do you know that she might have given me that money, yes, and she would have given it, too; she'd have been certain to give it, to be revenged on me, she'd have given it to satisfy her vengeance, to show her contempt for me, for hers is an infernal nature, too, and she's a woman of great wrath. I'd have taken the money, too, oh, I should have taken it; I should have taken it, and then, for the rest of my life ... oh, God! Forgive me, gentlemen, I'm making such an outcry because I've had that thought in my mind so lately, only the day before yesterday, that night when I was having all that bother with Lyagavy, and afterwards yesterday, all day yesterday, I remember, till that happened ..."

"Till what happened?" put in Nikolay Parfenovitch inquisitively, but Mitya did not hear it.

"I have made you an awful confession," Mitya said gloomily in conclusion. "You must appreciate it, and what's more, you must respect it, for if not, if that leaves your souls untouched, then you've simply no respect for me, gentlemen, I tell you that, and I shall die of shame at having confessed it to men like you! Oh, I shall shoot myself! Yes, I see, I see already that you don't believe me. What, you want to write that down, too?" he cried in dismay.

"Yes, what you said just now," said Nikolay Parfenovitch, looking at him in surprise, "that is, that up to the last hour you were still contemplating going to Katerina Ivanovna to beg that sum from her.... I assure you, that's a very important piece of evidence for us,

Dmitri Fyodorovitch, I mean for the whole case ... and particularly for you, particularly important for you."

"Have mercy, gentlemen!" Mitya flung up his hands. "Don't write that, anyway; have some shame. Here I've torn my heart asunder before you, and you seize the opportunity and are fingering the wounds in both halves.... Oh, my God!"

In despair he hid his face in his hands.

"Don't worry yourself so, Dmitri Fyodorovitch," observed the prosecutor, "everything that is written down will be read over to you afterwards, and what you don't agree to we'll alter as you like. But now I'll ask you one little question for the second time. Has no one, absolutely no one, heard from you of that money you sewed up? That, I must tell you, is almost impossible to believe."

"No one, no one, I told you so before, or you've not understood anything! Let me alone!"

"Very well, this matter is bound to be explained, and there's plenty of time for it, but meantime, consider; we have perhaps a dozen witnesses that you yourself spread it abroad, and even shouted almost everywhere about the three thousand you'd spent here; three thousand, not fifteen hundred. And now, too, when you got hold of the money you had yesterday, you gave many people to understand that you had brought three thousand with you."

"You've got not dozens, but hundreds of witnesses, two hundred witnesses, two hundred have heard it, thousands have heard it!" cried Mitya.

"Well, you see, all bear witness to it. And the word *all* means something."

"It means nothing. I talked rot, and every one began repeating it."

"But what need had you to 'talk rot,' as you call it?"

"The devil knows. From bravado perhaps ... at having wasted so much money.... To try and forget that money I had sewn up, perhaps ... yes, that was why ... damn it ... how often will you ask me that question? Well, I told a fib, and that was the end of it, once I'd said it, I didn't care to correct it. What does a man tell lies for sometimes?"

"That's very difficult to decide, Dmitri Fyodorovitch, what makes a man tell lies," observed the prosecutor impressively. "Tell me, though, was that 'amulet,' as you call it, on your neck, a big thing?"

"No, not big."

"How big, for instance?"

"If you fold a hundred-rouble note in half, that would be the size."

"You'd better show us the remains of it. You must have them somewhere."

"Damnation, what nonsense! I don't know where they are."

"But excuse me: where and when did you take it off your neck? According to your own evidence you didn't go home."

"When I was going from Fenya's to Perhotin's, on the way I tore it off my neck and took out the money."

"In the dark?"

"What should I want a light for? I did it with my fingers in one minute."

"Without scissors, in the street?"

"In the market-place I think it was. Why scissors? It was an old rag. It was torn in a minute."

"Where did you put it afterwards?"

"I dropped it there."

"Where was it, exactly?"

"In the market-place, in the market-place! The devil knows whereabouts. What do you want to know for?"

"That's extremely important, Dmitri Fyodorovitch. It would be material evidence in your favor. How is it you don't understand that? Who helped you to sew it up a month ago?"

"No one helped me. I did it myself."

"Can you sew?"

"A soldier has to know how to sew. No knowledge was needed to do that."

"Where did you get the material, that is, the rag in which you sewed the money?"

"Are you laughing at me?"

"Not at all. And we are in no mood for laughing, Dmitri Fyodorovitch."

"I don't know where I got the rag from—somewhere, I suppose."

"I should have thought you couldn't have forgotten it?"

"Upon my word, I don't remember. I might have torn a bit off my linen."

"That's very interesting. We might find in your lodgings to-morrow the shirt or whatever it is from which you tore the rag. What sort of rag was it, cloth or linen?"

"Goodness only knows what it was. Wait a bit.... I believe I didn't tear it off anything. It was a bit of calico.... I believe I sewed it up in a cap of my landlady's."

"In your landlady's cap?"

"Yes. I took it from her."

"How did you get it?"

"You see, I remember once taking a cap for a rag, perhaps to wipe my pen on. I took it without asking, because it was a worthless rag. I tore it up, and I took the notes and sewed them up in it. I believe it was in that very rag I sewed them. An old piece of calico, washed a thousand times."

"And you remember that for certain now?"

"I don't know whether for certain. I think it was in the cap. But, hang it, what does it matter?"

"In that case your landlady will remember that the thing was lost?"

"No, she won't, she didn't miss it. It was an old rag, I tell you, an old rag not worth a farthing."

"And where did you get the needle and thread?"

"I'll stop now. I won't say any more. Enough of it!" said Mitya, losing his temper at last.

"It's strange that you should have so completely forgotten where you threw the pieces in the market-place."

"Give orders for the market-place to be swept to-morrow, and perhaps you'll find it," said Mitya, sneering. "Enough, gentlemen, enough!" he decided, in an exhausted voice. "I see you don't believe me! Not for a moment! It's my fault, not yours. I ought not to have been so ready. Why, why did I degrade myself by confessing my secret to you? It's a joke to you. I see that from your eyes. You led me on to it, prosecutor? Sing a hymn of triumph if you can.... Damn you, you torturers!"

He bent his head, and hid his face in his hands. The lawyers were silent. A minute later he raised his head and looked at them almost vacantly. His face now expressed complete, hopeless despair, and he sat mute and passive as though hardly conscious of what was happening. In the meantime they had to finish what they were about. They had immediately to begin examining the witnesses. It was by now eight o'clock in the morning. The lights had been extinguished long ago. Mihail Makarovitch and Kalganov, who had been continually in and out of the room all the while the interrogation had been going on, had now both gone out again. The lawyers, too, looked very tired. It was a wretched morning, the whole sky was overcast, and the rain streamed down in bucketfuls. Mitya gazed blankly out of the window.

"May I look out of the window?" he asked Nikolay Parfenovitch, suddenly.

"Oh, as much as you like," the latter replied.

Mitya got up and went to the window.... The rain lashed against its little greenish panes. He could see the muddy road just below the house, and farther away, in the rain and mist, a row of poor, black, dismal huts, looking even blacker and poorer in the rain. Mitya thought of "Phœbus the golden-haired," and how he had meant to shoot himself at his first ray. "Perhaps it would be even better on a morning like this," he thought with a smile, and suddenly, flinging his hand downwards, he turned to his "torturers."

"Gentlemen," he cried, "I see that I am lost! But she? Tell me about her, I beseech you. Surely she need not be ruined with me? She's innocent, you know, she was out of her mind when she cried last night 'It's all my fault!' She's done nothing, nothing! I've been grieving over her all night as I sat with you.... Can't you, won't you tell me what you are going to do with her now?"

"You can set your mind quite at rest on that score, Dmitri Fyodorovitch," the prosecutor answered at once, with evident alacrity. "We have, so far, no grounds for interfering with the lady in whom you are so interested. I trust that it may be the same in the later development of the case.... On the contrary, we'll do everything that lies in our power in that matter. Set your mind completely at rest."

"Gentlemen, I thank you. I knew that you were honest, straight-forward people in spite of everything. You've taken a load off my heart.... Well, what are we to do now? I'm ready."

"Well, we ought to make haste. We must pass to examining the witnesses without delay. That must be done in your presence and therefore—"

"Shouldn't we have some tea first?" interposed Nikolay Parfenovitch, "I think we've deserved it!"

They decided that if tea were ready downstairs (Mihail Makarovitch had, no doubt, gone down to get some) they would have a glass and then "go on and on," putting off their proper breakfast until a more favorable opportunity. Tea really was ready below, and was soon brought up. Mitya at first refused the glass that Nikolay Parfenovitch politely offered him, but afterwards he asked for it himself and drank it greedily. He looked surprisingly exhausted. It might have been supposed from his Herculean strength that one night of carousing, even accompanied by the most violent emotions, could have had little effect on him. But he felt that he could hardly hold his head up, and from time to time all the objects about him seemed heaving and dancing before his eyes. "A little more and I shall begin raving," he said to himself.

The examination of the witnesses began. But we will not continue our story in such detail as before. And so we will not dwell on how Nikolay Parfenovitch impressed on every witness called that he must give his evidence in accordance with truth and conscience, and that he would afterwards have to repeat his evidence on oath, how every witness was called upon to sign the protocol of his evidence, and so on. We will only note that the point principally insisted upon in the examination was the question of the three thousand roubles, that is, was the sum spent here, at Mokroe, by Mitya on the first occasion, a month before, three thousand or fifteen hundred? And again had he spent three thousand or fifteen hundred yesterday? Alas, all the evidence given by every one turned out to be against Mitya. There was not one in his favor, and some witnesses introduced new, almost crushing facts, in contradiction of his, Mitya's, story.

The first witness examined was Trifon Borissovitch. He was not in the least abashed as he stood before the lawyers. He had, on the contrary, an air of stern and severe indignation with the accused, which gave him an appearance of truthfulness and personal dignity. He spoke little, and with reserve, waited to be questioned, answered precisely and deliberately. Firmly and unhesitatingly he bore witness that the sum spent a month before could not have been less than three thousand, that all the peasants about here would testify that they had heard the sum of three thousand mentioned by Dmitri Fyodorovitch himself. "What a lot of money he flung away on the gypsy girls alone! He wasted a thousand, I daresay, on them alone."

"I don't believe I gave them five hundred," was Mitya's gloomy comment on this. "It's a pity I didn't count the money at the time, but I was drunk...."

Mitya was sitting sideways with his back to the curtains. He listened gloomily, with a melancholy and exhausted air, as though he would say:

"Oh, say what you like. It makes no difference now."

"More than a thousand went on them, Dmitri Fyodorovitch," retorted Trifon Borissovitch firmly. "You flung it about at random and they picked it up. They were a rascally, thievish lot, horse-stealers, they've been driven away from here, or maybe they'd bear witness themselves how much they got from you. I saw the sum in your hands, myself—count it I didn't, you didn't let me, that's true enough—but by the look of it I should say it was far more than fifteen hundred ... fifteen hundred, indeed! We've seen money too. We can judge of amounts...."

As for the sum spent yesterday he asserted that Dmitri Fyodorovitch had told him, as soon as he arrived, that he had brought three thousand with him.

"Come now, is that so, Trifon Borissovitch?" replied Mitya. "Surely I didn't declare so positively that I'd brought three thousand?"

"You did say so, Dmitri Fyodorovitch. You said it before Andrey. Andrey himself is still here. Send for him. And in the hall, when you were treating the chorus, you shouted straight out that you would leave your sixth thousand here—that is with what you spent before, we must understand. Stepan and Semyon heard it, and Pyotr Fomitch Kalganov, too, was standing beside you at the time. Maybe he'd remember it...."

The evidence as to the "sixth" thousand made an extraordinary impression on the two lawyers. They were delighted with this new mode of reckoning; three and three made six, three thousand then and three now made six, that was clear.

They questioned all the peasants suggested by Trifon Borissovitch, Stepan and Semyon, the driver Andrey, and Kalganov. The peasants and the driver unhesitatingly confirmed Trifon Borissovitch's evidence. They noted down, with particular care, Andrey's account of the conversation he had had with Mitya on the road: " 'Where,' says he, 'am I, Dmitri Fyodorovitch, going, to heaven or to hell, and shall I be forgiven in the next world or not?' "

The psychological Ippolit Kirillovitch heard this with a subtle smile, and ended by recommending that these remarks as to where Dmitri Fyodorovitch would go should be "included in the case."

Kalganov, when called, came in reluctantly, frowning and ill-humored, and he spoke to the lawyers as though he had never met them before in his life, though they were acquaintances whom he had been meeting every day for a long time past. He began by saying that "he knew nothing about it and didn't want to." But it appeared that he had heard of the "sixth" thousand, and he admitted that he had been standing close by at the moment. As far as he could see he "didn't know" how much money Mitya had in his hands. He affirmed that the Poles had cheated at cards. In reply to reiterated questions he stated that, after the Poles had been turned out, Mitya's position with Agrafena Alexandrovna had certainly improved, and that she had said that she loved him. He spoke of Agrafena Alexandrovna with reserve and respect, as though she had been a lady of the best society, and did not once allow himself to call her Grushenka. In spite of the young man's obvious repugnance at giving evidence, Ippolit Kirillovitch examined him at great length, and only from him learnt all the details of what made up Mitya's "romance," so to say, on that night. Mitya did not once pull Kalganov up. At last they let the young man go, and he left the room with unconcealed indignation.

The Poles, too, were examined. Though they had gone to bed in their room, they had not slept all night, and on the arrival of the police officers they hastily dressed and got ready, realizing that they would certainly be sent for. They gave their evidence with dignity, though not without some uneasiness. The little Pole turned out to be a retired official of the twelfth class, who had served in Siberia as a veterinary surgeon. His name was Mussyalovitch. Pan Vrublevsky turned out to be an uncertificated dentist. Although Nikolay Parfenovitch asked them questions on entering the room they both addressed their answers to Mihail Makarovitch, who was standing on one side, taking him in their ignorance for the most important person and in command, and addressed him at every word as "Pan Colonel." Only after several reproofs from Mihail Makarovitch himself, they grasped that they had to address their answers to Nikolay Parfenovitch only. It turned out that they could speak Russian quite correctly except for their accent in some words. Of his relations with Grushenka, past and present, Pan Mussyalovitch spoke proudly and warmly, so that Mitya was roused at once and declared that he would not allow the "scoundrel" to speak like that in his presence! Pan Mussyalovitch at once called attention to the word "scoundrel" and begged that it should be put down in the protocol. Mitya fumed with rage.

"He's a scoundrel! A scoundrel! You can put that down. And put down, too, that, in spite of the protocol I still declare that he's a scoundrel!" he cried.

Though Nikolay Parfenovitch did insert this in the protocol, he showed the most praiseworthy tact and management. After sternly reprimanding Mitya, he cut short all further inquiry into the romantic aspect of the case, and hastened to pass to what was essential. One piece of evidence given by the Poles roused special interest in the lawyers: that was how, in that very room, Mitya had tried to buy off Pan Mussyalovitch, and had offered him three thousand roubles to resign his claims, seven hundred roubles down, and the remaining two thousand three hundred "to be paid next day in the town." He had sworn at the time that he had not the whole sum with him at Mokroe, but that his money was in the town. Mitya observed hotly that he had not said that he would be sure to pay him the remainder next day in the town. But Pan Vrublevsky confirmed the statement, and

Mitya, after thinking for a moment admitted, frowning, that it must have been as the Poles stated, that he had been excited at the time, and might indeed have said so.

The prosecutor positively pounced on this piece of evidence. It seemed to establish for the prosecution (and they did, in fact, base this deduction on it) that half, or a part of, the three thousand that had come into Mitya's hands might really have been left somewhere hidden in the town, or even, perhaps, somewhere here, in Mokroe. This would explain the circumstance, so baffling for the prosecution, that only eight hundred roubles were to be found in Mitya's hands. This circumstance had been the one piece of evidence which, insignificant as it was, had hitherto told, to some extent, in Mitya's favor. Now this one piece of evidence in his favor had broken down. In answer to the prosecutor's inquiry, where he would have got the remaining two thousand three hundred roubles, since he himself had denied having more than fifteen hundred, Mitya confidently replied that he had meant to offer the "little chap," not money, but a formal deed of conveyance of his rights to the village of Tchermashnya, those rights which he had already offered to Samsonov and Madame Hohlakov. The prosecutor positively smiled at the "innocence of this subterfuge."

"And you imagine he would have accepted such a deed as a substitute for two thousand three hundred roubles in cash?"

"He certainly would have accepted it," Mitya declared warmly. "Why, look here, he might have grabbed not two thousand, but four or six, for it. He would have put his lawyers, Poles and Jews, on to the job, and might have got, not three thousand, but the whole property out of the old man."

The evidence of Pan Mussyalovitch was, of course, entered in the protocol in the fullest detail. Then they let the Poles go. The incident of the cheating at cards was hardly touched upon. Nikolay Parfenovitch was too well pleased with them, as it was, and did not want to worry them with trifles, moreover, it was nothing but a foolish, drunken quarrel over cards. There had been drinking and disorder enough, that night.... So the two hundred roubles remained in the pockets of the Poles.

Then old Maximov was summoned. He came in timidly, approached with little steps, looking very disheveled and depressed. He had, all this time, taken refuge below with Grushenka, sitting dumbly beside her, and "now and then he'd begin blubbering over her and wiping his eyes with a blue check handkerchief," as Mihail Makarovitch described afterwards. So that she herself began trying to pacify and comfort him. The old man at once confessed that he had done wrong, that he had borrowed "ten roubles in my poverty," from Dmitri Fyodorovitch, and that he was ready to pay it back. To Nikolay Parfenovitch's direct question, had he noticed how much money Dmitri Fyodorovitch held in his hand, as he must have been able to see the sum better than any one when he took the note from him, Maximov, in the most positive manner, declared that there was twenty thousand.

"Have you ever seen so much as twenty thousand before, then?" inquired Nikolay Parfenovitch, with a smile.

"To be sure I have, not twenty, but seven, when my wife mortgaged my little property. She'd only let me look at it from a distance, boasting of it to me. It was a very thick bundle, all rainbow-colored notes. And Dmitri Fyodorovitch's were all rainbow-colored...."

He was not kept long. At last it was Grushenka's turn. Nikolay Parfenovitch was obviously apprehensive of the effect her appearance might have on Mitya, and he muttered a few words of admonition to him, but Mitya bowed his head in silence, giving him to understand "that he would not make a scene." Mihail Makarovitch himself led Grushenka in. She entered with a stern and gloomy face, that looked almost composed and sat down quietly on the chair offered her by Nikolay Parfenovitch. She was very pale, she seemed to be cold, and wrapped herself closely in her magnificent black shawl. She was suffering from a slight feverish chill—the first symptom of the long illness which followed that night. Her grave air, her direct earnest look and quiet manner made a very favorable impression on every one. Nikolay Parfenovitch was even a little bit "fascinated." He admitted himself, when talking about it afterwards, that only then had he seen "how handsome the woman was," for, though he had seen her several times before, he had always looked upon her as something of a "provincial hetaira." "She has the manners of the best society," he said enthusiastically, gossiping about her in a circle of ladies. But this was received with positive indignation by the ladies, who immediately called him a "naughty man," to his great satisfaction.

As she entered the room, Grushenka only glanced for an instant at Mitya, who looked at her uneasily. But her face reassured him at once. After the first inevitable inquiries and warnings, Nikolay Parfenovitch asked her, hesitating a little, but preserving the most courteous manner, on what terms she was with the retired lieutenant, Dmitri Fyodorovitch Karamazov. To this Grushenka firmly and quietly replied:

"He was an acquaintance. He came to see me as an acquaintance during the last month." To further inquisitive questions she answered plainly and with complete frankness, that, though "at times" she had thought him attractive, she had not loved him, but had won his heart as well as his old father's "in my nasty spite," that she had seen that Mitya was very jealous of Fyodor Pavlovitch and every one else; but that had only amused her. She had never meant to go to Fyodor Pavlovitch, she had simply been laughing at him. "I had no thoughts for either of them all this last month. I was expecting another man who had wronged me. But I think," she said in conclusion, "that there's no need for you to inquire about that, nor for me to answer you, for that's my own affair."

Nikolay Parfenovitch immediately acted upon this hint. He again dismissed the "romantic" aspect of the case and passed to the serious one, that is, to the question of most importance, concerning the three thousand roubles. Grushenka confirmed the statement that three thousand roubles had certainly been spent on the first carousal at Mokroe, and, though she had not counted the money herself, she had heard that it was three thousand from Dmitri Fyodorovitch's own lips.

"Did he tell you that alone, or before some one else, or did you only hear him speak of it to others in your presence?" the prosecutor inquired immediately.

To which Grushenka replied that she had heard him say so before other people, and had heard him say so when they were alone.

"Did he say it to you alone once, or several times?" inquired the prosecutor, and learned that he had told Grushenka so several times.

Ippolit Kirillovitch was very well satisfied with this piece of evidence. Further examination elicited that Grushenka knew, too, where that money had come from, and that Dmitri Fyodorovitch had got it from Katerina Ivanovna.

"And did you never, once, hear that the money spent a month ago was not three thousand, but less, and that Dmitri Fyodorovitch had saved half that sum for his own use?"

"No, I never heard that," answered Grushenka.

It was explained further that Mitya had, on the contrary, often told her that he hadn't a farthing.

"He was always expecting to get some from his father," said Grushenka in conclusion.

"Did he never say before you ... casually, or in a moment of irritation," Nikolay Parfenovitch put in suddenly, "that he intended to make an attempt on his father's life?"

"Ach, he did say so," sighed Grushenka.

"Once or several times?"

"He mentioned it several times, always in anger."

"And did you believe he would do it?"

"No, I never believed it," she answered firmly. "I had faith in his noble heart."

"Gentlemen, allow me," cried Mitya suddenly, "allow me to say one word to Agrafena Alexandrovna, in your presence."

"You can speak," Nikolay Parfenovitch assented.

"Agrafena Alexandrovna!" Mitya got up from his chair, "have faith in God and in me. I am not guilty of my father's murder!"

Having uttered these words Mitya sat down again on his chair. Grushenka stood up and crossed herself devoutly before the ikon. "Thanks be to Thee, O Lord," she said, in a voice thrilled with emotion, and still standing, she turned to Nikolay Parfenovitch and added:

"As he has spoken now, believe it! I know him. He'll say anything as a joke or from obstinacy, but he'll never deceive you against his conscience. He's telling the whole truth, you may believe it."

"Thanks, Agrafena Alexandrovna, you've given me fresh courage," Mitya responded in a quivering voice.

As to the money spent the previous day, she declared that she did not know what sum it was, but had heard him tell several people that he had three thousand with him. And to the question where he got the money, she said that he had told her that he had "stolen" it from Katerina Ivanovna, and that she had replied to that that he hadn't stolen it, and that he must pay the money back next day. On the prosecutor's asking her emphatically whether the money he said he had stolen from Katerina Ivanovna was what he had spent yesterday, or what he had squandered here a month ago, she declared that he meant the money spent a month ago, and that that was how she understood him.

Grushenka was at last released, and Nikolay Parfenovitch informed her impulsively that she might at once return to the town and that if he could be of any assistance to her, with horses for example, or if she would care for an escort, he ... would be—

"I thank you sincerely," said Grushenka, bowing to him, "I'm going with this old gentleman, I am driving him back to town with me, and meanwhile, if you'll allow me, I'll wait below to hear what you decide about Dmitri Fyodorovitch."

She went out. Mitya was calm, and even looked more cheerful, but only for a moment. He felt more and more oppressed by a strange physical weakness. His eyes were closing with fatigue. The examination of the witnesses was, at last, over. They proceeded to a final revision of the protocol. Mitya got up, moved from his chair to the corner by the curtain, lay down on a large chest covered with a rug, and instantly fell asleep.

He had a strange dream, utterly out of keeping with the place and the time.

He was driving somewhere in the steppes, where he had been stationed long ago, and a peasant was driving him in a cart with a pair of horses, through snow and sleet. He was cold, it was early in November, and the snow was falling in big wet flakes, melting as soon as it touched the earth. And the peasant drove him smartly, he had a fair, long beard. He was not an old man, somewhere about fifty, and he had on a gray peasant's smock. Not far off was a village, he could see the black huts, and half the huts were burnt down, there were only the charred beams sticking up. And as they drove in, there were peasant women drawn up along the road, a lot of women, a whole row, all thin and wan, with their faces a sort of brownish color, especially one at the edge, a tall, bony woman, who looked forty, but might have been only twenty, with a long thin face. And in her arms was a little baby crying. And her breasts seemed so dried up that there was not a drop of milk in them. And the child cried and cried, and held out its little bare arms, with its little fists blue from cold.

"Why are they crying? Why are they crying?" Mitya asked, as they dashed gayly by.

"It's the babe," answered the driver, "the babe weeping."

And Mitya was struck by his saying, in his peasant way, "the babe," and he liked the peasant's calling it a "babe." There seemed more pity in it.

"But why is it weeping?" Mitya persisted stupidly, "why are its little arms bare? Why don't they wrap it up?"

"The babe's cold, its little clothes are frozen and don't warm it."

"But why is it? Why?" foolish Mitya still persisted.

"Why, they're poor people, burnt out. They've no bread. They're begging because they've been burnt out."

"No, no," Mitya, as it were, still did not understand. "Tell me why it is those poor mothers stand there? Why are people poor? Why is the babe poor? Why is the steppe barren? Why don't they hug each other and kiss? Why don't they sing songs of joy? Why are they so dark from black misery? Why don't they feed the babe?"

And he felt that, though his questions were unreasonable and senseless, yet he wanted to ask just that, and he had to ask it just in that way. And he felt that a passion of pity, such as he had never known before, was rising in his heart, that he wanted to cry, that he wanted to do something for them all, so that the babe should weep no more, so that the dark-faced, dried-up mother should not weep, that no one should shed tears again from that moment, and he wanted to do it at once, at once, regardless of all obstacles, with all the recklessness of the Karamazovs.

"And I'm coming with you. I won't leave you now for the rest of my life, I'm coming with you," he heard close beside him Grushenka's tender voice, thrilling with emotion.

And his heart glowed, and he struggled forward towards the light, and he longed to live, to live, to go on and on, towards the new, beckoning light, and to hasten, hasten, now, at once!

"What! Where?" he exclaimed opening his eyes, and sitting up on the chest, as though he had revived from a swoon, smiling brightly. Nikolay Parfenovitch was standing over him, suggesting that he should hear the protocol read aloud and sign it. Mitya guessed that he had been asleep an hour or more, but he did not hear Nikolay Parfenovitch. He was suddenly struck by the fact that there was a pillow under his head, which hadn't been there when he had leant back, exhausted, on the chest.

"Who put that pillow under my head? Who was so kind?" he cried, with a sort of ecstatic gratitude, and tears in his voice, as though some great kindness had been shown him.

He never found out who this kind man was; perhaps one of the peasant witnesses, or Nikolay Parfenovitch's little secretary, had compassionately thought to put a pillow under his head; but his whole soul was quivering with tears. He went to the table and said that he would sign whatever they liked.

"I've had a good dream, gentlemen," he said in a strange voice, with a new light, as of joy, in his face.

When the protocol had been signed, Nikolay Parfenovitch turned solemnly to the prisoner and read him the "Committal," setting forth, that in such a year, on such a day, in such a place, the investigating lawyer of such-and-such a district court, having examined so-and-so (to wit, Mitya) accused of this and of that (all the charges were carefully written out) and having considered that the accused, not pleading guilty to the charges made against him, had brought forward nothing in his defense, while the witnesses, so-and-so, and so-and-so, and the circumstances such-and-such testify against him, acting in accordance with such-and-such articles of the Statute Book, and so on, has ruled, that, in order to preclude so-and-so (Mitya) from all means of evading pursuit and judgment he be detained in such-and-such a prison, which he hereby notifies to the accused and communicates a copy of this same "Committal" to the deputy prosecutor, and so on, and so on.

In brief, Mitya was informed that he was, from that moment, a prisoner, and that he would be driven at once to the town, and there shut up in a very unpleasant place. Mitya listened attentively, and only shrugged his shoulders.

"Well, gentlemen, I don't blame you. I'm ready.... I understand that there's nothing else for you to do."

Nikolay Parfenovitch informed him gently that he would be escorted at once by the rural police officer, Mavriky Mavrikyevitch, who happened to be on the spot....

"Stay," Mitya interrupted, suddenly, and impelled by uncontrollable feeling he pronounced, addressing all in the room:

"Gentlemen, we're all cruel, we're all monsters, we all make men weep, and mothers, and babes at the breast, but of all, let it be settled here, now, of all I am the lowest reptile! I've sworn to amend, and every day I've done the same filthy things. I understand now that such men as I need a blow, a blow of destiny to catch them as with a noose, and bind them by a force from without. Never, never should I have risen of myself! But the thunderbolt has fallen. I accept the torture of accusation, and my public shame, I want to suffer and by suffering I shall be purified. Perhaps I shall be purified, gentlemen? But listen, for the last time, I am not guilty of my father's blood. I accept my punishment, not because I killed him, but because I meant to kill him, and perhaps I really might have killed him. Still I mean to fight it out with you. I warn you of that. I'll fight it out with you to the end, and then God will decide. Good-by, gentlemen, don't be vexed with me for having shouted at you during the examination. Oh, I was still such a fool then.... In another minute I shall be a prisoner, but now, for the last time, as a free man, Dmitri Karamazov offers you his hand. Saying good-by to you, I say it to all men."

His voice quivered and he stretched out his hand, but Nikolay Parfenovitch, who happened to stand nearest to him, with a sudden, almost nervous movement, hid his hands behind his back. Mitya instantly noticed this, and started. He let his outstretched hand fall at once.

"The preliminary inquiry is not yet over," Nikolay Parfenovitch faltered, somewhat embarrassed. "We will continue it in the town, and I, for my part, of course, am ready to wish you all success ... in your defense.... As a matter of fact, Dmitri Fyodorovitch, I've always been disposed to regard you as, so to speak, more unfortunate than guilty. All of us here, if I may make bold to speak for all, we are all ready to recognize that you are, at bottom, a young man of honor, but, alas, one who has been carried away by certain passions to a somewhat excessive degree...."

Nikolay Parfenovitch's little figure was positively majestic by the time he had finished speaking. It struck Mitya that in another minute this "boy" would take his arm, lead him to another corner, and renew their conversation about "girls." But many quite irrelevant and inappropriate thoughts sometimes occur even to a prisoner when he is being led out to execution.

"Gentlemen, you are good, you are humane, may I see *her* to say 'good-by' for the last time?" asked Mitya.

"Certainly, but considering ... in fact, now it's impossible except in the presence of—"

"Oh, well, if it must be so, it must!"

Grushenka was brought in, but the farewell was brief, and of few words, and did not at all satisfy Nikolay Parfenovitch. Grushenka made a deep bow to Mitya.

"I have told you I am yours, and I will be yours. I will follow you for ever, wherever they may send you. Farewell; you are guiltless, though you've been your own undoing."

Her lips quivered, tears flowed from her eyes.

"Forgive me, Grusha, for my love, for ruining you, too, with my love."

Mitya would have said something more, but he broke off and went out. He was at once surrounded by men who kept a constant watch on him. At the bottom of the steps to which he had driven up with such a dash the day before with Andrey's three horses, two carts stood in readiness. Mavriky Mavrikyevitch, a sturdy, thick-set man with a wrinkled face, was annoyed about something, some sudden irregularity. He was shouting angrily. He asked Mitya to get into the cart with somewhat excessive surliness.

"When I stood him drinks in the tavern, the man had quite a different face," thought Mitya, as he got in. At the gates there was a crowd of people, peasants, women and drivers. Trifon Borissovitch came down the steps too. All stared at Mitya.

"Forgive me at parting, good people!" Mitya shouted suddenly from the cart.

"Forgive us too!" he heard two or three voices.

"Good-by to you, too, Trifon Borissovitch!"

But Trifon Borissovitch did not even turn round. He was, perhaps, too busy. He, too, was shouting and fussing about something. It appeared that everything was not yet ready in the second cart, in which two constables were to accompany Mavriky Mavrikyevitch. The peasant who had been ordered to drive the second cart was pulling on his smock, stoutly maintaining that it was not his turn to go, but Akim's. But Akim was not to be seen. They ran to look for him. The peasant persisted and besought them to wait.

"You see what our peasants are, Mavriky Mavrikyevitch. They've no shame!" exclaimed Trifon Borissovitch. "Akim gave you twenty-five copecks the day before yesterday. You've drunk it all and now you cry out. I'm simply surprised at your good-nature, with our low peasants, Mavriky Mavrikyevitch, that's all I can say."

"But what do we want a second cart for?" Mitya put in. "Let's start with the one, Mavriky Mavrikyevitch. I won't be unruly, I won't run away from you, old fellow. What do we want an escort for?"

"I'll trouble you, sir, to learn how to speak to me if you've never been taught. I'm not 'old fellow' to you, and you can keep your advice for another time!" Mavriky Mavrikyevitch snapped out savagely, as though glad to vent his wrath.

Mitya was reduced to silence. He flushed all over. A moment later he felt suddenly very cold. The rain had ceased, but the dull sky was still overcast with clouds, and a keen wind was blowing straight in his face.

"I've taken a chill," thought Mitya, twitching his shoulders.

At last Mavriky Mavrikyevitch, too, got into the cart, sat down heavily, and, as though without noticing it, squeezed Mitya into the corner. It is true that he was out of humor and greatly disliked the task that had been laid upon him.

"Good-by, Trifon Borissovitch!" Mitya shouted again, and felt himself, that he had not called out this time from good-nature, but involuntarily, from resentment.

But Trifon Borissovitch stood proudly, with both hands behind his back, and staring straight at Mitya with a stern and angry face, he made no reply.

"Good-by, Dmitri Fyodorovitch, good-by!" he heard all at once the voice of Kalganov, who had suddenly darted out. Running up to the cart he held out his hand to Mitya. He had no cap on.

Mitya had time to seize and press his hand.

"Good-by, dear fellow! I shan't forget your generosity," he cried warmly.

But the cart moved and their hands parted. The bell began ringing and Mitya was driven off.

Kalganov ran back, sat down in a corner, bent his head, hid his face in his hands, and burst out crying. For a long while he sat like that, crying as though he were a little boy instead of a young man of twenty. Oh, he believed almost without doubt in Mitya's guilt.

"What are these people? What can men be after this?" he exclaimed incoherently, in bitter despondency, almost despair. At that moment he had no desire to live.

"Is it worth it? Is it worth it?" exclaimed the boy in his grief.

Chapter Six
The Boys

"What do you think the doctor will say to him?" Kolya asked quickly. "What a repulsive mug, though, hasn't he? I can't endure medicine!"

"Ilusha is dying. I think that's certain," answered Alyosha, mournfully.

"They are rogues! Medicine's a fraud! I am glad to have made your acquaintance, though, Karamazov. I wanted to know you for a long time. I am only sorry we meet in such sad circumstances."

Kolya had a great inclination to say something even warmer and more demonstrative, but he felt ill at ease. Alyosha noticed this, smiled, and pressed his hand.

"I've long learned to respect you as a rare person," Kolya muttered again, faltering and uncertain. "I have heard you are a mystic and have been in the monastery. I know you are a mystic, but ... that hasn't put me off. Contact with real life will cure you.... It's always so with characters like yours."

"What do you mean by mystic? Cure me of what?" Alyosha was rather astonished.

"Oh, God and all the rest of it."

"What, don't you believe in God?"

"Oh, I've nothing against God. Of course, God is only a hypothesis, but ... I admit that He is needed ... for the order of the universe and all that ... and that if there were no God He would have to be invented," added Kolya, beginning to blush. He suddenly fancied that Alyosha might think he was trying to show off his knowledge and to prove that he was "grown up." "I haven't the slightest desire to show off my knowledge to him," Kolya thought indignantly. And all of a sudden he felt horribly annoyed.

"I must confess I can't endure entering on such discussions," he said with a final air. "It's possible for one who doesn't believe in God to love mankind, don't you think so? Voltaire didn't believe in God and loved mankind?" ("I am at it again," he thought to himself.)

"Voltaire believed in God, though not very much, I think, and I don't think he loved mankind very much either," said Alyosha quietly, gently, and quite naturally, as though he were talking to some one of his own age, or even older. Kolya was particularly struck by Alyosha's apparent diffidence about his opinion of Voltaire. He seemed to be leaving the question for him, little Kolya, to settle.

"Have you read Voltaire?" Alyosha finished.

"No, not to say read.... But I've read *Candide* in the Russian translation ... in an absurd, grotesque, old translation ... (At it again! again!)"

"And did you understand it?"

"Oh, yes, everything.... That is ... Why do you suppose I shouldn't understand it? There's a lot of nastiness in it, of course.... Of course I can understand that it's a philosophical novel and written to advocate an idea...." Kolya was getting mixed by now. "I am a Socialist, Karamazov, I am an incurable Socialist," he announced suddenly, apropos of nothing.

"A Socialist?" laughed Alyosha. "But when have you had time to become one? Why, I thought you were only thirteen?"

Kolya winced.

"In the first place I am not thirteen, but fourteen, fourteen in a fortnight," he flushed angrily, "and in the second place I am at a complete loss to understand what my age has to do with it? The question is what are my convictions, not what is my age, isn't it?"

"When you are older, you'll understand for yourself the influence of age on convictions. I fancied, too, that you were not expressing your own ideas," Alyosha answered serenely and modestly, but Kolya interrupted him hotly:

"Come, you want obedience and mysticism. You must admit that the Christian religion, for instance, has only been of use to the rich and the powerful to keep the lower classes in slavery. That's so, isn't it?"

"Ah, I know where you read that, and I am sure some one told you so!" cried Alyosha.

"I say, what makes you think I read it? And certainly no one told me so. I can think for myself.... I am not opposed to Christ, if you like. He was a most humane person, and if He were alive to-day, He would be found in the ranks of the revolutionists, and would perhaps play a conspicuous part.... There's no doubt about that."

"Oh, where, where did you get that from? What fool have you made friends with?" exclaimed Alyosha.

"Come, the truth will out! It has so chanced that I have often talked to Mr. Rakitin, of course, but ... old Byelinsky said that, too, so they say."

"Byelinsky? I don't remember. He hasn't written that anywhere."

"If he didn't write it, they say he said it. I heard that from a ... but never mind."

"And have you read Byelinsky?"

"Well, no ... I haven't read all of him, but ... I read the passage about Tatyana, why she didn't go off with Onyegin."

"Didn't go off with Onyegin? Surely you don't ... understand that already?"

"Why, you seem to take me for little Smurov," said Kolya, with a grin of irritation. "But please don't suppose I am such a revolutionist. I often disagree with Mr. Rakitin. Though I mention Tatyana, I am not at all for the emancipation of women. I acknowledge that women are a subject race and must obey. *Les femmes tricottent*, as Napoleon said." Kolya, for some reason, smiled, "And on that question at least I am quite of one mind with that pseudo-great man. I think, too, that to leave one's own country and fly to America is mean, worse than mean—silly. Why go to America when one may be of great service to humanity here? Now especially. There's a perfect mass of fruitful activity open to us. That's what I answered."

"What do you mean? Answered whom? Has some one suggested your going to America already?"

"I must own, they've been at me to go, but I declined. That's between ourselves, of course, Karamazov; do you hear, not a word to any one. I say this only to you. I am not at all anxious to fall into the clutches of the secret police and take lessons at the Chain bridge.

Long will you remember
The house at the Chain bridge.

Do you remember? It's splendid. Why are you laughing? You don't suppose I am fibbing, do you?" ("What if he should find out that I've only that one number of *The Bell* in father's bookcase, and haven't read any more of it?" Kolya thought with a shudder.)

"Oh, no, I am not laughing and don't suppose for a moment that you are lying. No, indeed, I can't suppose so, for all this, alas! is perfectly true. But tell me, have you read Pushkin—*Onyegin*, for instance?... You spoke just now of Tatyana."

"No, I haven't read it yet, but I want to read it. I have no prejudices, Karamazov; I want to hear both sides. What makes you ask?"

"Oh, nothing."

"Tell me, Karamazov, have you an awful contempt for me?" Kolya rapped out suddenly and drew himself up before Alyosha, as though he were on drill. "Be so kind as to tell me, without beating about the bush."

"I have a contempt for you?" Alyosha looked at him wondering. "What for? I am only sad that a charming nature such as yours should be perverted by all this crude nonsense before you have begun life."

"Don't be anxious about my nature," Kolya interrupted, not without complacency. "But it's true that I am stupidly sensitive, crudely sensitive. You smiled just now, and I fancied you seemed to—"

"Oh, my smile meant something quite different. I'll tell you why I smiled. Not long ago I read the criticism made by a German who had lived in Russia, on our students and schoolboys of to-day. 'Show a Russian schoolboy,' he writes, 'a map of the stars, which he knows nothing about, and he will give you back the map next day with corrections on it.' No knowledge and unbounded conceit—that's what the German meant to say about the Russian schoolboy."

"Yes, that's perfectly right," Kolya laughed suddenly, "exactly so! Bravo the German! But he did not see the good side, what do you think? Conceit may be, that comes from youth, that will be corrected if need be, but, on the other hand, there is an independent spirit almost from childhood, boldness of thought and conviction, and not the spirit of these sausage makers, groveling before authority.... But the German was right all the same. Bravo the German! But Germans want strangling all the same. Though they are so good at science and learning they must be strangled."

"Strangled, what for?" smiled Alyosha.

"Well, perhaps I am talking nonsense, I agree. I am awfully childish sometimes, and when I am pleased about anything I can't restrain myself and am ready to talk any stuff. But, I say, we are chattering away here about nothing, and that doctor has been a long time in there. But perhaps he's examining the mamma and that poor crippled Nina. I liked that Nina, you know. She whispered to me suddenly as I was coming away, 'Why didn't you come before?' And in such a voice, so reproachfully! I think she is awfully nice and pathetic."

"Yes, yes! Well, you'll be coming often, you will see what she is like. It would do you a great deal of good to know people like that, to learn to value a great deal which you will find out from knowing these people," Alyosha observed warmly. "That would have more effect on you than anything."

"Oh, how I regret and blame myself for not having come sooner!" Kolya exclaimed, with bitter feeling.

"Yes, it's a great pity. You saw for yourself how delighted the poor child was to see you. And how he fretted for you to come!"

"Don't tell me! You make it worse! But it serves me right. What kept me from coming was my conceit, my egoistic vanity, and the beastly wilfullness, which I never can get rid of, though I've been struggling with it all my life. I see that now. I am a beast in lots of ways, Karamazov!"

"No, you have a charming nature, though it's been distorted, and I quite understand why you have had such an influence on this generous, morbidly sensitive boy," Alyosha answered warmly.

"And you say that to me!" cried Kolya; "and would you believe it, I thought—I've thought several times since I've been here—that you despised me! If only you knew how I prize your opinion!"

"But are you really so sensitive? At your age! Would you believe it, just now, when you were telling your story, I thought, as I watched you, that you must be very sensitive!"

"You thought so? What an eye you've got, I say! I bet that was when I was talking about the goose. That was just when I was fancying you had a great contempt for me for being in such a hurry to show off, and for a moment I quite hated you for it, and began talking like a fool. Then I fancied—just now, here—when I said that if there were no God He would have to be invented, that I was in too great a hurry to display my knowledge, especially as I got that phrase out of a book. But I swear I wasn't showing off out of vanity, though I really don't know why. Because I was so pleased? Yes, I believe it was because I was so pleased ... though it's perfectly disgraceful for any one to be gushing directly they are pleased, I know that. But I am convinced now that you don't despise me; it was all my imagination. Oh, Karamazov, I am profoundly unhappy. I sometimes fancy all sorts of things, that every one is laughing at me, the whole world, and then I feel ready to overturn the whole order of things."

"And you worry every one about you," smiled Alyosha.

"Yes, I worry every one about me, especially my mother. Karamazov, tell me, am I very ridiculous now?"

"Don't think about that, don't think of it at all!" cried Alyosha. "And what does ridiculous mean? Isn't every one constantly being or seeming ridiculous? Besides, nearly all clever people now are fearfully afraid of being ridiculous, and that makes them unhappy. All I am surprised at is that you should be feeling that so early, though I've observed it for some time past, and not only in you. Nowadays the very children have begun to suffer from it. It's almost a sort of insanity. The devil has taken the form of that vanity and entered into the whole generation; it's simply the devil," added Alyosha, without a trace of the smile that Kolya, staring at him, expected to see. "You are like every one else," said Alyosha, in conclusion, "that is, like very many others. Only you must not be like everybody else, that's all."

"Even if every one is like that?"

"Yes, even if every one is like that. You be the only one not like it. You really are not like every one else, here you are not ashamed to confess to something bad and even ridiculous. And who will admit so much in these days? No one. And people have even ceased to feel the impulse to self-criticism. Don't be like every one else, even if you are the only one."

"Splendid! I was not mistaken in you. You know how to console one. Oh, how I have longed to know you, Karamazov! I've long been eager for this meeting. Can you really have thought about me, too? You said just now that you thought of me, too?"

"Yes, I'd heard of you and had thought of you, too ... and if it's partly vanity that makes you ask, it doesn't matter."

"Do you know, Karamazov, our talk has been like a declaration of love," said Kolya, in a bashful and melting voice. "That's not ridiculous, is it?"

"Not at all ridiculous, and if it were, it wouldn't matter, because it's been a good thing." Alyosha smiled brightly.

"But do you know, Karamazov, you must admit that you are a little ashamed yourself, now.... I see it by your eyes." Kolya smiled with a sort of sly happiness.

"Why ashamed?"

"Well, why are you blushing?"

"It was you made me blush," laughed Alyosha, and he really did blush. "Oh, well, I am a little, goodness knows why, I don't know..." he muttered, almost embarrassed.

"Oh, how I love you and admire you at this moment just because you are rather ashamed! Because you are just like me," cried Kolya, in positive ecstasy. His cheeks glowed, his eyes beamed.

"You know, Kolya, you will be very unhappy in your life," something made Alyosha say suddenly.

"I know, I know. How you know it all beforehand!" Kolya agreed at once.

"But you will bless life on the whole, all the same."

"Just so, hurrah! You are a prophet. Oh, we shall get on together, Karamazov! Do you know, what delights me most, is that you treat me quite like an equal. But we are not equals, no, we are not, you are better! But we shall get on. Do you know, all this last month, I've been saying to myself, 'Either we shall be friends at once, for ever, or we shall part enemies to the grave!' "

"And saying that, of course, you loved me," Alyosha laughed gayly.

"I did. I loved you awfully. I've been loving and dreaming of you. And how do you know it all beforehand? Ah, here's the doctor. Goodness! What will he tell us? Look at his face!"

The doctor came out of the room again, muffled in his fur coat and with his cap on his head. His face looked almost angry and disgusted, as though he were afraid of getting dirty. He cast a cursory glance round the passage, looking sternly at Alyosha and Kolya as he did so. Alyosha waved from the door to the coachman, and the carriage that had brought the doctor drove up. The captain darted out after the doctor, and, bowing apologetically, stopped him to get the last word. The poor fellow looked utterly crushed; there was a scared look in his eyes.

"Your Excellency, your Excellency ... is it possible?" he began, but could not go on and clasped his hands in despair. Yet he still gazed imploringly at the doctor, as though a word from him might still change the poor boy's fate.

"I can't help it, I am not God!" the doctor answered offhand, though with the customary impressiveness.

"Doctor ... your Excellency ... and will it be soon, soon?"

"You must be prepared for anything," said the doctor in emphatic and incisive tones, and dropping his eyes, he was about to step out to the coach.

"Your Excellency, for Christ's sake!" the terror-stricken captain stopped him again. "Your Excellency! but can nothing, absolutely nothing save him now?"

"It's not in my hands now," said the doctor impatiently, "but h'm!..." he stopped suddenly. "If you could, for instance ... send ... your patient ... at once, without delay" (the words "at once, without delay," the doctor uttered with an almost wrathful sternness that made the captain start) "to Syracuse, the change to the new be-ne-ficial climatic conditions might possibly effect—"

"To Syracuse!" cried the captain, unable to grasp what was said.

"Syracuse is in Sicily," Kolya jerked out suddenly in explanation. The doctor looked at him.

"Sicily! your Excellency," faltered the captain, "but you've seen"—he spread out his hands, indicating his surroundings—"mamma and my family?"

"N—no, Sicily is not the place for the family, the family should go to Caucasus in the early spring ... your daughter must go to the Caucasus, and your wife ... after a course of the waters in the Caucasus for her rheumatism ... must be sent straight to Paris to the mental specialist Lepelletier; I could give you a note to him, and then ... there might be a change—"

"Doctor, doctor! But you see!" The captain flung wide his hands again despairingly, indicating the bare wooden walls of the passage.

"Well, that's not my business," grinned the doctor. "I have only told you the answer of medical science to your question as to possible treatment. As for the rest, to my regret—"

"Don't be afraid, apothecary, my dog won't bite you," Kolya rapped out loudly, noticing the doctor's rather uneasy glance at Perezvon, who was standing in the doorway. There was a wrathful note in Kolya's voice. He used the word apothecary instead of doctor on purpose, and, as he explained afterwards, used it "to insult him."

"What's that?" The doctor flung up his head, staring with surprise at Kolya. "Who's this?" he addressed Alyosha, as though asking him to explain.

"It's Perezvon's master, don't worry about me," Kolya said incisively again.

"Perezvon?"[7] repeated the doctor, perplexed.

"He hears the bell, but where it is he cannot tell. Good-by, we shall meet in Syracuse."

"Who's this? Who's this?" The doctor flew into a terrible rage.

"He is a schoolboy, doctor, he is a mischievous boy; take no notice of him," said Alyosha, frowning and speaking quickly. "Kolya, hold your tongue!" he cried to Krassotkin. "Take no notice of him, doctor," he repeated, rather impatiently.

"He wants a thrashing, a good thrashing!" The doctor stamped in a perfect fury.

"And you know, apothecary, my Perezvon might bite!" said Kolya, turning pale, with quivering voice and flashing eyes. "*Ici*, Perezvon!"

"Kolya, if you say another word, I'll have nothing more to do with you," Alyosha cried peremptorily.

"There is only one man in the world who can command Nikolay Krassotkin—this is the man"; Kolya pointed to Alyosha. "I obey him, good-by!"

He stepped forward, opened the door, and quickly went into the inner room. Perezvon flew after him. The doctor stood still for five seconds in amazement, looking at Alyosha; then, with a curse, he went out quickly to the carriage, repeating aloud, "This is ... this is ... I don't know what it is!" The captain darted forward to help him into the carriage. Alyosha followed Kolya into the room. He was already by Ilusha's bedside. The sick boy was holding his hand and calling for his father. A minute later the captain, too, came back.

"Father, father, come ... we ..." Ilusha faltered in violent excitement, but apparently unable to go on, he flung his wasted arms round his father and Kolya, uniting them in one embrace, and hugging them as tightly as he could. The captain suddenly began to shake with dumb sobs, and Kolya's lips and chin twitched.

"Father, father! How sorry I am for you!" Ilusha moaned bitterly.

"Ilusha ... darling ... the doctor said ... you would be all right ... we shall be happy ... the doctor ..." the captain began.

"Ah, father! I know what the new doctor said to you about me.... I saw!" cried Ilusha, and again he hugged them both with all his strength, hiding his face on his father's shoulder.

"Father, don't cry, and when I die get a good boy, another one ... choose one of them all, a good one, call him Ilusha and love him instead of me...."

"Hush, old man, you'll get well," Krassotkin cried suddenly, in a voice that sounded angry.

"But don't ever forget me, father," Ilusha went on, "come to my grave ... and, father, bury me by our big stone, where we used to go for our walk, and come to me there with Krassotkin in the evening ... and Perezvon ... I shall expect you.... Father, father!"

His voice broke. They were all three silent, still embracing. Nina was crying quietly in her chair, and at last seeing them all crying, "mamma," too, burst into tears.

"Ilusha! Ilusha!" she exclaimed.

Krassotkin suddenly released himself from Ilusha's embrace.

"Good-by, old man, mother expects me back to dinner," he said quickly. "What a pity I did not tell her! She will be dreadfully anxious.... But after dinner I'll come back to you for the whole day, for the whole evening, and I'll tell you all sorts of things, all sorts of things. And I'll bring Perezvon, but now I will take him with me, because he will begin to howl when I am away and bother you. Good-by!"

And he ran out into the passage. He didn't want to cry, but in the passage he burst into tears. Alyosha found him crying.

"Kolya, you must be sure to keep your word and come, or he will be terribly disappointed," Alyosha said emphatically.

"I will! Oh, how I curse myself for not having come before!" muttered Kolya, crying, and no longer ashamed of it.

At that moment the captain flew out of the room, and at once closed the door behind him. His face looked frenzied, his lips were trembling. He stood before the two and flung up his arms.

"I don't want a good boy! I don't want another boy!" he muttered in a wild whisper, clenching his teeth. "If I forget thee, Jerusalem, may my tongue—" He broke off with a sob and sank on his knees before the wooden bench. Pressing his fists against his head, he began sobbing with absurd whimpering cries, doing his utmost that his cries should not be heard in the room.

Kolya ran out into the street.

"Good-by, Karamazov? Will you come yourself?" he cried sharply and angrily to Alyosha.

"I will certainly come in the evening."

"What was that he said about Jerusalem?... What did he mean by that?"

"It's from the Bible. 'If I forget thee, Jerusalem,' that is, if I forget all that is most precious to me, if I let anything take its place, then may—"

"I understand, that's enough! Mind you come! *Ici*, Perezvon!" he cried with positive ferocity to the dog, and with rapid strides he went home.

Chapter Seven
Ivan

Alyosha went towards the cathedral square to the widow Morozov's house to see Grushenka, who had sent Fenya to him early in the morning with an urgent message begging him to come. Questioning Fenya, Alyosha learned that her mistress had been particularly distressed since the previous day. During the two months that had passed since Mitya's arrest, Alyosha had called frequently at the widow Morozov's house, both from his own inclination and to take messages for Mitya. Three days after Mitya's arrest, Grushenka was taken very ill and was ill for nearly five weeks. For one whole week she was unconscious. She was very much changed—thinner and a little sallow, though she had for the past fortnight been well enough to go out. But to Alyosha her face was even more attractive than before, and he liked to meet her eyes when he went in to her. A look of firmness and intelligent purpose had developed in her face. There were signs of a spiritual transformation in her, and a steadfast, fine and humble determination that nothing could shake could be discerned in her. There was a small vertical line between her brows which gave her charming face a look of concentrated thought, almost austere at the first glance. There was scarcely a trace of her former frivolity.

It seemed strange to Alyosha, too, that in spite of the calamity that had overtaken the poor girl, betrothed to a man who had been arrested for a terrible crime, almost at the instant of their betrothal, in spite of her illness and the almost inevitable sentence hanging over Mitya, Grushenka had not yet lost her youthful cheerfulness. There was a soft light in the once proud eyes, though at times they gleamed with the old vindictive fire when she was visited by one disturbing thought stronger than ever in her heart. The object of that uneasiness was the same as ever—Katerina Ivanovna, of whom Grushenka had even raved when she lay in delirium. Alyosha knew that she was fearfully jealous of her. Yet Katerina Ivanovna had not once visited Mitya in his prison, though she might have done it whenever she liked. All this made a difficult problem for Alyosha, for he was the only person to whom Grushenka opened her heart and from whom she was continually asking advice. Sometimes he was unable to say anything.

Full of anxiety he entered her lodging. She was at home. She had returned from seeing Mitya half an hour before, and from the rapid movement with which she leapt up from her chair to meet him he saw that she had been expecting him with great impatience. A pack of cards dealt for a game of "fools" lay on the table. A bed had been made up on the leather sofa on the other side and Maximov lay, half-reclining, on it. He wore a dressing-gown and a cotton nightcap, and was evidently ill and weak, though he was smiling blissfully. When the homeless old man returned with Grushenka from Mokroe two months before, he had simply stayed on and was still staying with her. He arrived with her in rain and sleet, sat down on the sofa, drenched and scared, and gazed mutely at her with a timid, appealing smile. Grushenka, who was in terrible grief and in the first stage of fever, almost forgot his existence in all she had to do the first half-hour after her arrival. Suddenly she chanced to look at him intently: he laughed a pitiful, helpless little laugh. She called Fenya and told her to give him something to eat. All that day he sat in the same place, almost without stirring. When it got dark and the shutters were closed, Fenya asked her mistress:

"Is the gentleman going to stay the night, mistress?"

"Yes; make him a bed on the sofa," answered Grushenka.

Questioning him more in detail, Grushenka learned from him that he had literally nowhere to go, and that "Mr. Kalganov, my benefactor, told me straight that he wouldn't receive me again and gave me five roubles."

"Well, God bless you, you'd better stay, then," Grushenka decided in her grief, smiling compassionately at him. Her smile wrung the old man's heart and his lips twitched with grateful tears. And so the destitute wanderer had stayed with her ever since. He did not leave the house even when she was ill. Fenya and her grandmother, the cook, did not turn him out, but went on serving him meals and making up his bed on the sofa. Grushenka had grown used to him, and coming back from seeing Mitya (whom she had begun to visit in prison before she was really well) she would sit down and begin talking to "Maximushka" about trifling matters, to keep her from thinking of her sorrow. The old man turned out to be a good story-teller on occasions, so that at last he became necessary to her. Grushenka saw scarcely any one else beside Alyosha, who did not come every day and never stayed long. Her old merchant lay seriously ill at this time, "at his last gasp" as they said in the town, and he did, in fact, die a week after Mitya's trial. Three weeks before his death, feeling the end approaching, he made his sons, their wives and children, come upstairs to him at last and bade them not leave him again. From that moment he gave strict orders to his servants not to admit Grushenka and to tell her if she came, "The master wishes you long life and happiness and tells you to forget him." But Grushenka sent almost every day to inquire after him.

"You've come at last!" she cried, flinging down the cards and joyfully greeting Alyosha, "and Maximushka's been scaring me that perhaps you wouldn't come. Ah, how I need you! Sit down to the table. What will you have—coffee?"

"Yes, please," said Alyosha, sitting down at the table. "I am very hungry."

"That's right. Fenya, Fenya, coffee," cried Grushenka. "It's been made a long time ready for you. And bring some little pies, and mind they are hot. Do you know, we've had a storm over those pies to-day. I took them to the prison for him, and would you believe it, he threw them back to me: he would not eat them. He flung one of them on the floor and stamped on it. So I said to him: 'I shall leave them with the warder; if you don't eat them before evening, it will be that your venomous spite is enough for you!' With that I went away. We quarreled again, would you believe it? Whenever I go we quarrel."

Grushenka said all this in one breath in her agitation. Maximov, feeling nervous, at once smiled and looked on the floor.

"What did you quarrel about this time?" asked Alyosha.

"I didn't expect it in the least. Only fancy, he is jealous of the Pole. 'Why are you keeping him?' he said. 'So you've begun keeping him.' He is jealous, jealous of me all the time, jealous eating and sleeping! He even took it into his head to be jealous of Kuzma last week."

"But he knew about the Pole before?"

"Yes, but there it is. He has known about him from the very beginning, but to-day he suddenly got up and began scolding about him. I am ashamed to repeat what he said. Silly fellow! Rakitin went in as I came out. Perhaps Rakitin is egging him on. What do you think?" she added carelessly.

"He loves you, that's what it is: he loves you so much. And now he is particularly worried."

"I should think he might be, with the trial to-morrow. And I went to him to say something about to-morrow, for I dread to think what's going to happen then. You say that he is worried, but how worried I am! And he talks about the Pole! He's too silly! He is not jealous of Maximushka yet, anyway."

"My wife was dreadfully jealous over me, too," Maximov put in his word.

"Jealous of you?" Grushenka laughed in spite of herself. "Of whom could she have been jealous?"

"Of the servant girls."

"Hold your tongue, Maximushka, I am in no laughing mood now; I feel angry. Don't ogle the pies. I shan't give you any; they are not good for you, and I won't give you any vodka either. I have to look after him, too, just as though I kept an almshouse," she laughed.

"I don't deserve your kindness. I am a worthless creature," said Maximov, with tears in his voice. "You would do better to spend your kindness on people of more use than me."

"Ech, every one is of use, Maximushka, and how can we tell who's of most use? If only that Pole didn't exist, Alyosha. He's taken it into his head to fall ill, too, to-day. I've been to see him also. And I shall send him some pies, too, on purpose. I hadn't sent him any, but Mitya accused me of it, so now I shall send some! Ah, here's Fenya with a letter! Yes, it's from the Poles—begging again!"

Pan Mussyalovitch had indeed sent an extremely long and characteristically eloquent letter in which he begged her to lend him three roubles. In the letter was enclosed a receipt for the sum, with a promise to repay it within three months, signed by Pan Vrublevsky as well. Grushenka had received many such letters, accompanied by such receipts, from her former lover during the fortnight of her convalescence. But she knew that the two Poles had been to ask after her health during her illness. The first letter Grushenka got from them was a long one, written on large notepaper and with a big family crest on the seal. It was so obscure and rhetorical that Grushenka put it down before she had read half, unable to make head or tail of it. She could not attend to letters then. The first letter was followed next day by another in which Pan Mussyalovitch begged her for a loan of two thousand roubles for a very short period. Grushenka left that letter, too, unanswered. A whole series of letters had followed—one every day—all as pompous and rhetorical, but the loan asked for, gradually diminishing, dropped to a hundred roubles, then to twenty-five, to ten, and finally Grushenka received a letter in which both the Poles begged her for only one rouble and included a receipt signed by both.

Then Grushenka suddenly felt sorry for them, and at dusk she went round herself to their lodging. She found the two Poles in great poverty, almost destitution, without food or fuel, without cigarettes, in debt to their landlady. The two hundred roubles they had carried off from Mitya at Mokroe had soon disappeared. But Grushenka was surprised at their meeting her with arrogant dignity and self-assertion, with the greatest punctilio and pompous speeches. Grushenka simply laughed, and gave her former admirer ten roubles. Then, laughing, she told Mitya of it and he was not in the least jealous. But ever since, the Poles had attached themselves to Grushenka and bombarded her daily with requests for money and she had always sent them small sums. And now that day Mitya had taken it into his head to be fearfully jealous.

"Like a fool, I went round to him just for a minute, on the way to see Mitya, for he is ill, too, my Pole," Grushenka began again with nervous haste. "I was laughing, telling Mitya about it. 'Fancy,' I said, 'my Pole had the happy thought to sing his old songs to me to the guitar. He thought I would be touched and marry him!' Mitya leapt up swearing.... So, there, I'll send them the pies! Fenya, is it that little girl they've sent? Here, give her three roubles and pack a dozen pies up in a paper and tell her to take them. And you, Alyosha, be sure to tell Mitya that I did send them the pies."

"I wouldn't tell him for anything," said Alyosha, smiling.

"Ech! You think he is unhappy about it. Why, he's jealous on purpose. He doesn't care," said Grushenka bitterly.

"On purpose?" queried Alyosha.

"I tell you you are silly, Alyosha. You know nothing about it, with all your cleverness. I am not offended that he is jealous of a girl like me. I would be offended if he were not jealous. I am like that. I am not offended at jealousy. I have a fierce heart, too. I can be jealous myself. Only what offends me is that he doesn't love me at all. I tell you he is jealous now *on purpose*. Am I blind? Don't I see? He began talking to me just now of that woman, of Katerina, saying she was this and that, how she had ordered a doctor from Moscow for him, to try and save him; how she had ordered the best counsel, the most learned one, too. So he loves her, if he'll praise her to my face, more shame to him! He's treated me badly himself, so he attacked me, to make out I am in fault first and to throw it all on me. 'You were with your Pole before me, so I can't be blamed for Katerina,' that's what it amounts to. He wants to throw the whole blame on me. He attacked me on purpose, on purpose, I tell you, but I'll—"

Grushenka could not finish saying what she would do. She hid her eyes in her handkerchief and sobbed violently.

"He doesn't love Katerina Ivanovna," said Alyosha firmly.

"Well, whether he loves her or not, I'll soon find out for myself," said Grushenka, with a menacing note in her voice, taking the handkerchief from her eyes. Her face was distorted. Alyosha saw sorrowfully that from being mild and serene, it had become sullen and spiteful.

"Enough of this foolishness," she said suddenly; "it's not for that I sent for you. Alyosha, darling, to-morrow—what will happen to-morrow? That's what worries me! And it's only me it worries! I look at every one and no one is thinking of it. No one cares about it. Are you thinking about it even? To-morrow he'll be tried, you know. Tell me, how will he be tried? You know it's the valet, the valet killed him! Good heavens! Can they condemn him in place of the valet and will no one stand up for him? They haven't troubled the valet at all, have they?"

"He's been severely cross-examined," observed Alyosha thoughtfully; "but every one came to the conclusion it was not he. Now he is lying very ill. He has been ill ever since that attack. Really ill," added Alyosha.

"Oh, dear! couldn't you go to that counsel yourself and tell him the whole thing by yourself? He's been brought from Petersburg for three thousand roubles, they say."

"We gave these three thousand together—Ivan, Katerina Ivanovna and I—but she paid two thousand for the doctor from Moscow herself. The counsel Fetyukovitch would have charged more, but the case has become known all over Russia; it's talked of in all the papers and journals. Fetyukovitch agreed to come more for the glory of the thing, because the case has become so notorious. I saw him yesterday."

"Well? Did you talk to him?" Grushenka put in eagerly.

"He listened and said nothing. He told me that he had already formed his opinion. But he promised to give my words consideration."

"Consideration! Ah, they are swindlers! They'll ruin him. And why did she send for the doctor?"

"As an expert. They want to prove that Mitya's mad and committed the murder when he didn't know what he was doing"; Alyosha smiled gently; "but Mitya won't agree to that."

"Yes; but that would be the truth if he had killed him!" cried Grushenka. "He was mad then, perfectly mad, and that was my fault, wretch that I am! But, of course, he didn't do it, he didn't do it! And they are all against him, the whole town. Even Fenya's evidence went to prove he had done it. And the people at the shop, and that official, and at the tavern, too, before, people had heard him say so! They are all, all against him, all crying out against him."

"Yes, there's a fearful accumulation of evidence," Alyosha observed grimly.

"And Grigory—Grigory Vassilyevitch—sticks to his story that the door was open, persists that he saw it—there's no shaking him. I went and talked to him myself. He's rude about it, too."

"Yes, that's perhaps the strongest evidence against him," said Alyosha.

"And as for Mitya's being mad, he certainly seems like it now," Grushenka began with a peculiarly anxious and mysterious air. "Do you know, Alyosha, I've been wanting to talk to you about it for a long time. I go to him every day and simply wonder at him. Tell me, now, what do you suppose he's always talking about? He talks and talks and I can make nothing of it. I fancied he was talking of something intellectual that I couldn't understand in my foolishness. Only he suddenly began talking to me about a babe—that is, about some child. 'Why is the babe poor?' he said. 'It's for that babe I am going to Siberia now. I am not a murderer, but I must go to Siberia!' What that meant, what babe, I couldn't tell for the life of me. Only I cried when he said it, because he said it so nicely. He cried himself, and I cried, too. He suddenly kissed me and made the sign of the cross over me. What did it mean, Alyosha, tell me? What is this babe?"

"It must be Rakitin, who's been going to see him lately," smiled Alyosha, "though ... that's not Rakitin's doing. I didn't see Mitya yesterday. I'll see him to-day."

"No, it's not Rakitin; it's his brother Ivan Fyodorovitch upsetting him. It's his going to see him, that's what it is," Grushenka began, and suddenly broke off. Alyosha gazed at her in amazement.

"Ivan's going? Has he been to see him? Mitya told me himself that Ivan hasn't been once."

"There ... there! What a girl I am! Blurring things out!" exclaimed Grushenka, confused and suddenly blushing. "Stay, Alyosha, hush! Since I've said so much I'll tell the whole truth—he's been to see him twice, the first directly he arrived. He galloped here from Moscow at once, of course, before I was taken ill; and the second time was a week ago. He told Mitya not to tell you about it, under any circumstances; and not to tell any one, in fact. He came secretly."

Alyosha sat plunged in thought, considering something. The news evidently impressed him.

"Ivan doesn't talk to me of Mitya's case," he said slowly. "He's said very little to me these last two months. And whenever I go to see him, he seems vexed at my coming, so I've not been to him for the last three weeks. H'm!... if he was there a week ago ... there certainly has been a change in Mitya this week."

"There has been a change," Grushenka assented quickly. "They have a secret, they have a secret! Mitya told me himself there was a secret, and such a secret that Mitya can't rest. Before then, he was cheerful—and, indeed, he is cheerful now—but when he shakes his head like that, you know, and strides about the room and keeps pulling at the hair on his right temple with his right hand, I know there is something on his mind worrying him.... I know! He was cheerful before, though, indeed, he is cheerful to-day."

"But you said he was worried."

"Yes, he is worried and yet cheerful. He keeps on being irritable for a minute and then cheerful and then irritable again. And you know, Alyosha, I am constantly wondering at him—with this awful thing hanging over him, he sometimes laughs at such trifles as though he were a baby himself."

"And did he really tell you not to tell me about Ivan? Did he say, 'Don't tell him'?"

"Yes, he told me, 'Don't tell him.' It's you that Mitya's most afraid of. Because it's a secret: he said himself it was a secret. Alyosha, darling, go to him and find out what their secret is and come and tell me," Grushenka besought him with sudden eagerness. "Set my mind at rest that I may know the worst that's in store for me. That's why I sent for you."

"You think it's something to do with you? If it were, he wouldn't have told you there was a secret."

"I don't know. Perhaps he wants to tell me, but doesn't dare to. He warns me. There is a secret, he tells me, but he won't tell me what it is."

"What do you think yourself?"

"What do I think? It's the end for me, that's what I think. They all three have been plotting my end, for Katerina's in it. It's all Katerina, it all comes from her. She is this and that, and that means that I am not. He tells me that beforehand—warns me. He is planning to throw me over, that's the whole secret. They've planned it together, the three of them—Mitya, Katerina, and Ivan Fyodorovitch. Alyosha, I've been wanting to ask you a long time. A week ago he suddenly told me that Ivan was in love with Katerina, because he often goes to see her. Did he tell me the truth or not? Tell me, on your conscience, tell me the worst."

"I won't tell you a lie. Ivan is not in love with Katerina Ivanovna, I think."

"Oh, that's what I thought! He is lying to me, shameless deceiver, that's what it is! And he was jealous of me just now, so as to put the blame on me afterwards. He is stupid, he can't disguise what he is doing; he is so open, you know.... But I'll give it to him, I'll give it to him! 'You believe I did it,' he said. He said that to me, to me. He reproached me with that! God forgive him! You wait, I'll make it hot for Katerina at the trial! I'll just say a word then ... I'll tell everything then!"

And again she cried bitterly.

"This I can tell you for certain, Grushenka," Alyosha said, getting up. "First, that he loves you, loves you more than any one in the world, and you only, believe me. I know. I do know. The second thing is that I don't want to worm his secret out of him, but if he'll tell me of himself to-day, I shall tell him straight out that I have promised to tell you. Then I'll come to you to-day, and tell you. Only ... I fancy ... Katerina Ivanovna has nothing to do with it, and that the secret is about something else. That's certain. It isn't likely it's about Katerina Ivanovna, it seems to me. Good-by for now."

Alyosha shook hands with her. Grushenka was still crying. He saw that she put little faith in his consolation, but she was better for having had her sorrow out, for having spoken of it. He was sorry to leave her in such a state of mind, but he was in haste. He had a great many things to do still.

The first of these things was at the house of Madame Hohlakov, and he hurried there to get it over as quickly as possible and not be too late for Mitya. Madame Hohlakov had been slightly ailing for the last three weeks: her foot had for some reason swollen up, and though she was not in bed, she lay all day half-reclining on the couch in her boudoir, in a fascinating but decorous *déshabillé*. Alyosha had once noted with innocent amusement that, in spite of her illness, Madame Hohlakov had begun to be rather dressy—top-knots, ribbons, loose wrappers, had made their appearance, and he had an inkling of the reason, though he dismissed such ideas from his mind as frivolous. During the last two months the young official, Perhotin, had become a regular visitor at the house.

Alyosha had not called for four days and he was in haste to go straight to Lise, as it was with her he had to speak, for Lise had sent a maid to him the previous day, specially asking him to come to her "about something very important," a request which, for certain reasons, had interest for Alyosha. But while the maid went to take his name in to Lise, Madame Hohlakov heard of his arrival from some one, and immediately sent to beg him to come to her "just for one minute." Alyosha reflected that it was better to accede to the mamma's request, or else she would be sending down to Lise's room every minute that he was there. Madame Hohlakov was lying on a couch. She was particularly smartly dressed and was evidently in a state of extreme nervous excitement. She greeted Alyosha with cries of rapture.

"It's ages, ages, perfect ages since I've seen you! It's a whole week—only think of it! Ah, but you were here only four days ago, on Wednesday. You have come to see Lise. I'm sure you meant to slip into her room on tiptoe, without my hearing you. My dear, dear Alexey Fyodorovitch, if you only knew how worried I am about her! But of that later, though that's the most important thing, of that later. Dear Alexey Fyodorovitch, I trust you implicitly with my Lise. Since the death of Father Zossima—God rest his soul!" (she crossed herself)—"I look upon you as a monk, though you look charming in your new suit. Where did you find such a tailor in these parts? No, no, that's not the chief thing—of that later. Forgive me for sometimes calling you Alyosha; an old woman like me may take liberties," she smiled coquettishly; "but that will do later, too. The important thing is that I shouldn't forget what is important. Please remind me of it yourself. As soon as my tongue runs away with me, you just say 'the important thing?' Ach! how do I know now what is of most importance? Ever since Lise took back her promise—her childish promise, Alexey Fyodorovitch—to marry you, you've realized, of course, that it was only the playful fancy of a sick child who had been so long confined to her chair—thank God, she can walk now!... that new doctor Katya sent for from Moscow for your unhappy brother, who will to-morrow—But why speak of to-morrow? I am ready to die at the very thought of to-morrow. Ready to die of curiosity.... That doctor was with us yesterday and saw Lise.... I paid him fifty roubles for the visit. But that's not the point, that's not the point again. You see, I'm mixing everything up. I am in such a hurry. Why am I in a hurry? I don't understand. It's awful how I seem growing unable to understand anything. Everything seems mixed up in a sort of tangle. I am afraid you are so bored you will jump up and run away, and that will be all I shall see of you. Goodness! Why are we sitting here and no coffee? Yulia, Glafira, coffee!"

Alyosha made haste to thank her, and said that he had only just had coffee.

"Where?"

"At Agrafena Alexandrovna's."

"At ... at that woman's? Ah, it's she has brought ruin on every one. I know nothing about it though. They say she has become a saint, though it's rather late in the day. She had better have done it before. What use is it now? Hush, hush, Alexey Fyodorovitch, for I have so much to say to you that I am afraid I shall tell you nothing. This awful trial ... I shall certainly go, I am making arrangements. I shall be carried there in my chair; besides I can sit up. I shall have people with me. And, you know, I am a witness. How shall I speak, how shall I speak? I don't know what I shall say. One has to take an oath, hasn't one?"

"Yes; but I don't think you will be able to go."

"I can sit up. Ah, you put me out! Ah! this trial, this savage act, and then they are all going to Siberia, some are getting married, and all this so quickly, so quickly, everything's changing, and at last—nothing. All grow old and have death to look forward to. Well, so be it! I am weary. This Katya, *cette charmante personne*, has disappointed all my hopes. Now she is going to follow one of your brothers to Siberia, and your other brother is going to follow her, and will live in the nearest town, and they will all torment one another. It drives me out of my mind. Worst of all—the publicity. The story has been told a million times over in all the papers in Moscow and Petersburg. Ah! yes, would you believe it, there's a paragraph that I was 'a dear friend' of your brother's ——, I can't repeat the horrid word. Just fancy, just fancy!"

"Impossible! Where was the paragraph? What did it say?"

"I'll show you directly. I got the paper and read it yesterday. Here, in the Petersburg paper *Gossip*. The paper began coming out this year. I am awfully fond of gossip, and I take it in, and now it pays me out—this is what gossip comes to! Here it is, here, this passage. Read it."

And she handed Alyosha a sheet of newspaper which had been under her pillow.

It was not exactly that she was upset, she seemed overwhelmed and perhaps everything really was mixed up in a tangle in her head. The paragraph was very typical, and must have been a great shock to her, but, fortunately perhaps, she was unable to keep her mind fixed on any one subject at that moment, and so might race off in a minute to something else and quite forget the newspaper.

Alyosha was well aware that the story of the terrible case had spread all over Russia. And, good heavens! what wild rumors about his brother, about the Karamazovs, and about himself he had read in the course of those two months, among other equally credible items! One paper had even stated that he had gone into a monastery and become a monk, in horror at his brother's crime. Another contradicted this, and stated that he and his elder, Father Zossima, had broken into the monastery chest and "made tracks from the monastery." The present paragraph in the paper *Gossip* was under the heading, "The Karamazov Case at Skotoprigonyevsk." (That, alas! was the name of our little town. I had hitherto kept it concealed.) It was brief, and Madame Hohlakov was not directly mentioned in it. No names appeared, in fact. It was merely stated that the criminal, whose approaching trial was making such a sensation—retired army captain, an idle swaggerer, and reactionary bully—was continually involved in amorous intrigues, and particularly popular with certain ladies "who were pining in solitude." One such lady, a pining widow, who tried to seem young though she had a grown-up daughter, was so fascinated by him that only two hours before the crime she offered him three thousand roubles, on condition that he would elope with her to the gold mines. But the criminal, counting on escaping punishment, had preferred to murder his father to get the three thousand rather than go off to Siberia with the middle-aged charms of his pining lady. This playful paragraph finished, of course, with an outburst of generous indignation at the wickedness of parricide and at the lately abolished institution of serfdom. Reading it with curiosity, Alyosha folded up the paper and handed it back to Madame Hohlakov.

"Well, that must be me," she hurried on again. "Of course I am meant. Scarcely more than an hour before, I suggested gold mines to him, and here they talk of 'middle-aged charms' as though that were my motive! He writes that out of spite! God Almighty forgive him for the middle-aged charms, as I forgive him! You know it's— Do you know who it is? It's your friend Rakitin."

"Perhaps," said Alyosha, "though I've heard nothing about it."

"It's he, it's he! No 'perhaps' about it. You know I turned him out of the house.... You know all that story, don't you?"

"I know that you asked him not to visit you for the future, but why it was, I haven't heard ... from you, at least."

"Ah, then you've heard it from him! He abuses me, I suppose, abuses me dreadfully?"

"Yes, he does; but then he abuses every one. But why you've given him up I haven't heard from him either. I meet him very seldom now, indeed. We are not friends."

"Well, then, I'll tell you all about it. There's no help for it, I'll confess, for there is one point in which I was perhaps to blame. Only a little, little point, so little that perhaps it doesn't count. You see, my dear boy"—Madame Hohlakov suddenly looked arch and a charming, though enigmatic, smile played about her lips—"you see, I suspect ... You must forgive me, Alyosha. I am like a mother to you.... No, no; quite the contrary. I speak to you now as though you were my father—mother's quite out of place. Well, it's as though I were confessing to Father Zossima, that's just it. I called you a monk just now. Well, that poor young man, your friend, Rakitin (Mercy on us! I can't be angry with him. I feel cross, but not very), that frivolous young man, would you believe it, seems to have taken it into his head to fall in love with me. I only noticed it later. At first—a month ago—he only began to come oftener to see me, almost every day; though, of course, we were acquainted before. I knew nothing about it ... and suddenly it dawned upon me, and I began to notice things with surprise. You know, two months ago, that modest, charming, excellent young man, Pyotr Ilyitch Perhotin, who's in the service here, began to be a regular visitor at the house.

You met him here ever so many times yourself. And he is an excellent, earnest young man, isn't he? He comes once every three days, not every day (though I should be glad to see him every day), and always so well dressed. Altogether, I love young people, Alyosha, talented, modest, like you, and he has almost the mind of a statesman, he talks so charmingly, and I shall certainly, certainly try and get promotion for him. He is a future diplomat. On that awful day he almost saved me from death by coming in the night. And your friend Rakitin comes in such boots, and always stretches them out on the carpet.... He began hinting at his feelings, in fact, and one day, as he was going, he squeezed my hand terribly hard. My foot began to swell directly after he pressed my hand like that. He had met Pyotr Ilyitch here before, and would you believe it, he is always gibing at him, growling at him, for some reason. I simply looked at the way they went on together and laughed inwardly. So I was sitting here alone—no, I was laid up then. Well, I was lying here alone and suddenly Rakitin comes in, and only fancy! brought me some verses of his own composition—a short poem, on my bad foot: that is, he described my foot in a poem. Wait a minute—how did it go?

A captivating little foot.

It began somehow like that. I can never remember poetry. I've got it here. I'll show it to you later. But it's a charming thing—charming; and, you know, it's not only about the foot, it had a good moral, too, a charming idea, only I've forgotten it; in fact, it was just the thing for an album. So, of course, I thanked him, and he was evidently flattered. I'd hardly had time to thank him when in comes Pyotr Ilyitch, and Rakitin suddenly looked as black as night. I could see that Pyotr Ilyitch was in the way, for Rakitin certainly wanted to say something after giving me the verses. I had a presentiment of it; but Pyotr Ilyitch came in. I showed Pyotr Ilyitch the verses and didn't say who was the author. But I am convinced that he guessed, though he won't own it to this day, and declares he had no idea. But he says that on purpose. Pyotr Ilyitch began to laugh at once, and fell to criticizing it. 'Wretched doggerel,' he said they were, 'some divinity student must have written them,' and with such vehemence, such vehemence! Then, instead of laughing, your friend flew into a rage. 'Good gracious!' I thought, 'they'll fly at each other.' 'It was I who wrote them,' said he. 'I wrote them as a joke,' he said, 'for I think it degrading to write verses.... But they are good poetry. They want to put a monument to your Pushkin for writing about women's feet, while I wrote with a moral purpose, and you,' said he, 'are an advocate of serfdom. You've no humane ideas,' said he. 'You have no modern enlightened feelings, you are uninfluenced by progress, you are a mere official,' he said, 'and you take bribes.' Then I began screaming and imploring them. And, you know, Pyotr Ilyitch is anything but a coward. He at once took up the most gentlemanly tone, looked at him sarcastically, listened, and apologized. 'I'd no idea,' said he. 'I shouldn't have said it, if I had known. I should have praised it. Poets are all so irritable,' he said. In short, he laughed at him under cover of the most gentlemanly tone. He explained to me afterwards that it was all sarcastic. I thought he was in earnest. Only as I lay there, just as before you now, I thought, 'Would it, or would it not, be the proper thing for me to turn Rakitin out for shouting so rudely at a visitor in my house?' And, would you believe it, I lay here, shut my eyes, and wondered, would it be the proper thing or not. I kept worrying and worrying, and my heart began to beat, and I couldn't make up my mind whether to make an outcry or not. One voice seemed to be telling me, 'Speak,' and the other 'No, don't speak.' And no sooner had the second voice said that than I cried out, and fainted. Of course, there was a fuss. I got up suddenly and said to Rakitin, 'It's painful for me to say it, but I don't wish to see you in my house again.' So I turned him out. Ah! Alexey Fyodorovitch, I know myself I did wrong. I was putting it on. I wasn't angry with him at all, really; but I suddenly fancied—that was what did it—that it would be such a fine scene.... And yet, believe me, it was quite natural, for I really shed tears and cried for several days afterwards, and then suddenly, one afternoon, I forgot all about it. So it's a fortnight since he's been here, and I kept wondering whether he would come again. I wondered even yesterday, then suddenly last night came this *Gossip*. I read it and gasped. Who could have written it? He must have written it. He went home, sat down, wrote it on the spot, sent it, and they put it in. It was a fortnight ago, you see. But, Alyosha, it's awful how I keep talking and don't say what I want to say. Ah! the words come of themselves!"

"It's very important for me to be in time to see my brother to-day," Alyosha faltered.

"To be sure, to be sure! You bring it all back to me. Listen, what is an aberration?"

"What aberration?" asked Alyosha, wondering.

"In the legal sense. An aberration in which everything is pardonable. Whatever you do, you will be acquitted at once."

"What do you mean?"

"I'll tell you. This Katya ... Ah! she is a charming, charming creature, only I never can make out who it is she is in love with. She was with me some time ago and I couldn't get anything out of her. Especially as she won't talk to me except on the surface now. She is always talking about my health and nothing else, and she takes up such a tone with me, too. I simply said to myself, 'Well, so be it. I don't care'... Oh, yes. I was talking of aberration. This doctor has come. You know a doctor has come? Of course, you know it— the one who discovers madmen. You wrote for him. No, it wasn't you, but Katya. It's all Katya's doing. Well, you see, a man may be sitting perfectly sane and suddenly have an aberration. He may be conscious and know what he is doing and yet be in a state of aberration. And there's no doubt that Dmitri Fyodorovitch was suffering from aberration. They found out about aberration as soon as the law courts were reformed. It's all the good effect of the reformed law courts. The doctor has been here and questioned me about that evening, about the gold mines. 'How did he seem then?' he asked me. He must have been in a state of aberration. He came in shouting, 'Money, money, three thousand! Give me three thousand!' and then went away and immediately did the murder. 'I don't want to murder him,' he said, and he suddenly went and murdered him. That's why they'll acquit him, because he struggled against it and yet he murdered him."

"But he didn't murder him," Alyosha interrupted rather sharply. He felt more and more sick with anxiety and impatience.

"Yes, I know it was that old man Grigory murdered him."

"Grigory?" cried Alyosha.

"Yes, yes; it was Grigory. He lay as Dmitri Fyodorovitch struck him down, and then got up, saw the door open, went in and killed Fyodor Pavlovitch."

"But why, why?"

"Suffering from aberration. When he recovered from the blow Dmitri Fyodorovitch gave him on the head, he was suffering from aberration; he went and committed the murder. As for his saying he didn't, he very likely doesn't remember. Only, you know, it'll be better, ever so much better, if Dmitri Fyodorovitch murdered him. And that's how it must have been, though I say it was Grigory. It certainly was Dmitri Fyodorovitch, and that's better, ever so much better! Oh! not better that a son should have killed his father, I don't defend that. Children ought to honor their parents, and yet it would be better if it were he, as you'd have nothing to cry over then, for he did it when he was unconscious or rather when he was conscious, but did not know what he was doing. Let them acquit him— that's so humane, and would show what a blessing reformed law courts are. I knew nothing about it, but they say they have been so a long time. And when I heard it yesterday, I was so struck by it that I wanted to send for you at once. And if he is acquitted, make him come straight from the law courts to dinner with me, and I'll have a party of friends, and we'll drink to the reformed law courts. I don't believe he'd be dangerous; besides, I'll invite a great many friends, so that he could always be led out if he did anything. And then he might be made a justice of the peace or something in another town, for those who have been in trouble themselves make the best judges. And, besides, who isn't suffering from aberration nowadays?—you, I, all of us are in a state of aberration, and there are ever so many examples of it: a man sits singing a song, suddenly something annoys him, he takes a pistol and shoots the first person he comes across, and no one blames him for it. I read that lately, and all the doctors confirm it. The doctors are always confirming; they confirm anything. Why, my Lise is in a state of aberration. She made me cry again yesterday, and the day before, too, and to-day I suddenly realized that it's all due to aberration. Oh, Lise grieves me so! I believe she's quite mad. Why did she send for you? Did she send for you or did you come of yourself?"

"Yes, she sent for me, and I am just going to her." Alyosha got up resolutely.

"Oh, my dear, dear Alexey Fyodorovitch, perhaps that's what's most important," Madame Hohlakov cried, suddenly bursting into tears. "God knows I trust Lise to you with all my heart, and it's no matter her sending for you on the sly, without telling her mother.

But forgive me, I can't trust my daughter so easily to your brother Ivan Fyodorovitch, though I still consider him the most chivalrous young man. But only fancy, he's been to see Lise and I knew nothing about it!"

"How? What? When?" Alyosha was exceedingly surprised. He had not sat down again and listened standing.

"I will tell you; that's perhaps why I asked you to come, for I don't know now why I did ask you to come. Well, Ivan Fyodorovitch has been to see me twice, since he came back from Moscow. First time he came as a friend to call on me, and the second time Katya was here and he came because he heard she was here. I didn't, of course, expect him to come often, knowing what a lot he has to do as it is, *vous comprenez, cette affaire et la mort terrible de votre papa.* But I suddenly heard he'd been here again, not to see me but to see Lise. That's six days ago now. He came, stayed five minutes, and went away. And I didn't hear of it till three days afterwards, from Glafira, so it was a great shock to me. I sent for Lise directly. She laughed. 'He thought you were asleep,' she said, 'and came in to me to ask after your health.' Of course, that's how it happened. But Lise, Lise, mercy on us, how she distresses me! Would you believe it, one night, four days ago, just after you saw her last time, and had gone away, she suddenly had a fit, screaming, shrieking, hysterics! Why is it I never have hysterics? Then, next day another fit, and the same thing on the third, and yesterday too, and then yesterday that aberration. She suddenly screamed out, 'I hate Ivan Fyodorovitch. I insist on your never letting him come to the house again.' I was struck dumb at these amazing words, and answered, 'On what grounds could I refuse to see such an excellent young man, a young man of such learning too, and so unfortunate?'—for all this business is a misfortune, isn't it? She suddenly burst out laughing at my words, and so rudely, you know. Well, I was pleased; I thought I had amused her and the fits would pass off, especially as I wanted to refuse to see Ivan Fyodorovitch anyway on account of his strange visits without my knowledge, and meant to ask him for an explanation. But early this morning Lise waked up and flew into a passion with Yulia and, would you believe it, slapped her in the face. That's monstrous; I am always polite to my servants. And an hour later she was hugging Yulia's feet and kissing them. She sent a message to me that she wasn't coming to me at all, and would never come and see me again, and when I dragged myself down to her, she rushed to kiss me, crying, and as she kissed me, she pushed me out of the room without saying a word, so I couldn't find out what was the matter. Now, dear Alexey Fyodorovitch, I rest all my hopes on you, and, of course, my whole life is in your hands. I simply beg you to go to Lise and find out everything from her, as you alone can, and come back and tell me—me, her mother, for you understand it will be the death of me, simply the death of me, if this goes on, or else I shall run away. I can stand no more. I have patience; but I may lose patience, and then ... then something awful will happen. Ah, dear me! At last, Pyotr Ilyitch!" cried Madame Hohlakov, beaming all over as she saw Perhotin enter the room. "You are late, you are late! Well, sit down, speak, put us out of suspense. What does the counsel say. Where are you off to, Alexey Fyodorovitch?"

"To Lise."

"Oh, yes. You won't forget, you won't forget what I asked you? It's a question of life and death!"

"Of course, I won't forget, if I can ... but I am so late," muttered Alyosha, beating a hasty retreat.

"No, be sure, be sure to come in; don't say 'If you can.' I shall die if you don't," Madame Hohlakov called after him, but Alyosha had already left the room.

Going in to Lise, he found her half reclining in the invalid-chair, in which she had been wheeled when she was unable to walk. She did not move to meet him, but her sharp, keen eyes were simply riveted on his face. There was a feverish look in her eyes, her face was pale and yellow. Alyosha was amazed at the change that had taken place in her in three days. She was positively thinner. She did not hold out her hand to him. He touched the thin, long fingers which lay motionless on her dress, then he sat down facing her, without a word.

"I know you are in a hurry to get to the prison," Lise said curtly, "and mamma's kept you there for hours; she's just been telling you about me and Yulia."

"How do you know?" asked Alyosha.

"I've been listening. Why do you stare at me? I want to listen and I do listen, there's no harm in that. I don't apologize."

"You are upset about something?"

"On the contrary, I am very happy. I've only just been reflecting for the thirtieth time what a good thing it is I refused you and shall not be your wife. You are not fit to be a husband. If I were to marry you and give you a note to take to the man I loved after you, you'd take it and be sure to give it to him and bring an answer back, too. If you were forty, you would still go on taking my love-letters for me."

She suddenly laughed.

"There is something spiteful and yet open-hearted about you," Alyosha smiled to her.

"The open-heartedness consists in my not being ashamed of myself with you. What's more, I don't want to feel ashamed with you, just with you. Alyosha, why is it I don't respect you? I am very fond of you, but I don't respect you. If I respected you, I shouldn't talk to you without shame, should I?"

"No."

"But do you believe that I am not ashamed with you?"

"No, I don't believe it."

Lise laughed nervously again; she spoke rapidly.

"I sent your brother, Dmitri Fyodorovitch, some sweets in prison. Alyosha, you know, you are quite pretty! I shall love you awfully for having so quickly allowed me not to love you."

"Why did you send for me to-day, Lise?"

"I wanted to tell you of a longing I have. I should like some one to torture me, marry me and then torture me, deceive me and go away. I don't want to be happy."

"You are in love with disorder?"

"Yes, I want disorder. I keep wanting to set fire to the house. I keep imagining how I'll creep up and set fire to the house on the sly; it must be on the sly. They'll try to put it out, but it'll go on burning. And I shall know and say nothing. Ah, what silliness! And how bored I am!"

She waved her hand with a look of repulsion.

"It's your luxurious life," said Alyosha, softly.

"Is it better, then, to be poor?"

"Yes, it is better."

"That's what your monk taught you. That's not true. Let me be rich and all the rest poor, I'll eat sweets and drink cream and not give any to any one else. Ach, don't speak, don't say anything," she shook her hand at him, though Alyosha had not opened his mouth. "You've told me all that before, I know it all by heart. It bores me. If I am ever poor, I shall murder somebody, and even if I am rich, I may murder some one, perhaps— why do nothing! But do you know, I should like to reap, cut the rye? I'll marry you, and you shall become a peasant, a real peasant; we'll keep a colt, shall we? Do you know Kalganov?"

"Yes."

"He is always wandering about, dreaming. He says, 'Why live in real life? It's better to dream. One can dream the most delightful things, but real life is a bore.' But he'll be married soon for all that; he's been making love to me already. Can you spin tops?"

"Yes."

"Well, he's just like a top: he wants to be wound up and set spinning and then to be lashed, lashed, lashed with a whip. If I marry him, I'll keep him spinning all his life. You are not ashamed to be with me?"

"No."

"You are awfully cross, because I don't talk about holy things. I don't want to be holy. What will they do to one in the next world for the greatest sin? You must know all about that."

"God will censure you." Alyosha was watching her steadily.

"That's just what I should like. I would go up and they would censure me, and I would burst out laughing in their faces. I should dreadfully like to set fire to the house, Alyosha, to our house; you still don't believe me?"

"Why? There are children of twelve years old, who have a longing to set fire to something and they do set things on fire, too. It's a sort of disease."

"That's not true, that's not true; there may be children, but that's not what I mean."

"You take evil for good; it's a passing crisis, it's the result of your illness, perhaps."

"You do despise me, though! It's simply that I don't want to do good, I want to do evil, and it has nothing to do with illness."

"Why do evil?"

"So that everything might be destroyed. Ah, how nice it would be if everything were destroyed! You know, Alyosha, I sometimes think of doing a fearful lot of harm and everything bad, and I should do it for a long while on the sly and suddenly every one would find it out. Every one will stand round and point their fingers at me and I would look at them all. That would be awfully nice. Why would it be so nice, Alyosha?"

"I don't know. It's a craving to destroy something good or, as you say, to set fire to something. It happens sometimes."

"I not only say it, I shall do it."

"I believe you."

"Ah, how I love you for saying you believe me. And you are not lying one little bit. But perhaps you think that I am saying all this on purpose to annoy you?"

"No, I don't think that ... though perhaps there is a little desire to do that in it, too."

"There is a little. I never can tell lies to you," she declared, with a strange fire in her eyes.

What struck Alyosha above everything was her earnestness. There was not a trace of humor or jesting in her face now, though, in old days, fun and gayety never deserted her even at her most "earnest" moments.

"There are moments when people love crime," said Alyosha thoughtfully.

"Yes, yes! You have uttered my thought; they love crime, every one loves crime, they love it always, not at some 'moments.' You know, it's as though people have made an agreement to lie about it and have lied about it ever since. They all declare that they hate evil, but secretly they all love it."

"And are you still reading nasty books?"

"Yes, I am. Mamma reads them and hides them under her pillow and I steal them."

"Aren't you ashamed to destroy yourself?"

"I want to destroy myself. There's a boy here, who lay down between the railway lines when the train was passing. Lucky fellow! Listen, your brother is being tried now for murdering his father and every one loves his having killed his father."

"Loves his having killed his father?"

"Yes, loves it; every one loves it! Everybody says it's so awful, but secretly they simply love it. I for one love it."

"There is some truth in what you say about every one," said Alyosha softly.

"Oh, what ideas you have!" Lise shrieked in delight. "And you a monk, too! You wouldn't believe how I respect you, Alyosha, for never telling lies. Oh, I must tell you a funny dream of mine. I sometimes dream of devils. It's night; I am in my room with a candle and suddenly there are devils all over the place, in all the corners, under the table, and they open the doors; there's a crowd of them behind the doors and they want to come and seize me. And they are just coming, just seizing me. But I suddenly cross myself and they all draw back, though they don't go away altogether, they stand at the doors and in the corners, waiting. And suddenly I have a frightful longing to revile God aloud, and so I begin, and then they come crowding back to me, delighted, and seize me again and I cross myself again and they all draw back. It's awful fun. it takes one's breath away."

"I've had the same dream, too," said Alyosha suddenly.

"Really?" cried Lise, surprised. "I say, Alyosha, don't laugh, that's awfully important. Could two different people have the same dream?"

"It seems they can."

"Alyosha, I tell you, it's awfully important," Lise went on, with really excessive amazement. "It's not the dream that's important, but your having the same dream as me. You never lie to me, don't lie now: is it true? You are not laughing?"

"It's true."

Lise seemed extraordinarily impressed and for half a minute she was silent.

"Alyosha, come and see me, come and see me more often," she said suddenly, in a supplicating voice.

"I'll always come to see you, all my life," answered Alyosha firmly.

"You are the only person I can talk to, you know," Lise began again. "I talk to no one but myself and you. Only you in the whole world. And to you more readily than to myself. And I am not a bit ashamed with you, not a bit. Alyosha, why am I not ashamed with you, not a bit? Alyosha, is it true that at Easter the Jews steal a child and kill it?"

"I don't know."

"There's a book here in which I read about the trial of a Jew, who took a child of four years old and cut off the fingers from both hands, and then crucified him on the wall, hammered nails into him and crucified him, and afterwards, when he was tried, he said that the child died soon, within four hours. That was 'soon'! He said the child moaned, kept on moaning and he stood admiring it. That's nice!"

"Nice?"

"Nice; I sometimes imagine that it was I who crucified him. He would hang there moaning and I would sit opposite him eating pineapple *compote*. I am awfully fond of pineapple *compote*. Do you like it?"

Alyosha looked at her in silence. Her pale, sallow face was suddenly contorted, her eyes burned.

"You know, when I read about that Jew I shook with sobs all night. I kept fancying how the little thing cried and moaned (a child of four years old understands, you know), and all the while the thought of pineapple *compote* haunted me. In the morning I wrote a letter to a certain person, begging him *particularly* to come and see me. He came and I suddenly told him all about the child and the pineapple *compote*. *All* about it, *all*, and said that it was nice. He laughed and said it really was nice. Then he got up and went away. He was only here five minutes. Did he despise me? Did he despise me? Tell me, tell me, Alyosha, did he despise me or not?" She sat up on the couch, with flashing eyes.

"Tell me," Alyosha asked anxiously, "did you send for that person?"

"Yes, I did."

"Did you send him a letter?"

"Yes."

"Simply to ask about that, about that child?"

"No, not about that at all. But when he came, I asked him about that at once. He answered, laughed, got up and went away."

"That person behaved honorably," Alyosha murmured.

"And did he despise me? Did he laugh at me?"

"No, for perhaps he believes in the pineapple *compote* himself. He is very ill now, too, Lise."

"Yes, he does believe in it," said Lise, with flashing eyes.

"He doesn't despise any one," Alyosha went on. "Only he does not believe any one. If he doesn't believe in people, of course, he does despise them."

"Then he despises me, me?"

"You, too."

"Good," Lise seemed to grind her teeth. "When he went out laughing, I felt that it was nice to be despised. The child with fingers cut off is nice, and to be despised is nice...."

And she laughed in Alyosha's face, a feverish malicious laugh.

"Do you know, Alyosha, do you know, I should like—Alyosha, save me!" She suddenly jumped from the couch, rushed to him and seized him with both hands. "Save me!" she almost groaned. "Is there any one in the world I could tell what I've told you? I've told you the truth, the truth. I shall kill myself, because I loathe everything! I don't want to live, because I loathe everything! I loathe everything, everything. Alyosha, why don't you love me in the least?" she finished in a frenzy.

"But I do love you!" answered Alyosha warmly.

"And will you weep over me, will you?"

"Yes."

"Not because I won't be your wife, but simply weep for me?"

"Yes."

"Thank you! It's only your tears I want. Every one else may punish me and trample me under foot, every one, every one, not excepting *any one*. For I don't love any one. Do you hear, not any one! On the contrary, I hate him! Go, Alyosha; it's time you went to your brother"; she tore herself away from him suddenly.

"How can I leave you like this?" said Alyosha, almost in alarm.

"Go to your brother, the prison will be shut; go, here's your hat. Give my love to Mitya, go, go!"

And she almost forcibly pushed Alyosha out of the door. He looked at her with pained surprise, when he was suddenly aware of a letter in his right hand, a tiny letter folded up tight and sealed. He glanced at it and instantly read the address, "To Ivan Fyodorovitch Karamazov." He looked quickly at Lise. Her face had become almost menacing.

"Give it to him, you must give it to him!" she ordered him, trembling and beside herself. "To-day, at once, or I'll poison myself! That's why I sent for you."

And she slammed the door quickly. The bolt clicked. Alyosha put the note in his pocket and went straight downstairs, without going back to Madame Hohlakov; forgetting her, in fact. As soon as Alyosha had gone, Lise unbolted the door, opened it a little, put her finger in the crack and slammed the door with all her might, pinching her finger. Ten seconds after, releasing her finger, she walked softly, slowly to her chair, sat up straight in it and looked intently at her blackened finger and at the blood that oozed from under the nail. Her lips were quivering and she kept whispering rapidly to herself:

"I am a wretch, wretch, wretch, wretch!"

It was quite late (days are short in November) when Alyosha rang at the prison gate. It was beginning to get dusk. But Alyosha knew that he would be admitted without difficulty. Things were managed in our little town, as everywhere else. At first, of course, on the conclusion of the preliminary inquiry, relations and a few other persons could only obtain interviews with Mitya by going through certain inevitable formalities. But later, though the formalities were not relaxed, exceptions were made for some, at least, of Mitya's visitors. So much so, that sometimes the interviews with the prisoner in the room set aside for the purpose were practically *tête-à-tête*.

These exceptions, however, were few in number; only Grushenka, Alyosha and Rakitin were treated like this. But the captain of the police, Mihail Mihailovitch, was very favorably disposed to Grushenka. His abuse of her at Mokroe weighed on the old man's conscience, and when he learned the whole story, he completely changed his view of her. And strange to say, though he was firmly persuaded of his guilt, yet after Mitya was once in prison, the old man came to take a more and more lenient view of him. "He was a man of good heart, perhaps," he thought, "who had come to grief from drinking and dissipation." His first horror had been succeeded by pity. As for Alyosha, the police captain was very fond of him and had known him for a long time. Rakitin, who had of late taken to coming very often to see the prisoner, was one of the most intimate acquaintances of the "police captain's young ladies," as he called them, and was always hanging about their house. He gave lessons in the house of the prison superintendent, too, who, though scrupulous in the performance of his duties, was a kind-hearted old man. Alyosha, again, had an intimate acquaintance of long standing with the superintendent, who was fond of talking to him, generally on sacred subjects. He respected Ivan Fyodorovitch, and stood in awe of his opinion, though he was a great philosopher himself; "self-taught," of course. But Alyosha had an irresistible attraction for him. During the last year the old man had taken to studying the Apocryphal Gospels, and constantly talked over his impressions with his young friend. He used to come and see him in the monastery and discussed for hours together with him and with the monks. So even if Alyosha were late at the prison, he had only to go to the superintendent and everything was made easy. Besides, every one in the prison, down to the humblest warder, had grown used to Alyosha. The sentry, of course, did not trouble him so long as the authorities were satisfied.

When Mitya was summoned from his cell, he always went downstairs, to the place set aside for interviews. As Alyosha entered the room he came upon Rakitin, who was just taking leave of Mitya. They were both talking loudly. Mitya was laughing heartily as he saw him out, while Rakitin seemed grumbling. Rakitin did not like meeting Alyosha, especially of late. He scarcely spoke to him, and bowed to him stiffly. Seeing Alyosha enter now, he frowned and looked away, as though he were entirely absorbed in buttoning his big, warm, fur-trimmed overcoat. Then he began looking at once for his umbrella.

"I must mind not to forget my belongings," he muttered, simply to say something.

"Mind you don't forget other people's belongings," said Mitya, as a joke, and laughed at once at his own wit. Rakitin fired up instantly.

"You'd better give that advice to your own family, who've always been a slave-driving lot, and not to Rakitin," he cried, suddenly trembling with anger.

"What's the matter? I was joking," cried Mitya. "Damn it all! They are all like that," he turned to Alyosha, nodding towards Rakitin's hurriedly retreating figure. "He was sitting here, laughing and cheerful, and all at once he boils up like that. He didn't even nod to you. Have you broken with him completely? Why are you so late? I've not been simply waiting, but thirsting for you the whole morning. But never mind. We'll make up for it now."

"Why does he come here so often? Surely you are not such great friends?" asked Alyosha. He, too, nodded at the door through which Rakitin had disappeared.

"Great friends with Rakitin? No, not as much as that. Is it likely—a pig like that? He considers I am ... a blackguard. They can't understand a joke either, that's the worst of such people. They never understand a joke, and their souls are dry, dry and flat; they remind me of prison walls when I was first brought here. But he is a clever fellow, very clever. Well, Alexey, it's all over with me now."

He sat down on the bench and made Alyosha sit down beside him.

"Yes, the trial's to-morrow. Are you so hopeless, brother?" Alyosha said, with an apprehensive feeling.

"What are you talking about?" said Mitya, looking at him rather uncertainly. "Oh, you mean the trial! Damn it all! Till now we've been talking of things that don't matter, about this trial, but I haven't said a word to you about the chief thing. Yes, the trial is to-morrow; but it wasn't the trial I meant, when I said it was all over with me. Why do you look at me so critically?"

"What do you mean, Mitya?"

"Ideas, ideas, that's all! Ethics! What is ethics?"

"Ethics?" asked Alyosha, wondering.

"Yes; is it a science?"

"Yes, there is such a science ... but ... I confess I can't explain to you what sort of science it is."

"Rakitin knows. Rakitin knows a lot, damn him! He's not going to be a monk. He means to go to Petersburg. There he'll go in for criticism of an elevating tendency. Who knows, he may be of use and make his own career, too. Ough! they are first-rate, these people, at making a career! Damn ethics, I am done for, Alexey, I am, you man of God! I love you more than any one. It makes my heart yearn to look at you. Who was Karl Bernard?"

"Karl Bernard?" Alyosha was surprised again.

"No, not Karl. Stay, I made a mistake. Claude Bernard. What was he? Chemist or what?"

"He must be a savant," answered Alyosha; "but I confess I can't tell you much about him, either. I've heard of him as a savant, but what sort I don't know."

"Well, damn him, then! I don't know either," swore Mitya. "A scoundrel of some sort, most likely. They are all scoundrels. And Rakitin will make his way. Rakitin will get on anywhere; he is another Bernard. Ugh, these Bernards! They are all over the place."

"But what is the matter?" Alyosha asked insistently.

"He wants to write an article about me, about my case, and so begin his literary career. That's what he comes for; he said so himself. He wants to prove some theory. He wants to say 'he couldn't help murdering his father, he was corrupted by his environment,' and so on. He explained it all to me. He is going to put in a tinge of Socialism, he says. But there, damn the fellow, he can put in a tinge if he likes, I don't care. He can't bear Ivan, he hates him. He's not fond of you, either. But I don't turn him out, for he is a clever fellow. Awfully conceited, though. I said to him just now, 'The Karamazovs are not blackguards, but philosophers; for all true Russians are philosophers, and though you've studied, you are not a philosopher—you are a low fellow.' He laughed, so maliciously. And I said to him, 'De *ideabus non est disputandum.*' Isn't that rather good? I can set up for being a classic, you see!" Mitya laughed suddenly.

"Why is it all over with you? You said so just now," Alyosha interposed.

"Why is it all over with me? H'm!... The fact of it is ... if you take it as a whole, I am sorry to lose God—that's why it is."

"What do you mean by 'sorry to lose God'?"

"Imagine: inside, in the nerves, in the head—that is, these nerves are there in the brain ... (damn them!) there are sort of little tails, the little tails of those nerves, and as soon as they begin quivering ... that is, you see, I look at something with my eyes and then they begin quivering, those little tails ... and when they quiver, then an image appears ... it doesn't appear at once, but an instant, a second, passes ... and then something like a moment appears; that is, not a moment—devil take the moment!—but an image; that is, an object, or an action, damn it! That's why I see and then think, because of those tails, not at all because I've got a soul, and that I am some sort of image and likeness. All that is nonsense! Rakitin explained it all to me yesterday, brother, and it simply bowled me over. It's magnificent, Alyosha, this science! A new man's arising—that I understand.... And yet I am sorry to lose God!"

"Well, that's a good thing, anyway," said Alyosha.

"That I am sorry to lose God? It's chemistry, brother, chemistry! There's no help for it, your reverence, you must make way for chemistry. And Rakitin does dislike God. Ough! doesn't he dislike Him! That's the sore point with all of them. But they conceal it. They tell lies. They pretend. 'Will you preach this in your reviews?' I asked him. 'Oh, well, if I did it openly, they won't let it through,' he said. He laughed. 'But what will become of men then?' I asked him, 'without God and immortal life? All things are lawful then, they can do what they like?' 'Didn't you know?' he said laughing, 'a clever man can do what he likes,' he said. 'A clever man knows his way about, but you've put your foot in it, committing a murder, and now you are rotting in prison.' He says that to my face! A regular pig! I used to kick such people out, but now I listen to them. He talks a lot of sense, too. Writes well. He began reading me an article last week. I copied out three lines of it. Wait a minute. Here it is."

Mitya hurriedly pulled out a piece of paper from his pocket and read:

" 'In order to determine this question, it is above all essential to put one's personality in contradiction to one's reality.' Do you understand that?"

"No, I don't," said Alyosha. He looked at Mitya and listened to him with curiosity.

"I don't understand either. It's dark and obscure, but intellectual. 'Every one writes like that now,' he says, 'it's the effect of their environment.' They are afraid of the environment. He writes poetry, too, the rascal. He's written in honor of Madame Hohlakov's foot. Ha ha ha!"

"I've heard about it," said Alyosha.

"Have you? And have you heard the poem?"

"No."

"I've got it. Here it is. I'll read it to you. You don't know—I haven't told you—there's quite a story about it. He's a rascal! Three weeks ago he began to tease me. 'You've got yourself into a mess, like a fool, for the sake of three thousand, but I'm going to collar a hundred and fifty thousand. I am going to marry a widow and buy a house in Petersburg.' And he told me he was courting Madame Hohlakov. She hadn't much brains in her youth, and now at forty she has lost what she had. 'But she's awfully sentimental,' he says; 'that's how I shall get hold of her. When I marry her, I shall take her to Petersburg and there I shall start a newspaper.' And his mouth was simply watering, the beast, not for the widow, but for the hundred and fifty thousand. And he made me believe it. He came to see me every day. 'She is coming round,' he declared. He was beaming with delight. And then, all of a sudden, he was turned out of the house. Perhotin's carrying everything before him, bravo! I could kiss the silly old noodle for turning him out of the house. And he had written this doggerel. 'It's the first time I've soiled my hands with writing poetry,' he said. 'It's to win her heart, so it's in a good cause. When I get hold of the silly woman's fortune, I can be of great social utility.' They have this social justification for every nasty thing they do! 'Anyway it's better than your Pushkin's poetry,' he said, 'for I've managed to advocate enlightenment even in that.' I understand what he means about Pushkin, I quite see that, if he really was a man of talent and only wrote about women's feet. But wasn't Rakitin stuck up about his doggerel! The vanity of these fellows! 'On the convalescence of the swollen foot of the object of my affections'—he thought of that for a title. He's a waggish fellow.

A captivating little foot,
Though swollen and red and tender!
The doctors come and plasters put,
But still they cannot mend her.
Yet, 'tis not for her foot I dread—
A theme for Pushkin's muse more fit—
It's not her foot, it is her head:
I tremble for her loss of wit!
For as her foot swells, strange to say,
Her intellect is on the wane—
Oh, for some remedy I pray
That may restore both foot and brain!

He is a pig, a regular pig, but he's very arch, the rascal! And he really has put in a progressive idea. And wasn't he angry when she kicked him out! He was gnashing his teeth!"

"He's taken his revenge already," said Alyosha. "He's written a paragraph about Madame Hohlakov."

And Alyosha told him briefly about the paragraph in *Gossip*.

"That's his doing, that's his doing!" Mitya assented, frowning. "That's him! These paragraphs ... I know ... the insulting things that have been written about Grushenka, for instance.... And about Katya, too.... H'm!"

He walked across the room with a harassed air.

"Brother, I cannot stay long," Alyosha said, after a pause. "To-morrow will be a great and awful day for you, the judgment of God will be accomplished ... I am amazed at you, you walk about here, talking of I don't know what ..."

"No, don't be amazed at me," Mitya broke in warmly. "Am I to talk of that stinking dog? Of the murderer? We've talked enough of him. I don't want to say more of the stinking son of Stinking Lizaveta! God will kill him, you will see. Hush!"

He went up to Alyosha excitedly and kissed him. His eyes glowed.

"Rakitin wouldn't understand it," he began in a sort of exaltation; "but you, you'll understand it all. That's why I was thirsting for you. You see, there's so much I've been wanting to tell you for ever so long, here, within these peeling walls, but I haven't said a word about what matters most; the moment never seems to have come. Now I can wait no longer. I must pour out my heart to you. Brother, these last two months I've found in myself a new man. A new man has risen up in me. He was hidden in me, but would never have come to the surface, if it hadn't been for this blow from heaven. I am afraid! And what do I care if I spend twenty years in the mines, breaking ore with a hammer? I am not a bit afraid of that—it's something else I am afraid of now: that that new man may leave me. Even there, in the mines, under-ground, I may find a human heart in another convict and murderer by my side, and I may make friends with him, for even there one may live and love and suffer. One may thaw and revive a frozen heart in that convict, one may wait upon him for years, and at last bring up from the dark depths a lofty soul, a feeling, suffering creature; one may bring forth an angel, create a hero! There are so many of them, hundreds of them, and we are all to blame for them. Why was it I dreamed of that 'babe' at such a moment? 'Why is the babe so poor?' That was a sign to me at that moment. It's for the babe I'm going. Because we are all responsible for all. For all the 'babes,' for there are big children as well as little children. All are 'babes.' I go for all, because some one must go for all. I didn't kill father, but I've got to go. I accept it. It's all come to me here, here, within these peeling walls. There are numbers of them there, hundreds of them underground, with hammers in their hands. Oh, yes, we shall be in chains and there will be no freedom, but then, in our great sorrow, we shall rise again to joy, without which man cannot live nor God exist, for God gives joy: it's His privilege—a grand one. Ah, man should be dissolved in prayer! What should I be underground there without God? Rakitin's laughing! If they drive God from the earth, we shall shelter Him underground. One cannot exist in prison without God; it's even more impossible than out of prison. And then we men underground will sing from the bowels of the earth a glorious hymn to God, with Whom is joy. Hail to God and His joy! I love Him!"

Mitya was almost gasping for breath as he uttered his wild speech. He turned pale, his lips quivered, and tears rolled down his cheeks.

"Yes, life is full, there is life even underground," he began again. "You wouldn't believe, Alexey, how I want to live now, what a thirst for existence and consciousness has sprung up in me within these peeling walls. Rakitin doesn't understand that; all he cares about is building a house and letting flats. But I've been longing for you. And what is suffering? I am not afraid of it, even if it were beyond reckoning. I am not afraid of it now. I was afraid of it before. Do you know, perhaps I won't answer at the trial at all.... And I seem to have such strength in me now, that I think I could stand anything, any suffering, only to be able to say and to repeat to myself every moment, 'I exist.' In thousands of agonies—I exist. I'm tormented on the rack—but I exist! Though I sit alone on a pillar—I exist! I see the sun, and if I don't see the sun, I know it's there. And there's a whole life in that, in knowing that the sun is there. Alyosha, my angel, all these philosophies are the death of me. Damn them! Brother Ivan—"

"What of brother Ivan?" interrupted Alyosha, but Mitya did not hear.

"You see, I never had any of these doubts before, but it was all hidden away in me. It was perhaps just because ideas I did not understand were surging up in me, that I used to drink and fight and rage. It was to stifle them in myself, to still them, to smother them. Ivan is not Rakitin, there is an idea in him. Ivan is a sphinx and is silent; he is always silent. It's God that's worrying me. That's the only thing that's worrying me. What if He doesn't exist? What if Rakitin's right—that it's an idea made up by men? Then if He doesn't exist, man is the chief of the earth, of the universe. Magnificent! Only how is he going to be good without God? That's the question. I always come back to that. For whom is man going to love then? To whom will he be thankful? To whom will he sing the hymn? Rakitin laughs. Rakitin says that one can love humanity without God. Well, only a sniveling idiot can maintain that. I can't understand it. Life's easy for Rakitin. 'You'd better think about the extension of civic rights, or even of keeping down the price of meat. You will show your love for humanity more simply and directly by that, than by philosophy.' I answered him, 'Well, but you, without a God, are more likely to raise the price of meat, if it suits you, and make a rouble on every copeck.' He lost his temper. But after all, what is goodness? Answer me that, Alexey. Goodness is one thing with me and another with a Chinaman, so it's a relative thing. Or isn't it? Is it not relative? A treacherous question! You won't laugh if I tell you it's kept me awake two nights. I only wonder now how people can live and think nothing about it. Vanity! Ivan has no God. He has an idea. It's beyond me. But he is silent. I believe he is a free-mason. I asked him, but he is silent. I wanted to drink from the springs of his soul—he was silent. But once he did drop a word."

"What did he say?" Alyosha took it up quickly.

"I said to him, 'Then everything is lawful, if it is so?' He frowned. 'Fyodor Pavlovitch, our papa,' he said, 'was a pig, but his ideas were right enough.' That was what he dropped. That was all he said. That was going one better than Rakitin."

"Yes," Alyosha assented bitterly. "When was he with you?"

"Of that later; now I must speak of something else. I have said nothing about Ivan to you before. I put it off to the last. When my business here is over and the verdict has been given, then I'll tell you something. I'll tell you everything. We've something tremendous on hand.... And you shall be my judge in it. But don't begin about that now; be silent. You talk of to-morrow, of the trial; but, would you believe it, I know nothing about it."

"Have you talked to the counsel?"

"What's the use of the counsel? I told him all about it. He's a soft, city-bred rogue—a Bernard! But he doesn't believe me—not a bit of it. Only imagine, he believes I did it. I see it. 'In that case,' I asked him, 'why have you come to defend me?' Hang them all! They've got a doctor down, too, want to prove I'm mad. I won't have that! Katerina Ivanovna wants to do her 'duty' to the end, whatever the strain!" Mitya smiled bitterly. "The cat! Hard-hearted creature! She knows that I said of her at Mokroe that she was a woman of 'great wrath.' They repeated it. Yes, the facts against me have grown numerous as the sands of the sea. Grigory sticks to his point. Grigory's honest, but a fool. Many people are honest because they are fools: that's Rakitin's idea. Grigory's my enemy. And there are some people who are better as foes than friends. I mean Katerina Ivanovna. I am afraid, oh, I am afraid she will tell how she bowed to the ground after that four thousand. She'll pay it back to the last farthing. I don't want her sacrifice; they'll put me to shame at the trial. I wonder how I can stand it. Go to her, Alyosha, ask her not to speak of that in the court, can't you? But damn it all, it doesn't matter! I shall get through somehow. I don't pity her. It's her own doing. She deserves what she gets. I shall have my own story to tell, Alexey." He smiled bitterly again. "Only ... only Grusha, Grusha! Good Lord! Why should she have such suffering to bear?" he exclaimed suddenly, with tears. "Grusha's killing me; the thought of her's killing me, killing me. She was with me just now...."

"She told me she was very much grieved by you to-day."

"I know. Confound my temper! It was jealousy. I was sorry, I kissed her as she was going. I didn't ask her forgiveness."

"Why didn't you?" exclaimed Alyosha.

Suddenly Mitya laughed almost mirthfully.

"God preserve you, my dear boy, from ever asking forgiveness for a fault from a woman you love. From one you love especially, however greatly you may have been in fault. For a woman—devil only knows what to make of a woman! I know something about them, anyway. But try acknowledging you are in fault to a woman. Say, 'I am sorry, forgive me,' and a shower of reproaches will follow! Nothing will make her forgive you simply and directly, she'll humble you to the dust, bring forward things that have never happened, recall everything, forget nothing, add something of her own, and only then forgive you. And even the best, the best of them do it. She'll scrape up all the scrapings and load them on your head. They are ready to flay you alive, I tell you, every one of them, all these angels without whom we cannot live! I tell you plainly and openly, dear boy, every decent man ought to be under some woman's thumb. That's my conviction—not conviction, but feeling. A man ought to be magnanimous, and it's no disgrace to a man! No disgrace to a hero, not even a Cæsar! But don't ever beg her pardon all the same for anything. Remember that rule given you by your brother Mitya, who's come to ruin through women. No, I'd better make it up to Grusha somehow, without begging pardon. I worship her, Alexey, worship her. Only she doesn't see it. No, she still thinks I don't love her enough. And she tortures me, tortures me with her love. The past was nothing! In the past it was only those infernal curves of hers that tortured me, but now I've taken all her soul into my soul and through her I've become a man myself. Will they marry us? If they don't, I shall die of jealousy. I imagine something every day.... What did she say to you about me?"

Alyosha repeated all Grushenka had said to him that day. Mitya listened, made him repeat things, and seemed pleased.

"Then she is not angry at my being jealous?" he exclaimed. "She is a regular woman! 'I've a fierce heart myself!' Ah, I love such fierce hearts, though I can't bear any one's being jealous of me. I can't endure it. We shall fight. But I shall love her, I shall love her infinitely. Will they marry us? Do they let convicts marry? That's the question. And without her I can't exist...."

Mitya walked frowning across the room. It was almost dark. He suddenly seemed terribly worried.

"So there's a secret, she says, a secret? We have got up a plot against her, and Katya is mixed up in it, she thinks. No, my good Grushenka, that's not it. You are very wide of the mark, in your foolish feminine way. Alyosha, darling, well, here goes! I'll tell you our secret!"

He looked round, went close up quickly to Alyosha, who was standing before him, and whispered to him with an air of mystery, though in reality no one could hear them: the old warder was dozing in the corner, and not a word could reach the ears of the soldiers on guard.

"I will tell you all our secret," Mitya whispered hurriedly. "I meant to tell you later, for how could I decide on anything without you? You are everything to me. Though I say that Ivan is superior to us, you are my angel. It's your decision will decide it. Perhaps it's you that is superior and not Ivan. You see, it's a question of conscience, question of the higher conscience—the secret is so important that I can't settle it myself, and I've put it off till I could speak to you. But anyway it's too early to decide now, for we must wait for the verdict. As soon as the verdict is given, you shall decide my fate. Don't decide it now. I'll tell you now. You listen, but don't decide. Stand and keep quiet. I won't tell you everything. I'll only tell you the idea, without details, and you keep quiet. Not a question, not a movement. You agree? But, goodness, what shall I do with your eyes? I'm afraid your eyes will tell me your decision, even if you don't speak. Oo! I'm afraid! Alyosha, listen! Ivan suggests my *escaping*. I won't tell you the details: it's all been thought out: it can all be arranged. Hush, don't decide. I should go to America with Grusha. You know I can't live without Grusha! What if they won't let her follow me to Siberia? Do they let convicts get married? Ivan thinks not. And without Grusha what should I do there underground with a hammer? I should only smash my skull with the hammer! But, on the other hand, my conscience? I should have run away from suffering. A sign has come, I reject the sign. I have a way of salvation and I turn my back on it. Ivan says that in America, 'with the good-will,' I can be of more use than underground. But what becomes of our hymn from underground? What's America? America is vanity again! And there's a lot of swindling in America, too, I expect. I should have run away from crucifixion! I tell you, you know, Alexey, because you are the only person who can understand this. There's no one else. It's folly, madness to others, all I've told you of the hymn. They'll say I'm out of my mind or a fool. I am not out of my mind and I am not a fool. Ivan understands about the hymn, too. He understands, only he doesn't answer—he doesn't speak. He doesn't believe in the hymn. Don't speak, don't speak. I see how you look! You have already decided. Don't decide, spare me! I can't live without Grusha. Wait till after the trial!"

Mitya ended beside himself. He held Alyosha with both hands on his shoulders, and his yearning, feverish eyes were fixed on his brother's.

"They don't let convicts marry, do they?" he repeated for the third time in a supplicating voice.

Alyosha listened with extreme surprise and was deeply moved.

"Tell me one thing," he said. "Is Ivan very keen on it, and whose idea was it?"

"His, his, and he is very keen on it. He didn't come to see me at first, then he suddenly came a week ago and he began about it straight away. He is awfully keen on it. He doesn't ask me, but orders me to escape. He doesn't doubt of my obeying him, though I showed him all my heart as I have to you, and told him about the hymn, too. He told me he'd arrange it; he's found out about everything. But of that later. He's simply set on it. It's all a matter of money: he'll pay ten thousand for escape and give me twenty thousand for America. And he says we can arrange a magnificent escape for ten thousand."

"And he told you on no account to tell me?" Alyosha asked again.

"To tell no one, and especially not you; on no account to tell you. He is afraid, no doubt, that you'll stand before me as my conscience. Don't tell him I told you. Don't tell him, for anything."

"You are right," Alyosha pronounced; "it's impossible to decide anything before the trial is over. After the trial you'll decide of yourself. Then you'll find that new man in yourself and he will decide."

"A new man, or a Bernard who'll decide *à la* Bernard, for I believe I'm a contemptible Bernard myself," said Mitya, with a bitter grin.

"But, brother, have you no hope then of being acquitted?"

Mitya shrugged his shoulders nervously and shook his head. "Alyosha, darling, it's time you were going," he said, with a sudden haste. "There's the superintendent shouting in the yard. He'll be here directly. We are late; it's irregular. Embrace me quickly. Kiss me! Sign me with the cross, darling, for the cross I have to bear to-morrow."

They embraced and kissed.

"Ivan," said Mitya suddenly, "suggests my escaping; but, of course, he believes I did it."

A mournful smile came on to his lips.

"Have you asked him whether he believes it?" asked Alyosha.

"No, I haven't. I wanted to, but I couldn't. I hadn't the courage. But I saw it from his eyes. Well, good-by!"

Once more they kissed hurriedly, and Alyosha was just going out, when Mitya suddenly called him back.

"Stand facing me! That's right!" And again he seized Alyosha, putting both hands on his shoulders. His face became suddenly quite pale, so that it was dreadfully apparent, even through the gathering darkness. His lips twitched, his eyes fastened upon Alyosha.

"Alyosha, tell me the whole truth, as you would before God. Do you believe I did it? Do you, do you in yourself, believe it? The whole truth, don't lie!" he cried desperately.

Everything seemed heaving before Alyosha, and he felt something like a stab at his heart.

"Hush! What do you mean?" he faltered helplessly.

"The whole truth, the whole, don't lie!" repeated Mitya.

"I've never for one instant believed that you were the murderer!" broke in a shaking voice from Alyosha's breast, and he raised his right hand in the air, as though calling God to witness his words.

Mitya's whole face was lighted up with bliss.

"Thank you!" he articulated slowly, as though letting a sigh escape him after fainting. "Now you have given me new life. Would you believe it, till this moment I've been afraid to ask you, you, even you. Well, go! You've given me strength for to-morrow. God bless you! Come, go along! Love Ivan!" was Mitya's last word.

Alyosha went out in tears. Such distrustfulness in Mitya, such lack of confidence even to him, to Alyosha—all this suddenly opened before Alyosha an unsuspected depth of hopeless grief and despair in the soul of his unhappy brother. Intense, infinite compassion overwhelmed him instantly. There was a poignant ache in his torn heart. "Love Ivan!"—he suddenly recalled Mitya's words. And he was going to Ivan. He badly wanted to see Ivan all day. He was as much worried about Ivan as about Mitya, and more than ever now.

On the way to Ivan he had to pass the house where Katerina Ivanovna was living. There was light in the windows. He suddenly stopped and resolved to go in. He had not seen Katerina Ivanovna for more than a week. But now it struck him that Ivan might be with her, especially on the eve of the terrible day. Ringing, and mounting the staircase, which was dimly lighted by a Chinese lantern, he saw a man coming down, and as they met, he recognized him as his brother. So he was just coming from Katerina Ivanovna.

"Ah, it's only you," said Ivan dryly. "Well, good-by! You are going to her?"

"Yes."

"I don't advise you to; she's upset and you'll upset her more."

A door was instantly flung open above, and a voice cried suddenly:

"No, no! Alexey Fyodorovitch, have you come from him?"

"Yes, I have been with him."

"Has he sent me any message? Come up, Alyosha, and you, Ivan Fyodorovitch, you must come back, you must. Do you hear?"

There was such a peremptory note in Katya's voice that Ivan, after a moment's hesitation, made up his mind to go back with Alyosha.

"She was listening," he murmured angrily to himself, but Alyosha heard it.

"Excuse my keeping my greatcoat on," said Ivan, going into the drawing-room. "I won't sit down. I won't stay more than a minute."

"Sit down, Alexey Fyodorovitch," said Katerina Ivanovna, though she remained standing. She had changed very little during this time, but there was an ominous gleam in her dark eyes. Alyosha remembered afterwards that she had struck him as particularly handsome at that moment.

"What did he ask you to tell me?"

"Only one thing," said Alyosha, looking her straight in the face, "that you would spare yourself and say nothing at the trial of what" (he was a little confused) "... passed between you ... at the time of your first acquaintance ... in that town."

"Ah! that I bowed down to the ground for that money!" She broke into a bitter laugh. "Why, is he afraid for me or for himself? He asks me to spare—whom? Him or myself? Tell me, Alexey Fyodorovitch!"

Alyosha watched her intently, trying to understand her.

"Both yourself and him," he answered softly.

"I am glad to hear it," she snapped out maliciously, and she suddenly blushed.

"You don't know me yet, Alexey Fyodorovitch," she said menacingly. "And I don't know myself yet. Perhaps you'll want to trample me under foot after my examination to-morrow."

"You will give your evidence honorably," said Alyosha; "that's all that's wanted."

"Women are often dishonorable," she snarled. "Only an hour ago I was thinking I felt afraid to touch that monster ... as though he were a reptile ... but no, he is still a human being to me! But did he do it? Is he the murderer?" she cried, all of a sudden, hysterically, turning quickly to Ivan. Alyosha saw at once that she had asked Ivan that question before, perhaps only a moment before he came in, and not for the first time, but for the hundredth, and that they had ended by quarreling.

"I've been to see Smerdyakov.... It was you, you who persuaded me that he murdered his father. It's only you I believed!" she continued, still addressing Ivan. He gave her a sort of strained smile. Alyosha started at her tone. He had not suspected such familiar intimacy between them.

"Well, that's enough, anyway," Ivan cut short the conversation. "I am going. I'll come to-morrow." And turning at once, he walked out of the room and went straight downstairs.

With an imperious gesture, Katerina Ivanovna seized Alyosha by both hands.

"Follow him! Overtake him! Don't leave him alone for a minute!" she said, in a hurried whisper. "He's mad! Don't you know that he's mad? He is in a fever, nervous fever. The doctor told me so. Go, run after him...."

Alyosha jumped up and ran after Ivan, who was not fifty paces ahead of him.

"What do you want?" He turned quickly on Alyosha, seeing that he was running after him. "She told you to catch me up, because I'm mad. I know it all by heart," he added irritably.

"She is mistaken, of course; but she is right that you are ill," said Alyosha. "I was looking at your face just now. You look very ill, Ivan."

Ivan walked on without stopping. Alyosha followed him.

"And do you know, Alexey Fyodorovitch, how people do go out of their mind?" Ivan asked in a voice suddenly quiet, without a trace of irritation, with a note of the simplest curiosity.

"No, I don't. I suppose there are all kinds of insanity."

"And can one observe that one's going mad oneself?"

"I imagine one can't see oneself clearly in such circumstances," Alyosha answered with surprise.

Ivan paused for half a minute.

"If you want to talk to me, please change the subject," he said suddenly.

"Oh, while I think of it, I have a letter for you," said Alyosha timidly, and he took Lise's note from his pocket and held it out to Ivan. They were just under a lamp-post. Ivan recognized the handwriting at once.

"Ah, from that little demon!" he laughed maliciously, and, without opening the envelope, he tore it into bits and threw it in the air. The bits were scattered by the wind.

"She's not sixteen yet, I believe, and already offering herself," he said contemptuously, striding along the street again.

"How do you mean, offering herself?" exclaimed Alyosha.

"As wanton women offer themselves, to be sure."

"How can you, Ivan, how can you?" Alyosha cried warmly, in a grieved voice. "She is a child; you are insulting a child! She is ill; she is very ill, too. She is on the verge of insanity, too, perhaps.... I had hoped to hear something from you ... that would save her."

"You'll hear nothing from me. If she is a child I am not her nurse. Be quiet, Alexey. Don't go on about her. I am not even thinking about it."

They were silent again for a moment.

"She will be praying all night now to the Mother of God to show her how to act to-morrow at the trial," he said sharply and angrily again.

"You ... you mean Katerina Ivanovna?"

"Yes. Whether she's to save Mitya or ruin him. She'll pray for light from above. She can't make up her mind for herself, you see. She has not had time to decide yet. She takes me for her nurse, too. She wants me to sing lullabies to her."

"Katerina Ivanovna loves you, brother," said Alyosha sadly.

"Perhaps; but I am not very keen on her."

"She is suffering. Why do you ... sometimes say things to her that give her hope?" Alyosha went on, with timid reproach. "I know that you've given her hope. Forgive me for speaking to you like this," he added.

"I can't behave to her as I ought—break off altogether and tell her so straight out," said Ivan, irritably. "I must wait till sentence is passed on the murderer. If I break off with her now, she will avenge herself on me by ruining that scoundrel to-morrow at the trial, for she hates him and knows she hates him. It's all a lie—lie upon lie! As long as I don't break off with her, she goes on hoping, and she won't ruin that monster, knowing how I want to get him out of trouble. If only that damned verdict would come!"

The words "murderer" and "monster" echoed painfully in Alyosha's heart.

"But how can she ruin Mitya?" he asked, pondering on Ivan's words. "What evidence can she give that would ruin Mitya?"

"You don't know that yet. She's got a document in her hands, in Mitya's own writing, that proves conclusively that he did murder Fyodor Pavlovitch."

"That's impossible!" cried Alyosha.

"Why is it impossible? I've read it myself."

"There can't be such a document!" Alyosha repeated warmly. "There can't be, because he's not the murderer. It's not he murdered father, not he!"

Ivan suddenly stopped.

"Who is the murderer then, according to you?" he asked, with apparent coldness. There was even a supercilious note in his voice.

"You know who," Alyosha pronounced in a low, penetrating voice.

"Who? You mean the myth about that crazy idiot, the epileptic, Smerdyakov?"

Alyosha suddenly felt himself trembling all over.

"You know who," broke helplessly from him. He could scarcely breathe.

"Who? Who?" Ivan cried almost fiercely. All his restraint suddenly vanished.

"I only know one thing," Alyosha went on, still almost in a whisper, "*it wasn't you* killed father."

"'Not you'! What do you mean by 'not you'?" Ivan was thunderstruck.

"It was not you killed father, not you!" Alyosha repeated firmly.

The silence lasted for half a minute.

"I know I didn't. Are you raving?" said Ivan, with a pale, distorted smile. His eyes were riveted on Alyosha. They were standing again under a lamp-post.

"No, Ivan. You've told yourself several times that you are the murderer."

"When did I say so? I was in Moscow.... When have I said so?" Ivan faltered helplessly.

"You've said so to yourself many times, when you've been alone during these two dreadful months," Alyosha went on softly and distinctly as before. Yet he was speaking now, as it were, not of himself, not of his own will, but obeying some irresistible command. "You have accused yourself and have confessed to yourself that you are the murderer and no one else. But you didn't do it: you are mistaken: you are not the murderer. Do you hear? It was not you! God has sent me to tell you so."

They were both silent. The silence lasted a whole long minute. They were both standing still, gazing into each other's eyes. They were both pale. Suddenly Ivan began trembling all over, and clutched Alyosha's shoulder.

"You've been in my room!" he whispered hoarsely. "You've been there at night, when he came.... Confess ... have you seen him, have you seen him?"

"Whom do you mean—Mitya?" Alyosha asked, bewildered.

"Not him, damn the monster!" Ivan shouted, in a frenzy. "Do you know that he visits me? How did you find out? Speak!"

"Who is *he*! I don't know whom you are talking about," Alyosha faltered, beginning to be alarmed.

"Yes, you do know ... or how could you—? It's impossible that you don't know."

Suddenly he seemed to check himself. He stood still and seemed to reflect. A strange grin contorted his lips.

"Brother," Alyosha began again, in a shaking voice, "I have said this to you, because you'll believe my word, I know that. I tell you once and for all, it's not you. You hear, once for all! God has put it into my heart to say this to you, even though it may make you hate me from this hour."

But by now Ivan had apparently regained his self-control.

"Alexey Fyodorovitch," he said, with a cold smile, "I can't endure prophets and epileptics—messengers from God especially—and you know that only too well. I break off all relations with you from this moment and probably for ever. I beg you to leave me at this turning. It's the way to your lodgings, too. You'd better be particularly careful not to come to me to-day! Do you hear?"

He turned and walked on with a firm step, not looking back.

"Brother," Alyosha called after him, "if anything happens to you to-day, turn to me before any one!"

But Ivan made no reply. Alyosha stood under the lamp-post at the cross roads, till Ivan had vanished into the darkness. Then he turned and walked slowly homewards. Both Alyosha and Ivan were living in lodgings; neither of them was willing to live in Fyodor Pavlovitch's empty house. Alyosha had a furnished room in the house of some working people. Ivan lived some distance from him. He had taken a roomy and fairly comfortable lodge attached to a fine house that belonged to a well-to-do lady, the widow of an official. But his only attendant was a deaf and rheumatic old crone who went to bed at six o'clock every evening and got up at six in the morning. Ivan had become remarkably indifferent to his comforts of late, and very fond of being alone. He did everything for himself in the one room he lived in, and rarely entered any of the other rooms in his abode.

He reached the gate of the house and had his hand on the bell, when he suddenly stopped. He felt that he was trembling all over with anger. Suddenly he let go of the bell, turned back with a curse, and walked with rapid steps in the opposite direction. He walked a mile and a half to a tiny, slanting, wooden house, almost a hut, where Marya Kondratyevna, the neighbor who used to come to Fyodor Pavlovitch's kitchen for soup and to whom Smerdyakov had once sung his songs and played on the guitar, was now lodging. She had sold their little house, and was now living here with her mother. Smerdyakov, who was ill—almost dying—had been with them ever since Fyodor Pavlovitch's death. It was to him Ivan was going now, drawn by a sudden and irresistible prompting.

Chapter Eight
A Judicial Error

At ten o'clock in the morning of the day following the events I have described, the trial of Dmitri Karamazov began in our district court.

I hasten to emphasize the fact that I am far from esteeming myself capable of reporting all that took place at the trial in full detail, or even in the actual order of events. I imagine that to mention everything with full explanation would fill a volume, even a very large one. And so I trust I may not be reproached, for confining myself to what struck me. I may have selected as of most interest what was of secondary importance, and may have omitted the most prominent and essential details. But I see I shall do better not to apologize. I will do my best and the reader will see for himself that I have done all I can.

And, to begin with, before entering the court, I will mention what surprised me most on that day. Indeed, as it appeared later, every one was surprised at it, too. We all knew that the affair had aroused great interest, that every one was burning with impatience for the trial to begin, that it had been a subject of talk, conjecture, exclamation and surmise for the last two months in local society. Every one knew, too, that the case had become known throughout Russia, but yet we had not imagined that it had aroused such burning, such intense, interest in every one, not only among ourselves, but all over Russia. This became evident at the trial this day.

Visitors had arrived not only from the chief town of our province, but from several other Russian towns, as well as from Moscow and Petersburg. Among them were lawyers, ladies, and even several distinguished personages. Every ticket of admission had been snatched up. A special place behind the table at which the three judges sat was set apart for the most distinguished and important of the men visitors; a row of arm-chairs had been placed there—something exceptional, which had never been allowed before. A large proportion—not less than half of the public—were ladies. There was such a large number of lawyers from all parts that they did not know where to seat them, for every ticket had long since been eagerly sought for and distributed. I saw at the end of the room, behind the platform, a special partition hurriedly put up, behind which all these lawyers were admitted, and they thought themselves lucky to have standing room there, for all chairs had been removed for the sake of space, and the crowd behind the partition stood throughout the case closely packed, shoulder to shoulder.

Some of the ladies, especially those who came from a distance, made their appearance in the gallery very smartly dressed, but the majority of the ladies were oblivious even of dress. Their faces betrayed hysterical, intense, almost morbid, curiosity. A peculiar fact—established afterwards by many observations—was that almost all the ladies, or, at least the vast majority of them, were on Mitya's side and in favor of his being acquitted. This was perhaps chiefly owing to his reputation as a conqueror of female hearts. It was known that two women rivals were to appear in the case. One of them—Katerina Ivanovna—was an object of general interest. All sorts of extraordinary tales were told about her, amazing anecdotes of her passion for Mitya, in spite of his crime. Her pride and "aristocratic connections" were particularly insisted upon (she had called upon scarcely any one in the town). People said she intended to petition the Government for leave to accompany the criminal to Siberia and to be married to him somewhere in the mines. The appearance of Grushenka in court was awaited with no less impatience. The public was looking forward with anxious curiosity to the meeting of the two rivals—the proud aristocratic girl and "the hetaira." But Grushenka was a more familiar figure to the ladies of the district than Katerina Ivanovna. They had already seen "the woman who had ruined Fyodor Pavlovitch and his unhappy son," and all, almost without exception, wondered how father and son could be so in love with "such a very common, ordinary Russian girl, who was not even pretty."

In brief, there was a great deal of talk. I know for a fact that there were several serious family quarrels on Mitya's account in our town. Many ladies quarreled violently with their husbands over differences of opinion about the dreadful case, and it was only natural that the husbands of these ladies, far from being favorably disposed to the prisoner, should enter the court bitterly prejudiced against him. In fact, one may say pretty certainly that the masculine, as distinguished from the feminine, part of the audience were biased against the prisoner. There were numbers of severe, frowning, even vindictive faces. Mitya, indeed, had managed to offend many people during his stay in the town. Some of the visitors were, of course, in excellent spirits and quite unconcerned as to the fate of Mitya personally. But all were interested in the trial, and the majority of the men were certainly hoping for the conviction of the criminal, except perhaps the lawyers, who were more interested in the legal than in the moral aspect of the case.

Everybody was excited at the presence of the celebrated lawyer, Fetyukovitch. His talent was well known, and this was not the first time he had defended notorious criminal cases in the provinces. And if he defended them, such cases became celebrated and long remembered all over Russia. There were stories, too, about our prosecutor and about the President of the Court. It was said that Ippolit Kirillovitch was in a tremor at meeting Fetyukovitch, and that they had been enemies from the beginning of their careers in Petersburg, that though our sensitive prosecutor, who always considered that he had been aggrieved by some one in Petersburg because his talents had not been properly appreciated, was keenly excited over the Karamazov case, and was even dreaming of rebuilding his flagging fortunes by means of it, Fetyukovitch, they said, was his one anxiety. But these rumors were not quite just. Our prosecutor was not one of those men who lose heart in face of danger. On the contrary, his self-confidence increased with the increase of danger. It must be noted that our prosecutor was in general too hasty and morbidly impressionable. He would put his whole soul into some case and work at it as though his whole fate and his whole fortune depended on its result. This was the subject of some ridicule in the legal world, for just by this characteristic our prosecutor had gained a wider notoriety than could have been expected from his modest position. People laughed particularly at his passion for psychology. In my opinion, they were wrong, and our prosecutor was, I believe, a character of greater depth than was generally supposed. But with his delicate health he had failed to make his mark at the outset of his career and had never made up for it later.

As for the President of our Court, I can only say that he was a humane and cultured man, who had a practical knowledge of his work and progressive views. He was rather ambitious, but did not concern himself greatly about his future career. The great aim of his life was to be a man of advanced ideas. He was, too, a man of connections and property. He felt, as we learnt afterwards, rather strongly about the Karamazov case, but from a social, not from a personal standpoint. He was interested in it as a social phenomenon, in its classification and its character as a product of our social conditions, as typical of the national character, and so on, and so on. His attitude to the personal aspect of the case, to its tragic significance and the persons involved in it, including the prisoner, was rather indifferent and abstract, as was perhaps fitting, indeed.

The court was packed and overflowing long before the judges made their appearance. Our court is the best hall in the town—spacious, lofty, and good for sound. On the right of the judges, who were on a raised platform, a table and two rows of chairs had been put ready for the jury. On the left was the place for the prisoner and the counsel for the defense. In the middle of the court, near the judges, was a table with the "material proofs." On it lay Fyodor Pavlovitch's white silk dressing-gown, stained with blood; the fatal brass pestle with which the supposed murder had been committed; Mitya's shirt, with a blood-stained sleeve; his coat, stained with blood in patches over the pocket in which he had put his handkerchief; the handkerchief itself, stiff with blood and by now quite yellow; the pistol loaded by Mitya at Perhotin's with a view to suicide, and taken from him on the sly at Mokroe by Trifon Borissovitch; the envelope in which the three thousand roubles had been put ready for Grushenka, the narrow pink ribbon with which it had been tied, and many other articles I don't remember. In the body of the hall, at some distance, came the seats for the public. But in front of the balustrade a few chairs had been placed for witnesses who remained in the court after giving their evidence.

At ten o'clock the three judges arrived—the President, one honorary justice of the peace, and one other. The prosecutor, of course, entered immediately after. The President was a short, stout, thick-set man of fifty, with a dyspeptic complexion, dark hair turning gray and cut short, and a red ribbon, of what Order I don't remember. The prosecutor struck me and the others, too, as looking particularly pale, almost green. His face seemed to have grown suddenly thinner, perhaps in a single night, for I had seen him looking as usual only two days before. The President began with asking the court whether all the jury were present.

But I see I can't go on like this, partly because some things I did not hear, others I did not notice, and others I have forgotten, but most of all because, as I have said before, I have literally no time or space to mention everything that was said and done. I only know that neither side objected to very many of the jurymen. I remember the twelve jurymen— four were petty officials of the town, two were merchants, and six peasants and artisans of the town. I remember, long before the trial, questions were continually asked with some surprise, especially by ladies: "Can such a delicate, complex and psychological case be submitted for decision to petty officials and even peasants?" and "What can an official, still more a peasant, understand in such an affair?" All the four officials in the jury were, in fact, men of no consequence and of low rank. Except one who was rather younger, they were gray-headed men, little known in society, who had vegetated on a pitiful salary, and who probably had elderly, unpresentable wives and crowds of children, perhaps even without shoes and stockings. At most, they spent their leisure over cards and, of course, had never read a single book. The two merchants looked respectable, but were strangely silent and stolid. One of them was close-shaven, and was dressed in European style; the other had a small, gray beard, and wore a red ribbon with some sort of a medal upon it on his neck. There is no need to speak of the artisans and the peasants. The artisans of Skotoprigonyevsk are almost peasants, and even work on the land. Two of them also wore European dress, and, perhaps for that reason, were dirtier and more uninviting-looking than the others. So that one might well wonder, as I did as soon as I had looked at them, "what men like that could possibly make of such a case?" Yet their faces made a strangely imposing, almost menacing, impression; they were stern and frowning.

At last the President opened the case of the murder of Fyodor Pavlovitch Karamazov. I don't quite remember how he described him. The court usher was told to bring in the prisoner, and Mitya made his appearance. There was a hush through the court. One could have heard a fly. I don't know how it was with others, but Mitya made a most unfavorable impression on me. He looked an awful dandy in a brand-new frock-coat. I heard afterwards that he had ordered it in Moscow expressly for the occasion from his own tailor, who had his measure. He wore immaculate black kid gloves and exquisite linen. He walked in with his yard-long strides, looking stiffly straight in front of him, and sat down in his place with a most unperturbed air.

At the same moment the counsel for defense, the celebrated Fetyukovitch, entered, and a sort of subdued hum passed through the court. He was a tall, spare man, with long thin legs, with extremely long, thin, pale fingers, clean-shaven face, demurely brushed, rather short hair, and thin lips that were at times curved into something between a sneer and a smile. He looked about forty. His face would have been pleasant, if it had not been for his eyes, which, in themselves small and inexpressive, were set remarkably close together, with only the thin, long nose as a dividing line between them. In fact, there was something strikingly birdlike about his face. He was in evening dress and white tie.

I remember the President's first questions to Mitya, about his name, his calling, and so on. Mitya answered sharply, and his voice was so unexpectedly loud that it made the President start and look at the prisoner with surprise. Then followed a list of persons who were to take part in the proceedings—that is, of the witnesses and experts. It was a long list. Four of the witnesses were not present—Miüsov, who had given evidence at the preliminary inquiry, but was now in Paris; Madame Hohlakov and Maximov, who were absent through illness; and Smerdyakov, through his sudden death, of which an official statement from the police was presented. The news of Smerdyakov's death produced a sudden stir and whisper in the court. Many of the audience, of course, had not heard of the sudden suicide. What struck people most was Mitya's sudden outburst As soon as the statement of Smerdyakov's death was made, he cried out aloud from his place:

"He was a dog and died like a dog!"

I remember how his counsel rushed to him, and how the President addressed him, threatening to take stern measures, if such an irregularity were repeated. Mitya nodded and in a subdued voice repeated several times abruptly to his counsel, with no show of regret:

"I won't again, I won't. It escaped me. I won't do it again."

And, of course, this brief episode did him no good with the jury or the public. His character was displayed, and it spoke for itself. It was under the influence of this incident that the opening statement was read. It was rather short, but circumstantial. It only stated the chief reasons why he had been arrested, why he must be tried, and so on. Yet it made a great impression on me. The clerk read it loudly and distinctly. The whole tragedy was suddenly unfolded before us, concentrated, in bold relief, in a fatal and pitiless light. I remember how, immediately after it had been read, the President asked Mitya in a loud impressive voice:

"Prisoner, do you plead guilty?"

Mitya suddenly rose from his seat.

"I plead guilty to drunkenness and dissipation," he exclaimed, again in a startling, almost frenzied, voice, "to idleness and debauchery. I meant to become an honest man for good, just at the moment when I was struck down by fate. But I am not guilty of the death of that old man, my enemy and my father. No, no, I am not guilty of robbing him! I could not be. Dmitri Karamazov is a scoundrel, but not a thief."

He sat down again, visibly trembling all over. The President again briefly, but impressively, admonished him to answer only what was asked, and not to go off into irrelevant exclamations. Then he ordered the case to proceed. All the witnesses were led up to take the oath. Then I saw them all together. The brothers of the prisoner were, however, allowed to give evidence without taking the oath. After an exhortation from the priest and the President, the witnesses were led away and were made to sit as far as possible apart from one another. Then they began calling them up one by one.

I do not know whether the witnesses for the defense and for the prosecution were separated into groups by the President, and whether it was arranged to call them in a certain order. But no doubt it was so. I only know that the witnesses for the prosecution were called first. I repeat I don't intend to describe all the questions step by step. Besides, my account would be to some extent superfluous, because in the speeches for the prosecution and for the defense the whole course of the evidence was brought together and set in a strong and significant light, and I took down parts of those two remarkable speeches in full, and will quote them in due course, together with one extraordinary and quite unexpected episode, which occurred before the final speeches, and undoubtedly influenced the sinister and fatal outcome of the trial.

I will only observe that from the first moments of the trial one peculiar characteristic of the case was conspicuous and observed by all, that is, the overwhelming strength of the prosecution as compared with the arguments the defense had to rely upon. Every one realized it from the first moment that the facts began to group themselves round a single point, and the whole horrible and bloody crime was gradually revealed. Every one, perhaps, felt from the first that the case was beyond dispute, that there was no doubt about it, that there could be really no discussion, and that the defense was only a matter of form, and that the prisoner was guilty, obviously and conclusively guilty. I imagine that even the ladies, who were so impatiently longing for the acquittal of the interesting prisoner, were at the same time, without exception, convinced of his guilt. What's more, I believe they would have been mortified if his guilt had not been so firmly established, as that would have lessened the effect of the closing scene of the criminal's acquittal. That he would be acquitted, all the ladies, strange to say, were firmly persuaded up to the very last moment. "He is guilty, but he will be acquitted, from motives of humanity, in accordance with the new ideas, the new sentiments that had come into fashion," and so on, and so on. And that was why they had crowded into the court so impatiently. The men were more interested in the contest between the prosecutor and the famous Fetyukovitch. All were wondering and asking themselves what could even a talent like Fetyukovitch's make of such a desperate case; and so they followed his achievements, step by step, with concentrated attention.

But Fetyukovitch remained an enigma to all up to the very end, up to his speech. Persons of experience suspected that he had some design, that he was working towards some object, but it was almost impossible to guess what it was. His confidence and self-reliance were unmistakable, however. Every one noticed with pleasure, moreover, that he, after so short a stay, not more than three days, perhaps, among us, had so wonderfully succeeded in mastering the case and "had studied it to a nicety." People described with relish, afterwards, how cleverly he had "taken down" all the witnesses for the prosecution, and as far as possible perplexed them and, what's more, had aspersed their reputation and so depreciated the value of their evidence. But it was supposed that he did this rather by way of sport, so to speak, for professional glory, to show nothing had been omitted of the accepted methods, for all were convinced that he could do no real good by such disparagement of the witnesses, and probably was more aware of this than any one, having some idea of his own in the background, some concealed weapon of defense, which he would suddenly reveal when the time came. But meanwhile, conscious of his strength, he seemed to be diverting himself.

So, for instance, when Grigory, Fyodor Pavlovitch's old servant, who had given the most damning piece of evidence about the open door, was examined, the counsel for the defense positively fastened upon him when his turn came to question him. It must be noted that Grigory entered the hall with a composed and almost stately air, not the least disconcerted by the majesty of the court or the vast audience listening to him. He gave evidence with as much confidence as though he had been talking with his Marfa, only perhaps more respectfully. It was impossible to make him contradict himself. The prosecutor questioned him first in detail about the family life of the Karamazovs. The family picture stood out in lurid colors. It was plain to ear and eye that the witness was guileless and impartial. In spite of his profound reverence for the memory of his deceased master, he yet bore witness that he had been unjust to Mitya and "hadn't brought up his children as he should. He'd have been devoured by lice when he was little, if it hadn't been for me," he added, describing Mitya's early childhood. "It wasn't fair either of the father to wrong his son over his mother's property, which was by right his."

In reply to the prosecutor's question what grounds he had for asserting that Fyodor Pavlovitch had wronged his son in their money relations, Grigory, to the surprise of every one, had no proof at all to bring forward, but he still persisted that the arrangement with the son was "unfair," and that he ought "to have paid him several thousand roubles more." I must note, by the way, that the prosecutor asked this question whether Fyodor Pavlovitch had really kept back part of Mitya's inheritance with marked persistence of all the witnesses who could be asked it, not excepting Alyosha and Ivan, but he obtained no exact information from any one; all alleged that it was so, but were unable to bring forward any distinct proof. Grigory's description of the scene at the dinner-table, when Dmitri had burst in and beaten his father, threatening to come back to kill him, made a sinister impression on the court, especially as the old servant's composure in telling it, his parsimony of words and peculiar phraseology, were as effective as eloquence. He observed that he was not angry with Mitya for having knocked him down and struck him on the face; he had forgiven him long ago, he said. Of the deceased Smerdyakov he observed, crossing himself, that he was a lad of ability, but stupid and afflicted, and, worse still, an infidel, and that it was Fyodor Pavlovitch and his elder son who had taught him to be so. But he defended Smerdyakov's honesty almost with warmth, and related how Smerdyakov had once found the master's money in the yard, and, instead of concealing it, had taken it to his master, who had rewarded him with a "gold piece" for it, and trusted him implicitly from that time forward. He maintained obstinately that the door into the garden had been open. But he was asked so many questions that I can't recall them all.

At last the counsel for the defense began to cross-examine him, and the first question he asked was about the envelope in which Fyodor Pavlovitch was supposed to have put three thousand roubles for "a certain person." "Have you ever seen it, you, who were for so many years in close attendance on your master?" Grigory answered that he had not seen it and had never heard of the money from any one "till everybody was talking about it." This question about the envelope Fetyukovitch put to every one who could conceivably have known of it, as persistently as the prosecutor asked his question about Dmitri's inheritance, and got the same answer from all, that no one had seen the envelope, though many had heard of it. From the beginning every one noticed Fetyukovitch's persistence on this subject.

"Now, with your permission I'll ask you a question," Fetyukovitch said, suddenly and unexpectedly. "Of what was that balsam, or, rather, decoction, made, which, as we learn from the preliminary inquiry, you used on that evening to rub your lumbago, in the hope of curing it?"

Grigory looked blankly at the questioner, and after a brief silence muttered, "There was saffron in it."

"Nothing but saffron? Don't you remember any other ingredient?"

"There was milfoil in it, too."

"And pepper perhaps?" Fetyukovitch queried.

"Yes, there was pepper, too."

"Etcetera. And all dissolved in vodka?"

"In spirit."

There was a faint sound of laughter in the court.

"You see, in spirit. After rubbing your back, I believe, you drank what was left in the bottle with a certain pious prayer, only known to your wife?"

"I did."

"Did you drink much? Roughly speaking, a wine-glass or two?"

"It might have been a tumbler-full."

"A tumbler-full, even. Perhaps a tumbler and a half?"

Grigory did not answer. He seemed to see what was meant.

"A glass and a half of neat spirit—is not at all bad, don't you think? You might see the gates of heaven open, not only the door into the garden?"

Grigory remained silent. There was another laugh in the court. The President made a movement.

"Do you know for a fact," Fetyukovitch persisted, "whether you were awake or not when you saw the open door?"

"I was on my legs."

"That's not a proof that you were awake." (There was again laughter in the court.) "Could you have answered at that moment, if any one had asked you a question—for instance, what year it is?"

"I don't know."

"And what year is it, Anno Domini, do you know?"

Grigory stood with a perplexed face, looking straight at his tormentor. Strange to say, it appeared he really did not know what year it was.

"But perhaps you can tell me how many fingers you have on your hands?"

"I am a servant," Grigory said suddenly, in a loud and distinct voice. "If my betters think fit to make game of me, it is my duty to suffer it."

Fetyukovitch was a little taken aback, and the President intervened, reminding him that he must ask more relevant questions. Fetyukovitch bowed with dignity and said that he had no more questions to ask of the witness. The public and the jury, of course, were left with a grain of doubt in their minds as to the evidence of a man who might, while undergoing a certain cure, have seen "the gates of heaven," and who did not even know what year he was living in. But before Grigory left the box another episode occurred. The President, turning to the prisoner, asked him whether he had any comment to make on the evidence of the last witness.

"Except about the door, all he has said is true," cried Mitya, in a loud voice. "For combing the lice off me, I thank him; for forgiving my blows, I thank him. The old man has been honest all his life and as faithful to my father as seven hundred poodles."

"Prisoner, be careful in your language," the President admonished him.

"I am not a poodle," Grigory muttered.

"All right, it's I am a poodle myself," cried Mitya. "If it's an insult, I take it to myself and I beg his pardon. I was a beast and cruel to him. I was cruel to Æsop too."

"What Æsop?" the President asked sternly again.

"Oh, Pierrot ... my father, Fyodor Pavlovitch."

The President again and again warned Mitya impressively and very sternly to be more careful in his language.

"You are injuring yourself in the opinion of your judges."

The counsel for the defense was equally clever in dealing with the evidence of Rakitin. I may remark that Rakitin was one of the leading witnesses and one to whom the prosecutor attached great significance. It appeared that he knew everything; his knowledge was amazing, he had been everywhere, seen everything, talked to everybody, knew every detail of the biography of Fyodor Pavlovitch and all the Karamazovs. Of the envelope, it is true, he had only heard from Mitya himself. But he described minutely Mitya's exploits in the "Metropolis," all his compromising doings and sayings, and told the story of Captain Snegiryov's "wisp of tow." But even Rakitin could say nothing positive about Mitya's inheritance, and confined himself to contemptuous generalities.

"Who could tell which of them was to blame, and which was in debt to the other, with their crazy Karamazov way of muddling things so that no one could make head or tail of it?" He attributed the tragic crime to the habits that had become ingrained by ages of serfdom and the distressed condition of Russia, due to the lack of appropriate institutions. He was, in fact, allowed some latitude of speech. This was the first occasion on which Rakitin showed what he could do, and attracted notice. The prosecutor knew that the witness was preparing a magazine article on the case, and afterwards in his speech, as we shall see later, quoted some ideas from the article, showing that he had seen it already. The picture drawn by the witness was a gloomy and sinister one, and greatly strengthened the case for the prosecution. Altogether, Rakitin's discourse fascinated the public by its independence and the extraordinary nobility of its ideas. There were even two or three outbreaks of applause when he spoke of serfdom and the distressed condition of Russia.

But Rakitin, in his youthful ardor, made a slight blunder, of which the counsel for the defense at once adroitly took advantage. Answering certain questions about Grushenka, and carried away by the loftiness of his own sentiments and his success, of which he was, of course, conscious, he went so far as to speak somewhat contemptuously of Agrafena Alexandrovna as "the kept mistress of Samsonov." He would have given a good deal to take back his words afterwards, for Fetyukovitch caught him out over it at once. And it was all because Rakitin had not reckoned on the lawyer having been able to become so intimately acquainted with every detail in so short a time.

"Allow me to ask," began the counsel for the defense, with the most affable and even respectful smile, "you are, of course, the same Mr. Rakitin whose pamphlet, *The Life of the Deceased Elder, Father Zossima*, published by the diocesan authorities, full of profound and religious reflections and preceded by an excellent and devout dedication to the bishop, I have just read with such pleasure?"

"I did not write it for publication ... it was published afterwards," muttered Rakitin, for some reason fearfully disconcerted and almost ashamed.

"Oh, that's excellent! A thinker like you can, and indeed ought to, take the widest view of every social question. Your most instructive pamphlet has been widely circulated through the patronage of the bishop, and has been of appreciable service.... But this is the chief thing I should like to learn from you. You stated just now that you were very intimately acquainted with Madame Svyetlov." (It must be noted that Grushenka's surname was Svyetlov. I heard it for the first time that day, during the case.)

"I cannot answer for all my acquaintances.... I am a young man ... and who can be responsible for every one he meets?" cried Rakitin, flushing all over.

"I understand, I quite understand," cried Fetyukovitch, as though he, too, were embarrassed and in haste to excuse himself. "You, like any other, might well be interested in an acquaintance with a young and beautiful woman who would readily entertain the *élite* of the youth of the neighborhood, but ... I only wanted to know ... It has come to my knowledge that Madame Svyetlov was particularly anxious a couple of months ago to make the acquaintance of the younger Karamazov, Alexey Fyodorovitch, and promised you twenty-five roubles, if you would bring him to her in his monastic dress. And that actually took place on the evening of the day on which the terrible crime, which is the subject of the present investigation, was committed. You brought Alexey Karamazov to Madame Svyetlov, and did you receive the twenty-five roubles from Madame Svyetlov as a reward, that's what I wanted to hear from you?"

"It was a joke.... I don't see of what interest that can be to you.... I took it for a joke ... meaning to give it back later...."

"Then you did take— But you have not given it back yet ... or have you?"

"That's of no consequence," muttered Rakitin, "I refuse to answer such questions.... Of course I shall give it back."

The President intervened, but Fetyukovitch declared he had no more questions to ask of the witness. Mr. Rakitin left the witness-box not absolutely without a stain upon his character. The effect left by the lofty idealism of his speech was somewhat marred, and Fetyukovitch's expression, as he watched him walk away, seemed to suggest to the public "this is a specimen of the lofty-minded persons who accuse him." I remember that this incident, too, did not pass off without an outbreak from Mitya. Enraged by the tone in which Rakitin had referred to Grushenka, he suddenly shouted "Bernard!" When, after Rakitin's cross-examination, the President asked the prisoner if he had anything to say, Mitya cried loudly:

"Since I've been arrested, he has borrowed money from me! He is a contemptible Bernard and opportunist, and he doesn't believe in God; he took the bishop in!"

Mitya, of course, was pulled up again for the intemperance of his language, but Rakitin was done for. Captain Snegiryov's evidence was a failure, too, but from quite a different reason. He appeared in ragged and dirty clothes, muddy boots, and in spite of the vigilance and expert observation of the police officers, he turned out to be hopelessly drunk. On being asked about Mitya's attack upon him, he refused to answer.

"God bless him. Ilusha told me not to. God will make it up to me yonder."

"Who told you not to tell? Of whom are you talking?"

"Ilusha, my little son. 'Father, father, how he insulted you!' He said that at the stone. Now he is dying...."

The captain suddenly began sobbing, and plumped down on his knees before the President. He was hurriedly led away amidst the laughter of the public. The effect prepared by the prosecutor did not come off at all.

Fetyukovitch went on making the most of every opportunity, and amazed people more and more by his minute knowledge of the case. Thus, for example, Trifon Borissovitch made a great impression, of course, very prejudicial to Mitya. He calculated almost on his fingers that on his first visit to Mokroe, Mitya must have spent three thousand roubles, "or very little less. Just think what he squandered on those gypsy girls alone! And as for our lousy peasants, it wasn't a case of flinging half a rouble in the street, he made them presents of twenty-five roubles each, at least, he didn't give them less. And what a lot of money was simply stolen from him! And if any one did steal, he did not leave a receipt. How could one catch the thief when he was flinging his money away all the time? Our peasants are robbers, you know; they have no care for their souls. And the way he went on with the girls, our village girls! They're completely set up since then, I tell you, they used to be poor." He recalled, in fact, every item of expense and added it all up. So the theory that only fifteen hundred had been spent and the rest had been put aside in a little bag seemed inconceivable.

"I saw three thousand as clear as a penny in his hands, I saw it with my own eyes; I should think I ought to know how to reckon money," cried Trifon Borissovitch, doing his best to satisfy "his betters."

When Fetyukovitch had to cross-examine him, he scarcely tried to refute his evidence, but began asking him about an incident at the first carousal at Mokroe, a month before the arrest, when Timofey and another peasant called Akim had picked up on the floor in the passage a hundred roubles dropped by Mitya when he was drunk, and had given them to Trifon Borissovitch and received a rouble each from him for doing so. "Well," asked the lawyer, "did you give that hundred roubles back to Mr. Karamazov?" Trifon Borissovitch shuffled in vain.... He was obliged, after the peasants had been examined, to admit the finding of the hundred roubles, only adding that he had religiously returned it all to Dmitri Fyodorovitch "in perfect honesty, and it's only because his honor was in liquor at the time, he wouldn't remember it." But, as he had denied the incident of the hundred roubles till the peasants had been called to prove it, his evidence as to returning the money to Mitya was naturally regarded with great suspicion. So one of the most dangerous witnesses brought forward by the prosecution was again discredited.

The same thing happened with the Poles. They took up an attitude of pride and independence; they vociferated loudly that they had both been in the service of the Crown, and that "Pan Mitya" had offered them three thousand "to buy their honor," and that they had seen a large sum of money in his hands. Pan Mussyalovitch introduced a terrible number of Polish words into his sentences, and seeing that this only increased his consequence in the eyes of the President and the prosecutor, grew more and more pompous, and ended by talking in Polish altogether. But Fetyukovitch caught them, too, in his snares. Trifon Borissovitch, recalled, was forced, in spite of his evasions, to admit that Pan Vrublevsky had substituted another pack of cards for the one he had provided, and that Pan Mussyalovitch had cheated during the game. Kalganov confirmed this, and both the Poles left the witness-box with damaged reputations, amidst laughter from the public.

Then exactly the same thing happened with almost all the most dangerous witnesses. Fetyukovitch succeeded in casting a slur on all of them, and dismissing them with a certain derision. The lawyers and experts were lost in admiration, and were only at a loss to understand what good purpose could be served by it, for all, I repeat, felt that the case for the prosecution could not be refuted, but was growing more and more tragically overwhelming. But from the confidence of the "great magician" they saw that he was serene, and they waited, feeling that "such a man" had not come from Petersburg for nothing, and that he was not a man to return unsuccessful.

"To begin with, what was the source of this suspicion?" (Ippolit Kirillovitch began.) "The first person who cried out that Smerdyakov had committed the murder was the prisoner himself at the moment of his arrest, yet from that time to this he had not brought forward a single fact to confirm the charge, nor the faintest suggestion of a fact. The charge is confirmed by three persons only—the two brothers of the prisoner and Madame Svyetlov. The elder of these brothers expressed his suspicions only to-day, when he was undoubtedly suffering from brain fever. But we know that for the last two months he has completely shared our conviction of his brother's guilt and did not attempt to combat that idea. But of that later. The younger brother has admitted that he has not the slightest fact to support his notion of Smerdyakov's guilt, and has only been led to that conclusion from the prisoner's own words and the expression of his face. Yes, that astounding piece of evidence has been brought forward twice to-day by him. Madame Svyetlov was even more astounding. 'What the prisoner tells you, you must believe; he is not a man to tell a lie.' That is all the evidence against Smerdyakov produced by these three persons, who are all deeply concerned in the prisoner's fate. And yet the theory of Smerdyakov's guilt has been noised about, has been and is still maintained. Is it credible? Is it conceivable?"

Here Ippolit Kirillovitch thought it necessary to describe the personality of Smerdyakov, "who had cut short his life in a fit of insanity." He depicted him as a man of weak intellect, with a smattering of education, who had been thrown off his balance by philosophical ideas above his level and certain modern theories of duty, which he learnt in practice from the reckless life of his master, who was also perhaps his father—Fyodor Pavlovitch; and, theoretically, from various strange philosophical conversations with his master's elder son, Ivan Fyodorovitch, who readily indulged in this diversion, probably feeling dull or wishing to amuse himself at the valet's expense. "He spoke to me himself of his spiritual condition during the last few days at his father's house," Ippolit Kirillovitch explained; "but others too have borne witness to it—the prisoner himself, his brother, and the servant Grigory—that is, all who knew him well.

"Moreover, Smerdyakov, whose health was shaken by his attacks of epilepsy, had not the courage of a chicken. 'He fell at my feet and kissed them,' the prisoner himself has told us, before he realized how damaging such a statement was to himself. 'He is an epileptic chicken,' he declared about him in his characteristic language. And the prisoner chose him for his confidant (we have his own word for it) and he frightened him into consenting at last to act as a spy for him. In that capacity he deceived his master, revealing to the prisoner the existence of the envelope with the notes in it and the signals by means of which he could get into the house. How could he help telling him, indeed? 'He would have killed me, I could see that he would have killed me,' he said at the inquiry, trembling and shaking even before us, though his tormentor was by that time arrested and could do him no harm. 'He suspected me at every instant. In fear and trembling I hastened to tell him every secret to pacify him, that he might see that I had not deceived him and let me off alive.' Those are his own words. I wrote them down and I remember them. 'When he began shouting at me, I would fall on my knees.'

"He was naturally very honest and enjoyed the complete confidence of his master, ever since he had restored him some money he had lost. So it may be supposed that the poor fellow suffered pangs of remorse at having deceived his master, whom he loved as his benefactor. Persons severely afflicted with epilepsy are, so the most skillful doctors tell us, always prone to continual and morbid self-reproach. They worry over their 'wickedness,' they are tormented by pangs of conscience, often entirely without cause; they exaggerate and often invent all sorts of faults and crimes. And here we have a man of that type who had really been driven to wrong-doing by terror and intimidation.

"He had, besides, a strong presentiment that something terrible would be the outcome of the situation that was developing before his eyes. When Ivan Fyodorovitch was leaving for Moscow, just before the catastrophe, Smerdyakov besought him to remain, though he was too timid to tell him plainly what he feared. He confined himself to hints, but his hints were not understood.

"It must be observed that he looked on Ivan Fyodorovitch as a protector, whose presence in the house was a guarantee that no harm would come to pass. Remember the phrase in Dmitri Karamazov's drunken letter, 'I shall kill the old man, if only Ivan goes away.' So Ivan Fyodorovitch's presence seemed to every one a guarantee of peace and order in the house.

"But he went away, and within an hour of his young master's departure Smerdyakov was taken with an epileptic fit. But that's perfectly intelligible. Here I must mention that Smerdyakov, oppressed by terror and despair of a sort, had felt during those last few days that one of the fits from which he had suffered before at moments of strain, might be coming upon him again. The day and hour of such an attack cannot, of course, be foreseen, but every epileptic can feel beforehand that he is likely to have one. So the doctors tell us. And so, as soon as Ivan Fyodorovitch had driven out of the yard, Smerdyakov, depressed by his lonely and unprotected position, went to the cellar. He went down the stairs wondering if he would have a fit or not, and what if it were to come upon him at once. And that very apprehension, that very wonder, brought on the spasm in his throat that always precedes such attacks, and he fell unconscious into the cellar. And in this perfectly natural occurrence people try to detect a suspicion, a hint that he was shamming an attack *on purpose*. But, if it were on purpose, the question arises at once, what was his motive? What was he reckoning on? What was he aiming at? I say nothing about medicine: science, I am told, may go astray: the doctors were not able to discriminate between the counterfeit and the real. That may be so, but answer me one question: what motive had he for such a counterfeit? Could he, had he been plotting the murder, have desired to attract the attention of the household by having a fit just before?

"You see, gentlemen of the jury, on the night of the murder, there were five persons in Fyodor Pavlovitch's—Fyodor Pavlovitch himself (but he did not kill himself, that's evident); then his servant, Grigory, but he was almost killed himself; the third person was Grigory's wife, Marfa Ignatyevna, but it would be simply shameful to imagine her murdering her master. Two persons are left—the prisoner and Smerdyakov. But, if we are to believe the prisoner's statement that he is not the murderer, then Smerdyakov must have been, for there is no other alternative, no one else can be found. That is what accounts for the artful, astounding accusation against the unhappy idiot who committed suicide yesterday. Had a shadow of suspicion rested on any one else, had there been any sixth person, I am persuaded that even the prisoner would have been ashamed to accuse Smerdyakov, and would have accused that sixth person, for to charge Smerdyakov with that murder is perfectly absurd.

"Gentlemen, let us lay aside psychology, let us lay aside medicine, let us even lay aside logic, let us turn only to the facts and see what the facts tell us. If Smerdyakov killed him, how did he do it? Alone or with the assistance of the prisoner? Let us consider the first alternative—that he did it alone. If he had killed him it must have been with some object, for some advantage to himself. But not having a shadow of the motive that the prisoner had for the murder—hatred, jealousy, and so on—Smerdyakov could only have murdered him for the sake of gain, in order to appropriate the three thousand roubles he had seen his master put in the envelope. And yet he tells another person—and a person most closely interested, that is, the prisoner—everything about the money and the signals, where the envelope lay, what was written on it, what it was tied up with, and, above all, told him of those signals by which he could enter the house. Did he do this simply to betray himself, or to invite to the same enterprise one who would be anxious to get that envelope for himself? 'Yes,' I shall be told, 'but he betrayed it from fear.' But how do you explain this? A man who could conceive such an audacious, savage act, and carry it out, tells facts which are known to no one else in the world, and which, if he held his tongue, no one would ever have guessed!

"No, however cowardly he might be, if he had plotted such a crime, nothing would have induced him to tell any one about the envelope and the signals, for that was as good as betraying himself beforehand. He would have invented something, he would have told some lie if he had been forced to give information, but he would have been silent about that. For, on the other hand, if he had said nothing about the money, but had committed the murder and stolen the money, no one in the world could have charged him with murder for the sake of robbery, since no one but he had seen the money, no one but he knew of its existence in the house. Even if he had been accused of the murder, it could only have been thought that he had committed it from some other motive. But since no one had observed any such motive in him beforehand, and every one saw, on the contrary, that his master was fond of him and honored him with his confidence, he would, of course, have been the last to be suspected. People would have suspected first the man who had a motive, a man who had himself declared he had such motives, who had made no secret of it; they would, in fact, have suspected the son of the murdered man, Dmitri Fyodorovitch. Had Smerdyakov killed and robbed him, and the son been accused of it, that would, of course, have suited Smerdyakov. Yet are we to believe that, though plotting the murder, he told that son, Dmitri, about the money, the envelope, and the signals? Is that logical? Is that clear?

"When the day of the murder planned by Smerdyakov came, we have him falling downstairs in a *feigned* fit—with what object? In the first place that Grigory, who had been intending to take his medicine, might put it off and remain on guard, seeing there was no one to look after the house, and, in the second place, I suppose, that his master seeing that there was no one to guard him, and in terror of a visit from his son, might redouble his vigilance and precaution. And, most of all, I suppose that he, Smerdyakov, disabled by the fit, might be carried from the kitchen, where he always slept, apart from all the rest, and where he could go in and out as he liked, to Grigory's room at the other end of the lodge, where he was always put, shut off by a screen three paces from their own bed. This was the immemorial custom established by his master and the kind-hearted Marfa Ignatyevna, whenever he had a fit. There, lying behind the screen, he would most likely, to keep up the sham, have begun groaning, and so keeping them awake all night (as Grigory and his wife testified). And all this, we are to believe, that he might more conveniently get up and murder his master!

"But I shall be told that he shammed illness on purpose that he might not be suspected and that he told the prisoner of the money and the signals to tempt him to commit the murder, and when he had murdered him and had gone away with the money, making a noise, most likely, and waking people, Smerdyakov got up, am I to believe, and went in—what for? To murder his master a second time and carry off the money that had already been stolen? Gentlemen, are you laughing? I am ashamed to put forward such suggestions, but, incredible as it seems, that's just what the prisoner alleges. When he had left the house, had knocked Grigory down and raised an alarm, he tells us Smerdyakov got up, went in and murdered his master and stole the money! I won't press the point that Smerdyakov could hardly have reckoned on this beforehand, and have foreseen that the furious and exasperated son would simply come to peep in respectfully, though he knew the signals, and beat a retreat, leaving Smerdyakov his booty. Gentlemen of the jury, I put this question to you in earnest; when was the moment when Smerdyakov could have committed his crime? Name that moment, or you can't accuse him.

"But, perhaps, the fit was a real one, the sick man suddenly recovered, heard a shout, and went out. Well—what then? He looked about him and said, 'Why not go and kill the master?' And how did he know what had happened, since he had been lying unconscious till that moment? But there's a limit to these flights of fancy.

"'Quite so,' some astute people will tell me, 'but what if they were in agreement? What if they murdered him together and shared the money—what then?' A weighty question, truly! And the facts to confirm it are astounding. One commits the murder and takes all the trouble while his accomplice lies on one side shamming a fit, apparently to arouse suspicion in every one, alarm in his master and alarm in Grigory. It would be interesting to know what motives could have induced the two accomplices to form such an insane plan.

"But perhaps it was not a case of active complicity on Smerdyakov's part, but only of passive acquiescence; perhaps Smerdyakov was intimidated and agreed not to prevent the murder, and foreseeing that he would be blamed for letting his master be murdered, without screaming for help or resisting, he may have obtained permission from Dmitri Karamazov to get out of the way by shamming a fit—'you may murder him as you like; it's nothing to me.' But as this attack of Smerdyakov's was bound to throw the household into confusion, Dmitri Karamazov could never have agreed to such a plan. I will waive that point however. Supposing that he did agree, it would still follow that Dmitri Karamazov is the murderer and the instigator, and Smerdyakov is only a passive accomplice, and not even an accomplice, but merely acquiesced against his will through terror.

"But what do we see? As soon as he is arrested the prisoner instantly throws all the blame on Smerdyakov, not accusing him of being his accomplice, but of being himself the murderer. 'He did it alone,' he says. 'He murdered and robbed him. It was the work of his hands.' Strange sort of accomplices who begin to accuse one another at once! And think of the risk for Karamazov. After committing the murder while his accomplice lay in bed, he throws the blame on the invalid, who might well have resented it and in self-preservation might well have confessed the truth. For he might well have seen that the court would at once judge how far he was responsible, and so he might well have reckoned that if he were punished, it would be far less severely than the real murderer. But in that case he would have been certain to make a confession, yet he has not done so. Smerdyakov never hinted at their complicity, though the actual murderer persisted in accusing him and declaring that he had committed the crime alone.

"What's more, Smerdyakov at the inquiry volunteered the statement that it was *he* who had told the prisoner of the envelope of notes and of the signals, and that, but for him, he would have known nothing about them. If he had really been a guilty accomplice, would he so readily have made this statement at the inquiry? On the contrary, he would have tried to conceal it, to distort the facts or minimize them. But he was far from distorting or minimizing them. No one but an innocent man, who had no fear of being charged with complicity, could have acted as he did. And in a fit of melancholy arising from his disease and this catastrophe he hanged himself yesterday. He left a note written in his peculiar language, 'I destroy myself of my own will and inclination so as to throw no blame on any one.' What would it have cost him to add: 'I am the murderer, not Karamazov'? But that he did not add. Did his conscience lead him to suicide and not to avowing his guilt?

"And what followed? Notes for three thousand roubles were brought into the court just now, and we were told that they were the same that lay in the envelope now on the table before us, and that the witness had received them from Smerdyakov the day before. But I need not recall the painful scene, though I will make one or two comments, selecting such trivial ones as might not be obvious at first sight to every one, and so may be overlooked. In the first place, Smerdyakov must have given back the money and hanged himself yesterday from remorse. And only yesterday he confessed his guilt to Ivan Karamazov, as the latter informs us. If it were not so, indeed, why should Ivan Fyodorovitch have kept silence till now? And so, if he has confessed, then why, I ask again, did he not avow the whole truth in the last letter he left behind, knowing that the innocent prisoner had to face this terrible ordeal the next day?

"The money alone is no proof. A week ago, quite by chance, the fact came to the knowledge of myself and two other persons in this court that Ivan Fyodorovitch had sent two five per cent. coupons of five thousand each—that is, ten thousand in all—to the chief town of the province to be changed. I only mention this to point out that any one may have money, and that it can't be proved that these notes are the same as were in Fyodor Pavlovitch's envelope.

"Ivan Karamazov, after receiving yesterday a communication of such importance from the real murderer, did not stir. Why didn't he report it at once? Why did he put it all off till morning? I think I have a right to conjecture why. His health had been giving way for a week past: he had admitted to a doctor and to his most intimate friends that he was suffering from hallucinations and seeing phantoms of the dead: he was on the eve of the attack of brain fever by which he has been stricken down to-day. In this condition he suddenly heard of Smerdyakov's death, and at once reflected, 'The man is dead, I can throw the blame on him and save my brother. I have money. I will take a roll of notes and say that Smerdyakov gave them me before his death.' You will say that was dishonorable: it's dishonorable to slander even the dead, and even to save a brother. True, but what if he slandered him unconsciously? What if, finally unhinged by the sudden news of the valet's death, he imagined it really was so? You saw the recent scene: you have seen the witness's condition. He was standing up and was speaking, but where was his mind?

"Then followed the document, the prisoner's letter written two days before the crime, and containing a complete program of the murder. Why, then, are we looking for any other program? The crime was committed precisely according to this program, and by no other than the writer of it. Yes, gentlemen of the jury, it went off without a hitch! He did not run respectfully and timidly away from his father's window, though he was firmly convinced that the object of his affections was with him. No, that is absurd and unlikely! He went in and murdered him. Most likely he killed him in anger, burning with resentment, as soon as he looked on his hated rival. But having killed him, probably with one blow of the brass pestle, and having convinced himself, after careful search, that she was not there, he did not, however, forget to put his hand under the pillow and take out the envelope, the torn cover of which lies now on the table before us.

"I mention this fact that you may note one, to my thinking, very characteristic circumstance. Had he been an experienced murderer and had he committed the murder for the sake of gain only, would he have left the torn envelope on the floor as it was found, beside the corpse? Had it been Smerdyakov, for instance, murdering his master to rob him, he would have simply carried away the envelope with him, without troubling himself to open it over his victim's corpse, for he would have known for certain that the notes were in the envelope—they had been put in and sealed up in his presence—and had he taken the envelope with him, no one would ever have known of the robbery. I ask you, gentlemen, would Smerdyakov have behaved in that way? Would he have left the envelope on the floor?

"No, this was the action of a frantic murderer, a murderer who was not a thief and had never stolen before that day, who snatched the notes from under the pillow, not like a thief stealing them, but as though seizing his own property from the thief who had stolen it. For that was the idea which had become almost an insane obsession in Dmitri Karamazov in regard to that money. And pouncing upon the envelope, which he had never seen before, he tore it open to make sure whether the money was in it, and ran away with the money in his pocket, even forgetting to consider that he had left an astounding piece of evidence against himself in that torn envelope on the floor. All because it was Karamazov, not Smerdyakov, he didn't think, he didn't reflect, and how should he? He ran away; he heard behind him the servant cry out; the old man caught him, stopped him and was felled to the ground by the brass pestle.

"The prisoner, moved by pity, leapt down to look at him. Would you believe it, he tells us that he leapt down out of pity, out of compassion, to see whether he could do anything for him. Was that a moment to show compassion? No; he jumped down simply to make certain whether the only witness of his crime were dead or alive. Any other feeling, any other motive would be unnatural. Note that he took trouble over Grigory, wiped his head with his handkerchief and, convincing himself he was dead, he ran to the house of his mistress, dazed and covered with blood. How was it he never thought that he was covered with blood and would be at once detected? But the prisoner himself assures us that he did not even notice that he was covered with blood. That may be believed, that is very possible, that always happens at such moments with criminals. On one point they will show diabolical cunning, while another will escape them altogether. But he was thinking at that moment of one thing only—where was *she*? He wanted to find out at once where she was, so he ran to her lodging and learnt an unexpected and astounding piece of news—she had gone off to Mokroe to meet her first lover."

All was hushed as the first words of the famous orator rang out. The eyes of the audience were fastened upon him. He began very simply and directly, with an air of conviction, but not the slightest trace of conceit. He made no attempt at eloquence, at pathos, or emotional phrases. He was like a man speaking in a circle of intimate and sympathetic friends. His voice was a fine one, sonorous and sympathetic, and there was something genuine and simple in the very sound of it. But every one realized at once that the speaker might suddenly rise to genuine pathos and "pierce the heart with untold power." His language was perhaps more irregular than Ippolit Kirillovitch's, but he spoke without long phrases, and indeed, with more precision. One thing did not please the ladies: he kept bending forward, especially at the beginning of his speech, not exactly bowing, but as though he were about to dart at his listeners, bending his long spine in half, as though there were a spring in the middle that enabled him to bend almost at right angles.

At the beginning of his speech he spoke rather disconnectedly, without system, one may say, dealing with facts separately, though, at the end, these facts formed a whole. His speech might be divided into two parts, the first consisting of criticism in refutation of the charge, sometimes malicious and sarcastic. But in the second half he suddenly changed his tone, and even his manner, and at once rose to pathos. The audience seemed on the look-out for it, and quivered with enthusiasm.

He went straight to the point, and began by saying that although he practiced in Petersburg, he had more than once visited provincial towns to defend prisoners, of whose innocence he had a conviction or at least a preconceived idea. "That is what has happened to me in the present case," he explained. "From the very first accounts in the newspapers I was struck by something which strongly prepossessed me in the prisoner's favor. What interested me most was a fact which often occurs in legal practice, but rarely, I think, in such an extreme and peculiar form as in the present case. I ought to formulate that peculiarity only at the end of my speech, but I will do so at the very beginning, for it is my weakness to go to work directly, not keeping my effects in reserve and economizing my material. That may be imprudent on my part, but at least it's sincere. What I have in my mind is this: there is an overwhelming chain of evidence against the prisoner, and at the same time not one fact that will stand criticism, if it is examined separately. As I followed the case more closely in the papers my idea was more and more confirmed, and I suddenly received from the prisoner's relatives a request to undertake his defense. I at once hurried here, and here I became completely convinced. It was to break down this terrible chain of facts, and to show that each piece of evidence taken separately was unproved and fantastic, that I undertook the case."

So Fetyukovitch began.

"Gentlemen of the jury," he suddenly protested, "I am new to this district. I have no preconceived ideas. The prisoner, a man of turbulent and unbridled temper, has not insulted me. But he has insulted perhaps hundreds of persons in this town, and so prejudiced many people against him beforehand. Of course I recognize that the moral sentiment of local society is justly excited against him. The prisoner is of turbulent and violent temper. Yet he was received in society here; he was even welcome in the family of my talented friend, the prosecutor."

(N.B. At these words there were two or three laughs in the audience, quickly suppressed, but noticed by all. All of us knew that the prosecutor received Mitya against his will, solely because he had somehow interested his wife—a lady of the highest virtue and moral worth, but fanciful, capricious, and fond of opposing her husband, especially in trifles. Mitya's visits, however, had not been frequent.)

"Nevertheless I venture to suggest," Fetyukovitch continued, "that in spite of his independent mind and just character, my opponent may have formed a mistaken prejudice against my unfortunate client. Oh, that is so natural; the unfortunate man has only too well deserved such prejudice. Outraged morality, and still more outraged taste, is often relentless. We have, in the talented prosecutor's speech, heard a stern analysis of the prisoner's character and conduct, and his severe critical attitude to the case was evident. And, what's more, he went into psychological subtleties into which he could not have entered, if he had the least conscious and malicious prejudice against the prisoner. But there are things which are even worse, even more fatal in such cases, than the most malicious and consciously unfair attitude. It is worse if we are carried away by the artistic instinct, by the desire to create, so to speak, a romance, especially if God has endowed us with psychological insight. Before I started on my way here, I was warned in Petersburg, and was myself aware, that I should find here a talented opponent whose psychological insight and subtlety had gained him peculiar renown in legal circles of recent years. But profound as psychology is, it's a knife that cuts both ways." (Laughter among the public.) "You will, of course, forgive me my comparison; I can't boast of eloquence. But I will take as an example any point in the prosecutor's speech.

"The prisoner, running away in the garden in the dark, climbed over the fence, was seized by the servant, and knocked him down with a brass pestle. Then he jumped back into the garden and spent five minutes over the man, trying to discover whether he had killed him or not. And the prosecutor refuses to believe the prisoner's statement that he ran to old Grigory out of pity. 'No,' he says, 'such sensibility is impossible at such a moment, that's unnatural; he ran to find out whether the only witness of his crime was dead or alive, and so showed that he had committed the murder, since he would not have run back for any other reason.'

"Here you have psychology; but let us take the same method and apply it to the case the other way round, and our result will be no less probable. The murderer, we are told, leapt down to find out, as a precaution, whether the witness was alive or not, yet he had left in his murdered father's study, as the prosecutor himself argues, an amazing piece of evidence in the shape of a torn envelope, with an inscription that there had been three thousand roubles in it. 'If he had carried that envelope away with him, no one in the world would have known of that envelope and of the notes in it, and that the money had been stolen by the prisoner.' Those are the prosecutor's own words. So on one side you see a complete absence of precaution, a man who has lost his head and run away in a fright, leaving that clew on the floor, and two minutes later, when he has killed another man, we are entitled to assume the most heartless and calculating foresight in him. But even admitting this was so, it is psychological subtlety, I suppose, that discerns that under certain circumstances I become as bloodthirsty and keen-sighted as a Caucasian eagle, while at the next I am as timid and blind as a mole. But if I am so bloodthirsty and cruelly calculating that when I kill a man I only run back to find out whether he is alive to witness against me, why should I spend five minutes looking after my victim at the risk of encountering other witnesses? Why soak my handkerchief, wiping the blood off his head so that it may be evidence against me later? If he were so cold-hearted and calculating, why not hit the servant on the head again and again with the same pestle so as to kill him outright and relieve himself of all anxiety about the witness?

"Again, though he ran to see whether the witness was alive, he left another witness on the path, that brass pestle which he had taken from the two women, and which they could always recognize afterwards as theirs, and prove that he had taken it from them. And it is not as though he had forgotten it on the path, dropped it through carelessness or haste, no, he had flung away his weapon, for it was found fifteen paces from where Grigory lay. Why did he do so? Just because he was grieved at having killed a man, an old servant; and he flung away the pestle with a curse, as a murderous weapon. That's how it must have been, what other reason could he have had for throwing it so far? And if he was capable of feeling grief and pity at having killed a man, it shows that he was innocent of his father's murder. Had he murdered him, he would never have run to another victim out of pity; then he would have felt differently; his thoughts would have been centered on self-preservation. He would have had none to spare for pity, that is beyond doubt. On the contrary, he would have broken his skull instead of spending five minutes looking after him. There was room for pity and good-feeling just because his conscience had been clear till then. Here we have a different psychology. I have purposely resorted to this method, gentlemen of the jury, to show that you can prove anything by it. It all depends on who makes use of it. Psychology lures even most serious people into romancing, and quite unconsciously. I am speaking of the abuse of psychology, gentlemen."

Sounds of approval and laughter, at the expense of the prosecutor, were again audible in the court. I will not repeat the speech in detail; I will only quote some passages from it, some leading points.

This was how Fetyukovitch concluded his speech, and the enthusiasm of the audience burst like an irresistible storm. It was out of the question to stop it: the women wept, many of the men wept too, even two important personages shed tears. The President submitted, and even postponed ringing his bell. The suppression of such an enthusiasm would be the suppression of something sacred, as the ladies cried afterwards. The orator himself was genuinely touched.

And it was at this moment that Ippolit Kirillovitch got up to make certain objections. People looked at him with hatred. "What? What's the meaning of it? He positively dares to make objections," the ladies babbled. But if the whole world of ladies, including his wife, had protested he could not have been stopped at that moment. He was pale, he was shaking with emotion, his first phrases were even unintelligible, he gasped for breath, could hardly speak clearly, lost the thread. But he soon recovered himself. Of this new speech of his I will quote only a few sentences.

"... I am reproached with having woven a romance. But what is this defense if not one romance on the top of another? All that was lacking was poetry. Fyodor Pavlovitch, while waiting for his mistress, tears open the envelope and throws it on the floor. We are even told what he said while engaged in this strange act. Is not this a flight of fancy? And what proof have we that he had taken out the money? Who heard what he said? The weak-minded idiot, Smerdyakov, transformed into a Byronic hero, avenging society for his illegitimate birth—isn't this a romance in the Byronic style? And the son who breaks into his father's house and murders him without murdering him is not even a romance—this is a sphinx setting us a riddle which he cannot solve himself. If he murdered him, he murdered him, and what's the meaning of his murdering him without having murdered him—who can make head or tail of this?

"Then we are admonished that our tribune is a tribune of true and sound ideas and from this tribune of 'sound ideas' is heard a solemn declaration that to call the murder of a father 'parricide' is nothing but a prejudice! But if parricide is a prejudice, and if every child is to ask his father why he is to love him, what will become of us? What will become of the foundations of society? What will become of the family? Parricide, it appears, is only a bogy of Moscow merchants' wives. The most precious, the most sacred guarantees for the destiny and future of Russian justice are presented to us in a perverted and frivolous form, simply to attain an object—to obtain the justification of something which cannot be justified. 'Oh, crush him by mercy,' cries the counsel for the defense; but that's all the criminal wants, and to-morrow it will be seen how much he is crushed. And is not the counsel for the defense too modest in asking only for the acquittal of the prisoner? Why not found a charity in the honor of the parricide to commemorate his exploit among future generations? Religion and the Gospel are corrected—that's all mysticism, we are told, and ours is the only true Christianity which has been subjected to the analysis of reason and common sense. And so they set up before us a false semblance of Christ! 'What measure ye mete so it shall be meted unto you again,' cried the counsel for the defense, and instantly deduces that Christ teaches us to measure as it is measured to us—and this from the tribune of truth and sound sense! We peep into the Gospel only on the eve of making speeches, in order to dazzle the audience by our acquaintance with what is, anyway, a rather original composition, which may be of use to produce a certain effect—all to serve the purpose! But what Christ commands us is something very different: He bids us beware of doing this, because the wicked world does this, but we ought to forgive and to turn the other cheek, and not to measure to our persecutors as they measure to us. This is what our God has taught us and not that to forbid children to murder their fathers is a prejudice. And we will not from the tribune of truth and good sense correct the Gospel of our Lord, Whom the counsel for the defense deigns to call only 'the crucified lover of humanity,' in opposition to all orthodox Russia, which calls to Him, 'For Thou art our God!' "

At this the President intervened and checked the over-zealous speaker, begging him not to exaggerate, not to overstep the bounds, and so on, as presidents always do in such cases. The audience, too, was uneasy. The public was restless: there were even exclamations of indignation. Fetyukovitch did not so much as reply; he only mounted the tribune to lay his hand on his heart and, with an offended voice, utter a few words full of dignity. He only touched again, lightly and ironically, on "romancing" and "psychology," and in an appropriate place quoted, "Jupiter, you are angry, therefore you are wrong," which provoked a burst of approving laughter in the audience, for Ippolit Kirillovitch was by no means like Jupiter. Then, *à propos* of the accusation that he was teaching the young generation to murder their fathers, Fetyukovitch observed, with great dignity, that he would not even answer. As for the prosecutor's charge of uttering unorthodox opinions, Fetyukovitch hinted that it was a personal insinuation and that he had expected in this court to be secure from accusations "damaging to my reputation as a citizen and a loyal subject." But at these words the President pulled him up, too, and Fetyukovitch concluded his speech with a bow, amid a hum of approbation in the court. And Ippolit Kirillovitch was, in the opinion of our ladies, "crushed for good."

Then the prisoner was allowed to speak. Mitya stood up, but said very little. He was fearfully exhausted, physically and mentally. The look of strength and independence with which he had entered in the morning had almost disappeared. He seemed as though he had passed through an experience that day, which had taught him for the rest of his life something very important he had not understood till then. His voice was weak, he did not shout as before. In his words there was a new note of humility, defeat and submission.

"What am I to say, gentlemen of the jury? The hour of judgment has come for me, I feel the hand of God upon me! The end has come to an erring man! But, before God, I repeat to you, I am innocent of my father's blood! For the last time I repeat, it wasn't I killed him! I was erring, but I loved what is good. Every instant I strove to reform, but I lived like a wild beast. I thank the prosecutor, he told me many things about myself that I did not know; but it's not true that I killed my father, the prosecutor is mistaken. I thank my counsel, too. I cried listening to him; but it's not true that I killed my father, and he needn't have supposed it. And don't believe the doctors. I am perfectly sane, only my heart is heavy. If you spare me, if you let me go, I will pray for you. I will be a better man. I give you my word before God I will! And if you will condemn me, I'll break my sword over my head myself and kiss the pieces. But spare me, do not rob me of my God! I know myself, I shall rebel! My heart is heavy, gentlemen ... spare me!"

He almost fell back in his place: his voice broke: he could hardly articulate the last phrase. Then the judges proceeded to put the questions and began to ask both sides to formulate their conclusions.

But I will not describe the details. At last the jury rose to retire for consultation. The President was very tired, and so his last charge to the jury was rather feeble. "Be impartial, don't be influenced by the eloquence of the defense, but yet weigh the arguments. Remember that there is a great responsibility laid upon you," and so on and so on.

The jury withdrew and the court adjourned. People could get up, move about, exchange their accumulated impressions, refresh themselves at the buffet. It was very late, almost one o'clock in the night, but nobody went away: the strain was so great that no one could think of repose. All waited with sinking hearts; though that is, perhaps, too much to say, for the ladies were only in a state of hysterical impatience and their hearts were untroubled. An acquittal, they thought, was inevitable. They all prepared themselves for a dramatic moment of general enthusiasm. I must own there were many among the men, too, who were convinced that an acquittal was inevitable. Some were pleased, others frowned, while some were simply dejected, not wanting him to be acquitted. Fetyukovitch himself was confident of his success. He was surrounded by people congratulating him and fawning upon him.

"There are," he said to one group, as I was told afterwards, "there are invisible threads binding the counsel for the defense with the jury. One feels during one's speech if they are being formed. I was aware of them. They exist. Our cause is won. Set your mind at rest."

"What will our peasants say now?" said one stout, cross-looking, pock-marked gentleman, a landowner of the neighborhood, approaching a group of gentlemen engaged in conversation.

"But they are not all peasants. There are four government clerks among them."

"Yes, there are clerks," said a member of the district council, joining the group.

"And do you know that Nazaryev, the merchant with the medal, a juryman?"

"What of him?"

"He is a man with brains."

"But he never speaks."

"He is no great talker, but so much the better. There's no need for the Petersburg man to teach him: he could teach all Petersburg himself. He's the father of twelve children. Think of that!"

"Upon my word, you don't suppose they won't acquit him?" one of our young officials exclaimed in another group.

"They'll acquit him for certain," said a resolute voice.

"It would be shameful, disgraceful, not to acquit him!" cried the official. "Suppose he did murder him—there are fathers and fathers! And, besides, he was in such a frenzy.... He really may have done nothing but swing the pestle in the air, and so knocked the old man down. But it was a pity they dragged the valet in. That was simply an absurd theory! If I'd been in Fetyukovitch's place, I should simply have said straight out: 'He murdered him; but he is not guilty, hang it all!' "

"That's what he did, only without saying, 'Hang it all!' "

"No, Mihail Semyonovitch, he almost said that, too," put in a third voice.

"Why, gentlemen, in Lent an actress was acquitted in our town who had cut the throat of her lover's lawful wife."

"Oh, but she did not finish cutting it."

"That makes no difference. She began cutting it."

"What did you think of what he said about children? Splendid, wasn't it?"

"Splendid!"

"And about mysticism, too!"

"Oh, drop mysticism, do!" cried some one else; "think of Ippolit and his fate from this day forth. His wife will scratch his eyes out to-morrow for Mitya's sake."

"Is she here?"

"What an idea! If she'd been here she'd have scratched them out in court. She is at home with toothache. He he he!"

"He he he!"

In a third group:

"I dare say they will acquit Mitenka, after all."

"I should not be surprised if he turns the 'Metropolis' upside down to-morrow. He will be drinking for ten days!"

"Oh, the devil!"

"The devil's bound to have a hand in it. Where should he be if not here?"

"Well, gentlemen, I admit it was eloquent. But still it's not the thing to break your father's head with a pestle! Or what are we coming to?"

"The chariot! Do you remember the chariot?"

"Yes; he turned a cart into a chariot!"

"And to-morrow he will turn a chariot into a cart, just to suit his purpose."

"What cunning chaps there are nowadays! Is there any justice to be had in Russia?"

But the bell rang. The jury deliberated for exactly an hour, neither more nor less. A profound silence reigned in the court as soon as the public had taken their seats. I remember how the jurymen walked into the court. At last! I won't repeat the questions in order, and, indeed, I have forgotten them. I remember only the answer to the President's first and chief question: "Did the prisoner commit the murder for the sake of robbery and with premeditation?" (I don't remember the exact words.) There was a complete hush. The foreman of the jury, the youngest of the clerks, pronounced, in a clear, loud voice, amidst the deathlike stillness of the court:

"Yes, guilty!"

And the same answer was repeated to every question: "Yes, guilty!" and without the slightest extenuating comment. This no one had expected; almost every one had reckoned upon a recommendation to mercy, at least. The deathlike silence in the court was not broken—all seemed petrified: those who desired his conviction as well as those who had been eager for his acquittal. But that was only for the first instant, and it was followed by a fearful hubbub. Many of the men in the audience were pleased. Some were rubbing their hands with no attempt to conceal their joy. Those who disagreed with the verdict seemed crushed, shrugged their shoulders, whispered, but still seemed unable to realize this. But how shall I describe the state the ladies were in? I thought they would create a riot. At first they could scarcely believe their ears. Then suddenly the whole court rang with exclamations: "What's the meaning of it? What next?" They leapt up from their places. They seemed to fancy that it might be at once reconsidered and reversed. At that instant Mitya suddenly stood up and cried in a heartrending voice, stretching his hands out before him:

"I swear by God and the dreadful Day of Judgment I am not guilty of my father's blood! Katya, I forgive you! Brothers, friends, have pity on the other woman!"

He could not go on, and broke into a terrible sobbing wail that was heard all over the court in a strange, unnatural voice unlike his own. From the farthest corner at the back of the gallery came a piercing shriek—it was Grushenka. She had succeeded in begging admittance to the court again before the beginning of the lawyers' speeches. Mitya was taken away. The passing of the sentence was deferred till next day. The whole court was in a hubbub but I did not wait to hear. I only remember a few exclamations I heard on the steps as I went out.

"He'll have a twenty years' trip to the mines!"

"Not less."

"Well, our peasants have stood firm."

"And have done for our Mitya."

Chapter Nine
Epilogue

Very early, at nine o'clock in the morning, five days after the trial, Alyosha went to Katerina Ivanovna's to talk over a matter of great importance to both of them, and to give her a message. She sat and talked to him in the very room in which she had once received Grushenka. In the next room Ivan Fyodorovitch lay unconscious in a high fever. Katerina Ivanovna had immediately after the scene at the trial ordered the sick and unconscious man to be carried to her house, disregarding the inevitable gossip and general disapproval of the public. One of the two relations who lived with her had departed to Moscow immediately after the scene in court, the other remained. But if both had gone away, Katerina Ivanovna would have adhered to her resolution, and would have gone on nursing the sick man and sitting by him day and night. Varvinsky and Herzenstube were attending him. The famous doctor had gone back to Moscow, refusing to give an opinion as to the probable end of the illness. Though the doctors encouraged Katerina Ivanovna and Alyosha, it was evident that they could not yet give them positive hopes of recovery.

Alyosha came to see his sick brother twice a day. But this time he had specially urgent business, and he foresaw how difficult it would be to approach the subject, yet he was in great haste. He had another engagement that could not be put off for that same morning, and there was need of haste.

They had been talking for a quarter of an hour. Katerina Ivanovna was pale and terribly fatigued, yet at the same time in a state of hysterical excitement. She had a presentiment of the reason why Alyosha had come to her.

"Don't worry about his decision," she said, with confident emphasis to Alyosha. "One way or another he is bound to come to it. He must escape. That unhappy man, that hero of honor and principle—not he, not Dmitri Fyodorovitch, but the man lying the other side of that door, who has sacrificed himself for his brother," Katya added, with flashing eyes— "told me the whole plan of escape long ago. You know he has already entered into negotiations.... I've told you something already.... You see, it will probably come off at the third *étape* from here, when the party of prisoners is being taken to Siberia. Oh, it's a long way off yet. Ivan Fyodorovitch has already visited the superintendent of the third *étape*. But we don't know yet who will be in charge of the party, and it's impossible to find that out so long beforehand. To-morrow perhaps I will show you in detail the whole plan which Ivan Fyodorovitch left me on the eve of the trial in case of need.... That was when—do you remember?—you found us quarreling. He had just gone down-stairs, but seeing you I made him come back; do you remember? Do you know what we were quarreling about then?"

"No, I don't," said Alyosha.

"Of course he did not tell you. It was about that plan of escape. He had told me the main idea three days before, and we began quarreling about it at once and quarreled for three days. We quarreled because, when he told me that if Dmitri Fyodorovitch were convicted he would escape abroad with that creature, I felt furious at once—I can't tell you why, I don't know myself why.... Oh, of course, I was furious then about that creature, and that she, too, should go abroad with Dmitri!" Katerina Ivanovna exclaimed suddenly, her lips quivering with anger. "As soon as Ivan Fyodorovitch saw that I was furious about that woman, he instantly imagined I was jealous of Dmitri and that I still loved Dmitri. That is how our first quarrel began. I would not give an explanation, I could not ask forgiveness. I could not bear to think that such a man could suspect me of still loving that ... and when I myself had told him long before that I did not love Dmitri, that I loved no one but him! It was only resentment against that creature that made me angry with him. Three days later, on the evening you came, he brought me a sealed envelope, which I was to open at once, if anything happened to him. Oh, he foresaw his illness! He told me that the envelope contained the details of the escape, and that if he died or was taken dangerously ill, I was to save Mitya alone. Then he left me money, nearly ten thousand—those notes to which the prosecutor referred in his speech, having learnt from some one that he had sent them to be changed. I was tremendously impressed to find that Ivan Fyodorovitch had not given up his idea of saving his brother, and was confiding this plan of escape to me, though he was still jealous of me and still convinced that I loved Mitya. Oh, that was a sacrifice! No, you cannot understand the greatness of such self-sacrifice, Alexey Fyodorovitch. I wanted to fall at his feet in reverence, but I thought at once that he would take it only for my joy at the thought of Mitya's being saved (and he certainly would have imagined that!), and I was so exasperated at the mere possibility of such an unjust thought on his part that I lost my temper again, and instead of kissing his feet, flew into a fury again! Oh, I am unhappy! It's my character, my awful, unhappy character! Oh, you will see, I shall end by driving him, too, to abandon me for another with whom he can get on better, like Dmitri. But ... no, I could not bear it, I should kill myself. And when you came in then, and when I called to you and told him to come back, I was so enraged by the look of contempt and hatred he turned on me that—do you remember?—I cried out to you that it was he, he alone who had persuaded me that his brother Dmitri was a murderer! I said that malicious thing on purpose to wound him again. He had never, never persuaded me that his brother was a murderer. On the contrary, it was I who persuaded him! Oh, my vile temper was the cause of everything! I paved the way to that hideous scene at the trial. He wanted to show me that he was an honorable man, and that, even if I loved his brother, he would not ruin him for revenge or jealousy. So he came to the court ... I am the cause of it all, I alone am to blame!"

Katya never had made such confessions to Alyosha before, and he felt that she was now at that stage of unbearable suffering when even the proudest heart painfully crushes its pride and falls vanquished by grief. Oh, Alyosha knew another terrible reason of her present misery, though she had carefully concealed it from him during those days since the trial; but it would have been for some reason too painful to him if she had been brought so low as to speak to him now about that. She was suffering for her "treachery" at the trial, and Alyosha felt that her conscience was impelling her to confess it to him, to him, Alyosha, with tears and cries and hysterical writhings on the floor. But he dreaded that moment and longed to spare her. It made the commission on which he had come even more difficult. He spoke of Mitya again.

"It's all right, it's all right, don't be anxious about him!" she began again, sharply and stubbornly. "All that is only momentary, I know him, I know his heart only too well. You may be sure he will consent to escape. It's not as though it would be immediately; he will have time to make up his mind to it. Ivan Fyodorovitch will be well by that time and will manage it all himself, so that I shall have nothing to do with it. Don't be anxious; he will consent to run away. He has agreed already: do you suppose he would give up that creature? And they won't let her go to him, so he is bound to escape. It's you he's most afraid of, he is afraid you won't approve of his escape on moral grounds. But you must generously *allow* it, if your sanction is so necessary," Katya added viciously. She paused and smiled.

"He talks about some hymn," she went on again, "some cross he has to bear, some duty; I remember Ivan Fyodorovitch told me a great deal about it, and if you knew how he talked!" Katya cried suddenly, with feeling she could not repress, "if you knew how he loved that wretched man at the moment he told me, and how he hated him, perhaps, at the same moment. And I heard his story and his tears with sneering disdain. Brute! Yes, I am a brute. I am responsible for his fever. But that man in prison is incapable of suffering," Katya concluded irritably. "Can such a man suffer? Men like him never suffer!"

There was a note of hatred and contemptuous repulsion in her words. And yet it was she who had betrayed him. "Perhaps because she feels how she's wronged him she hates him at moments," Alyosha thought to himself. He hoped that it was only "at moments." In Katya's last words he detected a challenging note, but he did not take it up.

"I sent for you this morning to make you promise to persuade him yourself. Or do you, too, consider that to escape would be dishonorable, cowardly, or something ... unchristian, perhaps?" Katya added, even more defiantly.

"Oh, no. I'll tell him everything," muttered Alyosha. "He asks you to come and see him to-day," he blurted out suddenly, looking her steadily in the face. She started, and drew back a little from him on the sofa.

"Me? Can that be?" she faltered, turning pale.

"It can and ought to be!" Alyosha began emphatically, growing more animated. "He needs you particularly just now. I would not have opened the subject and worried you, if it were not necessary. He is ill, he is beside himself, he keeps asking for you. It is not to be reconciled with you that he wants you, but only that you would go and show yourself at his door. So much has happened to him since that day. He realizes that he has injured you beyond all reckoning. He does not ask your forgiveness—'It's impossible to forgive me,' he says himself—but only that you would show yourself in his doorway."

"It's so sudden...." faltered Katya. "I've had a presentiment all these days that you would come with that message. I knew he would ask me to come. It's impossible!"

"Let it be impossible, but do it. Only think, he realizes for the first time how he has wounded you, the first time in his life; he had never grasped it before so fully. He said, 'If she refuses to come I shall be unhappy all my life.' Do you hear? though he is condemned to penal servitude for twenty years, he is still planning to be happy—is not that piteous? Think—you must visit him; though he is ruined, he is innocent," broke like a challenge from Alyosha. "His hands are clean, there is no blood on them! For the sake of his infinite sufferings in the future visit him now. Go, greet him on his way into the darkness—stand at his door, that is all.... You ought to do it, you ought to!" Alyosha concluded, laying immense stress on the word "ought."

"I ought to ... but I cannot...." Katya moaned. "He will look at me.... I can't."

"Your eyes ought to meet. How will you live all your life, if you don't make up your mind to do it now?"

"Better suffer all my life."

"You ought to go, you ought to go," Alyosha repeated with merciless emphasis.

"But why to-day, why at once?... I can't leave our patient—"

"You can for a moment. It will only be a moment. If you don't come, he will be in delirium by to-night. I would not tell you a lie; have pity on him!"

"Have pity on *me!*" Katya said, with bitter reproach, and she burst into tears.

"Then you will come," said Alyosha firmly, seeing her tears. "I'll go and tell him you will come directly."

"No, don't tell him so on any account," cried Katya in alarm. "I will come, but don't tell him beforehand, for perhaps I may go, but not go in.... I don't know yet—"

Her voice failed her. She gasped for breath. Alyosha got up to go.

"And what if I meet any one?" she said suddenly, in a low voice, turning white again.

"That's just why you must go now, to avoid meeting any one. There will be no one there, I can tell you that for certain. We will expect you," he concluded emphatically, and went out of the room.

He hurried to the hospital where Mitya was lying now. The day after his fate was determined, Mitya had fallen ill with nervous fever, and was sent to the prison division of the town hospital. But at the request of several persons (Alyosha, Madame Hohlakov, Lise, etc.), Doctor Varvinsky had put Mitya not with other prisoners, but in a separate little room, the one where Smerdyakov had been. It is true that there was a sentinel at the other end of the corridor, and there was a grating over the window, so that Varvinsky could be at ease about the indulgence he had shown, which was not quite legal, indeed; but he was a kind-hearted and compassionate young man. He knew how hard it would be for a man like Mitya to pass at once so suddenly into the society of robbers and murderers, and that he must get used to it by degrees. The visits of relations and friends were informally sanctioned by the doctor and overseer, and even by the police captain. But only Alyosha and Grushenka had visited Mitya. Rakitin had tried to force his way in twice, but Mitya persistently begged Varvinsky not to admit him.

Alyosha found him sitting on his bed in a hospital dressing-gown, rather feverish, with a towel, soaked in vinegar and water, on his head. He looked at Alyosha as he came in with an undefined expression, but there was a shade of something like dread discernible in it. He had become terribly preoccupied since the trial; sometimes he would be silent for half an hour together, and seemed to be pondering something heavily and painfully, oblivious of everything about him. If he roused himself from his brooding and began to talk, he always spoke with a kind of abruptness and never of what he really wanted to say. He looked sometimes with a face of suffering at his brother. He seemed to be more at ease with Grushenka than with Alyosha. It is true, he scarcely spoke to her at all, but as soon as she came in, his whole face lighted up with joy.

Alyosha sat down beside him on the bed in silence. This time Mitya was waiting for Alyosha in suspense, but he did not dare ask him a question. He felt it almost unthinkable that Katya would consent to come, and at the same time he felt that if she did not come, something inconceivable would happen. Alyosha understood his feelings.

"Trifon Borissovitch," Mitya began nervously, "has pulled his whole inn to pieces, I am told. He's taken up the flooring, pulled apart the planks, split up all the gallery, I am told. He is seeking treasure all the time—the fifteen hundred roubles which the prosecutor said I'd hidden there. He began playing these tricks, they say, as soon as he got home. Serve him right, the swindler! The guard here told me yesterday; he comes from there."

"Listen," began Alyosha. "She will come, but I don't know when. Perhaps to-day, perhaps in a few days, that I can't tell. But she will come, she will, that's certain."

Mitya started, would have said something, but was silent. The news had a tremendous effect on him. It was evident that he would have liked terribly to know what had been said, but he was again afraid to ask. Something cruel and contemptuous from Katya would have cut him like a knife at that moment.

"This was what she said among other things; that I must be sure to set your conscience at rest about escaping. If Ivan is not well by then she will see to it all herself."

"You've spoken of that already," Mitya observed musingly.

"And you have repeated it to Grusha," observed Alyosha.

"Yes," Mitya admitted. "She won't come this morning." He looked timidly at his brother. "She won't come till the evening. When I told her yesterday that Katya was taking measures, she was silent, but she set her mouth. She only whispered, 'Let her!' She understood that it was important. I did not dare to try her further. She understands now, I think, that Katya no longer cares for me, but loves Ivan."

"Does she?" broke from Alyosha.

"Perhaps she does not. Only she is not coming this morning," Mitya hastened to explain again; "I asked her to do something for me. You know, Ivan is superior to all of us. He ought to live, not us. He will recover."

"Would you believe it, though Katya is alarmed about him, she scarcely doubts of his recovery," said Alyosha.

"That means that she is convinced he will die. It's because she is frightened she's so sure he will get well."

"Ivan has a strong constitution, and I, too, believe there's every hope that he will get well," Alyosha observed anxiously.

"Yes, he will get well. But she is convinced that he will die. She has a great deal of sorrow to bear..." A silence followed. A grave anxiety was fretting Mitya.

"Alyosha, I love Grusha terribly," he said suddenly in a shaking voice, full of tears.

"They won't let her go out there to you," Alyosha put in at once.

"And there is something else I wanted to tell you," Mitya went on, with a sudden ring in his voice. "If they beat me on the way or out there, I won't submit to it. I shall kill some one, and shall be shot for it. And this will be going on for twenty years! They speak to me rudely as it is. I've been lying here all night, passing judgment on myself. I am not ready! I am not able to resign myself. I wanted to sing a 'hymn'; but if a guard speaks rudely to me, I have not the strength to bear it. For Grusha I would bear anything ... anything except blows.... But she won't be allowed to come there."

Alyosha smiled gently.

"Listen, brother, once for all," he said. "This is what I think about it. And you know that I would not tell you a lie. Listen: you are not ready, and such a cross is not for you. What's more, you don't need such a martyr's cross when you are not ready for it. If you had murdered our father, it would grieve me that you should reject your punishment. But you are innocent, and such a cross is too much for you. You wanted to make yourself another man by suffering. I say, only remember that other man always, all your life and wherever you go; and that will be enough for you. Your refusal of that great cross will only serve to make you feel all your life an even greater duty, and that constant feeling will do more to make you a new man, perhaps, than if you went there. For there you would not endure it and would repine, and perhaps at last would say: 'I am quits.' The lawyer was right about that. Such heavy burdens are not for all men. For some they are impossible. These are my thoughts about it, if you want them so much. If other men would have to answer for your escape, officers or soldiers, then I would not have 'allowed' you," smiled Alyosha. "But they declare—the superintendent of that *étape* told Ivan himself—that if it's well managed there will be no great inquiry, and that they can get off easily. Of course, bribing is dishonest even in such a case, but I can't undertake to judge about it, because if Ivan and Katya commissioned me to act for you, I know I should go and give bribes. I must tell you the truth. And so I can't judge of your own action. But let me assure you that I shall never condemn you. And it would be a strange thing if I could judge you in this. Now I think I've gone into everything."

"But I do condemn myself!" cried Mitya. "I shall escape, that was settled apart from you; could Mitya Karamazov do anything but run away? But I shall condemn myself, and I will pray for my sin for ever. That's how the Jesuits talk, isn't it? Just as we are doing?"

"Yes." Alyosha smiled gently.

"I love you for always telling the whole truth and never hiding anything," cried Mitya, with a joyful laugh. "So I've caught my Alyosha being Jesuitical. I must kiss you for that. Now listen to the rest; I'll open the other side of my heart to you. This is what I planned and decided. If I run away, even with money and a passport, and even to America, I should be cheered up by the thought that I am not running away for pleasure, not for happiness, but to another exile as bad, perhaps, as Siberia. It is as bad, Alyosha, it is! I hate that America, damn it, already. Even though Grusha will be with me. Just look at her; is she an American? She is Russian, Russian to the marrow of her bones; she will be homesick for the mother country, and I shall see every hour that she is suffering for my sake, that she has taken up that cross for me. And what harm has she done? And how shall I, too, put up with the rabble out there, though they may be better than I, every one of them? I hate that America already! And though they may be wonderful at machinery, every one of them, damn them, they are not of my soul. I love Russia, Alyosha, I love the Russian God, though I am a scoundrel myself. I shall choke there!" he exclaimed, his eyes suddenly flashing. His voice was trembling with tears. "So this is what I've decided, Alyosha, listen," he began again, mastering his emotion. "As soon as I arrive there with Grusha, we will set to work at once on the land, in solitude, somewhere very remote, with wild bears. There must be some remote parts even there. I am told there are still Redskins there, somewhere, on the edge of the horizon. So to the country of the *Last of the Mohicans*, and there we'll tackle the grammar at once, Grusha and I. Work and grammar—that's how we'll spend three years. And by that time we shall speak English like any Englishman. And as soon as we've learnt it—good-by to America! We'll run here to Russia as American citizens. Don't be uneasy—we would not come to this little town. We'd hide somewhere, a long way off, in the north or in the south. I shall be changed by that time, and she will, too, in America. The doctors shall make me some sort of wart on my face—what's the use of their being so mechanical!—or else I'll put out one eye, let my beard grow a yard, and I shall turn gray, fretting for Russia. I dare say they won't recognize us. And if they do, let them send us to Siberia. I don't care. It will show it's our fate. We'll work on the land here, too, somewhere in the wilds, and I'll make up as an American all my life. But we shall die on our own soil. That's my plan, and it shan't be altered. Do you approve?"

"Yes," said Alyosha, not wanting to contradict him. Mitya paused for a minute and said suddenly:

"And how they worked it up at the trial! Didn't they work it up!"

"If they had not, you would have been convicted just the same," said Alyosha, with a sigh.

"Yes, people are sick of me here! God bless them, but it's hard," Mitya moaned miserably. Again there was silence for a minute.

"Alyosha, put me out of my misery at once!" he exclaimed suddenly. "Tell me, is she coming now, or not? Tell me? What did she say? How did she say it?"

"She said she would come, but I don't know whether she will come to-day. It's hard for her, you know," Alyosha looked timidly at his brother.

"I should think it is hard for her! Alyosha, it will drive me out of my mind. Grusha keeps looking at me. She understands. My God, calm my heart: what is it I want? I want Katya! Do I understand what I want? It's the headstrong, evil Karamazov spirit! No, I am not fit for suffering. I am a scoundrel, that's all one can say."

"Here she is!" cried Alyosha.

At that instant Katya appeared in the doorway. For a moment she stood still, gazing at Mitya with a dazed expression. He leapt impulsively to his feet, and a scared look came into his face. He turned pale, but a timid, pleading smile appeared on his lips at once, and with an irresistible impulse he held out both hands to Katya. Seeing it, she flew impetuously to him. She seized him by the hands, and almost by force made him sit down on the bed. She sat down beside him, and still keeping his hands pressed them violently. Several times they both strove to speak, but stopped short and again gazed speechless with a strange smile, their eyes fastened on one another. So passed two minutes.

"Have you forgiven me?" Mitya faltered at last, and at the same moment turning to Alyosha, his face working with joy, he cried, "Do you hear what I am asking, do you hear?"

"That's what I loved you for, that you are generous at heart!" broke from Katya. "My forgiveness is no good to you, nor yours to me; whether you forgive me or not, you will always be a sore place in my heart, and I in yours—so it must be...." She stopped to take breath. "What have I come for?" she began again with nervous haste: "to embrace your feet, to press your hands like this, till it hurts—you remember how in Moscow I used to squeeze them—to tell you again that you are my god, my joy, to tell you that I love you madly," she moaned in anguish, and suddenly pressed his hand greedily to her lips. Tears streamed from her eyes. Alyosha stood speechless and confounded; he had never expected what he was seeing.

"Love is over, Mitya!" Katya began again, "but the past is painfully dear to me. Know that you will always be so. But now let what might have been come true for one minute," she faltered, with a drawn smile, looking into his face joyfully again. "You love another woman, and I love another man, and yet I shall love you for ever, and you will love me; do you know that? Do you hear? Love me, love me all your life!" she cried, with a quiver almost of menace in her voice.

"I shall love you, and ... do you know, Katya," Mitya began, drawing a deep breath at each word, "do you know, five days ago, that same evening, I loved you.... When you fell down and were carried out ... All my life! So it will be, so it will always be—"

So they murmured to one another frantic words, almost meaningless, perhaps not even true, but at that moment it was all true, and they both believed what they said implicitly.

"Katya," cried Mitya suddenly, "do you believe I murdered him? I know you don't believe it now, but then ... when you gave evidence.... Surely, surely you did not believe it!"

"I did not believe it even then. I've never believed it. I hated you, and for a moment I persuaded myself. While I was giving evidence I persuaded myself and believed it, but when I'd finished speaking I left off believing it at once. Don't doubt that! I have forgotten that I came here to punish myself," she said, with a new expression in her voice, quite unlike the loving tones of a moment before.

"Woman, yours is a heavy burden," broke, as it were, involuntarily from Mitya.

"Let me go," she whispered. "I'll come again. It's more than I can bear now."

She was getting up from her place, but suddenly uttered a loud scream and staggered back. Grushenka walked suddenly and noiselessly into the room. No one had expected her. Katya moved swiftly to the door, but when she reached Grushenka, she stopped suddenly, turned as white as chalk and moaned softly, almost in a whisper:

"Forgive me!"

Grushenka stared at her and, pausing for an instant, in a vindictive, venomous voice, answered:

"We are full of hatred, my girl, you and I! We are both full of hatred! As though we could forgive one another! Save him, and I'll worship you all my life."

"You won't forgive her!" cried Mitya, with frantic reproach.

"Don't be anxious, I'll save him for you!" Katya whispered rapidly, and she ran out of the room.

"And you could refuse to forgive her when she begged your forgiveness herself?" Mitya exclaimed bitterly again.

"Mitya, don't dare to blame her; you have no right to!" Alyosha cried hotly.

"Her proud lips spoke, not her heart," Grushenka brought out in a tone of disgust. "If she saves you I'll forgive her everything—"

She stopped speaking, as though suppressing something. She could not yet recover herself. She had come in, as appeared afterwards, accidentally, with no suspicion of what she would meet.

"Alyosha, run after her!" Mitya cried to his brother; "tell her ... I don't know ... don't let her go away like this!"

"I'll come to you again at nightfall," said Alyosha, and he ran after Katya. He overtook her outside the hospital grounds. She was walking fast, but as soon as Alyosha caught her up she said quickly:

"No, before that woman I can't punish myself! I asked her forgiveness because I wanted to punish myself to the bitter end. She would not forgive me.... I like her for that!" she added, in an unnatural voice, and her eyes flashed with fierce resentment.

"My brother did not expect this in the least," muttered Alyosha. "He was sure she would not come—"

"No doubt. Let us leave that," she snapped. "Listen: I can't go with you to the funeral now. I've sent them flowers. I think they still have money. If necessary, tell them I'll never abandon them.... Now leave me, leave me, please. You are late as it is—the bells are ringing for the service.... Leave me, please!"

He really was late. They had waited for him and had already decided to bear the pretty flower-decked little coffin to the church without him. It was the coffin of poor little Ilusha. He had died two days after Mitya was sentenced. At the gate of the house Alyosha was met by the shouts of the boys, Ilusha's schoolfellows. They had all been impatiently expecting him and were glad that he had come at last. There were about twelve of them, they all had their school-bags or satchels on their shoulders. "Father will cry, be with father," Ilusha had told them as he lay dying, and the boys remembered it. Kolya Krassotkin was the foremost of them.

"How glad I am you've come, Karamazov!" he cried, holding out his hand to Alyosha. "It's awful here. It's really horrible to see it. Snegiryov is not drunk, we know for a fact he's had nothing to drink to-day, but he seems as if he were drunk ... I am always manly, but this is awful. Karamazov, if I am not keeping you, one question before you go in?"

"What is it, Kolya?" said Alyosha.

"Is your brother innocent or guilty? Was it he killed your father or was it the valet? As you say, so it will be. I haven't slept for the last four nights for thinking of it."

"The valet killed him, my brother is innocent," answered Alyosha.

"That's what I said," cried Smurov.

"So he will perish an innocent victim!" exclaimed Kolya; "though he is ruined he is happy! I could envy him!"

"What do you mean? How can you? Why?" cried Alyosha surprised.

"Oh, if I, too, could sacrifice myself some day for truth!" said Kolya with enthusiasm.

"But not in such a cause, not with such disgrace and such horror!" said Alyosha.

"Of course ... I should like to die for all humanity, and as for disgrace, I don't care about that—our names may perish. I respect your brother!"

"And so do I!" the boy, who had once declared that he knew who had founded Troy, cried suddenly and unexpectedly, and he blushed up to his ears like a peony as he had done on that occasion.

Alyosha went into the room. Ilusha lay with his hands folded and his eyes closed in a blue coffin with a white frill round it. His thin face was hardly changed at all, and strange to say there was no smell of decay from the corpse. The expression of his face was serious and, as it were, thoughtful. His hands, crossed over his breast, looked particularly beautiful, as though chiseled in marble. There were flowers in his hands and the coffin, inside and out, was decked with flowers, which had been sent early in the morning by Lise Hohlakov. But there were flowers too from Katerina Ivanovna, and when Alyosha opened the door, the captain had a bunch in his trembling hands and was strewing them again over his dear boy. He scarcely glanced at Alyosha when he came in, and he would not look at any one, even at his crazy weeping wife, "mamma," who kept trying to stand on her crippled legs to get a nearer look at her dead boy. Nina had been pushed in her chair by the boys close up to the coffin. She sat with her head pressed to it and she too was no doubt quietly weeping. Snegiryov's face looked eager, yet bewildered and exasperated. There was something crazy about his gestures and the words that broke from him. "Old man, dear old man!" he exclaimed every minute, gazing at Ilusha. It was his habit to call Ilusha "old man," as a term of affection when he was alive.

"Father, give me a flower, too; take that white one out of his hand and give it me," the crazy mother begged, whimpering. Either because the little white rose in Ilusha's hand had caught her fancy or that she wanted one from his hand to keep in memory of him, she moved restlessly, stretching out her hands for the flower.

"I won't give it to any one, I won't give you anything," Snegiryov cried callously. "They are his flowers, not yours! Everything is his, nothing is yours!"

"Father, give mother a flower!" said Nina, lifting her face wet with tears.

"I won't give away anything and to her less than any one! She didn't love Ilusha. She took away his little cannon and he gave it to her," the captain broke into loud sobs at the thought of how Ilusha had given up his cannon to his mother. The poor, crazy creature was bathed in noiseless tears, hiding her face in her hands.

The boys, seeing that the father would not leave the coffin and that it was time to carry it out, stood round it in a close circle and began to lift it up.

"I don't want him to be buried in the churchyard," Snegiryov wailed suddenly; "I'll bury him by the stone, by our stone! Ilusha told me to. I won't let him be carried out!"

He had been saying for the last three days that he would bury him by the stone, but Alyosha, Krassotkin, the landlady, her sister and all the boys interfered.

"What an idea, bury him by an unholy stone, as though he had hanged himself!" the old landlady said sternly. "There in the churchyard the ground has been crossed. He'll be prayed for there. One can hear the singing in church and the deacon reads so plainly and verbally that it will reach him every time just as though it were read over his grave."

At last the captain made a gesture of despair as though to say, "Take him where you will." The boys raised the coffin, but as they passed the mother, they stopped for a moment and lowered it that she might say good-by to Ilusha. But on seeing that precious little face, which for the last three days she had only looked at from a distance, she trembled all over and her gray head began twitching spasmodically over the coffin.

"Mother, make the sign of the cross over him, give him your blessing, kiss him," Nina cried to her. But her head still twitched like an automaton and with a face contorted with bitter grief she began, without a word, beating her breast with her fist. They carried the coffin past her. Nina pressed her lips to her brother's for the last time as they bore the coffin by her. As Alyosha went out of the house he begged the landlady to look after those who were left behind, but she interrupted him before he had finished.

"To be sure, I'll stay with them, we are Christians, too." The old woman wept as she said it.

They had not far to carry the coffin to the church, not more than three hundred paces. It was a still, clear day, with a slight frost. The church bells were still ringing. Snegiryov ran fussing and distracted after the coffin, in his short old summer overcoat, with his head bare and his soft, old, wide-brimmed hat in his hand. He seemed in a state of bewildered anxiety. At one minute he stretched out his hand to support the head of the coffin and only hindered the bearers, at another he ran alongside and tried to find a place for himself there. A flower fell on the snow and he rushed to pick it up as though everything in the world depended on the loss of that flower.

"And the crust of bread, we've forgotten the crust!" he cried suddenly in dismay. But the boys reminded him at once that he had taken the crust of bread already and that it was in his pocket. He instantly pulled it out and was reassured.

"Ilusha told me to, Ilusha," he explained at once to Alyosha. "I was sitting by him one night and he suddenly told me: 'Father, when my grave is filled up crumble a piece of bread on it so that the sparrows may fly down, I shall hear and it will cheer me up not to be lying alone.'"

"That's a good thing," said Alyosha, "we must often take some."

"Every day, every day!" said the captain quickly, seeming cheered at the thought.

They reached the church at last and set the coffin in the middle of it. The boys surrounded it and remained reverently standing so, all through the service. It was an old and rather poor church; many of the ikons were without settings; but such churches are the best for praying in. During the mass Snegiryov became somewhat calmer, though at times he had outbursts of the same unconscious and, as it were, incoherent anxiety. At one moment he went up to the coffin to set straight the cover or the wreath, when a candle fell out of the candlestick he rushed to replace it and was a fearful time fumbling over it, then he subsided and stood quietly by the coffin with a look of blank uneasiness and perplexity. After the Epistle he suddenly whispered to Alyosha, who was standing beside him, that the Epistle had not been read properly but did not explain what he meant. During the prayer, "Like the Cherubim," he joined in the singing but did not go on to the end. Falling on his knees, he pressed his forehead to the stone floor and lay so for a long while.

At last came the funeral service itself and candles were distributed. The distracted father began fussing about again, but the touching and impressive funeral prayers moved and roused his soul. He seemed suddenly to shrink together and broke into rapid, short sobs, which he tried at first to smother, but at last he sobbed aloud. When they began taking leave of the dead and closing the coffin, he flung his arms about, as though he would not allow them to cover Ilusha, and began greedily and persistently kissing his dead boy on the lips. At last they succeeded in persuading him to come away from the step, but suddenly he impulsively stretched out his hand and snatched a few flowers from the coffin. He looked at them and a new idea seemed to dawn upon him, so that he apparently forgot his grief for a minute. Gradually he seemed to sink into brooding and did not resist when the coffin was lifted up and carried to the grave. It was an expensive one in the churchyard close to the church, Katerina Ivanovna had paid for it. After the customary rites the grave-diggers lowered the coffin. Snegiryov with his flowers in his hands bent down so low over the open grave that the boys caught hold of his coat in alarm and pulled him back. He did not seem to understand fully what was happening. When they began filling up the grave, he suddenly pointed anxiously at the falling earth and began trying to say something, but no one could make out what he meant, and he stopped suddenly. Then he was reminded that he must crumble the bread and he was awfully excited, snatched up the bread and began pulling it to pieces and flinging the morsels on the grave.

"Come, fly down, birds, fly down, sparrows!" he muttered anxiously.

One of the boys observed that it was awkward for him to crumble the bread with the flowers in his hands and suggested he should give them to some one to hold for a time. But he would not do this and seemed indeed suddenly alarmed for his flowers, as though they wanted to take them from him altogether. And after looking at the grave, and as it were, satisfying himself that everything had been done and the bread had been crumbled, he suddenly, to the surprise of every one, turned, quite composedly even, and made his way homewards. But his steps became more and more hurried, he almost ran. The boys and Alyosha kept up with him.

"The flowers are for mamma, the flowers are for mamma! I was unkind to mamma," he began exclaiming suddenly.

Some one called to him to put on his hat as it was cold. But he flung the hat in the snow as though he were angry and kept repeating, "I won't have the hat, I won't have the hat." Smurov picked it up and carried it after him. All the boys were crying, and Kolya and the boy who discovered about Troy most of all. Though Smurov, with the captain's hat in his hand, was crying bitterly too, he managed, as he ran, to snatch up a piece of red brick that lay on the snow of the path, to fling it at the flock of sparrows that was flying by. He missed them, of course, and went on crying as he ran. Half-way, Snegiryov suddenly stopped, stood still for half a minute, as though struck by something, and suddenly turning back to the church, ran towards the deserted grave. But the boys instantly overtook him and caught hold of him on all sides. Then he fell helpless on the snow as though he had been knocked down, and struggling, sobbing, and wailing, he began crying out, "Ilusha, old man, dear old man!" Alyosha and Kolya tried to make him get up, soothing and persuading him.

"Captain, give over, a brave man must show fortitude," muttered Kolya.

"You'll spoil the flowers," said Alyosha, "and mamma is expecting them, she is sitting crying because you would not give her any before. Ilusha's little bed is still there—"

"Yes, yes, mamma!" Snegiryov suddenly recollected, "they'll take away the bed, they'll take it away," he added as though alarmed that they really would. He jumped up and ran homewards again. But it was not far off and they all arrived together. Snegiryov opened the door hurriedly and called to his wife with whom he had so cruelly quarreled just before:

"Mamma, poor crippled darling, Ilusha has sent you these flowers," he cried, holding out to her a little bunch of flowers that had been frozen and broken while he was struggling in the snow. But at that instant he saw in the corner, by the little bed, Ilusha's little boots, which the landlady had put tidily side by side. Seeing the old, patched, rusty-looking, stiff boots he flung up his hands and rushed to them, fell on his knees, snatched up one boot and, pressing his lips to it, began kissing it greedily, crying, "Ilusha, old man, dear old man, where are your little feet?"

"Where have you taken him away? Where have you taken him?" the lunatic cried in a heartrending voice. Nina, too, broke into sobs. Kolya ran out of the room, the boys followed him. At last Alyosha too went out.

"Let them weep," he said to Kolya, "it's no use trying to comfort them just now. Let us wait a minute and then go back."

"No, it's no use, it's awful," Kolya assented. "Do you know, Karamazov," he dropped his voice so that no one could hear them, "I feel dreadfully sad, and if it were only possible to bring him back, I'd give anything in the world to do it."

"Ah, so would I," said Alyosha.

"What do you think, Karamazov? Had we better come back here to-night? He'll be drunk, you know."

"Perhaps he will. Let us come together, you and I, that will be enough, to spend an hour with them, with the mother and Nina. If we all come together we shall remind them of everything again," Alyosha suggested.

"The landlady is laying the table for them now—there'll be a funeral dinner or something, the priest is coming; shall we go back to it, Karamazov?"

"Of course," said Alyosha.

"It's all so strange, Karamazov, such sorrow and then pancakes after it, it all seems so unnatural in our religion."

"They are going to have salmon, too," the boy who had discovered about Troy observed in a loud voice.

"I beg you most earnestly, Kartashov, not to interrupt again with your idiotic remarks, especially when one is not talking to you and doesn't care to know whether you exist or not!" Kolya snapped out irritably. The boy flushed crimson but did not dare to reply.

Meantime they were strolling slowly along the path and suddenly Smurov exclaimed:

"There's Ilusha's stone, under which they wanted to bury him."

They all stood still by the big stone. Alyosha looked and the whole picture of what Snegiryov had described to him that day, how Ilusha, weeping and hugging his father, had cried, "Father, father, how he insulted you," rose at once before his imagination.

A sudden impulse seemed to come into his soul. With a serious and earnest expression he looked from one to another of the bright, pleasant faces of Ilusha's schoolfellows, and suddenly said to them:

"Boys, I should like to say one word to you, here at this place."

The boys stood round him and at once bent attentive and expectant eyes upon him.

"Boys, we shall soon part. I shall be for some time with my two brothers, of whom one is going to Siberia and the other is lying at death's door. But soon I shall leave this town, perhaps for a long time, so we shall part. Let us make a compact here, at Ilusha's stone, that we will never forget Ilusha and one another. And whatever happens to us later in life, if we don't meet for twenty years afterwards, let us always remember how we buried the poor boy at whom we once threw stones, do you remember, by the bridge? and afterwards we all grew so fond of him. He was a fine boy, a kind-hearted, brave boy, he felt for his father's honor and resented the cruel insult to him and stood up for him. And so in the first place, we will remember him, boys, all our lives. And even if we are occupied with most important things, if we attain to honor or fall into great misfortune—still let us remember how good it was once here, when we were all together, united by a good and kind feeling which made us, for the time we were loving that poor boy, better perhaps than we are. My little doves—let me call you so, for you are very like them, those pretty blue birds, at this minute as I look at your good dear faces. My dear children, perhaps you won't understand what I am saying to you, because I often speak very unintelligibly, but you'll remember it all the same and will agree with my words some time. You must know that there is nothing higher and stronger and more wholesome and good for life in the future than some good memory, especially a memory of childhood, of home. People talk to you a great deal about your education, but some good, sacred memory, preserved from childhood, is perhaps the best education. If a man carries many such memories with him into life, he is safe to the end of his days, and if one has only one good memory left in one's heart, even that may sometime be the means of saving us. Perhaps we may even grow wicked later on, may be unable to refrain from a bad action, may laugh at men's tears and at those people who say as Kolya did just now, 'I want to suffer for all men,' and may even jeer spitefully at such people. But however bad we may become—which God forbid—yet, when we recall how we buried Ilusha, how we loved him in his last days, and how we have been talking like friends all together, at this stone, the cruelest and most mocking of us—if we do become so—will not dare to laugh inwardly at having been kind and good at this moment! What's more, perhaps, that one memory may keep him from great evil and he will reflect and say, 'Yes, I was good and brave and honest then!' Let him laugh to himself, that's no matter, a man often laughs at what's good and kind. That's only from thoughtlessness. But I assure you, boys, that as he laughs he will say at once in his heart, 'No, I do wrong to laugh, for that's not a thing to laugh at.'"

"That will be so, I understand you, Karamazov!" cried Kolya, with flashing eyes.

The boys were excited and they, too, wanted to say something, but they restrained themselves, looking with intentness and emotion at the speaker.

"I say this in case we become bad," Alyosha went on, "but there's no reason why we should become bad, is there, boys? Let us be, first and above all, kind, then honest and then let us never forget each other! I say that again. I give you my word for my part that I'll never forget one of you. Every face looking at me now I shall remember even for thirty years. Just now Kolya said to Kartashov that we did not care to know whether he exists or not. But I cannot forget that Kartashov exists and that he is not blushing now as he did when he discovered the founders of Troy, but is looking at me with his jolly, kind, dear little eyes. Boys, my dear boys, let us all be generous and brave like Ilusha, clever, brave and generous like Kolya (though he will be ever so much cleverer when he is grown up), and let us all be as modest, as clever and sweet as Kartashov. But why am I talking about those two? You are all dear to me, boys, from this day forth, I have a place in my heart for you all, and I beg you to keep a place in your hearts for me! Well, and who has united us in this kind, good feeling which we shall remember and intend to remember all our lives? Who, if not Ilusha, the good boy, the dear boy, precious to us for ever! Let us never forget him. May his memory live for ever in our hearts from this time forth!"

"Yes, yes, for ever, for ever!" the boys cried in their ringing voices, with softened faces.

"Let us remember his face and his clothes and his poor little boots, his coffin and his unhappy, sinful father, and how boldly he stood up for him alone against the whole school."

"We will remember, we will remember," cried the boys. "He was brave, he was good!"

"Ah, how I loved him!" exclaimed Kolya.

"Ah, children, ah, dear friends, don't be afraid of life! How good life is when one does something good and just!"

"Yes, yes," the boys repeated enthusiastically.

"Karamazov, we love you!" a voice, probably Kartashov's, cried impulsively.

"We love you, we love you!" they all caught it up. There were tears in the eyes of many of them.

"Hurrah for Karamazov!" Kolya shouted ecstatically.

"And may the dead boy's memory live for ever!" Alyosha added again with feeling.

"For ever!" the boys chimed in again.

"Karamazov," cried Kolya, "can it be true what's taught us in religion, that we shall all rise again from the dead and shall live and see each other again, all, Ilusha too?"

"Certainly we shall all rise again, certainly we shall see each other and shall tell each other with joy and gladness all that has happened!" Alyosha answered, half laughing, half enthusiastic.

"Ah, how splendid it will be!" broke from Kolya.

"Well, now we will finish talking and go to his funeral dinner. Don't be put out at our eating pancakes—it's a very old custom and there's something nice in that!" laughed Alyosha. "Well, let us go! And now we go hand in hand."

"And always so, all our lives hand in hand! Hurrah for Karamazov!" Kolya cried once more rapturously, and once more the boys took up his exclamation: "Hurrah for Karamazov!"

Footnotes

1. In Russian, "silen."
2. A proverbial expression in Russia.
3. Grushenka.
4. i.e. setter dog.
5. Probably the public event was the Decabrist plot against the Tsar, of December 1825, in which the most distinguished men in Russia were concerned.—TRANSLATOR'S NOTE.
6. When a monk's body is carried out from the cell to the church and from the church to the graveyard, the canticle "What earthly joy..." is sung. If the deceased was a priest as well as a monk the canticle "Our Helper and Defender" is sung instead.
7. i.e. a chime of bells.
8. Literally: "Did you get off with a long nose made at you?"—a proverbial expression in Russia for failure.
9. Gogol is meant.

Made in the USA
Columbia, SC
29 January 2019